Joys and Desires

'Tasha's young,' Peter said. 'I mean, young in the head. She's got this great family, they probably smother her but she doesn't know it yet –' And then he cut off, as he always did – as Kristin did, too – when they started to talk about Tasha. It seemed disloyal.

And after all, Kristin reminded herself, I have a lot to thank Tasha for. Peter most of all. She hoped it hadn't hurt Tasha too much to give him up. She was almost on the point of saying Tasha really didn't need to: that they could manage, somehow . . .

But no. Share him? It was lunacy. Better, she supposed, to leave things as they were.

Lucy Kidd was born in New York in 1965 and educated at Harvard and in France. She first came to England in 1987 to write her first novel, *A Rose Without Thorns*. She now lives in Scotland with her husband and daughter.

LUCY KIDD

Joys
and
Desires

Mandarin

A Mandarin Paperback
JOYS AND DESIRES

First published in Great Britain 1996
by Mandarin Paperbacks
an imprint of Reed Books Ltd
Michelin House, 81 Fulham Road, London SW3 6RB
and Auckland, Melbourne, Singapore and Toronto

Copyright © Lucy Kidd 1996
The author has asserted her moral rights

A CIP catalogue record for this title
is available from the British Library
ISBN 0 7493 2042 7

Typeset by Deltatype Ltd, Ellesmere Port, Wirral
Printed and bound in Great Britain
by Cox & Wyman Ltd, Reading, Berks

For Susan

May she have many happy friendships

I went to the Garden of Love,
And saw what I never had seen:
A Chapel was built in the midst,
Where I used to play on the green.

And the gates of this Chapel were shut,
And 'Thou shalt not' writ over the door;
So I turn'd to the Garden of Love,
That so many sweet flowers bore,

And I saw it was filled with graves,
And tomb-stones where flowers should be:
And Priests in black gowns were walking their
   rounds,
And binding with briars my joys & desires.

– William Blake, *The Garden of Love*

Norfolk, 1994

Tasha walked up the slow rise where the cliff parted from the shore, above the slate-coloured edge of the sea. She was probably wasting her time here. It was a dull day at the end of March, dense cloud hanging low in a sky which had always seemed to her vaster, yet more oppressive than any other in this country.

But then, she reminded herself, that sky was the very reason he liked this place: the reason why he came here.

And since she didn't know where else to begin her search, she persisted. For ten, perhaps fifteen minutes, she kept to the sandy path, glancing occasionally, warily, at the signs punctuating its edges: *Danger! Landslides – Falling Rock*. She continued to climb until the shore lay a good thirty feet below her. And then she stopped.

A tiny figure stood ahead of her, erect against the wind. Pale gold hair like fluffy cotton blew about her face, and she wrapped her arms, in a thick green jumper, around herself for warmth.

Kristin had always felt the cold: Tasha remembered that.

She opened her mouth to shout, but Kristin's voice reached her first.

'Stay back! Go away.'

'What are you doing here?'

Kristin only looked at her coldly. Tasha started to walk forward again.

'I told you. Don't come up here.'

'I will if I want to. What's going on anyway?'

'Well, then, don't say I didn't warn you.' Kristin's voice rang out, light and clear.

'For Christ's sake, I'm not going to bite you.' Tasha stood just a few feet away from her now. 'How'd you get here, anyway?' Her own car, Tasha remembered, had been the only one parked at the edge of the beach.

Kristin didn't answer. Her hands were clenched, white-knuckled, around her upper arms. She had never learnt the art of relaxing: too afraid, perhaps, hedged round by her various phobias. Food. Men. Flying, driving, touching too close.

Compulsive. That had been Zeke's word for her, Tasha remembered. Back then, she had doubted her brother's view of things. She didn't, now.

She ventured a few steps closer to the cliff's edge.

'Don't! I told you.'

Tasha turned her head. 'What the hell is going on?'

'It'll be better for you if you keep out of this. It's for your own good.'

But because nothing Kristin was saying made any sense, and because a glimmer of something down below on the rocks had caught her eye, Tasha leaned forward.

She felt a sudden, sick lurch in her stomach, and rocked backwards, landing, sitting, on the edge of the path. She drew her hands up to cover her eyes.

'I told you. It'll be better if you just go. I can take care of myself.'

'Just tell me what happened.' Tasha's voice was weak. She was not sure she wanted to know.

'It was – an accident.'

'I don't believe you.'

'Well, you can believe me or not.' Kristin spoke sharply. 'It doesn't matter.'

Strangely, Tasha's eyes were dry. She supposed it was the shock: the tears came later. She lifted her head. 'An – accident,' she said.

'He had it coming.'

'Kristin, how can you say that? Are you crazy?'

Kristin tilted back her head and let out a lone note of laughter.

And Tasha knew the answer then. She knew she should

get away from here. That Kristin was dangerous: that there could be no helping her. Tasha brushed off the knees of her jeans and started, unsteadily, to stand. 'Right,' she said. She took a step back, and another.

'Tasha, are you going?'

She saw the panic in Kristin's eyes then. 'You said you wanted me to.'

'Are you going to – tell people?'

Tasha took a deep breath. 'I don't see – ' *I don't see why not*, she had been about to say. She was glad she had caught herself. 'I don't think so.'

'Because it really was an accident. I didn't mean it to come out this way. I mean, I did – ' Kristin looked suddenly away, out to sea.

'I don't think you ought to tell me.' More than anything, Tasha wanted to run. Run now. Run and tell all the usual people. The police. People who would know what to do.

'You're part of it, too.'

'Oh, no,' said Tasha. But she knew it was true. She was part of it, and soon she would be in too deep to escape. She made one last try. 'Listen. This is nothing to do with me. I don't want to know what you've got to tell me because it'll all be lies. All of it, Kristin. I should have known from the first day I met you never to believe a single word you say.' She drew breath, but the words were boiling over, surging up inside her. 'You don't understand what friendship is. You don't care about other people's feelings. All your life you've been heading for something like this. Haven't you?' Tasha squinted because the tears were coming, coming at last, and in her blurred sight Kristin's hair took on an unnatural glow, her angelic face a surreal fixity. 'I should have left you alone back at Elliott. I'd be a hell of a lot happier now.'

'And Peter?'

The sound of the name stung. 'Peter's nothing to do with it. This is all you. Your fault. God, how I wish I'd never known you.'

5

Fife, 1994

'What do you mean, he's dead? Who are you?'

Kate called into the silent phone, after the voice, which had already gone. She tried, now, to remember what, exactly, the voice had told her; but it was hard, shaken out of her sleep at eight in the morning. She remembered only its cold, official tone. And yet it had not identified itself as police, or hospital, or any of the members of officialdom who would normally make such a call. Could it be a hoax? But then, why? She had no enemies.

Nor, she thought, did Peter. Though perhaps he deserved them. The art world was full of rivalries: even of outright nastiness, which was, in part, the reason she had hidden herself away from it, up here.

Peter. Dead. The thought made her shake: now slightly, then gradually, increasingly, uncontrollably. It couldn't be true. It must be some sort of joke, or mistake.

If only she could ring him, right now, and know he was all right. Again, with an echo of the old resentment, she wished he trusted her enough to give her his phone number. Or numbers: both of them. Since he had two houses now.

But she knew that, as so often, there was nothing she could do but wait. She drew back the curtains of the one big room that filled the attic of her cottage, looking out at the blue-grey dawn above the roofs of Crail and trying to be calm. For a moment, she even prayed. *Holy Mary, sweet Jesus, let it be a lie.* Peter was all right. He had to be. He would explain it to her when he came home. He would hug her and nuzzle against her neck, like the wee boy he had always been to her. The smile-lines would crinkle round his dark eyes and he would laugh at it: some silly joke. Some accident. More likely than not, he would have some ripe words for it. *See, Kate? It's rubbish. Here I am.*

And then, briefly, she would hate him; she would feel a second's sharp hurt. Simply because it had to be like this: she had to trust him so much. But then, she loved him.

Oxfordshire, 1977

From the back garden, the path led up two uneven stone stairs, and in through a doorway – the secret door, Kristin liked to call it, because it was so low – and then through a dark, winding corridor, from one ancient chamber to another: the scullery, the kitchen, the breakfast room, the library. Today the corridor smelt slightly of mould and dust. Kristin let the door bang shut behind her.

'Daddy!' she called, and already there was suspicion in her voice. *He isn't here, he's out. He's run away just like I did.* She smiled at the thought. She had run away from London, because she couldn't bear living with Mama anymore: and because she knew he must need her. She hadn't really understood until yesterday morning.

She remembered how a superior expression had crossed Anastasia Woolnoth's prim mouth as she pronounced, at the beginning of break, 'The *Telegraph* says your father's gone bankrupt.'

Kristin had only stared back. Anastasia was fifteen, two years above her at St Paul's, and seemed infinitely worldly. 'I don't know what you mean.'

'It means he'll have to sell all his houses and cars. And maybe you won't be able to come to school here anymore.' The slant of Anastasia's eyes had turned cruel.

All that evening Kristin had pondered Anastasia's pronouncement, knowing that it was no use asking her mother about it. Her mother was always tired these days, frazzled, sipping at cups of cold coffee and snapping whenever Kristin asked her questions. So Kristin knew there was only one thing to do. The next morning, she had waited in front of the school until Mama drove away out of sight. She ran to the Tube station and then, almost too easily, an hour later was on the train from Paddington to Thame.

She could explain it all later, at school. Because she simply had to see Daddy. She was worried, now, after what Anastasia had told her. And he had to know she still loved him: that it didn't matter.

She shouted again into the corridor. He must be here, because the door had been open. *'Daddy?'*

She remembered the one, odd article, on a back business page of *The Times*, last year; she had glimpsed it, here on the kitchen table, before Cook snatched the paper away. *On Top of the World?* said the headline; and there had been a picture of her father. She had wanted to ask Cook what it was about, but the older woman only snatched the paper out of her sight, snapping, 'Lies and rubbish.'

And then Cook had gone – retired, Daddy had said, although she wasn't really that old. And then so had the butler and finally everyone else except the weekly cleaner. And Mama and Daddy had started fighting again, and finally Mama took Kristin away to London; but still Daddy stayed here, though the house grew emptier and emptier. Every time Kristin came out for a weekend, more of its contents – sometimes even her own things, like the antique chest by her bed, and then finally even her pony in the stables – had gone.

Now, when she walked down this hall, which had once felt warm and cosy with its long Oriental carpet, she heard only a strange echo.

On Top of the World? She had felt strangely betrayed when she read that. She remembered how, when she was little, she used to go in to see her father in his office, at the top of Ward Tower. He would hoist her up on to his shoulders and show her his view of the Thames, and say, 'Look! We're on top of the world.'

She remembered his voice, deep and warm, its slight accent barely detectable beneath his Oxford English; his broad shoulders, and strong arms which set her down on the ground again. He had shiny black hair and deep brown eyes. He was the handsomest man in the world. The other girls at school all admired him. 'My father's *Hungarian*,' Kristin had boasted to them once. She had been about to say that his name wasn't really Leslie Ward but Laszlo Vary, and that his family had fled Hungary before the war. It seemed terribly romantic. But, 'We know *that*,' Anastasia had pronounced, in a way that silenced Kristin and made her wonder: maybe it was really no better to be half-Hungarian and half-Danish, as she was, than to be, say, Jewish, or just ordinary English with nobody famous among your ancestors. Was that why Daddy never talked about Hungary – always insisted that he was not, in fact, Hungarian but English?

Her father's study was the last room along the corridor.

'Daddy?'

Of course there were other rooms: nine bedrooms, a dining room, a formal parlour. Most of them Tudor, a few Jacobean; there was a guest suite, Edwardian, off to one side of the house, which was never used because the Wards never had any guests. Kristin supposed that compared to the other people in the village, her parents kept very much to themselves. But it never occurred to her to ask her father why they lived in such a large house if they didn't need the space; she knew that he loved The Priory just as she did, and would no more think of selling it than of selling his great tower on the Thames.

Ward Construction: Reach for the Sky. That had been his slogan in the late-sixties – before he replaced it with *On Top of the World*. Kristin had not minded him using *their* private phrase in his advertisements. He had built hundreds of towers all over London, so it was true.

But somehow it had hurt when *The Times* had used those same words against him. Just as it had hurt, a few years before, when some of the papers had turned against her father's projects, calling them 'monstrosities'.

'Daddy?'

His car had been in the drive; he should be able to hear her by now, surely? She walked into the dining room. It was empty now, even the floorboards bare: the rugs, the table, the Sheraton chairs, all sold. There were pale squares on the blue wallpaper where pictures had hung.

Maybe Anastasia was right. At the thought, Kristin began to shiver. *Bankrupt.* The last few times she had come to visit, her father and she had spent all their time in the living room, which still had some of its furniture. They had huddled, in thick sweaters, by the fireplace, playing chequers. Her father was drinking a bit – two whiskies before lunch, three before dinner. His hair looked matted; his hands shook and his face was lined. 'Do you see' – he had cracked a smile – 'what terrible care I take of myself? Honestly, Kirsti, you're better off with your mother.'

It was June now, so Kristin didn't notice the chill in the rooms as she had the last time. She opened the study door, about to call for him again. Then she saw a shape above the desk which took on a terrible clarity, and she opened her mouth and found she couldn't scream.

New York, 1977

Dodging across a solid line of yellow cabs at the corner of Central Park West and 86th Street, Tasha clutched her package close to her chest: brown-papered, rectangular and almost as long as she was tall. She was sure her parents would be impressed. They had to be. After all, hadn't Mr Ferranti, her painting teacher, told her she was the most talented person he'd met in his whole five years of running the summer school? And the class had sixteen- and even eighteen-year-olds in it. Tasha was only thirteen, though she knew she looked older. In the last year or so she had begun to develop what her mother, in slightly disparaging tones, called 'your Grandma Natasha's figure'. Since Grandma Natasha was seventy-six, black-haired and massively fat, and Tasha was honey-blonde and slim – well, more or less – she knew her mother could mean only one thing. Boobs. Well, then, she was glad she had them. She supposed biggish hips, which she had, unfortunately, also started to develop, were the inevitable accompaniment; but according to what her brothers said, that didn't matter at all.

As she swung in under the awning of the turreted Neo-Gothic building which was her home, she thought she saw Gabe, the doorman, giving her the eye. She eyed him back, and spoke before he did.

'Finished, Gabe.' She jiggled her parcel.

'Work of art. Michelangelo, right?' He cracked his chewing gum.

'You got it.' Tasha gave her hips, in their cut-off jeans, an experimental twitch as she moved beyond him.

As she stepped out of the lift on the twenty-third floor, a grey cat attempted to slither in past her. She kicked it back

19

out into the apartment. She wasn't sure of the cat's name. At last count twelve felines lived with the Seidelmans, but they seemed to keep on multiplying. Her mother, Rona, blamed it on Grandma Natasha, who brought in another stray almost every time she visited.

Inside the apartment's dark foyer, everything seemed unnaturally quiet. Tasha still couldn't get used to all her brothers being away: David in medical school, J.L. at Yale, Nat far off now in California. Even Zeke, the youngest, was away staying with friends before starting his third year at Elliott. Elliott Academy, in Lawrencetown, Massachusetts, was America's oldest and probably best boarding school. A few years back, it had started admitting girls, and so Tasha was determined to go there next year, when she was fourteen, just as all her brothers had. She had even started writing her application essay: '*I want to come to Elliott Academy because my four brothers . . .*' Nat, home from Elliott last Easter, had caught her at it and laughed: 'I *think* they're looking for something a little more individual. About, you know, your goals and aspirations?'

So Tasha had tried to start up again, taking his advice, but she was stumped. What were her goals and aspirations? She hadn't a clue.

Well, she thought, thudding happily through to the living room, *now I do*.

Her parents were exactly where she found them every night: Rona, petite, black-haired and newly manicured, reading a copy of *Bazaar* at one end of the sofa; Maurice at the other end, frowning through his spectacles at one of his medical journals.

Tasha planted herself in the doorway, waiting for them both to look up and notice her. When they did, she hefted up her package. '*Ta-da!*' she sang. 'Finished! I bet it's bigger than you thought.'

'Your painting, huh? Let's see.' Her father looked mildly amused.

'Mr Ferranti said it was the best in the whole class!'

20

Tasha started to rip off the paper. She turned the canvas round, beaming, awaiting approval.

'Uh-*huh*?' her father said.

'Well, honey,' said her mother.

'It's a still life,' said Tasha. 'In the style of Cézanne.'

'Oh,' said Rona. 'I see.'

There was a silence.

'Very nice, honey,' said Maurice.

Rona smiled brightly. 'Why don't we hang it up in your bedroom?'

'But I thought you might want to hang it in here,' said Tasha, 'with all these others.'

Her mother laughed. 'Honey, these are *Braques*, from your grandfather's collection. But I'll tell you what we can do. We'll get your picture a nice frame – '

'You don't like it.'

'Of course we do!' Rona stood up and glanced at her husband.

'Sure,' said Maurice, over-enthusiastically. 'It's wonderful, Natasha, and so are you. So let's eat dinner.'

As they sat at the large, empty dining table, Tasha repeated what Mr Ferranti had said. 'I could be a professional! He really said that. He said it would take a lot of training . . . He said I should find my medium, but I think it's probably oil, because I've done watercolour and printmaking . . . I could go to art school! I mean, after Elliott. I can't believe it. Mr Ferranti really thinks I have the talent.'

'He does, does he?' And then, inexplicably, her father chuckled; his pink face wrinkled up and he shook his head.

'He did!' said Tasha. 'And it's what I want to do. I'll go to Elliott –' She felt her heart starting to race – 'and then I'll go to art school, and be an artist.'

'Artists don't make much of a living,' said her father. 'Anyway, honey, you've got years to make up your mind.'

Tasha stared at both her parents, back and forth. 'But I'm serious.'

21

'Of course you are,' said her mother. 'I think your painting's very pretty.'

'It's not supposed to be *pretty*.'

Tasha's parents looked at her blankly.

'Never mind. Can I be excused?'

'It's ice cream for dessert,' said her mother.

'No, thanks. I'm full.'

Her parents looked after her, puzzled, as she left the dining room. For a while she sat next door, stroking one of the cats and staring at the prints and paintings – the Braques – that lined the walls. *They* weren't exactly 'pretty'. They were more than that. Didn't her parents understand?

Of course those pictures were old, and Braque was famous. Maybe *that* was what her parents meant. So did they look at the paintings, or just at the names in the corners? Had they really looked at hers?

The more she looked around her, the more confused she felt. And then she remembered Mr Ferranti's words, his praise, and knew suddenly: *They might be wrong. I might be right.* It was an odd feeling. She had never disagreed with her parents over anything serious before.

Lawrencetown, 1980

1 By now, Tasha knew the place almost as well as Central Park West, and home: the green maple leaves shifting and fluttering in the breeze, the broad main road that led to Boston, the clapboard houses and brick dormitories. In the middle of it all, above a wide stretch of grass, stood Hy El, the oldest of the school buildings, with its tall tower named after Hyam, one of the brothers Elliott who had founded the Academy in the eighteenth century. From Hy El a network of brick paths radiated outwards, as far as the wide Boston Road. Here Tasha crossed, having just climbed down from the city bus with her duffel bag and suitcase. She felt a second's oppression, as if the world had just closed in on her; and then a familiar relief. Nothing had changed.

A few minutes later she was hoisting her luggage up the stairs of Hobson House.

'Hello?' she shouted. 'Anybody home?'

Nobody answered. That was weird. The place must be empty. Well, it wouldn't be for long. She scanned the grubby doors around her, with their faint traces of last year's graffiti, looking for her name on the door: the door of her very own room, a single. At last. They'd promised her.

There was definitely something wrong here. She saw two names: hers and someone else's. Someone else she didn't even know. She nudged the door open. Two desks, two chairs, two lamps and lampshades. Two beds – and on the farther one, by the window, a girl. She had very blonde frizzy hair, and sat with her back straight, looking out-wards.

'Hello,' said Tasha loudly, again. She wished the girl

would at least acknowledge her. 'I guess somebody screwed up. I was supposed to have a single.'

The other girl glanced over at her briefly. She had big eyes, thin lips and an upturned nose, and she was wearing the kind of outfit only new girls wore: a Fair Isle sweater with a matching tartan skirt. One of her feet was curled up under her.

'Are you new?' said Tasha.

The other girl didn't answer.

'That's okay,' said Tasha, 'we're all new sometime.' The continuing silence made her uneasy. 'The thing is, about roommates . . . I asked not to have one this year because I don't seem to have much luck with them.' She was beginning to feel oddly self-conscious, and the more she felt it, the more she talked: she always had. 'You see, my first roommate had this, like, nervous breakdown and had to go home. And the second, well, that one was pretty weird. It's a long story.' Tasha took a few steps towards the far bed, hopeful that the other girl might prompt her to go on.

The other girl didn't. She slowly turned her head again. Her eyes were blue, Tasha noticed now: a strangely matte, unrevealing blue, like turquoise. 'I expect,' she said, 'you'll get your single. I shan't be here long. I could move out now, if you want me to.'

Her tone was polite; foreign. 'You – can't move out yet.' Tasha fumbled for words. 'If you want a room transfer you have to ask the Dean, and she won't give one to anybody for at least three weeks. That's the rules.'

The other girl laughed suddenly, briefly. 'Really.'

Feeling even more self-conscious, Tasha started emptying the contents of her duffel bag out on to the remaining bed. She decided to give conversation one last go. 'So where do you come from?'

The answer came in a wary voice, after a second or so. 'London.'

'Really? That's immensely cool. I've never been to

Europe.' Tasha waited for a response. Silence again. 'So did you just fly over, or what?'

'I've been staying in Baltimore. With my mother.'

'Oh. Your parents divorced, then?'

When she heard no answer, Tasha turned her head and saw the other girl nod. 'You got any brothers and sisters?'

The other girl shook her head.

Minimally encouraged, Tasha started to talk again. 'I've got four brothers. They all came to Elliott before me. My parents didn't want me to come at fourteen like they did, they thought I should be older. You know how parents get. Possessive. It's the worst when you're the youngest.' She was about to launch into a detailed description of each of her brothers' school careers, when the thump of a door behind her interrupted her, along with a low, unmistakable bellow.

'Yo! Tash.'

She spun around and ran straight up against a broad chest and a pair of stringily muscled arms. 'Schirm! Baby!' For a moment she savoured the bulk of his body and his mild, sweaty scent. Adam Schirmerhorn, her last spring's boyfriend, grinned, gap-toothed, down at her. Then she remembered, and detached herself slightly. 'Schirm, I've got a roommate.'

'Oh. Bummer.'

'Schirm, uh, this is . . .' She had forgotten the other girl's name, from the door.

Schirm, looking over at the other girl, seemed to brighten. 'Hey. Cool.'

The other girl gave the barest of nods, and Tasha, tugging Schirm out of the room and down the stairs, couldn't be sure whether she was annoyed because her roommate had been almost rude to Schirm – or because, even without being nice, she so obviously had made an impression.

Thank God, thought Kristin as her apparent roommate and

27

that creature, Schirm, galloped away down the stairs. She had not counted on a roommate, and the reality was more horrible than anything she had imagined on first glimpsing that second name-plate on the door. *Natasha Seidelman*. She had imagined someone small, dark and Jewish. Not this gabbling, honey-coloured centrefold. And that boyfriend! Kristin gave a small shudder. She wondered what it was about Americans. Why were they all so big – and so loud?

She ran her hands, in a habitual, comforting gesture, up and down the sides of her own arms. She wasn't big: there was nothing in excess about her. She could feel the comforting hardness of muscle and bone beneath her jumper.

She wondered what further horrors lay in store. She had glimpsed one or two other girls heaving trunks up the stairs earlier, though they seemed to be gone now. Around noon, the housemistress who lived downstairs, a thirtyish woman with a hippie bandanna around her head, had knocked on the door to invite her down for hot chocolate that night with all the other girls. Kristin had not told her that she found the idea of hot chocolate repugnant. What she wanted, and was just on the point of allowing herself, was a cigarette.

Yes. She had resisted long enough. It was time. She slipped open the latches of her suitcase and probed among the layers of folded clothing. When she had extracted her lighter and a single Carlton, she fastened everything up again. She made herself wait a torturing moment, the filter tip teasing her lips.

Then the flick of her lighter: the bliss of the first deep breath in. She would open the window in a second: not yet. Smoking was against the rules here, unless you had parental permission, which she, of course, had not obtained. She made it her policy to talk to her stepfather, John Borson – or Borson, as she thought of him – as little as possible.

He had sent her here; she wondered how long it would take her to get kicked out. How long, before he understood that she had no intention, either, of living peacefully with him, her mother, and his ghastly sons in Baltimore.

She thought with distaste of his ploddingly rational lectures. *Look. Elliott Academy is a very good school. You performed well on the entrance exams, and you're obviously not happy here at home . . .*

This isn't my home, she had snapped back, and then held her tongue before the urge to demolish his asinine views overcame her. *Happy? Happy, here?* Since when was happiness part of the human condition?

But she had learnt long ago that such observations were lost on Borson – on Americans in general.

She wondered about Natasha Seidelman. The other girl looked, of course, appallingly like all those students in the Academy's glossy prospectus: blond, suntanned, monstrously healthy. In fact, she possessed this typical look to such a degree that, Kristin realised now, she had failed to take in the other girl's features in any detail. She remembered a roundish oval face and a mouthful of straight teeth. Brown eyes, so far as she could recall, rather than the expected blue. She had registered Natasha Seidelman's height as somewhere near her own, five foot six; now she tried to gauge her weight. She was rarely wrong at this. Natasha, she thought, must be a good deal heavier than she: perhaps nine stone? Even ten?

Yes, Kristin thought, and took a long, polluting, satisfying drag of her cigarette. Natasha Seidelman was just a little bit fat.

She had opened the window to clear the smoke. Now, as she stubbed out her cigarette on the grid of the fire escape outside, she could see the low blaze of the setting sun at the top of the road: beyond all the other teeming, adolescent-inhabited houses. Soon, she registered, it would be six or so, and all their inmates – grinning their vacuous smiles and babbling away in their nasal voices – would troop off up that hill towards school supper in the dining hall. And then, since she had no intention of dining, Kristin would go out and find a phone. She had tried Aunt Poppy two nights ago. Aunt Poppy had said no. But Adrian, who was at Cambridge, her oldest friend – surely he would understand?

Tasha ran up the stone steps into the welcoming heat of Commons. It felt like coming home. Clusters of students gathered in the downstairs hall, beneath the stern portraits of Hyam and Silas Elliott. Voices rose everywhere in greeting, echoing each other in their delighted shrieks.

'Courtney!'

'Sarah-Jane!'

'Lorenzo, man! How've you been?'

The girls squealed and hugged; the more assured among the boys squeezed and kissed them back, while the more reticent grinned at each other and stuck close to the walls. Tasha rushed, beaming, into the mêlée.

'Tash!'

'Tasha!'

Her name joined the others among the echoes. For a moment she thought of her roommate – *Kristin* . . . Kristin Ward, that was her name – and wondered where she was. Maybe she should have gone back to Hobson to fetch her.

Then, absorbed into a group which made its way, shouting and laughing, along the stairs to the upper dining hall, Tasha forgot all about Kristin Ward.

2 Antony Czerny stood alone in the studio. Tasha picked him out at once, dressed in faded black and hunched over a clipboard, counting down names in a column, evidently, in a language she did not understand.

He turned at the sound of her footsteps and gave a fleeting smile. 'Hello there, Tasha. Goddamned class lists. The Dean wants me to take twenty-seven pupils for drawing. I tell her, no way. And so how are you? How is your work?'

Faced with his straightforward faith in her, Tasha felt, as ever, ashamed. She should have done more over the summer. 'Well, I did a few watercolours when we were up in Nova Scotia.'

'Watercolour is not your medium, surely?' Mr Czerny never smiled from politeness, but only when he was amused; he was not smiling now.

'Well, you're right, but . . .'

'Never mind.' He beckoned her towards his coffee machine, which stood alone in the middle of an unusually neat white counter. Soon it would be covered by jars full of brushes standing in muddy tins of turpentine.

'I was wanting to ask you,' said Tasha, 'can I come in tonight and get started?'

'For you' – Czerny gave a half-smile – 'I suppose. Since you seem to be incapable of working in normal hours. Only *you* will be the one to explain when you stay too late and have to climb up your fire escape after curfew. Okay?'

'It's a deal.' Tasha reached for her coffee. 'Anyway, I've made a resolution. This year I'm not breaking any more rules.'

'*That* we will have to see.'

They sipped their coffee and talked over their summers, and finally Mr Czerny asked her the inevitable question.

'And so, your parents. You have told them you wish to go to art school?'

'Not in so many words, exactly – '

'Tasha.' Czerny looked grave.

'Well – ' She shrugged. 'It's the year after *next*. My parents – well, they're pretty keen for me to go to Yale. Since two of my brothers went there.'

Czerny brightened. 'The Yale School of Art?'

'Yeah, maybe,' said Tasha evasively, knowing that was not what her parents meant at all. They meant the University, where, preferably, she would study something like biology or political science, and come to her senses. To change the subject, she said, 'I've got a new roommate.'

'How is she? You like her?'

'I don't really know her yet.' Tasha put down her empty mug and grinned mischievously. 'She's really beautiful.'

Czerny was not immune to a bit of flirtation. 'I am sure you have no cause to be jealous.'

'Nah, she's too weird for me to be jealous of. She doesn't talk.' In the last two days, Tasha and Kristin had exchanged even fewer words than on the first day they met. When Tasha came back at night, she always found Kristin reading in bed, or asleep; when she woke in the mornings, she found Kristin gone.

'Maybe she is jealous of *you*.' Czerny smiled.

For a second Tasha wondered if he had a point; then she dismissed the idea. 'Couldn't be. Anyway, I can come in tonight?'

'For you' – the teacher offered a mock-courtly bow – 'I will open these doors at any hour.' Then he added intently, '*If* you will begin to be serious.'

'I am. I am really, really going to work.' Tasha grinned and backed away. She knew Mr Czerny wouldn't believe her. She wasn't even sure she believed herself.

She walked away, down the long corridor of the art

block. The paint-spattered floors creaked, and as usual the whole barnlike structure looked in need of a few repairs. Evidently the school governors didn't see much point in pouring much money into art. As Mr Czerny was always saying, it didn't pay.

Tasha wondered for a moment, as she crossed the scrubby grass dividing the art block from Commons, whether in fact Mr Czerny was her best friend here. For all that they rarely spoke of anything personal, he seemed to understand her in ways her other friends – Schirm, Rachel, Courtney, Lorenzo – somehow did not. Her other friends, in fact, all thought Mr Czerny slightly ridiculous; and Tasha minded that. They thought all the Academy teachers were failures. *Why?* Tasha wanted to ask them. Antony Czerny had his integrity, his freedom to paint: what was so despicable about being a teacher? Not everyone had family money, like Schirm, or model good looks like Courtney, or bravado and acting talent, like Lorenzo. She had known all of them since their first weeks here, as new pupils, fourteen-year-olds. She ought to know them well, and they her; except sometimes all they had to say to each other sounded like hollow flattery. Courtney and Rachel, who roomed together in one of the big dorms up on the main campus, were always telling her, 'You're just so *radical*, Tash, staying down there in Hobson. Let's face it, if you wanted to be up here with us, you could. You'd fit right in. Everyone knows you.'

Tasha hadn't told them her main reason for staying at Hobson was that the housemistress there, Sarah, was too lazy about her job to notice how many hours Tasha spent behind a closed bedroom door with Schirm. She figured she needed her privacy. That was another good reason for staying at Hobson: but one she suspected Courtney and Rachel wouldn't understand at all. *You should run for Class President next year, really,* they told her sometimes. *You're so popular.*

That might be true, Tasha thought now as she rounded

the back of Commons, or it might not. It didn't stop her feeling, occasionally, oddly lonely.

Hurrying towards the row of doors, she nearly collided with Kristin Ward.

'Hey.' She smiled automatically. 'I haven't seen you in, like, *days*. What've you been up to?'

Kristin backed away slightly. 'The usual, I suppose.' She was wearing a navy blue woollen coat and clutching a styrofoam cup of something steaming.

Tasha watched her. Was it really worth making the effort? Kristin always seemed so prickly . . . She gave an inward sigh. 'So. I guess you've already eaten?'

Kristin nodded. 'Sort of. I'm in a bit of a hurry.'

'Oh, well. I'll probably end up alone, and with the dregs of the food.' Tasha tossed her head. 'Sure you don't feel like coming in again?'

'Well. All right.'

Tasha held the door open while Kristin balanced her drink, thinking what a remarkable voice the other girl had. She wouldn't mind being English and having a voice like that: soft, yet cool and elegant as if you owned the world. Moving past the upstairs steam tables, she was trying to think how to tell Kristin that, when, surprising her, Kristin spoke first.

'Somehow I don't believe what you said about eating alone.'

Tasha turned her head. She noticed that Kristin had picked up a tray too, and was gathering cutlery behind her. 'Sure, I get stuck on my own sometimes. Everybody does.' Actually, she couldn't remember eating alone since her first year, but she thought the lie might make Kristin feel better. 'Hey, I mean Commons is so huge.' She headed out towards the near-empty dining room, with its panelled walls and high windows. The four chambers of Commons were elegant but intimidating places; anyone who emerged from the serving rooms unaccompanied was

34

forced to stand, vulnerable and visible, scanning the wide spaces for a table to join.

Tasha glanced back. Kristin was digging among the near-empty bins of the salad bar.

She would, thought Tasha, feeling a stab of irritation. Kristin looked just the kind of impossibly thin girl who would insist on surviving on leaves. As Kristin joined her, Tasha glanced down at her own plate of soggy spaghetti and said, feeling a little mean, 'I thought you already ate.'

Kristin looked edgy. 'No. I didn't say that.'

Suddenly Tasha felt guilty for needling her. 'Hey, well, it doesn't matter. Nobody counts. Some of the guys who play football come in here like five times a day.'

Kristin gave a thin smile and said nothing.

Tasha planted her tray on a table. 'So did you go to Registration?'

Kristin nodded.

'I'm going this afternoon. English Poetry and History 42, right?'

'They told me I had to do both. What's History 42?'

'American history. It's *the* hardest course. It's notorious.'

'Then I suppose it'll be my duty as a loyal subject to fail it.' Kristin looked down studiously, dipping a carrot stick in her cottage cheese.

'Yeah, well, some people do, but they have to repeat. Oh.' Tasha grinned, feeling foolish. 'You mean 'cause you're not American.'

'Of course, if I failed *everything*' – Kristin still looked down, digging furrows in her cheese – 'they should have to kick me out. Shouldn't they?'

'That depends –' Tasha began.

'So perhaps,' Kristin went on, 'that would be the simplest way out of here? Fail everything.' She looked up with a sudden, conspiratorial smile.

Tasha grinned back. Something touched her in that smile of Kristin's: the earnestness in the slight overlap, so

35

rarely exposed, of the two small front teeth. 'Well –' She began again to explain. 'Like I said. It depends.'

'On what?'

'Well, for one thing, on how rich your parents are. And how many generations of your family have been to Elliott. They don't like to kick out legacies.'

'Legacies?'

'People with a family history here. Like, take Schirm. His grandfather and great-grandfather and great-*great*-grandfather all went here. So he'd have to just about commit murder to get kicked out. But for most people, if you break enough rules –'

'Such as?' Kristin's uptilted nose wrinkled.

'Oh, there're rules about everything.' Tasha was warming to the subject. 'Firearms, keeping a pet, setting off the smoke alarms, breaking curfew, drinking, drugs . . . They don't mind about sex so long as no one breaks curfew. I mean, basically, they don't want to know. And if you want to have boys in your room after curfew, there's always the fire escapes.'

'Fire escapes?'

'They climb up them. Weekends, for parties. Sarah's too spaced out to notice. Every Saturday night she smokes some dope and tries to get going on her novel. She's been writing it for three years. So, basically, you can do anything on a Saturday night. She doesn't want to hear you.'

Kristin frowned. 'I see.' She forked some lettuce into her mouth. Tasha couldn't tell whether Kristin disapproved or just didn't get it. Not, she thought suddenly, that Kristin could be all *that* pure. She'd definitely smelled smoke in their room a few times.

'I don't know,' said Tasha suddenly, 'how you can eat that stuff naked. Anyway, why do you bother? You're so skinny.'

Kristin shrugged, abashed, but also looked faintly

pleased. 'I suppose it runs in the family. My mother was a dancer.'

'Really? What kind?'

'In the Royal Ballet.'

'You're kidding! That's great. What does your dad do?'

'He – was in construction.'

Noting Kristin's constraint, Tasha took over. 'My dad's a doctor. Well, actually he does research, in neurology. My mom shops for a living. She's always saying Dad could make more money if he went into private practice, but he won't. Having five kids is kind of a strain on the old pocketbook, I guess.'

Kristin smiled. 'So everyone who comes here isn't fantastically rich.'

'Oh, no. This school prides itself on how *democratic* it is.' Tasha gave a quirky smile. 'It gives out scholarships and everything. But, yeah, there are a lot of rich people here, too. You've got your old-money types like Schirm. Then there are the diplomat brats and the UN babies. My friend Lorenzo's one of those. His dad's Dutch and his mom's Italian. All the UN people live on the East Side though, back in New York. I'm across the Great Divide.'

'How's that?' Kristin looked amused.

'Central Park. I'm from the West Side, but you don't get many West Siders here.'

'A bit like the river,' said Kristin suddenly.

'What?'

'In London. Almost everyone lives north of it. My Aunt Poppy doesn't, she lives in Putney, but that's almost as nice.' Kristin looked down and seemed to take a deep breath. 'I . . . used to want to go back home, to London. To live with her.'

'Would, um . . . I mean, you don't anymore?' Tasha felt she had to tread carefully.

'Well, I couldn't. I realise that now. She really hasn't the space.' Kristin smiled as she looked up, but her eyes were oddly bright. 'I also . . . had this notion of going to stay with my friend Adrian.'

'Oh. Is that your boyfriend?'

Kristin gave a slight laugh. 'Oh, no. He's an old, old friend. We practically grew up together in the country. But anyway, he's at Cambridge now, at university, so I couldn't actually stay with him. I mean, I understand.'

Tasha, puzzled by this narrative, didn't respond.

'It was a silly idea, I suppose. He said . . . I couldn't stay at his college for very long, and what would I do for money? And things like that.'

'So you really do want to go back to England.'

'I did. I *do*.' Kristin seemed to correct herself.

'What about your father? Couldn't you go back and live with him?' Tasha regretted the words as soon as they were out. Immediately Kristin started fidgeting with her fork and knife.

'My father's dead,' she said, and wiped her fingers and stood up.

'I'm sorry.' Tasha rose, too. 'I didn't mean to be nosy.'

Kristin gave an edgy smile, but still stood holding her tray. 'I don't suppose there's any point in my telling you all this. I don't suppose there's even any point getting kicked out. I'd only have to go back to Baltimore, which is even more horrid than here.' She gave a brief, forced smile and Tasha saw her eyes shining strangely again. 'Anyway.' She turned quickly. 'I really ought to go now. Thanks for lunch.'

Dumbfounded, Tasha watched her walk away. She thought she had been doing the right thing, trying to break through. But had she blundered in too far? Would it be better just to leave Kristin Ward alone? She wondered now.

Damn! Kristin stared at the ground as she walked down the hill, the clapboard walls and gables of Hobson House just in sight now. She hadn't meant to say all that to Tasha. What was the point of confiding – making friends? She'd only get pulled up again, and lose them. After four different schools in as many years, she'd learnt not to need friends: first St Paul's, then the comprehensive, then that girls' school in Baltimore, now here. The last time she'd had proper friends was at St Paul's. They had all said it wouldn't matter when she switched to the comprehensive – that they would keep in touch. They hadn't.

The comprehensive had been a fashionable one, in such a good part of London that her mother had only been able to afford a dank basement flat there. 'I'm sure this school is *quite* as good as St Paul's, darling,' Kari Ward told her daughter brightly. 'Cabinet ministers have sent their children here.'

But if they had, those days were long gone. Gangs in black leather smoked hash in the bathrooms and lined the corridors, ready to pounce on newcomers. On the first day, two of the older girls burnt a cigarette hole in the arm of Kristin's coat just to show who was in charge. But still, she could bear it, because at least she was still at home: still in London. She counted the weeks and years until she could do her A-levels; and then she would go to university and be free . . .

And then her mother had gone away on one of her weekends and come home, pink-faced and excited. 'Darling, John and I are going to be married.'

Kristin, who had adapted to her new school and was dressed from head to toe in rebel black, had looked up at her and snarled, in her best school voice, 'Bloody quick of you.'

'Darling.' Kari's thin lips pressed together. 'I don't think you should be so ungrateful. John is willing for you to come and live with us in Baltimore. Even to pay your school fees, he says so. Beggars can't be choosers.'

'I'd rather be a beggar.'

Later Kristin began to understand – though she never admitted it to her mother – that Kari Ward was saving them both in the only way she knew. She had never worked since her days in the Ballet; she had never expected to need to work again.

Still, Kristin thought, if *she* had been her mother, she would have taken the most boring, the most menial job, rather than marry fat-faced John Borson and go to live in suburban Maryland in the monstrosity he called a 'Tudor house'. She would have stayed single for the rest of her life, rather than shame Daddy's memory that way.

On the flight over to Washington, DC, a little more than a year ago, Kristin had exulted at the first turbulence. *Maybe we'll crash.* If they crashed, she would never have to land in America. She would die, and join Daddy, and Mummy would die and be punished for betraying him.

And then she looked out of the window, and was afraid. She had flown often enough before, but now, for the first time, she felt the vulnerability of their aircraft's perch in the sky. Why did they stay up? Why didn't they fall? Maybe they *would* fall.

And she knew then that she didn't want to crash. She wanted to live. She clung to the arms of her seat and closed her eyes, feeling queasy. She had learnt fear.

So that was how it had come about: flying first, then being driven in other people's cars. Then people, and making friends: but it didn't matter. None of it mattered. She was only here marking time, only waiting. Sometimes it seemed to her she had lost track of what for.

3 It was nearing the end of October, now, and in the evenings, when gusts of wind blew in through the cracks of the windows of Hobson House, Kristin would put on the kettle in their room and make tea. She had begun to convince Tasha of the therapeutic effects of Earl Grey, especially. As the kettle started to boil, inevitably, Tasha would let her books slip off her lap and start to talk: about her family, or the other girls in Hobson House, or even, occasionally, about the homework she claimed to be struggling through – though Kristin suspected that Tasha was cleverer, and found it all easier, than she would admit.

'"Binding with briars my joys & desires".' Tasha looked up one night from the blank page that was supposed to contain the next day's poetry essay. 'What the heck do you think that's all about? S and M?'

Kristin laughed. 'You're incorrigible.'

'"I went to the Garden of Love, And saw what I never had seen . . ." Well, that makes enough sense. I get that. But then this later stuff –'

Kristin smiled slightly to herself. She had written her essay on 'The Tyger'. She wasn't going anywhere near 'The Garden of Love', precisely because the poem set off strange vibrations in her that she did not care to analyse.

She supposed that for Tasha it all seemed straightforward: plain and easy. She thought of last Saturday night, when the three boys – Tasha's friends – had climbed up the fire escape into their bedroom, at two a.m. Schirm, the theatrical Lorenzo de Maas, and another from Lorenzo's dorm, Steve Steifel. Kristin supposed she had liked Steve the best of the three. While Lorenzo drank vodka and

41

attempted verbal fireworks, Steve sat back against the wall, a bottle of bourbon idling against his hand, watching the scene around him: the incense Tasha had lit in her small brass burner, the red scarf she had thrown over a lamp for dramatic effect, the wild shadows cast against the wall by Lorenzo's waving arms. Two of the younger girls from Hobson House were there, too, listening wide-eyed to Lorenzo's pronouncements on devil-worship.

Kristin had felt mildly bored, and began to squirm, her bottom aching against the hard floor. Steve glanced over at her. 'Cigarette?' he said, easing a pack out of his jacket pocket.

'Oh, yes, please.' Kristin looked up gratefully. He wasn't bad-looking, this Steve. He had light curly hair, a straight nose, chiselled lips.

'You English, or what?'

'Mm-hm.'

So they had started, rather lazily, talking. Steve came from Atlanta, where his father owned a furniture factory. A bottle of rum did the rounds of the room again, and Kristin declined it.

'You smoke, but you don't drink?' said Steve.

She shook her head. In fact, she abhorred alcohol – the calories, the bitter formaldehyde taste, the danger of losing control. But she smiled now, for she felt she ought to make an effort. Steve was polite at least, and didn't do anything like drape his arm around her – Schirm had tried that a few minutes before, making her cringe.

She smoothed her skirt. Its navy pleats looked formal and out of place here. She was beginning to think she ought to get some jeans, like everyone else wore. Steve seemed to read her thoughts.

'You look nice,' he said. 'Maybe I'm old-fashioned, or maybe it's my southern blood, but I like it when girls wear dresses.'

'Thanks.' Kristin looked down.

42

'How'd you like to clear out of here? I'm getting kind of hot.'

Kristin shrugged. 'All right.'

So they went next door, into the two younger girls' unoccupied bedroom, and, after laying a tentative hand on Kristin's arm and mumbling something about 'going out sometime', to which Kristin – she was not sure why – agreed, Steve Steifel kissed her.

It felt like nothing in particular, neither agreeable nor disagreeable: only wet.

'Hey,' Steve said, withdrawing, 'I've never kissed an English girl before.'

Kristin had no idea how she was supposed to answer that, and so she didn't.

She had let Steve kiss her twice more before one of the room's rightful occupants came in; and after that, standing in the corridor, she found herself accepting an invitation to dinner at the Elliott Inn.

Tasha was impressed. 'That's a pricey place. Schirm's *never* taken me there,' she said, when Kristin reported the news. 'You must be psyched.'

Kristin winced at the Academy jargon. 'Psyched,' she repeated. 'Mm, yes. I suppose.' She wondered to herself: was that, what she had experienced with Steve, what everyone got so worked up about? The reason for all the art and music and poetry, through all these centuries . . .

She had never, in fact, really kissed a boy before. She didn't know why. Perhaps because in the last few years she had never made friends, enough to be invited to parties.

Later that week, when she read 'The Garden of Love' for the first time, she felt a queer stirring somewhere in her that she knew had nothing to do with Steve Steifel, nor ever would. She wasn't sure what it meant. She wasn't sure what Blake was all about, really. It seemed no reason to ditch Steve. Tasha, after all, seemed to approve of him. He was one of the gang she half-jokingly called the Beautiful People, which seemed to include Lorenzo and

43

two rather haughty girls called Courtney and Rachel as well as Schirm and, sometimes these days, Tasha and Kristin. They always ate together in the upper hall of Commons – Kristin had quickly learnt that downstairs was only for nobodies. Which she supposed she would be herself, if it weren't for Tasha. Not that she cared. She wondered, sometimes, why Tasha had bothered to make friends, except for the fact that when Tasha relinquished the blandly optimistic Academy world-view for a moment or two, she could actually be rather clever. Even discriminating. She knew all kinds of things about art which she rarely let on: she made more of a show of knowing all the words to Simon and Garfunkel's songs. The younger girls in Hobson House would wander into her room to borrow records, or items from Tasha's well-worn and mainly second-hand wardrobe. 'Let's ask Tasha,' Kristin would sometimes hear one of them saying, whenever they faced some dilemma over boys, friends, or parents. 'Tasha's so cool.'

Cool was the ultimate accolade at Elliott, and Tasha seemed to earn it in spades. For looking good without taking much notice of her hair or ever bothering with makeup; for beating most boys at arm-wrestling and admitting loudly to her weight – 'One thirty-eight. All muscle.' She would stroll stark naked around the corridors of the house, and the funny thing, Kristin realised when she saw her then, was that in that state she did not look in the least fat – only voluptuous. Tasha talked with a startling frankness of her breasts – 36C, she claimed – and her periods. Or, sometimes, the lack of them.

Kristin had been sitting on her bed doing homework, a month or so after the start of school, when Tasha spun in, singing one of the songs from her Herman's Hermits album.

Kristin looked up. 'What on earth's the good news?'

'Major, major relief, Kris. I'm not pregnant. God, I never

44

really did believe I was, but you can't be sure, can you?' Tasha pirouetted, then collapsed heavily on to her bed.

'*What?*'

'I'm okay! I just got my period. I've never been so grateful in my life. What do you say we go out for ice cream and celebrate?'

'Wait,' said Kristin, as Tasha was starting to rise again. 'You really thought you could have been . . .'

'I was so stupid, I forgot my diaphragm, and then I was late. I was going crazy.'

'I didn't know.' Kristin's eyes widened.

'Well, I'm superstitious. Didn't want to talk about it and make it true.'

'But,' said Kristin, still grappling with the truth, 'you really thought there was a chance that –'

'There's always a *chance*. Except with the pill. Maybe I should go on the pill.'

'But do you mean you and – Adam –' Kristin still couldn't bring herself to use Schirm's silly nickname out loud.

'Sure. What did you think?'

Kristin felt foolish now. 'I don't know.' She smiled across at Tasha. 'I guess I didn't think.'

'What, are you a virgin?' said Tasha suddenly.

Kristin made no answer at first. Then she nodded, shamefaced.

'Hey,' said Tasha. 'What about that ice cream?'

They walked down the Boston Road into the middle of Lawrencetown, to Brougham's; and there Kristin heard it all: how Tasha had held out for the whole of her first two years at the Academy, then finally taken the plunge, just short of her sixteenth birthday. 'When I went to visit my brother Zeke at Yale,' she said matter-of-factly, 'his roommate devirginised me.'

Kristin stifled a laugh at Tasha's choice of words. 'But – wasn't it awful, since you didn't know him well? Embarrassing?'

'Nah.' Tasha waved a chocolate-covered spoon in the air. 'Matt seemed pretty experienced. I couldn't tell, then, but looking back . . .'

Kristin supposed some prompting was expected. 'You mean, after Adam?'

Tasha laughed. '"Adam". That cracks me up. But, yeah, I suppose, compared to him . . . and, well, I had a couple of flings in between. . . .'

'Flings?'

Tasha rolled her eyes in exasperation. 'You know!'

'Do you mean you've – slept with – other men, besides Adam and this Matt?' Kristin was still reeling slightly. Old-fashioned she might be, but she had only just grown used to the notion that her roommate was not a virgin.

'I had to know what it was like!' said Tasha cheerfully. 'But I've settled down a *lot* now. Hey.' She looked harder at Kristin, and shoved her sundae dish towards her. 'You look like you're in shock. Eat.'

Kristin, who had been sipping slowly on a diet soda and trying to avert her eyes from Tasha's ice cream, felt her resistance give way. She picked up a clean spoon, and in under thirty seconds, the sundae was gone. Then, without explaining, she walked up to the counter and ordered another.

'I'm glad to see you eating for once,' said Tasha.

When the second sundae was gone, Kristin sat back with a gasp. 'Oh, my God. I feel ghastly. Why did you let me do that?'

Tasha only looked on with a puzzled smile.

Kristin started gathering up her coat. 'We've got to go home. If I don't get out of here, I think I'll burst open and die. When I get home, I'll take some Ex-Lax. Then I'll be okay.'

Tasha followed her to the counter, where they paid. Then Kristin marched out and up the street, ferociously fast.

'Wait a minute,' said Tasha. 'Ex-Lax? That's, like –'

'Why not?' Kristin tossed her head. 'I do it all the time.'

'What? Take laxatives?'

Kristin nodded, walking even faster.

'But you can't! That's crazy. It screws up your system.'

'My system can manage.' Kristin took a deep breath. 'For heaven's sake. They just flush you out, that's all.' She didn't look at Tasha, but talked as they walked along. 'I hate ice cream really.'

'Then why was the guy behind the counter in Brougham's talking to you like he knew you?'

Kristin sighed and shook her head. 'Well –'

'You've been in there before. He said, "See you round."'

'Well, yes, I have. Once. Twice.' Kristin sighed again. She was building speed. 'I went in once, the night I tried to phone Adrian and he said I couldn't stay with him.' Her face turned bleak and inscrutable. 'I ate ice cream then. Three of those chocolate things. Yes. I know it's mad. I was depressed.'

'Oh,' said Tasha dully.

'Are you shocked?' Kristin looked over and smiled.

'Why not just, like, eat when you're hungry?'

'Tasha, if I did that I'd be enormous.'

They had almost reached the turning for Hobson House.

'Promise me one thing?' said Tasha. 'You won't take Ex-Lax. My dad told me what's in that stuff. Do you have any idea. . . .'

Kristin laughed: a high thin sound. 'I don't see much choice. If I don't, I'll be sick.'

'We'll walk instead, all right? We can walk around campus until you feel better.'

And so they had walked: up the Boston Road as far as Hy El and Commons and the sports pavilion; then further on, into the fields beyond; and then even further because Kristin said she still felt ill – she couldn't go back yet. So they circled the field until the sky was pitch black. It was long after curfew when they got back to Hobson House: luckily Sarah rarely bothered with sign-in.

Walking, they had talked of little things and big things, boys and brothers and food and men. Probably, Kristin realised later, that was the night they had begun to be friends.

Tasha invited Kristin to come to her parents' in New York for Thanksgiving. Kristin, having made no plans for the holiday, beyond a certainty that she would not go back to Baltimore, was glad to accept.

There were bowlfuls of *borscht* and a gigantic turkey, cooked and carved by the dark and immense Grandma Natasha, who browbeat all and sundry into eating three times as much as they would have otherwise, and interrupted her son Maurice's attempts at political discussion with an unstoppable determination: '*Tashka*, you and your friend are too thin! You must take more of this strange American bird. I find it dry. You know, Tashka, your friend, Christine – she reminds me of myself when I was young! When I was a model in Paris . . . I knew all the great ones then. Don't laugh, Ezekiel! It is true. I knew them all. Braque, Picasso, Derain . . .'

The Seidelmans were like no other family Kristin had yet encountered. Loud, uninhibited, as diverse in their appearance as the multitude of cats that roamed through the apartment, they seemed to swallow her up amongst them and yet not quite notice her. Tasha's two eldest brothers held forth on their jobs in medicine and banking; the youngest, Zeke, was plump, dark and nosy; the remaining brother, Nat, was the only one absent from the gathering, because he had defied family tradition to go and study in California.

Kristin supposed the Seidelmans must be well off, to judge from the collection of art on their walls. Rona was constantly referring to her father's furniture business: 'Loeb's, the largest on Long Island'. Yet the wallpaper behind the drawings and paintings was soot-darkened and the carpets bore a distinct smell of cat. Kristin imagined that the Seidelmans could afford to change all that, but simply didn't notice.

She had not really known any Jews before. Some of the girls at St Paul's had come from Jewish families, but then their parents had made scrupulous efforts to be more English than the English. As, she reflected, her own father had. She remembered the forced solemnity of holiday meals at Littledene: just herself and her parents. Cook would bring in soup, a roast, plum pudding. It had never occurred to Kristin to wonder what her parents had eaten on Christmas or New Year's Day, as children: what smells and flavours they had left behind in Hungary and Denmark, with their pasts, forever. Kari and Leslie never, ever spoke of their pasts: as if to remember them too clearly would make them foreign all over again.

She realised with a start that Zeke was asking her a question.

'So, Kristin. What's your ambition in life?'

She laughed. 'I suppose, to go back to England.'

He shrugged. 'Okay. Sure. But I mean career-wise.'

'That's rather secondary.'

'How can you say that?' Zeke paused to shovel into a dish of potatoes. 'Suppose you do get back to England, what are you going to do there?'

Kristin was not about to start explaining. 'I don't know, Zeke. What do you do? What are you studying?'

But he was not to be deterred. He went on questioning.

The next morning, Tasha and Kristin rushed out into the city. Tasha took Kristin to see the dinosaur skeletons at the Museum of Natural History; then they went down to Rockefeller Center and watched the skaters from the warmth of the café beside the ice rink.

'I'd like to take a picture of all this,' Kristin said suddenly. She didn't mean the tall buildings or the sky beyond: just the tangle of dark legs against ice.

'I didn't know you took photographs.'

49

Abashed, Kristin admitted, 'I don't. The urge just came over me all of a sudden.' In fact, New York had taken her by surprise today. She had expected to feel crowded, overwhelmed: to find it ugly. When instead, through the haze of cold winter air, it looked quite beautiful: the outsized grandeur of the glass boxes, the slim Art Deco towers. Kristin found herself thinking unexpectedly that she should like to capture it.

Tasha was eating chocolate cake, and clearly thinking about something else. 'It's funny,' she said. 'I just realised, I haven't thought about Schirm for two days. Have you missed Steve?' She tucked her flopping straight hair back behind an ear.

'Actually, he hasn't crossed my mind.' Kristin didn't particularly want to think about the Academy – or Steve, she realised. Steve, with his slow, gentlemanly kisses that failed to arouse her. She didn't like to think of this weekend's coming to an end. 'If I had a family like yours,' she said suddenly, 'I'd *hate* going back to school. Don't you mind it?'

Tasha smiled, bemused. 'No way! If I lived at home all the time, my folks would drive me crazy.'

'But your parents are wonderful!'

Tasha only shook her head. 'In small doses.'

That night before dinner, they sat lazily in Tasha's bedroom – which was big and square, like an artist's studio, nestled in the attic above the rest of the apartment – and leafed through the pages of her collection of art books. Outside the windows, the light of the setting sun caught the leafless trees of Central Park and the distant stone and brick mansion blocks of the East Side.

'I've always wanted to paint that,' said Tasha, standing up to look where Kristin did: at the sun-tinted silhouettes of buildings, the spacious sky. 'Sometimes I think Canaletto would have liked to paint New York. If he could have seen it.'

'The man who did all those paintings of Venice?'

'Yeah. But he painted other places, too. Like London. He had a way with bricks, and sky. Made them look better than they were, maybe. Kind of perfect and ancient.' Tasha smiled, self-conscious, as she shoved back her flopping hair. 'Me, I can't even make up my mind who I want to be. Cézanne, Canaletto, Whistler . . .'

'Why should you?' Kristin smiled back.

'Mr Czerny says you've got to get all the copying out of your system before you find out what your style really is.'

'I'm sure you'll get there.'

'But then, Mr Czerny doesn't trust me not to go into banking or something. Which my parents would be delighted about.'

'So? Prove them all wrong.' Kristin looked oddly determined.

'So what do you want to do?' said Tasha. 'You know. When you're older.'

'Everyone in your family keeps asking me that! I haven't a clue.' Kristin flopped down on the floor again, where she had been looking at Tasha's photo books. Some of them still lay open: Ansel Adams's western landscapes, Eugene Atget's Paris. She had never thought photographs could do so much.

'Well, what did you used to want to do?' Tasha persisted. 'When you were little?'

'I never thought about it.' Kristin met Tasha's astonished stare. 'Really and truly! No one ever asked. I thought I'd just grow up and go on living at Littledene. There was a lot to do there.' She spoke defensively now. 'We had ponies . . . and dogs and things. Most of the women in the neighbourhood didn't have jobs, anyway. They had houses to look after, and children.'

'Oh,' said Tasha, dumbfounded.

'Don't you want children?'

'Maybe. I want to paint, though. That's the main thing.'

Tasha turned towards the window and didn't seem to realise Kristin was staring.

To be so certain: to have such concrete ambitions. Kristin envied her. What kind of a hope was it – to want to go home? To restore what had been hers before? To belong again – with scarcely a thought for something so mundane as a 'career', which could only be peripheral to her real desires . . . It was surely not the sort of ambition an American would understand.

Tasha turned over in bed, puzzled. It made no sense, what Zeke had murmured to her, a few minutes ago.

'I'd watch out for that girl,' he said over his shoulder as they foraged together in the fridge. 'She's compulsive.'

Tasha had only laughed. 'Right.'

'You'd just better watch yourself. She'll use people.'

'Uh-huh.'

'I'm not kidding. Believe you me, that little-girl-lost act's just a put-on. She wants money. Money and status. And she'll trample all over people to get them, so watch out.'

Tasha laughed again. 'Thanks for the amateur psychology.' When Zeke started to protest, she waved him good night. He didn't have a clue. For heaven's sake, Kristin didn't *have* an ambition. If she found one, so much the better for her. Even then, Tasha doubted that she would trample all over anyone to get what she wanted: Kristin was too gentle, too polite. She'd never really hurt anyone else. Tasha was sure of that.

The five days had to come to an end. Kristin had tried to prepare herself. On Friday, and especially today, she had warned herself, *You'll have to go back*. After Thanksgiving dinner, the Seidelmans' apartment had slowly emptied, Grandma Natasha, David and J.L. returning to their own homes in the city; for the rest of the weekend only Zeke and Tasha were left. Now, on Sunday night, as Tasha was upstairs packing her suitcase, the phone rang.

Kristin answered it. She was nearest to it, reading in the living room.

'Hallo?'

'Hi, there. Are you Kristin?'

'How – who – who is this?'

'I think you've got to be Kristin. I could tell just from the way you said that one word. "Hallo?"' The voice on the other end laughed, and before Kristin could gather her wits for a rejoinder, went on, in oddly soothing tones, 'Hey, don't hang up yet. This is Nat.'

'That's what I thought.'

Nat – the brother Tasha talked about the most, the one who hadn't come home for Thanksgiving because he was too far away – seemed in no hurry to speak to his family, but started talking to Kristin instead. Later, she wasn't sure what they had talked about: only that there was something calm and un-Seidelmanlike about Nat. Something which invited inconsequential chat, as if it mattered: as if, long distance or not, he had all the time in the world.

After a few minutes Tasha came bounding into the room. 'Yo! Is that Nat?' She grabbed the phone before Kristin could answer, then scolded into it: 'Nathaniel. Stop flirting with my roommate.' Tasha grinned at Kristin while a series of unintelligible protests poured into her ear.

Tasha stayed on the phone almost an hour longer, while Kristin wandered upstairs to pack. She was curious about this Nat, who, she gathered, was the token black sheep of the family: for a Seidelman, leaving the East Coast and opting to study psychology instead of medicine amounted to a major rebellion. Half-overhearing Tasha's voice, then others joining it in the living room, Kristin fought the urge to go downstairs again. *After all, they're not my family.* She thought of Lawrencetown, and catching the train back tomorrow, and loneliness flooded her.

'If you like it,' Tasha was insisting into the phone, 'just get it. So what if the dealer says –'

'Nathaniel,' Zeke broke in, 'buy the car.'

'How much does it cost?' Maurice demanded.

'Your father's right,' Rona chimed in. 'Try to bargain him down. And by the way, how long have you been on the phone, Nathaniel? Are you running up your bill?'

'Rona, leave him alone, he's a grown-up boy –'

Kristin closed the bedroom door on the cacophony of voices, then leaned back against it and made herself take a deep breath. *They're not your family.* They might have been kind – Tasha's father might even have engaged her in several heart-to-heart conversations over the weekend, of his own peculiar psycho-political variety, while Rona had counselled her earnestly on New York bargain-hunting – but still, they were not her parents. Nor were Tasha's brothers her brothers. She was as alone as she had ever been. Anything else was just pretending.

She hated tears: hated the way they made her lose control. She stood in the light of the window, forcing them back, making herself look clearly at the park: Tasha's Canaletto Manhattan.

Immediately, arriving upstairs, Tasha knew something had gone wrong. The lights were all out and it was dark. 'Kris? Where are you?'

'Here.' The voice came, subdued, from near the window.

Tasha approached hesitantly. 'Kris? Is something wrong?'

'Nothing, really.' Kristin's voice was shaky. 'I'll be all right.'

'Are you feeling homesick?' Tasha laid a hand on Kristin's straight back; she felt it tremble, bony and warm, like a wary small animal's.

'How could I be homesick?' Kristin sniffed. 'I hate Baltimore, and I hate my family.' She took a deep breath. 'It's just . . . you're all so *happy*.' She looked over, with brimming eyes.

54

'We're not.' Tasha forced a smile. 'Not much more than most families.'

'Then mine – must be the exception.' Kristin twitched her head away.

'Hey. It's all right.' Tasha stroked her back and moved closer.

'I hate – getting emotional about it. It's no use really.'

'You have to let things out.'

Kristin gave a small smile, and sniffed. 'Do I?'

'Is it . . . Do you miss your father?'

Kristin's body shook for a second, but she didn't answer.

'How did he die?' Tasha heard the words come out: cold, brutal – and for a second she regretted them. But she felt suddenly that she had to know. Kristin talked so little about her parents: her past. Tasha had pieced together something of her history: the fact that she had been forced to move around, to go to many different schools. The fact that something had gone wrong with her father's business.

Kristin said almost coldly, 'He shot himself.' She paused. 'At the house – at Littledene. He was in the study. I found him.'

'Oh, Kris.' But Tasha found that no words sufficed: that when she tried to draw Kristin closer, the other girl didn't want to be held. 'Kris, I'm sorry. I'm sorry I asked like that. I –'

Kristin seemed not to hear her. 'He'd – lost all his money. And us. My mother had left him. I didn't understand why, at the time. I went out to the country one day, to see him. It was an impulse –' Her mouth tightened into a grimace, her body straightening, stiffening.

And then she took a gulp of air, a deep breath, and it all came out. A long, disjointed story: office towers and Budapest and a self-absorbed Danish dancer; money and belonging and not belonging. And at times Tasha thought she began to understand, and at times she didn't at all; and when Kristin had finished, and took a deep breath again and said, 'You see, don't you? Why I need to go back. Why I have to?' Tasha nodded. Though she didn't really see.

'Because it was *mine*, Littledene, it was meant to be mine. And if I give up – that means he lost. Still foreign. A failure. He's there, in the churchyard at Littledene. He's waiting.'

Tasha stroked Kristin's arm. 'I'm sure he can wait a while longer.' She looked worriedly at her friend. 'You're not going back – right away, anymore, are you?'

Kristin shrugged and gave a narrow smile. 'I don't suppose I can.'

'You're not going to leave Elliott, are you?'

'I suppose there are worse places.'

'Because I don't *want* you to go, you know. You're the best roommate I ever had. I mean it.'

A smile quivered on Kristin's lips.

'We're going to have a good time there! You'll see. It wouldn't be the same without you.'

'Thanks.' Kristin smiled again. As she plunged towards Tasha the other girl's arms enfolded her, and they both clung on, very tight.

1982

4 Kristin hurried up the hill, through the fresh snow that had already filled the furrows dug yesterday by feet and shovels. It was eight a.m. and she felt all alone in the world, and happy. However late they all stayed up at Hobson House, she had never lost her habit of getting up early. Sometimes she woke up red-eyed, but if the sky was light she could not sleep, and so she made her way up to the darkroom in the art block, to work.

She had started photography classes last winter. At first she had been disheartened by how little she could do: whatever she saw in her mind's eye, it always failed somehow to emerge in her prints. But perhaps the very fact that she knew what she *wanted*, made her persevere when the others gave up. Also, she had become mildly addicted to the intense red-lit quiet of the darkroom.

As she climbed the slope of lawn towards the shining white peak of Hy El, it seemed hard to believe that she had belonged to this place for only a little more than a year. She had spent a long, dreary summer in Baltimore, working in a clothing store so that she wouldn't have to ask Borson for money; after that, she had not returned home again, but spent Thanksgiving and last Christmas with the Seidelmans. She didn't think her mother and Borson missed her particularly; somewhat to her surprise, they had accepted, without protest, her announcement that she wanted to go to Paris next year to study photography. Borson had even agreed to pay. But then, it occurred to her in her more cynical moments, the school she was proposing to go to was cheaper than an American university – and also much farther away.

Next year Tasha would probably be going to art school in

New York – though she had agreed, at her parents' urging, to apply to Yale. She didn't expect to get in. The other people in Tasha's gang had their plans made, too: Lorenzo was studying drama at Yale, and Courtney, now Class President, was into Harvard. Steve was taking a year off . . .

Kristin still didn't like to think about Steve. She and Steve were friends now: at least that was the accepted Elliott terminology. Their explorations – to Tasha's astonishment – had never gone much beyond kissing. For some reason, Kristin had not wanted them to, and had evaded Steve's invitations up to his room until eventually he stopped asking. Kissing bored her. She would sit rigidly on the bed beside him, tongues trawling, and wonder how much longer it could go on.

Tasha, for her part, could hardly believe that was as far as it had gone. '*What*? He doesn't turn you on? But he's so good-looking, Kris. What's the matter?'

Kristin couldn't begin to explain, and it made her feel no better when last spring Steve took up with Rachel, Courtney's roommate, and the two of them were hardly ever seen outdoors for the rest of that year.

Tasha said not to let it bother her. Maybe, for her and Steve, the chemistry just hadn't been there. Maybe it hadn't; but the lack troubled Kristin. Was something frozen in her, that she couldn't respond physically to men – could never seem to desire them on sight, as Tasha did? Kristin lost count of the boyfriends Tasha had gone through in the last year. She and Schirm had drifted apart just after Thanksgiving, and after that had come Gerard, an intense, square-browed aspiring physicist; Kev, who swam on the school team and smelt of chlorine; Wallace, with the Navajo nose, who read Beat poetry and knew where to find psychedelic mushrooms . . .

Often Kristin wondered how Tasha did it: found something to attract her in all of them, different as they were.

'You've just got to open your eyes!' Tasha would answer. 'There are guys at this school practically lining up to go out with you, Kris, if you'd just, like, drop them a hint.'

'Who, then?'

Tasha had named names, and Kristin was mildly troubled to realise that she had never given the attractions of any of these candidates a moment's thought. What was wrong with her?

'You've got to give guys a chance,' said Tasha. 'They're intimidated by you.'

'By me?' Kristin gave an incredulous laugh.

'Because of your looks, and maybe . . . because you're kind of reserved, you know? You've got to help guys along. Talk to them, laugh at their jokes . . . You know, seduce them.'

Kristin only laughed again. She hadn't the remotest idea of how to seduce someone. Besides, she didn't want to. She wanted to *be* seduced: taken, surely and swiftly. Without embarrassment, without affection. Desire only. Virginity dispensed with.

She didn't know how to put this to Tasha, and so every time she tried, the words evaded her.

'An older man?' said Tasha.

'Maybe. But it's not essential.'

'I'm sure we could find you an older man . . .'

Kristin shook her head. This was the last thing she wanted to be thinking about on her way up the hill to the darkroom. Surely, somewhere in the world, other seventeen-year-old girls were virgins and not filled with embarrassment at the fact. Maybe, after all, she should let Tasha arrange something, with some Academy boy.

The thought filled her with repugnance. *What is wrong with me?*

She threw open the creaky front door of the art block. With any luck, after a good couple of hours' work, she would have forgotten all about this. Someone was studying the photos on display on the wall – most of which were hers – but she barely looked to see who it was.

Then he spun to face her. He had a crooked smile under shaggy, almost black hair, and something about the shadows around his eyes gave him away as too old to be an Academy student. Though not far too old. He was wearing jeans and an oversized, slightly grubby Aran jumper.

'Sorry,' he said, stepping back. 'I thought you were my boss. But I can see I'm okay. You're not.' He smiled briefly.

'Your boss?' Kristin repeated. The man's smile seemed to change the look of his whole face: the shape of it, even. Thin and angular before, with hollows beneath prominent cheekbones, it filled out when he smiled. The cheeks creased; the dark eyes twinkled and lost their hunted look.

'Aye. Antony Czerny. Do you know him?'

He was Scots, then. She recognised the accent. 'Sort of,' she said.

'He'll be after me by now. I've been in hiding.' The smile again.

'Oh, I shouldn't worry.' Kristin wondered why she said that. She didn't really know Mr Czerny well; nor had she the faintest idea who this man was, or what he was supposed to be doing. 'Hiding from what?' she said now.

'You lot,' he said, with a nod in her direction. 'Young Americans.'

'I'm not American,' said Kristin, offended.

'Aye, I know that. Thought you wouldn't like it if I said you were.'

'Why did you say it, then?'

But the man only shrugged, infuriatingly. He turned towards the wall, and the display of photographs on the bulletin board. Kristin noticed the curve to the bridge of his nose, more pronounced in profile than it had been straight on. Wavy hair fell over his forehead and down on to his collar. She wondered what he was supposed to be doing for Mr Czerny. Maybe he was a sort of workman. He had the hands of one: large and square, the backs of them tanned and nicked and scarred, the fingers burying themselves just now in his jeans pockets. 'These aren't bad,' he said, jerking his head towards the wall.

'Thank you.' Kristin tried to give an ironical ring to her voice. 'Actually, I took them.'

His gaze flickered over her for a moment with something like respect. 'You did?'

'Does that surprise you?'

He only laughed. 'Are you dead set on being offended no matter what I say?'

'I don't know what you mean.'

'I should have guessed. It's always like that with the English.'

'So it comes down to that.' Kristin gave him a long look, and a thin smile. 'The Scots versus the English. That *is* old.' She wondered, momentarily, why she was having this discussion. She could be well into her developing by now.

But, when he looked at her, the expression in his eyes – half-obscured though they were by all that hair – was meeker than before. 'Could we start again by any chance? I'm Peter Conaway.'

'Hello.' She smiled slightly. 'I'm Kristin.'

'Do you have a last name?'

'Ward.' She looked past him. His eyes made her nervous. 'Are you . . . working here?'

'Supposed to be. They gave me something they're calling a teaching fellowship. Czerny thought the thing up, I don't know what I'm supposed to do yet.'

'I see.'

'I'm a sculptor and Czerny thought it might help give me time to get started here, get some work together, I've got a show coming up this spring.' Peter Conaway locked his fingers together and stretched his arms out in front of him.

'Good for you,' said Kristin. She was torn between politeness and a desire to escape. There was something about this man's presence that pressed in upon her: a vividness, an ebullience, a sense that he would talk on forever, unless positively discouraged.

63

'See, this place is weird for me.' Peter Conaway glanced around, then stepped closer to Kristin with a conspiratorial look. 'All these rich Americans. Like, for instance, do you ever wonder how they all get those teeth?'

'What?' Kristin gave a bemused smile.

'I think they shoot elephants and pull out the ivory or something. Walruses, maybe. They aren't *real* teeth, I know that for sure.' Peter smiled again.

Kristin almost said that there seemed to her to be nothing wrong with his own teeth; but that seemed a bit personal. 'I – ought to go,' she said.

'Where?'

She gave a slight, puzzled frown. 'The darkroom. I was on my way in, when . . .'

'So tell me.' He half-turned towards the wall. 'These photos. How do you get them to come out, when there's no light?'

He was pointing at two shots of Hy El at dusk. Kristin felt a small tremor of pleasure, that her work had been noticed, appreciated. 'Oh, it's not so hard,' she said. 'I used a tripod and fast film and waited. But then on two nights people wandered into the frame and I ruined it, so I had to go back again.'

'You're a perfectionist.'

'I don't know. Maybe.'

'I wouldn't have the patience for photography.' Peter Conaway paused, his thumbs hooked into the pockets of his jeans. 'Great thing about sculpture, you can even do something with your failures. Paint them an interesting colour, tack on a few scraps more. Might even sell it to some no-hoper.' He grinned.

'I'm not sure I believe you're an artist,' said Kristin archly. 'You don't seem to take it very seriously.'

For a moment, neither of them spoke. Peter's eyes travelled over her. She had the odd feeling that he was taking her in for the first time: noticing more than the fact that she was a certain age, a certain sex. Measuring her.

Finding her – what? Desirable? Not? She couldn't tell. His eyes were a dark, flat brown, strangely impenetrable, and now they travelled slowly up from somewhere in the middle of her body, towards her face.

'So do you eat breakfast?' he said.

What an odd question, she thought. Either it was purely hypothetical, or he was asking her out. Somehow she didn't want to take the risk of a definite answer. She shrugged. 'I really ought to go now.'

'Aye, well then.' Peter Conaway nodded and said no more.

Feeling foolish, even unkind, for having rejected his offer – if, indeed, he meant one – Kristin turned abruptly towards the darkroom. 'Goodbye.'

'See you round, then, Kristin.'

There was something mocking, she thought, in his voice. For a moment she wondered if she had confirmed his every stereotypical Scottish notion of the English: cold, aloof, unapproachable. Oh, well, if she had, that wasn't *her* problem.

Normally she told Tasha about every new person she met, just as Tasha always told her. New faces were scarce enough at Elliott. But for some reason Kristin did not tell Tasha about Peter Conaway. She reasoned that they would meet soon enough, for Tasha had already signed up for sculpture class: this was the first time sculpture was being offered by the art department, and now Kristin knew why.

She had the uneasy feeling that Peter was the sort of man Tasha would fancy like mad. Well, she would have every reason to. Kristin remembered the queer sensation, like a rush of warmth through her body, that she had experienced, ever so briefly, as Peter's gaze travelled upwards and met hers.

She rather wished she would run into him again. Just by accident. But at the same time, over the next few days, she shied away from the art block. She had no new rolls of film to develop, she told herself. So she had no good reason to go there.

In the end, she was running up the steps of Commons when she saw Peter again, so fast she almost missed him.

'Kristin!' he called: not particularly loudly, his voice guttural in the wind. He was at the far end of the long row of doors, and students in ski jackets flew in and out and down the steps between them. He was wearing, Kristin noticed, only the jeans and jumper she had seen him in before, though snow was piled high on the ground.

'Hello.' She smiled and moved slightly closer. 'Aren't you cold?'

'What?'

'No coat.'

'Ach, I don't own one. Don't need it.'

'Oh.' She felt suddenly foolish. Was he, perhaps, too poor to afford one? She shouldn't have mentioned it.

As if he had read her mind, he went on, 'Where I come from, we never get anything but rain. Never gets this cold either, though. Out by the coast we used to have palm trees.'

'Where's that?'

'Dornoch, on the Firth of Clyde.' He smiled. 'You know where that is?'

Kristin shrugged. 'Of course. In . . . Scotland.'

'See you southerners – you'd all be shocked if I didn't know where, like, Guildford was, or Chipping-in-the-Marsh or what have you. But when it comes to Scotland . . .'

'I haven't,' Kristin said crisply, 'lived in England for two and a half years.'

'Counting the days, are you? So what brought you here?'

'Oh, various things.'

He studied her. She thought that she would rather he talked.

'Haven't seen you round the darkroom,' he said.

'I haven't had any pictures to develop.' She allowed herself to meet his eyes just for a second; they looked as obscure and brown-black in the daylight as they had indoors.

He dug his hands into his pockets. 'You know, people here . . . Does it ever seem to you, like –' Then he shook his head. 'Never mind.'

'What?'

'Like you can't have a conversation 'cause they just flit away from you before it's started? Except these teachers Antony's always introducing me to. They're a dreich lot. Heaven help me from teaching for a living by the time I'm forty.'

'Have you taught before?'

'Sure, all over. Place I just left was a posh school down in New York, on the Upper East Side, but that was easy. Bunch of twelve-year-old boys. They didn't care about art, so I gave up. We cleared the room and played football.'

Kristin laughed; Peter went on without stopping. 'See, they were all, like, only children. Try telling that to people in Dornoch: one kid, that's all you get, can't afford any more. The Pope'd have fits. 'Course these New York kids, their parents were all divorced. I felt a bit sorry for them, actually. Most of them had drivers coming to pick them up in the afternoon. And, Jesus! You should have seen some of those cars. Great big Mercedes – what I would have given for a run down Fifth Avenue on a Sunday in one of those. Or out on a highway . . . Isn't it amazing, don't you think, sometimes, Kristin? The way you get out on the road here and there's just nobody around you. So big and straight – you start going eighty, ninety – you hardly notice.'

A little dazed by the sudden stream of words, Kristin only laughed again. 'Actually I hate being in cars. They make me feel ill.'

'Come on.' Peter was mocking her. 'You're in America!'

'Well, I'm afraid that wasn't my choice. If it had been, I wouldn't be here.'

'How do you mean?'

But something made Kristin draw back from telling him. She remembered, suddenly, where she was: the fact that she had a class soon and that Courtney Abbott was staring at her curiously from the middle of a clump of people further along the steps. 'Oh, it's a long story,' she said.

Peter seemed not to mind how she answered. 'Wish me luck,' he said. 'I'm taking my first class here tonight. Think they'll be any good?'

'Why ask me?'

'I've seen your pictures. Thought since you had some talent yourself, you ought to know.' Peter looked at her, unsmiling, for a moment, and she had the feeling that, in the middle of what had most probably been a series of exaggerations, flights of fancy – he was telling her the truth.

'Thanks.'

He shrugged.

'Actually, my roommate's going to be in your class. Tasha Seidelman. She paints. Most people think she's very good.'

'I'll look out for her, then.' Peter nodded goodbye as Kristin headed, belatedly, for the door and pulled it open. She would be late for her next class now, if she took time to get a coffee, but she would have felt foolish backing away. She smiled through the glass at him, but already he was moving down the steps. *Towards Tasha*, she thought: she knew absurdly. Of course he was going to meet her sometime. He was going to meet plenty of people. Obviously he wanted to – he had more or less said he was lonely.

For a second, she wished she had done something – said something more. But what could she have said? She

68

almost wished she had gone out to breakfast that time when he asked her. But it was too late for that.

5 Tasha had seen handsomer men, she reflected as she cleared up after that first sculpture class; she had seen men better built, more symmetrically formed. So what could explain the way she had felt when Peter Conaway walked into the room?

She had had no doubt. She had known at once. *I want him.*

She could try to tear that instant attraction into pieces: to analyse it. She remembered the broad shoulders and long arms, muscular out of all proportion to the rest of him; the dark wavy hair he kept shaking out of his eyes. The smile that filled out the hollows of his face and seemed to say he loved the whole world, himself included – and especially you.

It didn't even matter that, thanks to his accent, she could only understand about two-thirds of what he said. He had talked a blue streak, all through sculpture class. He had made them laugh, a few at a time, as this group or that group of students managed to make out what he'd said. Tasha had strained her ears to hear. She had come away feeling exhausted.

When he had asked for a volunteer to demonstrate a few points he was trying to make about the human body, she had immediately leapt forward. He had touched her, she supposed, as little as he reasonably could, adjusting her position, and then walking around her. 'I had an old teacher,' he said, 'at the Glasgow School of Art. Told us we all end up portraying ourselves. And he was right. So, see, Tasha, don't get offended at what we come up with. Just tell yourself if it was Picasso you'd have two heads.'

Then for five minutes everyone had sketched – except,

Tasha noticed, for Peter Conaway. Every time she glanced in his direction, she seemed to catch his eye; his gaze, bright and dark, upon her. As he had predicted, the sketches all looked different from one another, and nothing like her. Thanking her again, he touched her on the shoulder. She felt strangely warm there, still.

Just before the class adjourned, he mentioned that he was looking for a regular model for the class: the department would pay.

'Dressed or undressed?' said a joker at the back of the room.

'That you volunteering? No? So, okay, I'm in Quincy Adams House. If anyone knows anyone, tell them to get in touch.'

Tasha made sure she was the last to leave after class, lingering over the jammed drawer of a cabinet.

'Never mind, I'll get that.' Peter gave it a careless shove, and it slid in.

'You're pretty strong.'

He shrugged. 'Work with enough heavy stuff and you get to be. So, thanks again.'

'Are you really from Glasgow?'

He looked amused. 'No, I'm just a small-town boy. So are you really from New York?'

'How did you know?'

'Your voice. I used to teach there.'

To Tasha's amazement, he had taught at the very school her brothers had gone to when they were younger: before high school. 'Wow,' she said, and told him, 'that's, like, such a coincidence.'

'Is it? Seems to me the rich folk move about in a pretty small world, even in America.'

'I'm not rich,' said Tasha automatically. Peter only laughed.

'No, really. I'm not. It's like . . .'

He shook his head then. 'It's too late to argue this one,

71

Tasha. It'd take us all night, and I've got to close up this place. Don't you lot have a curfew or something?'

'Yeah, um . . .' Tasha searched her mind for something else to say, to keep the conversation going. Then a notion struck. 'I might know someone who could model. My roommate, actually.'

'Good. Just let her know where I am, then.'

This seemed, somehow, an unsatisfactory way of concluding the conversation, but, faced with curfew and nothing else pressing to say, Tasha turned and nodded. 'See you next week.'

'Aye, Tasha. See you then.' For some reason, that amused look was playing around Peter's lips again.

'You *what*?' Kristin almost shrieked.

Tasha repeated herself.

'Tasha, that's ridiculous. I couldn't possibly.'

'He said there was money. A couple of dollars an hour. I thought since you said your stepfather'd been giving you problems about your allowance . . .'

'But – standing up in front of all those people? Wearing – what?'

'A leotard. Whatever you wear for dance.'

'I couldn't. I'd be mortified.' How fat am I these days? Kristin wondered with a sudden desperation. Last summer, when she had gone back to Baltimore, she had been horrified to find out she weighed over eight and a half stone. Her period, which hadn't troubled her for over a year, had returned, and stayed with her through most of the summer though she dieted ferociously. She had come back to school almost a stone lighter, but, what with Hobson House's mass excursions to the pizzeria and the ice-cream parlour – and then this Christmas, at the Seidelmans' . . .

She didn't know if she could contemplate exposing herself in her current state. Tasha was chattering on about sculpture class.

'. . . and so I volunteered to model just this once, but, God! I felt stupid, and Peter's really, really gorgeous . . .'

'What?'

'Black eyes, black hair – he's got these real muscular arms. He's Scottish but he looks kind of Italian to me. Or Irish. You know, like, dark Irish.'

'Oh,' said Kristin. She heard the stunned note in her voice but hoped that Tasha didn't.

'The weird thing is, I hadn't seen him around here anywhere before. Have you?'

'What? Oh, um, no.'

'Oh, well. I'm sure he's taken. Probably got a girlfriend back home. All the good ones do.' Tasha gave an exaggerated yawn. 'Hey, I've got bagels and cream cheese in the fridge. Do you want some?'

'No!' Kristin almost snapped. 'No, thanks.'

Tasha gave her a funny look. 'Only asking.'

The next time Kristin saw Peter, she was hurrying past Hy El on her way to French; she really was in a hurry, or so she told herself, for when Peter waved and called hello to her, she didn't stop, only called back, 'Hi,' a little breathlessly.

'How are you, Kris?' he shouted.

'Fine. And you?' She knew then that she had the chance to mention it. *Tasha – my roommate – said you needed a model . . .*

But she hadn't the nerve. So they passed and went their separate ways. Kristin felt a momentary regret, as at an opportunity missed, or perhaps never really grasped in the first place. Peter must be getting to know more people around the Academy now. Soon he would forget he had met her first; what might have been friendship would drift back into ordinary acquaintanceship – and then, perhaps, nothing at all. Which was all right. She told herself it was all right. What difference did it make whom she met or what she did here, since this was not her world and she was leaving it so soon?

Tasha overheard the phone call, later that night, and smiled.

'Hello. Um . . . Peter?' Kristin's voice sounded polite and excessively formal. 'Yes. Yes, it is me.' She gave a small nervous laugh. 'Well, actually, um, my roommate – Tasha Seidelman, she's in your sculpture class? – mentioned to me that you might be needing a – model . . .'

It only dawned on Tasha as she heard the phone click down and watched Kristin re-enter their room, pink-faced, that there had been something odd in her first few words. *Yes. Yes, it is me.*

She sounded as if she and Peter knew each other, from somewhere. And if they did – even if they had met just once – why had Kristin never mentioned it?

That Thursday night, Tasha walked into the studio a few minutes early. She felt proud of herself for not being jealous. Peter was bound to notice Kristin's looks: everyone did. But, Tasha told herself, she was secure enough to handle that. She had come to the private conclusion that Kristin was too shy around men to make anything happen with them. *Look, but don't touch*: that was the message she gave off. And Peter would be no different.

A few of the other students trickled in, and she made an effort to start up a conversation, all the while keeping an eye out for Peter. When at last he arrived, it was in the midst of a group of students – chatting, laughing. Tasha felt jealous, as she had not before. *She* should have been with them, talking to him. Surreptitiously she watched him as he split off from the group and shed his slightly mud-stained thick white sweater. When he rolled up his shirtsleeves, Tasha could see the cords of muscle in his arms. She thought of him bare-chested, hewing stone: of Michelangelo's *Slaves*. And she swallowed, as a warm jolt of desire ran straight through her.

Tasha, she warned herself, *you're going to have to let this one die down a little. You're going to have to control it.*

74

Kristin knew she was ready. She must resist the temptation to cover herself up again: to run away, to go home. She was dressed as if for dance. She must pretend this was a dance class. She must simply go out.

She looked down, and saw fat on her stomach; she knew it was behind her, too, on her hips and thighs. The cold made her nipples stand out. She wished she had worn a bra.

For the fourteenth or fifteenth time she wished that she could have contrived some other way of getting near Peter again: that she had resisted that momentary impulse to phone him. Then, since there was nothing else to do, she opened the supply room door, with a tense, brief smile. 'Sorry for holding you up.' She glanced along the row of students and caught Tasha's eye. She didn't dare catch Peter's.

She heard only his voice, disembodied. 'No problem, Kristin. We appreciate your coming. Today you'll just have to bear with us while we work out a pose. Can everyone see?'

Good Lord, he was walking straight towards her. She felt her skin rise up into bumps, every pore, every hair on edge. He was going to touch her.

They walked down the hill together after class.

'Did you get awfully stiff, standing like that?'

'What? . . . Oh, no. We do it in dance enough. I'm used to it.'

'He *is* gorgeous, isn't he?'

'Who? Peter?'

Tasha giggled. 'Of course Peter.'

'His teeth are crooked.'

'I'm sick of straight teeth. Do you remember what he said about dentists in Scotland, giving kids caramel bars when they finished filling their cavities? My dad would have a fit. Have you ever been to Scotland?'

For a moment Kristin wondered who had talked longer

and more disconnectedly this evening: Tasha or Peter. They were both unstoppable once they got going. And they *had* got going – both of them – tonight after class. Cracking jokes, telling ghastly stories of teeth going missing and operations going awry – Kristin didn't even know what had started them off. While she herself had stood by, smiling painfully, wishing something, anything, would free her to join in, too . . .

'Hey.' Tasha gave her a nudge. 'Did you hear me?'

'Yeah. I've been to Scotland. Only Edinburgh, though.'

'So are all Scots so sexy?'

'Not,' said Kristin drily, 'to my recollection.' For a moment it occurred to her that Peter was unlike any Scot she had ever met, and she wondered why.

By the end of January, Peter Conaway had started to be noticed. Male teachers under fifty were a rarity at the Academy, and so never failed to find devoted admirers, especially among the younger girls. The first- and second-year girls at Hobson House were no exception. Having tried, unsuccessfully, to sign up for sculpture class, they took to pestering Kristin and Tasha with questions. How old did they think Mr Conaway was? Did he seem interested in younger women?

The sudden attention amused Tasha, but discomfited Kristin. Ever since Tasha had started gushing about Peter's looks, she had been forced to accept that he was not her unique discovery. But now, to find out that someone who had inspired in her such unsettling feelings was adored from afar by a vast, undiscriminating mass of girls . . .

It made her all the more certain that nothing could ever actually happen between her and Peter. She was not about to let him know how she felt. The very thought of it made her go red and hot in the face, and all over. Every Thursday night she trailed through the slush to sculpture class in a mixture of expectation and dread. She wished she had never taken on this modelling, yet she couldn't think of stopping it. At least it meant that for a few minutes here and there, she had Peter's attention. He would touch her to indicate how she should position herself. On the back, below the chin, on the elbow . . . He never touched anyone else. So she had at least that privilege.

He *talked* to Tasha, though. Oh, how they talked. Tasha led him on, in her usual way: she probably didn't even think about how she did it. Kristin would go into the supply room to change, and hear Peter talking about Scotland and the town where he'd grown up, where, he claimed, there was a sausage factory and a biscuit factory and everyone went into one or the other. 'Guess it's a bit like that in New York, eh? When you leave school you have your choice. Chase Manhattan, Goldman Sachs, Milton Friedman . . .'

Kristin had heard Tasha shriek with laughter. 'Milton Friedman's not a bank. He's an economist.'

'Ach, Tasha, I'm too skint to know these things.'

And Kristin would emerge and the conversation would die down, or flatten and go quiet with the efforts of the other two to include her. Kristin hated herself then.

I must get over this, she decided, and reminded herself that Peter didn't matter: no one here did. She was going to Paris and, eventually, home to England, and would never see anyone from the Academy again, except, perhaps, for Tasha. If Tasha and Peter hit it off, fine.

She told herself this, but she did not believe it.

She walked into Commons and almost didn't see them. They were sitting at a corner table of one of the downstairs dining halls: the 'uncool' chambers where only first-year girls and spotty, studious boys ate. What were they doing there?

Kristin stopped in the doorway, looking, just to be sure, until belatedly Tasha glanced up and beckoned. Kristin picked up an apple and a knife and wound her way over.

'That's not much of a lunch,' said Peter. 'Here, have this.

I took three.' He handed her a plate containing a giant chocolate chip cookie.

'Oh, no, thanks. I already ate.'

'No, you didn't,' said Tasha. 'You had French.'

Kristin ignored this and smiled politely at Peter.

'Four hamburgers and french fries and three cookies. That's this guy's *lunch*,' said Tasha. 'I hate to contemplate dinner.'

'More,' said Peter, grinning and munching, 'of the same.'

'It makes me sick how guys can do that and stay so skinny. You'd think they never ate.'

'In a way of speaking, Tash, I didn't. Twenty-two years in the fish-and-chip and coronary capital of the world. Got to make up for lost time.'

Kristin cut into her apple, feeling tongue-tied. But Peter didn't seem to notice. He just talked more.

'I was just saying, Kristin, your roommate here should be going to art school. What's she doing talking about Yale? Why's she want to go there and study, like, Latin and philosophy for four more years? She's an artist!'

Tasha sighed. 'It's my parents. They insisted I had to apply. Anyway, I won't get in.'

Peter dumped three sugar cubes into his coffee. 'My parents couldn't believe the state would actually give me money to hang about at university.'

'So they didn't mind your going to art school?' said Tasha.

He grinned. 'They couldn't care less. It was that or the sausage factory. Anyway, Kristin, I don't suppose it was like that for you, eh?'

'What?' Kristin was startled.

'I'll bet you were down there with your horses and your golden retrievers. Couple of butlers, maybe.'

She tried to sound cheerful: unguarded. 'I see you know all about where I come from.'

He shrugged; his eyes glinted, amused.

'Actually,' she said, cutting her apple, 'only one butler. One is quite enough.' She looked up at him; their eyes seemed to meet, as if across a barrier that only he and Kristin were aware of. Tasha had put on the tolerant smile that Kristin knew well as the one she wore when she didn't quite understand, or necessarily like, what was going on around her. But suddenly Kristin didn't care. She blotted Tasha out. She looked levelly at Peter. 'And I'm allergic to golden retrievers.'

'You going to go back then?'

'I expect so. Are you?'

He shook his head. 'Never. I'm done with Britain. I like it too much here.'

Tasha looked back and forth from Kristin to Peter. As they talked, she had been searching her mind for an excuse that might get her out of ski practice, which started in ten minutes, but she could come up with nothing. Reluctantly, now, she rose. 'I've got to go. Where are you guys heading?'

Kristin glanced, startled, from Tasha back to Peter, the ghost of a smile on her lips as if, Tasha thought, something wonderful had happened. Tasha wondered what it was.

'Actually,' said Peter, 'I had a favour to ask Kristin here. Won't take long. Will we see you tomorrow night, Tash?'

'Sure.' Tasha nodded and picked up her tray and trailed slowly away. *Favour? What favour?*

When she had gone, Kristin looked up slowly at Peter, and saw that he was watching her: intently yet calmly, his chin on his wrist. She cut a fine sliver of apple and studied it, and found all of her nervousness had gone. 'So. How can I help you?'

Quincy Adams was a long two-storeyed yellow house at the back of campus, its upper floor a faculty apartment, its ground floor a vacant garage-like space occupied, just now, by Peter's sculptures.

'Sorry about the light,' he said. 'If it could've waited another month we could have done it outdoors, but this crazy gallery's given me exactly ten days to get the shots to them. The exhibit's for Easter.'

'Provincetown,' said Kristin, setting up her tripod. 'Now is that the place on Cape Cod that's supposed to be full of artists?'

Peter's laugh was a low growl. 'Art dealers more like. It's too expensive for us plebs, we only turn the stuff out.'

Kristin glanced up from her work, a smile playing on her lips. 'We're in America,' she said neutrally. 'Land of opportunity. Sort of place chips fall *off* people's shoulders.'

He laughed. 'Who, me? I'm not the one with the mysterious past.'

'There's no mystery. Shall we start with the black and white shots?'

Oddly, for him, Peter didn't answer, so she looked up expectantly. He was sitting on something shrouded by a dropcloth, his arms, in their well-worn denim shirt, folded. She had registered already that it was about fifty degrees in here and that, as usual, Peter was wearing several layers less clothing than any normal person would have done.

'Black and white first?' she said again.

'What is it about you?' he said. 'It keeps bugging me. What are you doing here? A person like you. You should be at, I don't know, Benenden or somewhere.'

She laughed. 'I'll make a deal. Photos first, and then you can ask me anything you want.'

'Anything?'

'I don't have to answer.'

He gave an amicable shrug then, and started to point out and unwrap the pieces of work he wanted photographed. He needed pictures mainly of the larger ones, the ones that weren't travelling to Provincetown, so as to give an overall impression of what he did.

Kristin went to work, pleased that he had chosen her: pleased that he thought of her as a professional. He had said he was hopeless at taking pictures; she doubted that, but decided not to question it. The bare, big room made a better studio than she had expected. She spent nearly two hours moving from one piece of sculpture to the next: the Modigliani-like bronzes, the chunky amalgams of stone and metal. Some of them incorporated bits of what looked like used machinery, and bore absurd combinations of consonants for names: *Kwylnydyd, Bkosnofi.*

'Where do you get the names from?' said Kristin. 'They sound like old Welsh kings. Or African ones, or something.'

Peter laughed. 'I close my eyes and punch the keys on my computer.'

She nodded at a large object in the corner still covered in drapery. 'Do you want that photographed, too?'

'Why not? What the heck.' Peter whipped off the cover. The object beneath stood on blocks, coloured partly a rusty blue, partly gunmetal-grey, its nose ornamented with what looked like a fender and headlamps.

'That's . . . different,' said Kristin, at a loss.

Peter's face cracked into laughter. 'Sure! Why not take its picture. We'll show it at the gallery. ''64 Corvette. Probably better than any of my stuff.'

'Oh.' Kristin felt her face flush deep red. 'I'm sorry. I . . .'

'Never mind, Kristin.' He came over and hugged her suddenly around the shoulders. For a second she caught the scent of him, pine and skin and fresh plaster. He let her go. 'Do you think you could do me?'

Kristin turned her head away. She was sure she was horribly, hideously pink. 'You mean . . .'

'You know. Take my picture.'

'Oh! Of course.' Relief flooded her. 'I've not had a lot of practice with people . . .'

'Just the one. Alexei wants to stick it up somewhere. Look, I'll stand here against this wall, you just fire away. Okay?'

Kristin lifted her camera off the tripod. 'The light's all on your left there. If you moved . . .'

He shrugged and went where she told him to. He seemed not to mind the camera: just went on talking, as she took her first, tentative shots, about Alexei and his gallery and how, once the show was over, he was going to spend the rest of the Easter break getting his car ready for the road.

'Do you know all about cars, then?' Kristin squinted into her viewfinder.

'A little.' He shrugged. 'My father used to fix them up in his spare time. My brothers, too.'

'Do you have lots of brothers and sisters?'

'Four sisters, two brothers. You?'

She shook her head. 'None. Only child. Do you think you could lean towards me a bit? Yes.' The flash went off.

'I think Alexei wants something kind of far out. Can you make me look weird, you know?' Peter grinned.

Kristin smiled back. 'Easy.' And so, again, she arranged him. She knelt down to photograph him from below; from this angle, she knew, the lens would distort and fore-shorten him. Make him almost monkeylike, perhaps, with his long arms. But he didn't protest. 'No, don't smile,' she said. So now he looked down at her, his face angular and narrow, even slightly forbidding.

'That could be a good one,' she said, rising. 'You don't mind being photographed, do you?'

'No.' He looked puzzled at the idea. 'Do you mind modelling? You know, in class.'

'A little. I don't like to know I'm being watched.'

'But there are probably men looking at you all the time.'

'What?' She looked up, discomfited. And then, 'Don't,' she said.

'Sorry.' He looked over evenly, leaning against the wall, waiting for the camera to flash again. 'But it's probably true.'

'Do you want to . . . try one more shot?' She didn't like this line of conversation. 'Now,' she said, 'if you lean back a little, and look this way, past me . . .'

There was something young and vulnerable in the squinting eyes; and yet something old, guarded, in the stance, knotty hands clenched against a crossbeam on the walls. *This is the one*, Kristin thought, *the one for me*. The one she would keep for herself: probably it wouldn't suit Alexei.

She wondered just why she should be thinking about hanging on to a photo of Peter Conaway.

'Good,' she said, and he smiled, and she shot again. 'Now look at me.'

He was doing what she wanted: responding. Obeying. Nothing had prepared her for the sheer erotic charge of it: not just of desiring him, but of knowing, for a few seconds at least, that she was in control.

'And then?' said Tasha. She blew into her mug of hot chocolate, her face flushed, discomposed.

'Well, and that was it. I finished the photos and came home.'

'But what did he *say*?' prodded Tasha.

'Oh, I don't know. We talked about his show, and about photography. A little about London. He lived there for a while, before he came here.' She had not, Kristin remembered, got around to telling her own story: Peter seemed to have forgotten her promise. Thank goodness.

'So what's his place like?'

'I only saw the ground floor.'

'What were his sculptures like, then?'

'Honestly, Tasha, if you're so curious, why don't you invite yourself over there?'

Instantly Kristin regretted her words. For of course Tasha *would* invite herself, and from there it would be all too easy. Once Tasha went, she, Kristin, would have lost her chance forever. And yet perhaps she must bear that fact, and live with it, because for Peter to become her own lover was so much what she wanted that she knew now it could never be.

6   Painting again felt to Tasha like plunging into a welcoming warm bath, liquid and easy. She started with a clean canvas, and dipped her brush into a pool of tomato red on her palette. Soon the brushstrokes were crossing and recrossing the whiteness in front of her. She did not know what she intended to portray; she thought of a film she had seen once, of Joan Miró at work – one swirl, one squiggle spawning another.

As ever when she was painting, she did not feel the hours pass. She had a dim impression that it had grown dark outside. She only half-heard the steps behind her in the studio.

'Czerny said you were good. Now I believe him.'

Tasha froze; she rarely blushed, but now she felt a warmth creeping up the back of her neck. 'Oh, hi, Peter.' She turned. 'I didn't know you were there. Have you been watching?'

'Only for a few seconds. Have you ever seen that film of Joan Miró? You know, with the glass?'

'That's amazing. I was just thinking about that.'

'I love the way there's nothing, and then a few minutes later, all this colour . . .'

'You know, I saw that at summer school when I was just thirteen. I think it was one of the things that decided me about painting.'

'I saw it on telly. As usual, my parents thought I had a few screws loose, watching that artsy stuff.'

'Have you seen many of his paintings? I mean, in real life . . .'

It seemed to Tasha that they talked for hours. She stood there, her brush drying in the air above the can of

84

turpentine, raking back her hair with paint-stained hands. It was so exciting: she hardly ever met anyone who really understood. Who knew every painting that came into her head, and saw it in his own mind just as clearly. It seemed like she could mention anything – from Canaletto to the Tiffany windows at the Metropolitan, to the Edward Hopper of that couple inside their apartment seen from a subway train . . . He knew it.

Finally she glanced in the direction of the window and saw that it was dark out. 'Wow. Do you know what time it is?'

'No.' Peter smiled. 'I don't wear watches.'

'Me neither. Gee. I was supposed to meet Lorenzo at five but I think I've already missed him.'

'Who's Lorenzo? Your boyfriend?'

'No, no.' Tasha shook her head and looked down.

'That sounds pretty definite.'

'I think he's . . .' Tasha realised that perhaps she should not pronounce on Lorenzo's sexuality, since he never had.

Peter ignored the evasion. 'You have lots of friends, don't you, Tasha?'

'Yeah.' She looked at him evenly. 'But not so many real ones. There's really only Kristin, and . . .' *You*, she was about to say. But she couldn't. She didn't know how he would take it. 'I was wondering,' she said at last, 'is there any chance I could have a look at your sculptures?'

They broke a path across the crisp, icy shell of snow that covered the ground between the art block and Quincy Adams. The stars were out; their breath dispersed in clouds of vapour.

'I wish it was always like this,' Tasha said suddenly.

'Christ, you know you're lucky, Tasha. Four years here. When I first got here, I thought it looked like paradise. And New York – that was out of this world.'

'Why didn't you stay there?'

'I would have. Job was only for a year, so I had to move on. When I first got to New York I thought, Jesus, what a rich place it is. But in a way it's nothing on Lawrence-town.'

'Do you care about money?'

Peter only laughed. 'It's something you start to care about when you don't have enough of it.'

'But it's not important. I mean, it only buys you things. Pays the rent and stuff.'

'Aye, and when you can't buy things, you see how you like to do without it! But I'll tell you, being poor in America is like being rich other places. Like, if you want a car you can buy one for two hundred dollars' – Peter was warming up, talking and walking faster – 'and you've got all these fantastic roads, you can cross the country if you want to – '

'If your two-hundred-dollar car doesn't break down!'

'Or suppose you're hungry at midnight, or two a.m., there's always food. I can't get over it. French fries. Cheesecake. Macadamia nut ice cream. I'll tell you, they've never *heard* of macadamia nuts in Dornoch.'

'So what's it like there?'

He laughed. 'Pretty grey. Mostly council houses.'

'What's a council house?'

He only laughed again. 'Never mind. Do you like spaghetti, Tasha?'

They had reached Quincy Adams, and stamped the snow off their shoes and climbed the stairs. Peter directed her into his living room, where Tasha set about building a fire in the cast-iron stove that seemed to provide the only heat. Meanwhile, Peter started to fry onions and garlic in the kitchen. He cooked, Tasha noticed, with the same male abandon as her brothers, throwing in whole cloves of garlic, a whole tin of anchovies, two huge tins of tomatoes.

'I'll bet this isn't what they eat in Scotland.'

Peter came to the doorway and cocked an eyebrow. 'How do you know? Actually, you're right, Tash. I learnt to cook from my girlfriend, my first year at art school. She was Italian.'

'So what was her name?'

86

'Rosa. She had this tremendous black hair, went all the way down her back. So what about you, Tash? You have a boyfriend? I mean, leaving out Lorenzo.'

He asked matter-of-factly, but Tasha was pleased to hear the words. 'Nope. Not at the moment.'

After that he armed them both with big glasses of red wine and took her downstairs to see the sculptures.

'Wow,' said Tasha, after a few minutes' mute staring. 'These are *big*. Did you make them all here?'

'Some of them came with me from London.' Peter took a swig of wine. 'Cost a fortune to bring them, believe me. But I don't like to leave them behind.' He gave her a half-smile. 'Sentimental.'

'No. That makes sense. I understand.'

'Though I fancy I could part with sentiment in exchange for a bit of hard cash. I live in hope.'

'Have you sold anything yet?'

He shrugged. 'Sure. Some small ones.'

Tasha was impressed. 'That's really good. How do you do it? My parents are always telling me I'm crazy, wanting to paint. That I'll never sell anything.'

Peter put down his glass. 'My folks, too. Just the same. But they don't know. There's all kinds of ways.' He started talking about fellowships and grants and teaching. Tasha listened, nodding, feeling heartened. There *was* a way. And he knew it. She drank in the words.

'Not,' he said finally, 'that you'll get rich.' He laughed. 'That's me, twenty-five, and I'm still scraping by.'

'You're doing what you want to do.'

He shrugged and led the way upstairs again.

Tasha noticed that by the time he poured out the rest of the wine the bottle was empty. Funny, she didn't feel drunk: only blissfully relaxed. She looked around her at the bright, bare room while Peter served up the spaghetti. This, she thought, was the life. Wine, painting, sex with a handsome man ... Well, maybe. He hadn't exactly dropped any definite hints. She mustn't, she reminded herself, jump to conclusions.

When they had polished off the spaghetti, Peter brought out half a chocolate cake. It looked suspiciously like the ones served up on Fridays in Commons.

'How'd you get that out?'

He tapped the side of his nose and grinned. 'My friend Maureen. Works in the kitchen. She's Irish. Comes from the same part of the world as I do.'

'But you're not Irish, you're Scottish.'

'Same difference. My grandparents were Irish.'

Tasha digested this. 'Mine were Lithuanian and Polish and French.'

'You know, it was a weird thing to me, New York. You get so many Jews.'

Tasha only laughed.

'What? Well, you're Jewish, right?'

She shook her head. 'Sure. But that's just New York for you. It's, like, taken for granted.'

'So do you go to synagogue? Did you have a bar mitzvah and all of that?' Peter's eyes were bright with a sudden curiosity.

'Bas mitzvah. I'm a girl. But I didn't have one. My parents aren't religious.' Tasha was smiling, for Peter seemed all at once so naïve: so keen to learn. So she told him about her parents, and her Grandma Natasha's days in Paris; Peter's eyes lit up even more when he heard about Braque and Derain and all the rest. 'I can't tell you it's a hundred percent true,' Tasha warned him. 'My brothers think she's made it up.'

'Who cares?' He laughed. 'Paris in the twenties. I could fair go a few months of that.'

'Paris in the eighties can't be bad either.' *Kristin's going there*, Tasha thought.

'Too true.' Peter eased himself back against the wall, running a hand through the shaggy hair that fell over his

88

forehead. It had grown even longer than it had been at the start of term.

'Are you, um, growing your hair out for something?' Tasha said suddenly.

'For what? A ponytail?' He grinned. 'No. Not really. Just can't be bothered to get it cut. Costs money.'

'I could cut your hair. I do my brothers'.'

Peter only smiled back. He looked a little tipsy, Tasha thought.

'Have you got scissors?'

'Kitchen.' He struggled to pronounce the word clearly.

'I love your accent. The way you say that like there's no "t" in it.' Tasha got up, weaving slightly, and went to look through the kitchen drawers. 'Got 'em!' she shouted a minute later, in triumph. Then she came back to kneel beside Peter. 'So have you got a comb?'

With a teasing smile he slid his hand down over hers, on to the scissors. 'I'm not so sure about this. Tell you what, I'll do yours instead.'

'No!' Tasha almost screamed. 'No way.' But she was laughing, too, as she crawled backwards.

He pursued her on hands and knees. 'It'd be great. You know, like Mia Farrow in *Rosemary's Baby* . . .'

Tasha screamed again.

'Come on.' His Scots accent had a lurching laziness about it now that Tasha found tremendously sexy. 'Give it a go. You'd still look terrific.'

But though she might have been drunk, Tasha was not *that* drunk. She would never part with her long hair. Letting out something between a laugh and a cry, she fled backwards, crawling all the way around the crate Peter used as a coffee table. Then she fell back against the sofa, exhausted.

He caught up. He pinched a lock of her hair between his fingers, and she thought he was about to do it: chop it off. 'No,' he said, letting go. 'Couldn't. I couldn't imagine you without all that hair.'

'Thank goodness.' Tasha closed her eyes. Her heart's thumping reverberated through her head.

And now Peter was easing his hands up her back, over her sweater, which was an old worn-out cashmere, one of Zeke's: she could feel the flat, hard tips of Peter's fingers through it. She might have asked him what he was doing, to break the silence, but she didn't dare. She didn't want him to stop. His fingers eased their way up to the nape of her neck, the roots of her hair; he combed his fingers through the long, straight locks. Strangely, it did not hurt at all. He moved very gently. Then he lifted the hair and planted a kiss on her neck.

'Oh,' she said.

'You know this place better than I do, Tash.'

'And?' She half-turned her head.

'What do they do about students who sleep with their teachers?'

She laughed. 'Nothing. Unless they find out.' Smiling, she turned her head a little to look at him, and saw his dark eyes facing the window, shining with an obscure light. Why was it that those eyes looked older than the eyes of a twenty-five-year-old? The wrinkles around them, maybe. Tasha laid her hand on his and he brought it up to his mouth: drawing the index finger in between his lips, letting the others splay against his cheeks; licking; biting.

She drew back instinctively.

'But they won't find out,' he said.

'Of course not.'

'I've heard about you. I've heard you've broken every rule this place has to offer.'

'Who told you?'

He only smiled. 'Word gets round.'

'I've never' – she tilted back her head – 'slept with a teacher.'

'What makes you think you're going to now?' He drew back and held her hand against his cheek.

90

Tasha only smiled. She felt bold and confident. Stretching, catlike, she tugged off her sweater, then unhooked her bra. It was skin-coloured, transparent, and hardly concealed much. But, still. Peter studied her, his expression unchanged, except for a tug, a twitch at the corner of his mouth. He reached across, and his thumbs brushed her nipples. And again.

'Hadn't you better go home now?' he said.

'What? You're kidding.'

'It's late,' he said, and moved away. 'Honestly.' He glanced back. 'Maybe you'd better.'

Tasha felt her face go red. She threw her sweater on quickly and bundled her bra into a pocket of her jeans. She felt a fool; she only wanted to leave, and quickly. But then he caught her in both arms as she started to rise. 'No hurry. I'll see you to the door.'

'What are you –'

He touched a finger to his lips. 'Trust me. I'll see you out.' He smiled.

So she rattled down the stairs ahead of him, nervous, and as he reached for the door-latch he caught her against him with one arm and gave her a long, hard kiss. Twice she tried to break away, but he wouldn't let her.

She was flustered. 'Peter, what was that for?'

'For next time.'

'But –'

'When you come back.' He turned the latch and held the door open for her. 'Will you be okay getting home?'

'Sure.' She debated saying 'no', so that he would escort her back to Hobson House, and discarded the idea. There was no surer way of being found out. If there was going to be anything to find out. She still wondered. She had never known a man to hold off that way before.

If he wanted her, why was he playing games?

'So how was it?' Kristin looked up from a cup of tea.

'What?'

91

'Peter's.'

'How'd you know?' Tasha shoved her hair back. It was probably messed up and tangled.

'It's written all over your face.' Kristin smiled.

'Oh, well, yeah, fine.'

'Fine? That's it?' Kristin's eyebrows lifted.

'Nothing happened, if that's what you mean.' Tasha wondered why Kristin's smile had the look of relief about it. Was she jealous? Did she like Peter?

Thinking it over for a second, Tasha ruled that idea out. Kristin had never given the slightest hint that she did. And she had had her chance, surely. That photography session . . .

Tasha wiped a hand across her brow. 'Anyway. What did *you* do tonight?'

As Kristin shrugged and related her doings – she had spent most of the evening downstairs, talking about Paris with Sarah – Tasha heaved an inward sigh of relief. She wasn't going to have to explain any more. It made her uncomfortable to think that her evasions had already come close to being lies.

'I'm glad you came back, Tash.'

'What, did you think I wouldn't?'

Peter shrugged. 'Thought I might have annoyed you.'

'Nah, I like a man who plays hard to get.'

He laughed, his thumb rotating on her shoulder: a steady, soothing motion.

'So,' Tasha said.

He still said nothing.

'Are we going to?'

'I'd better hope I don't get chucked out of my job.' He shook his head and ran a hand through his hair.

'You won't. Trust me. As long as I get in by curfew . . . Sarah's blind as a bat about this kind of thing, anyway.'

He frowned. 'Now, who's Sarah?'

Tasha giggled. 'Our housemistress. Brown hair, big

glasses? You mean you haven't even noticed her? She's got a huge crush on you. So does about half our house.'

Peter rubbed his forehead, looking sheepish. Tasha wanted to throw her arms around him and smother him in a great big hug. She felt braver than usual, too. '*I've* got a huge crush on you, too,' she said, 'but I guess that's okay. 'Cause here I am.'

'Aye, of course it's okay.' Peter squeezed her around the shoulders, and then his hands slid lower. He started working at the buttons of her shirt. 'Christ. How's this get undone?'

Tasha giggled. 'I would have thought you'd know. It's a man's shirt.'

'Ah.'

'Does that mean you have more practice with the other kind?'

He laughed. 'No comment.'

'You didn't leave a girlfriend behind in Scotland?' Tasha turned her head, suddenly curious. She ran her fingers through the dark hair that fell over Peter's forehead.

'Aye. Wife and three kids.' He grinned. 'Two wives actually. One in London, one in Liverpool.'

'Right.'

The rough stubble on his cheek grazed her and then his mouth found hers. Somehow, kissing, his lips felt thicker, softer than they looked: as if they had some deceptive elasticity about them. 'Actually, I have to admit,' he said, 'I'm not the marrying kind.'

'What?' She spluttered a laugh. 'Who cares?'

They kissed again.

'I don't want to get married either,' she said. 'Never. What's the point? It only ties you down.'

'A woman after my own heart,' he said. 'I figure my family's done enough in the line of marriage and kids. Not that that stops them sticking their noses in what I'm getting up to. Speaking of which . . .' He had shuffled sideways and now held her at arm's length, her shirt

93

unbuttoned. 'How'd I get so lucky, I wonder? You belong on the cover of some magazine, Tasha Seidelman.'

'I hate to think what kind you mean.'

'I could just about fall in love.' He looked straight at her.

'Stop it,' she said, but it seemed to her that she had to kiss him again just then. He lay back on the rug, crooking one arm around her neck, drawing her down on top of him.

A second later he released her, twitching his head. 'Let me see you.'

'I'm not the bashful type. You might have guessed.' Tasha sat up and threw off her shirt. She wasn't wearing a bra this time, and her breasts spilled out, round, smooth, slightly pendulous: *your best feature*, some boyfriend or other had teased her, she couldn't remember which one now.

Peter's expression didn't change, but his eyes widened. 'I saw that.'

'Jesus. You really do have a gorgeous body.'

As quickly as she could, then, she slid out of her jeans and panties. 'Am I better naked than with clothes on?'

'That I'm not telling you. Spoilt New York brat that you are.' He reached out and slapped her playfully on the thigh. She caught his hand.

'Hey. You'll pay for that. I can arm-wrestle. I'm strong.'

'Not as strong as I am.' And he shook his head and suddenly was up above her: pinning her shoulders to the floor with one hand while he tugged off his belt and his jeans with the other and scattered the line of her jaw with small kisses that were almost more like bites. Tasha gave a slight push against him, trying to rise, and, finding she couldn't, felt a surge of warm wetness between her legs. All at once she knew that she was with a real man, not a boy, and that it felt like nothing she had experienced before, but when she tried to put the words together to explain this to Peter, she found she couldn't. Her face felt hot. His body was hard, muscular, heavy above hers. For a

94

moment she wished she could see more of it, but then, when she tried to lift her head towards him, he let her, and at the same time slid his hands round behind her buttocks. Then, unexpectedly, almost roughly, he entered her, and she forgot every word she had wanted to say.

She wondered later what his secret was: how he had held off so long, when they were both – or at least she herself had felt – on the verge of explosion. How he could go on moving so hard and fiercely, and so long – and then slow down when she least expected it, and linger inside her, and then build again, his mouth and hands deliberate at the same time as the rest of him lost all patience? All she knew was that, three or four times, she had fallen back, exhausted, thinking it was all over, and yet it wasn't; and he had laughed, and now, when she asked him why he held out that way, he said, 'It's only the first time once.'

'I think that's the usual reason guys give for coming too quickly.'

He laughed. 'So how many have there been, Tash?'

'You really want to know?'

He nodded, then shrugged.

'I'm not sure. Well, let me count. Seven, I think. Are you counting flings?'

He seemed to be laughing at something again. Her seriousness, perhaps, she thought, or her difficulty in remembering.

'What's a fling?' he said.

'This, I guess.'

'Oh, no, Natasha Seidelman.' He picked up her hand. 'This is no fling.'

'What is it, then?' She felt absurdly pleased.

'Let's play it by ear.' His fingers were playing with the ends of her hair. It was, she thought, a perfect moment. She wanted it to last, or, even better, to live it over and over again. She wondered in passing if Peter felt the same way; and then, more alarmingly, if this was what it was like to fall in love. She never had, before. Or at least it had taken her until now to realise it.

7 Soon, Tasha told herself, she would tell Kristin. She definitely would.

The time never seemed right: Kristin was rushing around, to the darkroom, to the language lab, worrying about the state of her French; Tasha was rushing around, too, though to a different purpose. She had cut cross-country skiing so many times that the coach was threatening to evict her from the squad. She missed meals, because often Peter cooked for them both. By now, Kristin must be noticing.

Feeling vaguely guilty, Tasha made a definite plan to meet Kristin in Commons for dinner, one Saturday a week before the Easter holidays. And then, despite her good intentions, she overslept. She woke up in Peter's bed and glanced at the clock: it was already six-thirty. Commons closed in half an hour. As she rushed into her clothes, he watched her. There was an amused curl to his mouth.

'Why the rush?'

'It's not funny. I'm late for meeting Kristin.'

'I'm sure she can put two and two together.'

Tasha only shook her head as she zipped up her coat.

'Hold on,' he said. 'She's probably found somebody else to eat with by now.'

'That's not the point.'

'So you think she doesn't know?'

Tasha shook her head distractedly. 'She probably . . . I mean, maybe . . . Peter, I don't want her to find out the wrong way, I'm not sure how she'd take it.'

'Whoa, hold on. What do you mean?'

'I don't know. She might . . . mind.'

Peter studied her for a second with an interested look,

then shrugged and fell back under the covers. Tasha ran down the stairs and across the grass towards the art block. Halfway there, she saw a small figure with a halo of hair coming towards her. She shouted, and Kristin caught sight of her and stopped. She didn't speak until Tasha was closer.

'Lorenzo told me he'd seen you heading for Quincy Adams.' Kristin's expression was inscrutable.

'I'm sorry.' Tasha was gasping. 'Sorry I'm late.'

Kristin gave a small shrug. 'Never mind.'

'No. Really. It's all my fault. Kristin – I'm sorry. I . . . There's something I should have told you before.'

'That's all right.' Kristin's voice was crisp. 'Are you and Peter having an affair, then? Or – what do you call them – a "fling"?'

Tasha could almost hear the quotation marks bristling around the word. 'To tell you the truth, I'm not sure. I keep telling myself it's going to end, because I know it has to –'

'Of course it's really none of my business.'

Kristin had cut her off, Tasha realised. 'I always meant to tell you. I was just afraid.'

Kristin gave a short laugh. 'Afraid! Why?'

'Well, I thought you sort of liked him.'

Kristin looked across with light, blank eyes. 'I do like him. Of course. But what does that matter?'

'Kris, you know what I mean. I was never sure if – you know, that time you went over to take pictures for him . . . And before. Before sculpture class started. I had the impression you knew him – from before,' Tasha finished lamely.

'Oh, I'd spoken to him a couple of times.' Kristin shrugged.

'I guess I felt guilty.'

'But why?'

'You know why!'

Kristin smiled and gave her head a slight shake. 'Honestly. Do as you like.'

'Kristin, don't punish me. At least tell me what you think.'

'Why should I think anything?'

Tasha sighed, and took a few steps forward. 'You don't . . . disapprove, do you? Of him being older and a teacher and all that.'

Kristin gave a high laugh. 'No! Of course not.'

'Just I thought you might . . .' Tasha shook her head, snarled up in her own words all of a sudden. 'Never mind. Are we still going into Commons? Have you eaten yet?'

'I've heard dinner's dire tonight.'

'Then let's go to Brougham's.' Tasha leapt at the chance: privacy. Time for confessions. She might feel better if at least Kristin would allow her to tell all: the minute details, the acts and times and places.

Kristin shrugged. 'Actually, I'm not in the mood for Brougham's.'

So, silently, they trudged along to Commons.

A few days later, Kristin announced that instead of coming to New York, as they had planned, for the Easter holidays, she thought she would go down to Baltimore. Her mother had been complaining that she never visited.

Tasha didn't try to argue. 'My parents'll miss you,' she said. 'So will Nat. He's been dying to meet you after all the times you two have talked on the phone.'

Kristin gave her a blank smile. 'That's sweet of him. I can't think what he means. We never talk about anything much.'

'Exactly,' said Tasha. She had always wondered what Kristin and her brother found to chatter about, keeping her waiting every time Nat rang. 'So are you really sure you can't come, Kris?'

Kristin nodded silently, firmly.

The two weeks in Borson's mock-Tudor house in suburban Maryland felt very long indeed. At times Kristin almost wished she'd relented and gone to New York. It was just too bad she simply couldn't stand to be around Tasha lately.

She had managed, for the most part, to keep out of their room for the few days that remained of term. When she was there, Tasha tended to pad around, casting occasional, mournful glances in her direction, which annoyed Kristin and made her want to snipe.

Sometimes Kristin wondered exactly what Tasha had done to seduce Peter. She thought she knew fairly well. She had seen Tasha practise her charms on other men: the easy laugh at the most feeble of jokes, the long strawy hair tossed from side to side until wisps of it clung, electric, to their hapless faces. She had thought Peter was more sophisticated than to fall for something so obvious. And yet, he was a man. They were all the same. No doubt, failing everything else, Tasha would happily have stripped off her clothes and shown off that great, blowsy bosom. *God*, Kristin thought, *I hate her sometimes, I hate what she can do*.

She would simply have to stick out the rest of the year at Elliott. She would be gone soon enough – her real life would begin, and then none of this would matter.

Perhaps that was why Kristin found herself minding less about what Tasha had done. Unpacking in their bedroom after Easter, she heard Tasha's steps come thumping up the stairs, and a kind of residual affection took hold of her, prompting her to say, 'Hi. You're back early.'

'You, too.' Tasha pulled back her hair, looking a little surprised. 'So how was Baltimore?'

'Oh, ghastly,' said Kristin, 'as usual. It's good to be back.' A smile cracked her face, and she ran forward into Tasha's arms.

A few weeks into the final term of school, university admissions came. Up and down the mailroom, long thin white envelopes and square brown fat ones were torn open, in hushed silence, followed sometimes by shrieks and hugs and tears. Everyone pretended not to care, but they did. The rumours flew. Harvard was trying to tempt Lorenzo de Maas away from Yale. Steve and Courtney and Rachel were into Stanford. Courtney was into Harvard, too.

Kristin couldn't care less. She cared a little on Tasha's behalf, since Tasha hadn't heard yet from Yale, which meant, probably, that the news was bad. Or good, depending on how you looked at it: Tasha still protested that she didn't want to go there.

And yet, on the day the inevitable, thin white envelope came, Tasha came tearing down the hill to Hobson House and thrust it at Kristin. 'Here. Do it for me. I can't open it.'

Kristin studied the blue letterhead on the corner of the envelope.

'Go on!'

And so Kristin tore it open. Tasha's brown eyes gaped wide: she seemed to have stopped breathing.

Kristin glanced at the letter. She wondered whether it was kindest to convey bad news quietly, or more matter-of-factly. And then, 'Oh,' she said. 'You're in.'

'I'm in?' Tasha seized the letter.

'Yes. Looks like. Read it –'

But Tasha was already reading it, and then jumping up and down and squealing.

'Tasha,' Kristin protested, 'I thought you didn't care.'

But almost before the words were out, Tasha had flown out of their room and down the stairs.

'So,' said Peter, 'Yale,' and kissed her under the chin and bit her earlobe. They lay stretched out together, naked, on a quilt in front of the wood-burning stove. 'You of all people, Tash. Are you sure you're that clever?'

She punched him half-heartedly in the stomach.

'So,' he said, his breath in her ear, 'you're some kind of fucking genius and you never even told me. Better hurry up and tell your parents, they'll be happy. Least till you tell them you're not going.'

'Peter . . .' Tasha squirmed. She felt two of his fingers sliding towards her, into her. 'You're really sure I shouldn't? I mean, that it'd be the end of me as an artist if I *did* go?'

He shrugged.

'Anyway, I'm not going to think about that now.' Tasha lifted his hand. 'How about the real thing?'

He obliged. She stretched back and let her back arch beneath him. 'Say it again,' she said.

'What?'

'Yale.'

He laughed. 'It's going to your head.' Then he bent his head to her breasts and, between licks, repeated the name. 'Yale. Fucking Yale.'

'I think it's starting to wear off,' she said, and pulled him closer. Yet the high lasted, so that even when the climax had throbbed inside her and she should have felt sleepy and relaxed, she hummed with energy. She stood up while Peter still lay beneath her, surveying the scene she knew so well by now: the battered sofa, the neat stacks of art magazines on either side of it; the doorway into the bedroom, with the square pine bed they rarely used because of the cold, and the computer Peter would never let her play with. He said he used it for letters and occasionally to conjure up designs. The idea that a computer could draw intrigued her, but he kept putting her off. She didn't mind, just now. She padded into the kitchen to make coffee, and when she came back with it he sat up and sketched her – he often did, making her look sometimes like a Renoir bather, sometimes like a Picasso or even like a Lichtenstein. 'Why don't you draw it like you? Peter Conaway?' she had asked him once, and he only laughed. 'There is no me. Not on paper. I only sculpt.'

She remembered that now, and tilted back her head. 'So what should I do about Yale?'

'I can't tell you that.' Peter was serious, concentrating on his drawing.

'But you really think it would be a bad move? I mean, if I went, I could still take art classes. I could paint during the vacations ... I know you said that from eighteen to twenty-one or whatever is the most important time ...'

Glancing up and down, Peter didn't answer at first. 'Your parents are the problem, right? 'Cause they've got to pay.'

'Yeah.' Tasha sighed. 'They don't want me to go to art school. That's why it would have been easier if I *didn't* get into Yale.'

'But there's financial aid, right?'

'Peter, I'd never get that. I haven't been independent for long enough –'

He shrugged. 'But you could move out, right? Put off college a couple of years. Then you could apply where you want, and ...'

'I couldn't do that,' said Tasha instantly. The whole idea seemed unspeakably scary. A second or so later, it occurred to her that Peter might have meant something also scary, but more inviting: that she should move in with *him*. Could he mean that? But she didn't see how she could ask, exactly.

When his drawing emerged, it looked less like her than a sort of Martian, little-girlish, with great wide eyes. She privately thought it the ugliest yet. 'I don't look like that,' she said.

'You're right,' he said. 'Experiment.' He crumpled it up. 'I'm better sticking to machines.'

'I didn't say it wasn't good,' she said hastily. But she felt a peculiar surge of confidence. Peter was an artist, a professional artist, and yet there were areas – drawing, for example – where she knew she was just as good as he was. She supposed she had never been in the habit of thinking of them as equals, just because of the difference in their ages. Yet that would gradually shrink as they got older.

When he's thirty, she thought, I'll be twenty-three: that seemed not such a huge difference. Not impossible. The notion that they might live together came into her head again. *Not now*, she thought, *but one day*. She liked it so much, she kept it to herself.

Kristin felt strangely aimless now, as everyone else's acceptances came and they learned about their futures. Since she had applied to, and been accepted by, the American College in Paris four months ago, the novelty of imagining her own future had largely worn off.

Sometimes she even wondered whether she was hurrying back towards England too quickly. She thought of Tasha at Yale – not so far from here, in Connecticut – and Peter in Boston or New York. That, at least, was where she supposed he'd be; she had never had occasion to ask him.

She knew he and Tasha were still seeing each other two or three times a week. She knew also that it would be more if it weren't for the need to keep up appearances. There was nothing in the school rule book, needless to say, about students who slept with their teachers.

At least Tasha no longer tried to flood her with details. She had started to, two or three times; at last Kristin burst out, 'Believe it or not, but I don't really want to know, Tash. What his penis looks like or how long he does X, Y or Z. You've told me about every other man you've screwed, so can't you at least keep this one to yourself?'

She had repented that; Tasha had looked ashamed and beleaguered, but at least the revelations stopped.

Kristin was still modelling. She supposed it would look queer to stop suddenly; besides, she could use the money. *I am going to leave school still a virgin*, she told herself. There didn't seem much chance, now, of anything else. Most of the time, she put it out of her mind. She wished Tasha would, too.

One night, a few days after the letter from Yale had come, they were both drinking tea. 'Don't you think,' said

Tasha, 'you just ought to get it over with before you go to France?'

Kristin studied the steam that rose up from her cup. 'Get *what* over with?'

'You know! Sleep with someone. I mean, just for practice.'

Kristin laughed. 'I didn't know that it required practising.'

'Tons of people have flings,' Tasha persisted, 'at the end of senior year.'

Kristin's mouth twisted. 'Suppose they do. There's no one I fancy, so will you shut up about it, please?'

'What about Peter?'

Kristin stared at Tasha. Then she brushed an imaginary hair out of her eye. 'For heaven's sake. Peter doesn't count. He's taken.'

'You never said you didn't like him. I know . . . I didn't give you much of a chance.'

'Well – it's nothing now. Over and done with.'

'You *do* like him. I knew it. Trust me, I had to go blundering in there . . . Kristin, I'm sorry.'

'Nothing to be sorry about.'

'But if you had the choice, would you . . .'

'What are you talking about?'

'If you could – would Peter be the one?'

Kristin wiped a hand across her forehead, which felt damp.

'There's no point talking about "ifs".'

'But there is. I mean, Kris, I know he likes you. I used to think . . .' Tasha hesitated, and tossed her hair nervously back. 'I used to think he liked you more than me. It even seemed like there was something between you. I could see it – when I was around you both.'

Kristin looked down into her lap.

'He's said things to me – about how beautiful you are.'

Kristin looked up, hopeful for a second. 'Has he?'

Tasha's face was serious. 'Yeah. He has. I guess what I'm

trying to say is . . .' Her fingers played nervously with the fringe of the blanket on her bed, braiding and unbraiding. 'If you want him – if you want me to let him know . . .'

Kristin stared back at her, astounded. 'But what about you? And besides, we can't just carve him up between us.'

A smile played around Tasha's mouth. 'Somehow I don't think he'd mind. Being carved up. He'd probably just love to hear us talking now.'

'But . . . *you* care about him, too.'

Tasha gave an exaggerated shrug. 'Sure. But we're young. We'll be going our separate ways. The year's almost over.' She shrugged again. *'Que sera, sera.'* She met Kristin's gaze. 'I'll tell him. How you feel. If you want.'

'Tasha, no.' Kristin took a deep breath. 'I'd hate him to think I was mooning over him like some lovesick school-girl. I'm not.'

'I'll tell him you want just a fling, then.' Tasha shrugged.

'But – why?' Kristin looked over at her friend, perplexed by her generosity. If it could be called generosity, when it implicated someone else and his feelings, too . . .

'You're my best friend.' Tasha looked at her evenly. She felt noble and brave.

'What are you smiling at?'

'Nothing.' Tasha shook her head. 'I'll talk to him. The way I figure it, men come and go. You can't count on them. But you can count on your friends.' She gave a broad smile.

Kristin nodded. 'Tash, I'm still not sure –'

But she knew the deed was done.

The next Friday, a note appeared in Kristin's mailbox.

Dear Kris
Could you manage a few more photos? Maybe
today around four if you can drop by – sorry such
short notice.

P.

She realised that she had never seen his handwriting before. It was black and angular, all stylised capitals, like, she thought, an architect's or a draughtsman's.

She knew she had time to catch Tasha at Hobson House, and ask her one last time if she really minded. But she didn't. She went to dance, then to the darkroom, and by the time she finished there, it was already after four. Now or never.

8 She peeled off her jacket. 'I got your note. I –'

'Good. In this way, then.' He ushered her in through the narrow hall, touching her arm lightly. For the third or fourth time since arriving downstairs she wondered how this could possibly work. *Tasha*, she thought, *you're mad*. She would make her excuses. . . .

'Photos,' she said. 'You said something about photos. I – I brought my camera.'

'Fine.' Peter smiled back as he dropped her jacket on a sofa and went over to a table, where a bottle of wine and two glasses were standing. 'But you won't be needing it. I wasn't meaning it that way.'

'What were you meaning, then?'

'That I'd take the pictures. Of you.' He poured, and moved easily over.

'Of me?' She smiled, abashed. 'Well, I'm not very good at that sort of thing.'

'Oh, I don't see why you shouldn't be.'

'What sort of photos?'

'Nude ones.'

'I see.' She swallowed, and felt something like a small stone drop down through her body and give a single beat between her legs. 'Well, I. . . .'

'Only for me to look at. No one else.'

She wondered how he had come up with this elaborate ploy: if it was that. Or perhaps it was real. Perhaps he wanted the photos, or simply fancied taking them. In any case, she felt oddly freed by the thought that it would be, after all, just a sort of experiment. 'All right,' she said coolly. 'What do I do?'

'Take off your clothes, then.' Peter was watching her,

not intently, but with a certain aesthetic indifference, his head tilted. 'We can start here.'

'Here?' She didn't like to seem nervous: to ask to go somewhere more private than the sitting room, though she noticed now that the blinds were drawn.

'Aye.' He grinned. 'If that's all right with your ladyship?'

'Don't start,' she said.

'Start what?'

But she didn't say. For a moment it flashed through her mind how odd it all was, that she should find herself here, about to lose her virginity to this impulsive Scotsman, with his hard hairy arms and guttural voice: the sort of man whose path, in the normal course of things, would never have crossed hers. And she knew it and he knew it, and perhaps that was what was making him smile with one eyebrow raised, knowing, as he drank his wine. He said, 'I want you, Kristin.'

She had started to peel down the top of the leotard that she wore for dance. She said, startled, 'Thank you.'

'Don't thank me.' He laughed. 'I'm not doing you any favours. Of course I want you. Always have. I didn't need Tasha to tell me to. Just stand there like that. Don't move.'

She stood with her back to him, hiding her nakedness; her breasts were so small she never bothered wearing a bra, and yet they didn't seem to her worthy of display either. She thought with a momentary jealousy of Tasha's – round and golden. Then she heard the click of a lens, and saw a bulb flash out of the corner of her eye. When she turned her head, then gradually her body, she saw the black face of the camera, covering Peter's. A mechanical face, with his voice behind it, talking to her. She felt suddenly bolder. Looking away, she peeled off her tights, then stood and stretched. Tiny her breasts might be, but she liked the rest of her body, pale and thin – though not, perhaps, as thin as it might be – with bones protruding in places, childlike and delicate.

'You liked it that time,' Peter said, 'when you took my picture. You liked telling me what to do.'

'I guess so.'

'So fair's fair. I'm going to tell you what to do now.'

'What?' She felt alert, on edge.

He strolled closer. 'For now? Just stay there.' The camera-face was coming uncomfortably close to her. He told her to lean back against the wall: turn her head, raise her arms. Then to lower them again. The flash shot off light: two, three times more. He knelt in front of her, aiming upwards.

She felt nervous again. 'I don't see what you're doing this for.'

'Does it matter?' He inched closer. She wondered what was appearing in the viewfinder, for it couldn't be all of her; but she couldn't be sure. 'I use photos in my work sometimes,' he said.

'Will you use these?'

'Maybe. Why don't you go in the bedroom now? Just through there.' He nodded and she turned in the direction he indicated. The room was dark, but immediately he turned on a bright, almost harsh light overhead. And then a lamp by the bed which softened the effect of it slightly. For a moment as he let the camera rest on the floor beside him, she could see his face. Then he raised it again, aiming, smiling. 'Sit down on the bed. Aye, there you are.' He paused. Another click, another flash. 'Shall I fuck you there, Kristin?'

'What?'

'You heard me.'

Kristin saw the curl of his smile and was thankful again that she couldn't see his face.

'Don't you want me to?' he said.

'I –'

'That's what Tasha told me. It's no problem. Like I told you, I want to fuck you like crazy. Always have. Even when I met you that morning up by the darkroom. Remember?'

She remembered. 'Why do you use that word?'

'What word?' He grinned, and the camera flashed again. 'You know.'

'Because I think it turns you on, Kristin Ward. You like me to say it. I'll say it again if you want me to.' He paused. 'Do you want me to?'

'Yes. Okay.'

He moved closer. He started to put the camera down.

'No – don't stop. Not yet.' She wanted him to go on talking. Using that word. She liked it. It appalled her, how she liked it, and yet she could no more stop listening for it, wanting to hear it in Peter's voice, than she could get up now and dress and run away. She had to stay: to know where it all was leading.

So then, as if he could read her mind, he talked to her. He used words that shocked her, that no man had dared to speak to her face before; and he smiled and chuckled, as if he knew. 'I want to get inside your cunt,' he said, 'and fuck you silly.'

Her breath ran out in a small rush.

'And that won't be the end of it. I want to stay there and do it again and again until you've had enough, till you don't want it anymore. But I won't stop, Kristin. I'll just go on, because I never want to stop fucking you.'

Words came to her feebly, belatedly, because she felt a warmth, down below, and a strange trickling. 'Oh, God.'

'Does that mean you want me too, Kristin?'

'Yes, of course, you know I do.' Her voice sounded impatient, almost sharp.

'Then show me.'

'What do you mean?'

'Open your legs and show me.' He spoke patiently, as if to a small child.

I can't, she almost said. But she knew she could, and would, and wanted to. She leaned back against the mattress and let her knees drop apart. The flash went bright again.

'Now,' she said. 'Do it to me now.' *Get it over with*, she thought.

Peter shook his head. 'No. Not yet.'

He took more pictures. He came closer, until she knew that all that could show in the photographs would be that furled, wet, unrecognisable part of her. And then, when it seemed to her that she had waited minutes, hours, he lowered the camera. 'Now?' he said.

She was surprised, for a moment, by the vulnerable blinking of his eyes, in the light. She tried not to notice them: to hear only the implacable voice. 'Yes. Now.'

The camera strap riffled through his hair as he pulled it off over his head. And then, very quickly, he undressed. For a moment she blinked at his nakedness; he seemed larger than she had imagined, his skin tawnier. 'Come down here,' he said, 'on the floor.'

She moved down, obedient and unquestioning. And then, to her surprise, he turned her round, touching her lightly just as he did to move her into position in sculpture class. She leaned her head and arms on the bed. His hands spread over her buttocks, a finger sliding in, piercing the folds of her wetness, and then, too quickly for her to notice or fear anything, he entered her.

All at once her every feeling rushed in towards the one place where they met and joined. She felt the sharp thrust of him into her, and her own following warmth. He eased himself back, and in again, harder, his hands light on her waist.

'I thought,' he said, 'you might like it like this. None of the rot about love. Nothing romantic. Just this.'

She felt a moment's obscure pain at the words, then forgot it. What he said was true, and she didn't care. She arched her back and opened herself to meet his strokes, feeling his hands clasp tight under her ribs. 'Harder,' she said.

He laughed. 'Say it again.'

'Harder?'

And still he went on, and she cried out, but she thought not in pain, not exactly, and then his weight sank against her body. She collapsed beneath him. 'Is it – over?'

He smiled and twisted above her until they were separate once again, and she lay on her back beside him. 'That not enough for you?'

Her breath was coming in deep, fevered pants. She still was not entirely – satisfied, she realised. She felt ravenous. She wanted more. 'Mm. Yes, of course.' She looked down and away.

His fingers approached her and played for a second or two in the hungry wetness. 'I'll have to see what else I can do, then.'

They lay like that for some time, silent. Then, curious but too ashamed to look, she reached down towards his organ. It was somewhere, she thought, halfway. He sighed and chuckled a little, but said nothing, and then gradually, she thought, it revived. He climbed above her: entered her again. By now, she thought, he must feel as if he were swimming in a great sea of wetness. He leaned on his hands above her; he strove and gasped and thrust hard against her, and at last she felt a faint throbbing.

He fell back. 'Jesus, Kristin,' he said. 'You're a hard woman to please.'

'No –' she protested.

But then he smiled and leaned over her and, for the first time, kissed her. Not on the mouth but on the forehead.

'How did you know?' she said some time later, when they were dressed again, and drinking tea in his living room. She had reached for her clothes quickly once they both lay calm, for she had begun to feel the cold, and did not have Tasha's unselfconsciousness.

'Know what?' He smiled over towards her.

'To do all those things. Say those things.'

113

He shrugged. 'Just guessed.'

'But how did you guess?'

He shrugged. 'I'd say experience, except I wouldn't say I have so much of that. No more than average. But I've always thought it's the quiet girls you've got to watch out for.'

She half-smiled, studying his hands clasped round a mug. Flecks of something white, paint or plaster, clung to the edges of his nails. 'Am I one of the quiet ones, then?'

He didn't answer.

'So what's – Tasha?'

'How did I know you'd ask me that?' Peter slid a bare arm across towards Kristin's and began to play, absent-mindedly, with her fingers.

'Well, it's natural enough, I guess. This is such a strange situation.'

'I don't know. The world's full of situations.'

For a moment Kristin felt the gulf in their experience again, as she hadn't since that time – it seemed hours ago now – when Peter had started taking photographs. 'I suppose it is,' she said meekly.

'Tasha's awful innocent,' he said.

She laughed. 'Innocent?' It seemed hardly the word for someone of her roommate's much-boasted carnal knowledge.

'Aye, and it's sweet, and I mean well with her, I really do. But – maybe it's just because she's American. There are some things she doesn't understand.'

'Like?'

'Oh, she thinks it's romantic to be poor. And that if you're talented enough you'll get to be successful. I've been in this business long enough to know that's exactly the opposite of the case, but I hate to tell her . . . Heck, I shouldn't be saying this to you, Kristin. I know you two are friends.'

'But *we*'re friends, too,' she said. 'At least we are now, I hope.'

'Aye. More than friends.' He pinched her on the cheek but didn't kiss her, and she was glad of that. She hadn't minded – she had almost liked it – when he kissed her, quickly, before. But now they only looked at each other, known and knowing, and for now, for her, that was enough.

She found she did not want to discuss it, much as Tasha tried to fish for confidences. The questions began as soon as Kristin glided into their room that night, smiling secretly to herself.

'You're blushing,' said Tasha.

'No, I'm not,' said Kristin blithely.

'So where've you been?'

'Peter's.'

'And?'

'And that's that.'

'What do you mean, that's that? It can't be.'

'Tasha, I'm not like you.' Kristin sat down on her bed and undid her coat very slowly. 'I can't talk about details. I'm sorry to disappoint you.'

Tasha was staring: her big brown-eyed puppy-doggish begging stare. She would have whimpered and yelped, thought Kristin, if that would help. Instead, she turned her attention towards an end of her hair. 'But – no regrets?' she said.

Kristin shook her head. 'No regrets.'

'So are you going to see him again?'

Kristin turned her head towards Tasha with a quizzical look. 'Well, that wouldn't really be on, would it?'

'I don't know. That's up to you.'

'But, Tasha, this is crazy. We can't both –'

'No. I guess you're right.'

They heard an insistent rap on the door, then: it was a party of younger girls wanting to go out to Brougham's. To Kristin's puzzlement, Tasha eagerly accepted their invitation, and by the time she got back Kristin was in bed. It

115

wasn't late, but she had felt suddenly cold, and huddled under the covers.

'Hey,' whispered Tasha across the darkness. 'You can't be asleep.'

Kristin gave an answering moan. Tasha came over and perched on the end of the bed. 'You okay?'

'Mm. Just cold.' Kristin's teeth clenched.

'I'll climb in with you.' Not waiting for an invitation, Tasha threw off her shoes and slid under the covers. Sometimes she did this when neither of them could sleep, if it was winter and really, really cold.

For a minute or two they huddled in the narrow bed. Kristin, Tasha thought, felt very small and fragile. When she touched her elbow to see if she was still awake, she felt a knob of bone. 'You've still got your sweater on.'

'Tasha? What are we going to do?'

'About what?'

'You know.' Kristin's voice was muffled. 'This afternoon – it was scary.'

'Why?'

'It didn't feel like me. It felt as if someone else had taken over.'

Tasha stroked her back. 'That's okay. That happens.'

'No – you don't know. I –' Kristin shook her head.

'People do all kinds of things. You know, heat of passion and all . . . I'm sure nothing would have fazed Peter.' Tasha felt Kristin stiffen against her. 'Sorry. I just meant –'

'No. I know what you mean.' Kristin took a deep breath. 'But what are we going to do? About all of us.'

'I don't know.'

Kristin gave a small laugh. 'Is that all you have to say? Not even any suggestions?'

'Let's sleep on it.'

'And?'

'Well – maybe we'll have an answer by the morning.'

But by the morning no answer had presented itself; and

116

when Tasha, who had drifted back to her own bed in the middle of the night, suggested that they both just lie low and avoid Peter Conaway for a while, Kristin agreed. She couldn't think of any better solution.

That afternoon she went to the school infirmary and got herself a tube of jelly and a diaphragm. She told herself that it was just so she would have them on hand, and not take any more stupid risks, as she had the afternoon before. Her period was due in two days, so she wasn't seriously worried. But she felt foolish. And now she was sexually active – perhaps. To think of it gave her a strange thrill.

Not that she would be seeing Peter again. She supposed she had half-promised Tasha she wouldn't. Thursday's sculpture class came and went, much the same as ever. Though she had felt sure she couldn't go through with it, as soon as she changed and walked into the studio and saw Peter smile and wave at her as if nothing had happened, she knew that she could keep up the façade. That he and Tasha could, too. After class, while she changed again, Peter and Tasha chatted; they said good night; she and Tasha walked home.

That night she tossed and turned in bed and couldn't sleep. She thought about Peter, and knew now that she wished he had given her just one secret look: one sign. Though why should he – any more than he should to Tasha? They had both been . . .

No. She didn't want to think of it.

That Saturday morning, Peter caught her arm outside Commons. She hadn't even seen him. She jumped.

'Kristin.' His hand was tight around her wrist, then gone. 'This is getting ridiculous.'

'What do you mean?' She glanced nervously around. No one she knew was about. But then, what did she care? Tasha was the one who cared about Academy gossip: not she.

'I tried to talk to Tasha the other day and she ran away. What's going on with the two of you?'

'Um, nothing.' Kristin's gaze slid away from his.

'I'm starting to feel a little bit used.'

'Oh. Well . . .' Kristin smiled uneasily, thrown off balance. She and Tasha had never thought about Peter, she realised. Not in himself: his own feelings.

'Is that the end of it, eh? Your fling with a bit of rough trade.' His voice was tense and low, but on his face there was a hint of a smile.

'Peter.' She forced a laugh. 'You know I –'

'I've got the photographs.'

She looked at him hard. 'What are you saying?'

'They're good.'

She felt the blood rising to her face. 'You know I wish that hadn't happened.'

'What do you think I'm going to do? Blackmail you?' He laughed. 'Honest, I might be hard up, but I'd never do a thing like that. Besides.' He paused. 'They're special. You're special.'

'Oh.' She smiled and looked down. 'Thanks.'

'For Christ's sake, stop thanking me.'

'All right, then. I take it back. And I won't thank you again for anything, believe me.' Kristin tossed her head, annoyed, and stepped back.

'That a promise?' Peter smiled.

She didn't answer. Instead she said, as deliberately as she could, 'Those photos. You didn't develop them in the darkroom here, I hope.'

'I did, but don't worry. I went at midnight.'

Unbidden, the image of her naked self emerging from beneath the developing fluid filled Kristin's mind, and as Peter touched her arm she felt something swell and seep slightly, low down. 'Bloody hell,' she said, shaking him off.

'Do you want to come and see them?'

She smiled, a little. 'I guess I'd better.'

'This afternoon?'

'I've got dance class.'

'Fuck dance class.'

Her eyes crinkled and flashed. 'Exactly.'

Again, they drank tea, after. Peter seemed to see nothing incongruous in it, and she liked that. Perhaps the fact that they came from the same country meant that they shared certain things automatically. 'Do you have a cigarette?' she ventured.

'You're a bad girl, Kristin,' he scolded as he dug out a dusty pack from a drawer. 'Now, I bet you don't have permission.'

'Christ.' She rolled her eyes. 'This bloody school. They treat us as if we were all ten years old.'

'Count yourself lucky you're not still at Benenden, then.' Peter smiled slightly.

'For your information it was a day school. St Paul's.' She stopped, realising that she was about to go into all that – the past – without intending to.

'So what happened?'

She told him, a little. She found she did not mind telling it, now. It had become to seem more distant, just lately: more safely enclosed in the past. Even the worst bits. *My father died. It was suicide, actually*. She could say it.

'I see,' was Peter's only response. And then he said, 'What was it like, growing up with all that money?'

'I couldn't say. It just seemed natural. I didn't know what it was like for other people, if you know what I mean.'

'So do you miss it now?' He had taken a cigarette when she did, and now sucked on it contemplatively, not inhaling but screwing up his face as he blew out puffs of smoke. Through the haze he looked older than usual, his face craggier, five-o'clock-shadowed. Watching him, Kristin found herself wanting him slightly, again, and debated telling him. 'Miss it?' she repeated. 'No. Not exactly. But I still feel – displaced. As if I'll never be quite right until I'm

119

living in England again. Till I have another house like Littledene.'

'A modest ambition.' Peter smiled. 'So how're you going to get that? Marry someone rich?'

She tilted her head, embarrassed that he had seen, so quickly, the way out that had occurred to her more than once. 'Sure,' she demurred. 'Easy.'

'Easier for a woman.' He twirled his cigarette between his fingers. 'If you start working as a photographer, you'll meet people. Men have a harder time going up in the world that way.'

'Why?' she teased. 'Do *you* want to marry a rich woman?'

He grinned and shrugged. 'Send one my way. I'll see.' He stubbed out his cigarette and lay back, one hand fingering the cleft between her buttocks. 'Hungry?' he said.

'No. Not particularly.'

'Then what?'

She didn't answer. She thought back over the photographs: black and white, more amateurish and obscure than she had imagined. Thankfully obscure. But she had known well enough what she was seeing: what he, through the lens, had seen. As she thought of it, something seeped inside her. She half-closed her eyes.

'If you want that again,' he said neutrally, 'you're going to have to make me.'

'How?' she said.

'I'll tell you how. Come here.' He stroked her thigh and nudged her up above him. For a moment, before he said anything else, he just lay there, one hand reaching up to touch her lips. 'You're so beautiful. Sometimes I think I'm dreaming.'

She flinched.

'You'll have heard that before.'

'It's not true.'

''Course it is.'

'Don't.'

So he obeyed, and touched her mouth again, more quickly, and told her what she should do with it, and did not try to flatter her again.

She went back, and back again, to Quincy Adams, because, she finally admitted to herself, she was hooked. She was glad, now, that she had waited so long, because sex was so *good*. It seemed an odd word to use for the bare lust, the near-obscenity of their acts together. But she was beginning to accept this new side of herself, and not to feel ashamed. She thought of that poem, 'The Garden of Love'. Maybe she needed to feel the dirtiness of what she was doing: the abasement. *And the gates of this chapel were shut, And 'Thou Shalt Not' writ over the door* ... Maybe that was why she liked to hear Peter repeat the rude words. And didn't like to hear him talk of love, or even admire her looks. She wasn't beautiful. She didn't deserve it. She hoped that they could be more honest than that: that they were friends. There could be affection between friends: caresses, even. Sometimes Peter would run a comb through her hair, or massage her whole body with oils. Sometimes he told her about his former girlfriends: the high-school one from Dornoch, the Italian girl at art school. Rosa had, he said, opened his eyes. There was a whole world beyond Dornoch and even Glasgow: tastes and smells he had never thought of: far more enjoyments than their dour little corner of the earth had to offer.

A curiosity took hold of Kristin when he talked about Dornoch. He talked of it easily, scathingly, laughing as he went on: about the coal-smoke smell of the place, the sausage factory and the drunken men out of work who beat up on their wives; the women who had seven, eight kids by different men. He made it all sound more fantastical than grim. Kristin started to feel, almost, as if she had met them: Peter's father, loudmouthed, eyes half-closed on the sofa; his sisters and their babies; the neighbours; the drunks up the road; the worndown, decent teacher at the comprehensive who told Peter he ought to go to art school. To escape.

'But you can't,' he said, and shrugged, when he told her. 'Do you miss it?'

He laughed. 'Miss it! Christ, it's etched in my memory. Like steel. I don't need to see it again. Come on, Miss Ward. Downstairs. I'll show you my motor. She's nearly done, just needs a paint job.' He scooped her up in his arms and off the bed, smiling. She felt weightless in his arms. 'Christ,' he murmured, still smiling, 'if anybody'd ever told me ten years ago I was going to be going to bed with a girl like you . . .'

Kristin felt guilty about Tasha, because she still hadn't told her she was seeing Peter again. She tried hard to fit her visits to Quincy Adams into the middle of the day, when no one would notice, except perhaps her dance instructor, whom she could always wheedle with an excuse. Tasha, anyway, seemed so busy these days, catching up with her friends, like Lorenzo and Courtney, and filling in forms for Yale. She had decided to go, after all. Kristin supposed it had been decided as soon as Tasha got on the phone to New York to tell her parents the good news. Kristin had heard their ecstatic cries, even through the receiver in Tasha's hand. Tasha would not, she'd supposed then, hold out.

Peter had said as much, too. 'Tasha's young,' he said. 'I mean, young in the head. She's got this great family, they probably smother her but she doesn't know it yet –' And then he cut off, as he always did – as Kristin did, too – when they started to talk about Tasha. It seemed disloyal.

And after all, Kristin reminded herself, I have a lot to thank Tasha for. Peter most of all. She hoped it hadn't hurt Tasha too much to give him up. She was almost on the point of saying Tasha really didn't need to: that they could manage, somehow . . .

But, no. Share him? It was lunacy. Better, she supposed, to leave things as they were.

9 'So there you are.'

A silhouette blocked Tasha's exit from the studio: wide shoulders, arms stretched from one side of the doorframe to the other.

'Peter.'

'Aye. Thought I'd gone walkabout, did you?'

'Gone what?'

'Done a runner. Never mind. Where have you been? Doing anything right now?'

'Well, um . . .'

'Sneaked a whole sheet of brownies out of Commons this morning.' He winked. 'Back at my place. Coffee. What do you say?'

'Actually, I should be getting back for –'

'Tasha.' His voice was patient: reproachful.

'Oh, what the heck.' She smiled. 'Okay.'

As they walked side by side through the echoing corridors of the art block, deserted at four on a Sunday afternoon, and then out across the soggy grass, they hedged round the subject which Tasha, at least, sensed was the real one on their minds. They talked about Peter's show in Provincetown and an upcoming one in Chicago in July. They came to Quincy Adams and he unlocked the bottom door. As she started up the stairs ahead of him, she felt arms clamp round her waist.

'Hey,' she said, 'what's that for?'

'I've missed you.'

She let herself turn to face him. As she stood one step above him, their eyes were almost on a level. She smiled and fingered one of the buttons of his collar, feeling strangely shy. 'Me, too.'

'So then where've you been?'

'It's complicated. I meant to try to talk to you, but –'

'Is it to do with Kristin?'

Tasha nodded.

'Just set me straight here, Tasha. I wasn't the one who got me into that situation, remember? It was your idea.' He curled a finger under her chin and held it, to make her look at him. 'Am I being punished, or what?'

'Peter, no. Don't be crazy.'

''Cause that's the way I feel. As if you thought, well, I've had enough of him. Let's just drop him and not tell him about it. So much for my little tangle with the rough trade.'

'The what?'

'Never mind.' Peter's gaze was hostile, puzzled, forgiving: one of these things or all of them at once, Tasha couldn't be sure.

She sighed. 'Kristin and I sort of said we'd – figure out what to do. But we never really did.'

He nodded.

'Have you seen Kristin since – I mean, since . . .'

'Actually, I have.' He looked at her evenly. But still his arms were warm and close around her, and he didn't let go.

Tasha swallowed, and felt a pain in her chest. She hadn't guessed it would hurt like that. Kristin could at least have told her. 'Oh. Well, I guess I understand. I ought to go . . .'

'That's not it, Tasha.' Peter was staring hard at her. Then he smiled, coaxing, as if she were a simple child who refused to get the point. 'For Christ's sake, I want you back. That's why I wanted to see you.'

'But why? Oh –' Tasha shook her head and let out a curse. 'I wish I'd never gotten into this.'

'But you have, Tash. So here we are.'

'What about Kristin?'

'Never mind Kristin. I'll take care of her.' He leaned towards her and took one of her earlobes into his mouth.

'So,' he murmured around it, 'are you coming upstairs? You know, it's actually true, what I said about the coffee.'

She laughed and melted against him. Her eyes felt teary, she didn't know why. 'Okay,' she said. 'You have the brownies. I just ate.'

'Not hungry?' Peter pulled her close again. 'That's not like you, Tasha Seidelman.'

She didn't tell Kristin; she didn't need to. Kristin merely caught her eye in Commons and said, 'I think I know where you've been.'

Tasha tossed back her hair, feeling sheepish – and then, remembering, defiant. 'Well. So have you.'

Kristin nodded and studied her glass of Diet Coke. Then she looked up, clear-eyed. 'Are you angry?'

'No. Well –'

'Good. I'm sorry I never told you.'

'No, that's okay. Well, I mean, you could have . . .'

'I know. I just find these things difficult.'

'It's not going to get any easier.'

'Why? What do you mean?'

Kristin, Tasha thought, could be infuriatingly self-contained sometimes. Didn't she have any feelings about all this? Any at all? 'I mean we can't just . . . You know, go on, both of us . . .'

'I don't see why not.'

'For one thing, Peter's pretty confused.'

'Is that what he told you?' Kristin had started pleating her paper napkin. 'Well.' She gave a slight laugh. 'Perhaps he is. Perhaps we all are. But what does it matter, really, Tasha? In a month we'll be scattering in all directions. Can't we just go on as we are till then? I don't suppose *he* minds.'

'No.' Tasha laughed a little, too. 'I don't suppose so.' She looked over at her friend. Kristin looked casual, nonchalant in her faded leotard and long print skirt, her hair longer and wilder than it used to be, sweeping past her shoulders. Maybe it was just Tasha's imagination, but she didn't seem so contained, so neat, so . . . virginal anymore. Maybe, deep down, Kristin was the wild one. The thought discomfited Tasha, and, for once, words failed her.

At the end of May, Peter got his Corvette on the road at last. It wasn't a red Corvette, but a brilliant royal blue one, midway between slate and fluorescent: the same colour, in fact, as several of the sculptures reposing on the ground floor of Quincy Adams.

He swung it round to the front of the art block where Tasha and Kristin were waiting.

'Wow.' Tasha paced round it, giving it an appraising stroke of the hand. 'Not bad, Conaway.'

'So come in.' He grinned up at them. Tasha swung open the door and plunked herself onto the seat beside him.

'And you, Kris,' he said.

'Oh – no, thanks.'

Tasha groaned and opened the door again. 'Come on. He'll go about forty. Tell her, Peter.'

'I'll tell her no such thing.' He revved the engine. 'In with you, Kris, or you won't know what you're missing.'

So, looking doubtful, Kristin squeezed into the same seat as Tasha. Sitting in the front made her feel queasy with apprehension, but she didn't like to admit it. She forced a smile on to her face; Peter swung out, down the lane from the main campus to the Boston Road. Soon Hy El and the Elliott Inn were slipping past them. Tasha turned up the radio: Bruce Springsteen. Peter shook his head, smiling to himself. 'So isn't this just the life? Someday, you know, I'm going to take off and drive clear across this country. All the way to California.'

'Man,' said Tasha, 'that's what I want to do. Take me with you.'

And Kristin held her face still, not minding what Tasha said, knowing that she no more meant it than half the other wild, enthusiastic things she came out with; but at

Peter's words, she felt her own heart start to soar: at the thought of that great long drive. That freedom. Even though this was not her own country and she had never cared, before, for seeing any more of it, she suddenly knew how he felt.

They drove on past the tail end of Lawrencetown: the cinema and the Chinese restaurant Academy students never visited, because they were too far to walk to.

Peter said, 'Let's go to Boston.'

'Now?' said Tasha. 'I'm not so sure. I've got a Spanish exam tomorrow . . .'

Kristin looked coolly over at her. 'You know you'll pass it.'

'Aye,' said Peter. 'Come on. You're the one that got into Yale, remember?'

They drove on into the darkening evening, Kristin's heart rising with a sense of escape: of freedom. That night they drove all over Boston: through Cambridge and Watertown and almost as far as the shore, past neon-lit strips of restaurants shaped like towers and ships and ranches. They bought Chinese food and beer and ate and drank them on the drive home; Peter dropped them off around the corner from Hobson House, where Sarah awaited them in the doorway, glowering and tapping her watch.

Tasha made the excuses for both of them: said they'd been up at the art block and forgotten the time. Kristin could tell Sarah didn't believe her.

'Well,' she said at last, 'all right. Who was that driving you?'

'Driving?' said Tasha innocently. 'Oh! Yeah. Driving. Well, that was Peter Conaway. He was up at the art block and gave us a lift home.' She beamed at Sarah for a second. 'Thanks for being so understanding.'

Kristin had her doubts about how understanding Sarah was, as opposed to calculatingly lazy.

'Anyway,' Tasha said that night as they got ready for

128

bed, 'we won't be doing it again. But wasn't it fun? I hadn't realised. It's like, even with all this crazy stuff going on, we could still be friends. I wish we *could* go out driving again. Don't you?'

It seemed, now, as the year wore to its close, that Peter had caught the travel bug, grown restless: that Lawrencetown could scarcely contain him. He was constantly inventing new drives, new destinations, and inviting Kristin and Tasha along. They had a hard time refusing. He drove Tasha out to an art fair in the neighbouring town of Selby, and Kristin up to the New Hampshire border; one sunny Saturday he drove them both out to Crane's Beach, where they drank lemonade and talked about the year to come and their separate, wandering ways, a little sad, a little unbelieving, as if nothing beyond these next few weeks was really going to happen.

As the inevitable end of the year drew nearer, Tasha wondered at Kristin's nonchalance. Of course, it was just possible that Kristin was a little cold-blooded. Or – since that sounded cruel – that she was just the kind of person who didn't fall in love easily. And so she hadn't fallen in love with Peter. Somehow they had arranged, in an amicable, half-acknowledged way, to share him. The hours they had free were different ones: Tasha, up till now a late sleeper, had very few morning classes, and Kristin could usually manage to cut dance in the afternoons. Night-times, because of curfew, were out of bounds for both of them.

Peter laughed about it all with Tasha. 'Rather be sleeping, would you?' he would say, gathering her up in his arms as she stumbled, still bleary-eyed, across the threshold of Quincy Adams at nine in the morning. Tasha tried not to think that he must hug Kristin the same way sometimes – joke with her the same way. Or did he?

She rubbed a finger across his chin. 'I don't notice you falling asleep. What's your secret?'

'Secret? I have too many of those these days.'

'Don't I know it.' She raised an eyebrow. 'Too much of a good thing, maybe. Lucky we're all leaving soon.'

'Now, don't say that.'

'Will you miss me?'

He looked at her briefly, seriously. ''Course. What do you think?'

Tasha considered for a moment, then took the plunge. 'Do you . . . have any idea where you're going to be next year?'

'I was thinking back in New York, maybe.'

'Yale's just two hours away from there.'

He smiled but said nothing. Which was unusual, Tasha thought: normally Peter Conaway was an open book, chattering away about his past and his present and his feelings, lightheartedly, even inconsequentially – evading the main topic at hand sometimes – but still talking. The only secret he still seemed to keep from her was how to work his computer. It tantalised Tasha, perched there on the upturned crate in his bedroom. The discs sat in a shoebox beside it. Those, Tasha had examined surreptitiously: they all bore neat labels. *London, 1980*; *New York, 1981*; *Lawrencetown, 1981-*. What came next? she wondered. After Lawrencetown? But she supposed Peter didn't know, himself.

'What's on the Lawrencetown disc?' she had even asked him, once. He had been working on the machine when she came into his flat; he switched it off and turned round to pull her into his lap.

'Boring stuff. Letters, couple of drawings.'

'Who do you write letters to?'

'Oh, my stepfather, sisters.'

'Stepfather?'

'Yeah, my mother remarried.' He curled a lock of hair round Tasha's finger.

'Your parents got divorced? You never told me.'

He shrugged. 'Not much to tell.'

'So is that all the people you write to?'

'Oh, no. I write to my wife, kids. Grandchildren.'

'Yeah, right.' Tasha smiled. 'Only one wife? You sure?'

'Too many women in my life! That's my problem.' He kissed a path up the arc of her throat.

'That doesn't sound like a problem to me.' For a fraction of a second, Tasha wondered what it would feel like to be in Peter's position. Pretty good, she thought. Too good. She was almost jealous.

'Depends' – his mouth lingered by her ear – 'how you look at it.'

Sarah had found a publisher for her book. In a gregarious mood, she invited all the girls from Hobson House down to her flat and handed out bottles of beer, which was, of course, against the rules. She got very giggly.

Weaving her way over to Tasha and Kristin, pink-cheeked behind her round spectacles, Sarah said, 'I don't suppose *you* two are looking forward to graduation.'

It was Kristin's turn to act innocent. 'What do you mean?'

'How well do you two know Peter Conaway?' Sarah eyed them up and down. 'You know, it's really weird. He won't talk at all to us teachers. Yet people say he and some of his students are *real* friendly.'

'I wouldn't know,' said Tasha coolly. A little while later, Sarah left them. When she was safely away, Kristin whispered, 'Do you think she knows?'

'Who cares? People in this place have nothing to talk about. Lorenzo told me last week there was a rumour going around that we were having threesomes out at the TraveLodge in Selby. People have seen us going out in the car.'

Kristin gulped, then smiled faintly. 'I don't think I'd choose the TraveLodge.'

Tasha studied her for a moment. 'Do you think we would ever . . .'

Kristin looked knowing, behind her haze of hair. 'What?'

'Never mind.'

'The important thing is to keep people like Sarah quiet.'

'You're right.'

'This place is so ridiculously claustrophobic. It runs on rumours. Doesn't anyone have anything else to talk about? Anything else to do?'

But Sarah had come into the room again, so Tasha didn't answer her.

'I'm not in love with you,' Kristin said. She sat on the floor, naked, winding and unwinding a tie of Peter's around her wrist. She had found it in his closet, among his very few clothes; it was made of a luscious deep plum silk, Italian, probably expensive, and she wondered where he had got it.

He squinted down at her. He was sketching. 'I didn't say you were.'

'You almost said it. You've no right to assume,' she said.

'Why not? 'Cause I'm beneath you? And if you came right down to it you'd never want Daddy to know we've been screwing each other?'

Her whole body tensed. 'Don't say that.'

'Say what?' He saw her expression and stopped drawing.

'Daddy.'

He put down his paper and charcoal, and slid from his chair to the ground. 'Sorry.' He laid a hand on her hair. 'I was just shooting off my mouth. You know I didn't mean . . . Hey, after all, I remember it, Kristin. All that stuff you told me, about your dad. What I said now – it just came out.'

Kristin stroked her arms, and felt the goosebumps rise. 'That's okay, I guess.'

'Cold?' he said.

She nodded, and he inched closer, behind her, and put his arms around her. She shivered a little.

'You feel such a fragile thing sometimes, Kris,' he said. 'To hold. Just like a wee girl.'

She gave a short laugh and stretched her neck back, letting her head rest against his shoulder. It was easy, she thought: too easy to let go. To let herself be held, and comforted, and warmed: but she mustn't. She had been alone this long, and that wasn't going to change. Not for a long time. 'Let go,' she said, twisting in his arms.

'Why?'

She could feel him smiling: hear the smile in his voice without looking. 'Because.'

'You can let me hold you, Kristin. It won't hurt you.'

She thought now that he was no longer smiling. 'But that's where you're wrong.'

'Why?' His arms loosened.

'Because I'd get used to it,' she said simply.

'Is that so bad?'

'For me? Yes.'

'And if I wasn't going to disappear? If I were going to stick around . . . Suppose –' He planted a kiss below her ear. 'Suppose I were coming to Paris, and I could be with you. What then, Kristin Ward?'

'Oh, don't talk rubbish.' There were tears in her eyes. She didn't want him to see them.

'It's not rubbish.'

'So how would you get to Paris?'

'I haven't a clue.'

'So.' She turned around, and composed her face and jabbed his chest with an accusing finger. 'You are talking rubbish, and I'm right. It's better not to. So just stop, Peter. All right? Just stop.'

Tasha knew she shouldn't do it. She was on her own in Peter's flat only because he had been called out suddenly by Mr Czerny. Some supplies had gone missing from the studio, or something. 'Be back soon,' he had said. 'Behave yourself.' And run off.

She didn't know how long that would give her. Half an hour, maybe. She went into the bedroom and sat, experimentally, on the lopsided stool in front of the computer. Then she tried the switch at the back.

The monitor hummed and the screen glowed green. Well, that had been easy. Now, a disc. It would never work without a disc. She knew that much: she wasn't prying.

She flipped through them: London, New York, Lawrencetown. *Lawrencetown*. Once her hand landed there she couldn't pull away. She knew where to slide the disc in: she had seen Peter do it. And whenever you wanted to go on, you pressed 'Return'.

So she waited. She pressed 'Return' a few times. Then she tried some other things she thought she had seen Peter doing.

All at once words filled up the screen.

> *My darling Katey – you know me through & thru*
> *so youll know Im not putting it on when I say Im*
> *in trouble again. Youll have no sympathy probably*
> *& youd be right in that. But dear Kate here we are*
> *–*
>
> *You remember those 2 girls. Well its still going, I*
> *dont seem to know how to stop it. My own fault*
> *maybe but I think they put me there too. You*
> *remember how lonely I was in this place, so many*
> *thick rich kids & dim faculty & they were both*
> *different.*

At the top of the stairs, the door slammed.

Tasha punched buttons – *Return, Exit, Cancel* – in a frantic rush to wipe the words off the screen. But they wouldn't go.

'Tash? Where are you?'

'Just a minute –'

'Tasha?' Peter came through the bedroom doorway. Then he half-crossed the room and stopped. 'What the hell are you doing?'

She turned around, redfaced. 'Sorry. Peter, I . . . I was just fooling around. I was curious. I wanted to see your drawings.'

His face was expressionless. He leaned down and saw what was on the screen. 'Christ, Tasha. Did I ever say you could go fucking around in my things? Did I ever, ever say that?'

'Peter.' Tasha felt as if her heart had stopped. He looked so strange. She backed away from the computer, and now he was jabbing at keys. In a few strokes the words had all disappeared. But Tasha remembered them. Her composure was coming back, slowly. 'Who's Katey?'

Peter slid out the disc and switched off the machine. 'A friend.'

'What friend? Peter, you were writing to her about *us*.'

He didn't answer her. He walked away and stood at the window.

'Peter, I'm sorry. I know it was none of my business –'

He turned suddenly. 'She's dead, all right? If you have to know.'

'What?'

'Dead,' he said. 'We were friends, back in Dornoch. She died years ago.'

'I'm sorry.'

He sighed and walked back over to her and laid a hand on her shoulder. 'We all have our secrets, eh? It's not much of one. Not really a secret. Just one of these weird things. And so . . .'

'Why do you write her letters?' Tasha turned her face up to look at him.

'I'll tell you.' He pulled her up against him, and led her over to the bed, where they lay side by side. He took her hand in his and played almost absentmindedly with the fingers as he talked. 'See, back then when I was about

135

fourteen, fifteen, she was the only person who understood me. She lived in Dornoch but she wasn't like us. Her family were rich, she went away in the car every day to a posh private school. But somehow we ran into each other – down by the bus stop, I remember. I'd never seen her before, she was reading a book. Chagall. A book about Chagall. So we started talking.'

Peter wrapped an arm around Tasha's shoulders. 'See, people in Dornoch who cared about art were pretty few and far between. Like you might guess. So we got to be friends. She wasn't my girlfriend. She was two, three years older. And, all right, I guess I was in love with her, a little, but there wasn't anything going to come of it. She was a serious girl. She had long hair and these great big thick dark eyebrows.' He shook his head, smiling. 'I remember once I asked her why she let them grow like that and she gave me this speech about male supremacy.' He smiled again. 'And, see, she was the one who made me want to go to art school. Not just that teacher I told you about. I felt so – kind of fond of her. She listened to me. In my family, it was crazy, everybody talking all the time. With Kate it was, like, quiet. I know we would have kept in touch.

'She was nineteen, all set to go to the Uni in Glasgow – and then she went out to some party with her father. I don't know what it was, they had lots of friends far out of the town. So then they were driving home and they had this – head-on collision. Her father'd been drinking. Must have been.'

'Oh, Peter . . .'

He hadn't finished. 'They were both killed right away. At least that was what I heard. Nobody ever told me personally.' He looked down at his hands.

'That's such an awful thing to have happen. To a friend. I really am sorry.'

He looked up quickly. 'Well, it was a long time ago.'

'Not that long. What, ten years?'

He didn't seem to hear her. 'I write to her just because

sometimes I like to have somebody to write to. You know, like a diary.' He smiled faintly. 'Like, this thing with you and Kristin. It's so crazy, but I couldn't tell any of my sisters, not in a million years. Or my brothers – no way.'

'I've told Nat.'

'You have?' Peter looked wary.

'You don't mind, do you?'

'I guess not. Figure we're even. I've told Kate. But then I don't write to old Kate all that often. Sometimes I just like to think of her up there listening. Kind of like an angel.' His face cracked into a smile. 'That sounds crazy.'

'No, it's not.' Tasha put an arm around Peter's shoulders. 'I think it's sweet. And I think it's sad, what happened. It makes me feel like . . .' She searched for words. Peter waited, only watching her. 'My relationships with men have all been kind of – superficial. I don't mean you.' She added the last words quickly.

'I hope not.' He grinned and pulled her above him on the bed. 'I want you to know, Tasha. Whatever happens, with this crazy business with us and Kristin – you're one terrific person.'

She felt bashful. 'Thanks.'

'I'll never forget all this.'

'Stop. You're making me feel – nostalgic for something that isn't over.'

'Sorry.' He pulled her head down against his chest and stroked her hair.

'Peter, have you thought about where you're going to be next year?'

'A little.'

'If it's New York –'

'I don't know if it's going to be New York. I don't want to make promises.' His voice softened. 'Only because I wouldn't want to disappoint you. If it wasn't New York, I might have to get another teaching job. Wherever they'll take me, basically.'

'Sure. I understand.' Tasha drew a deep breath. 'If

you're far away – do you think you could write me sometimes?'

'Sure.' He hugged her. 'And if I'm not far away, we might do even better, eh?'

Tasha felt, suddenly, like flying. She lifted her head and their two mouths collided in a messy, exuberant kiss.

After that, Tasha lost the urge to search among Peter's computer discs. She knew, somehow, that if there was anything she really wanted to know, he would tell her.

What she had learnt about Kate and the letters – the diary – she kept to herself. She told herself that she did so because the story wasn't hers but Peter's to tell. Not because she would keep any real secret from Kristin.

Now there were only three weeks left of school; by the middle of June, it would all be over. The sun grew hot, as it had every year before, and students sprawled on the grass of the great lawn, listening to Bob Marley. Every other year, Tasha had joined them, but this year she walked past Lorenzo, Schirm, Courtney and the rest of the old gang with the barest of waves. She felt she had moved beyond the Academy already: that no one else in it was quite real anymore, except for Kristin and Peter.

Some afternoons, Peter took her out in the Corvette, driving very fast into the country. The radio played *Night Moves* and they pulled over to kiss, and sometimes do more, in the shade of a layby. She came back to Hobson House with her sundress creased and Kristin would look at her knowingly. Or sometimes it would be Kristin who came in, flushed and beaming.

'No,' Tasha would tell her. 'Don't say.'

'I wasn't going to.'

'Do you completely believe this is happening, Kris?'

'I don't know.'

'Sometimes I think I'm making it all up. That it's just too weird to be true.'

'Does it matter?'

Tasha almost spoke the inevitable next words, the words she had spoken before, in a dozen such conversations, but she stopped herself. *It's all going to end soon. The year will end. It'll all be over.*

As if, by not saying them, they might not prove true.

Two nights running, they went up to Peter's house together and drank wine and came back late for curfew. And Tasha knew that they were testing the limits, and didn't care. But even she was astonished at what Peter suggested next. She just didn't see how they could get away with it.

'Come up to Maine with me, you two,' he said. 'At the weekend.' He was jangling keys in his hand, ready to lock up. It was a Thursday night, after sculpture.

'What?' said Kristin.

'Maine?' said Tasha. 'How are we going to –'

He dug his hands into his pockets and grinned knowingly, glancing from one of them to the other. 'Just hang on,' he said. 'Alexei's given me the keys to his cottage. There's bound to be a way.'

'Alexei, the one from Provincetown?' said Kristin.

'Listen,' said Peter. 'What we can do is . . .'

As she listened, Tasha remembered the scruffy, shaggier, more eager and hungry Peter Conaway she had seen for the first time in sculpture class less than six months ago. He hadn't changed, really. He still looked the same. So why did he suddenly seem so different? His voice – she was sure of it – was smoother; his manner more confident. Sure of himself.

Because of us, she thought.

As Peter finished speaking, she heard her own heart pounding. *All of us. The three of us, together. In Maine.* She didn't know quite what it would mean, but she wanted it, and because she wanted to go so much, she was afraid. 'I'm not sure I can pull this one off,' she said.

'Come on, Tasha,' he said. 'Sure you can.'

'I can talk to Sarah, too,' said Kristin. Her eyes were

bright. 'You know she couldn't care less, Tasha. She'll believe what we tell her. She can't be bothered to do anything else.'

'I guess so,' said Tasha, doubtful, but swept along by Kristin's blithe determination, and Peter's knowing, twinkling gaze on her. 'Okay,' she said.

They would go to Maine.

10 In the dark they unloaded the boot of the car and made their way up the unlit path. The drive from Lawrencetown had taken from six p.m. till past midnight. Peter's torch was broken; Kristin caught her foot and tripped.

She let out a curse. The other two burst out into peals of laughter, echoing off each other.

'What is it?' said Kristin grouchily.

'You. Swearing,' Peter shouted back.

'Very funny,' she said. 'I'll probably get poison ivy now.'

The other two tossed back disembodied retorts from either side of her.

'You won't, Kris, you're wearing so many clothes. Do you really think it's cold here?'

'Leave her alone, Tash. Alexei said it can get bloody freezing, even in June.'

'You weren't carrying the wine, were you, Kris?'

It was Peter's turn to swear, at that possibility.

'Is that all you two care about? You disgusting alcoholics.' As she picked herself up, Kristin remembered for a brief, delicious moment how they had escaped along the Boston Road: just driven off. With no excuses, no preparations, and very little luggage. Tasha had fretted and wanted to phone Hobson House when they got to New Hampshire; Peter and Kristin had talked her out of it. They had agreed on their plan: it was the only way. After curfew, Tasha would phone and say they were at her parents', in New York: that they were really, really sorry, but something had come over them and they had climbed on the wrong bus after their day out in Boston . . .

Tasha had pointed out when they first came up with the

plan that if she said that, Sarah would think they'd been drinking.

'Of course she will,' Kristin had answered. 'But who cares? Look, we graduate in two weeks. We're not her responsibility then. She just wants to see us out of the Academy without getting *her* in any trouble.'

Up ahead, now, a light flicked on inside the house; Kristin could see Peter's silhouette leaning against the doorframe. Tasha ran ahead, her feet crunching on the cinder path, and Kristin, too, started to move faster. For now, she would put the Academy out of her mind. They were away from it. Alone. The only thing that could make it more perfect would be if . . .

It was a cruel thought. She tried to pretend it had not come to her, but it had, and now she could not rid her mind of it. Not completely. *If Tasha weren't here, too.*

Never mind. She could not begin to guess what would happen, now that they were here, and on their own: what it meant, the three of them, staying in a house together. Neither of the others had spoken of it, but she supposed they must think of it, too. *Three days.*

Tasha and Peter had been standing in the doorway; now they turned towards the inside of the house as she approached.

'Wait!' Kristin shouted. 'Isn't there an outside light? I can't see a bloody thing. I'm afraid of the dark.'

They both laughed, and Kristin knew what Peter would say, even before he ran down the steps and pulled her up in his arms.

'Afraid? Don't give us that, Kristin Ward. You're not afraid of anything.'

They stayed up for most of that night, lying, unsleeping, on a blanket on the sand-and-shingle beach of the house's private cove. Lights blinked on and off along the water.

'What are they? Boats?' Kristin said.

'Fishermen, maybe,' said Peter.

142

'Drug traffickers,' said Tasha, from his other side.

'Hey,' he said, 'how do you suppose they do it? How do they find each other? The one who's dropping off and the one picking up. Does one of them flash a light so the other knows who they are?'

'Peter.' Tasha gave an indulgent sigh. 'Mellow out, will you? I thought we were supposed to be trying to sleep.'

'Speak for yourself. I can't sleep on rocks. Has either of you two ever played that game where –'

Giggling, looking up and catching each other's eyes, Kristin and Tasha pounced on him. Tasha covered his mouth. '*Shh,*' said Kristin.

He acquiesced. Tasha lit a clove cigarette and they passed it back and forth, more for its scent than its taste. The end of it glowed orange.

'Hey,' said Peter, 'if you look here at the ashes, you can see wee folk dancing.'

Tasha gave a great yawn.

'I remember,' said Kristin, 'we used to have big fires in one of our rooms. At Littledene. I used to sit there watching the people dancing in the flames. It's one of my first memories, actually.'

'Mine,' said Peter, 'is of cracking my head on the pavement. My sister was supposed to be looking after me. She just dragged me home, bleeding everywhere. I had to go to hospital for stitches.'

'I hate hospitals,' said Tasha.

'But your father's a doctor.' Peter laughed.

Kristin said, 'Do you have a scar from it?'

It was like that all night. Their conversation waved and wandered; whenever it looked like dying, Peter, sleepless, would stir it up again.

'Don't you ever,' said Tasha, 'run out of energy?'

He only laughed.

'Don't you sleep much?'

'Not every night. Sometimes I only catch a few hours. I'm kind of an insomniac.'

'I guess we never knew that,' said Tasha. She sounded thoughtful. 'Isn't that funny? That we could know you all this time but not know what you were like at night.'

Icy water lapped at the soles of their feet.

'I wish we could stay like this forever,' said Kristin. But no one answered her. She felt Peter's hand reach out to clasp hers; then, as it loosened, his little finger stroked her palm.

'Me, too.' Tasha yawned and propped her head against Peter's shoulder. In fact, she yearned for her bed. But the other two seemed happy here.

She felt his fingers stroking her shoulder, then coming to rest just above her breast. Her heartbeat quickening, she turned towards him, reaching out. But then she heard the gentle rise and fall of his breathing, and realised he was asleep. So was Kristin.

Tasha woke at first light, groggy, to find Kristin gone. He was still there beside her, though. Shivering, she curled up and rested her head on his chest.

Gradually an arm snaked round her; she felt his body waking, the limbs first. His two hands joined to clasp round her, and now he pressed his front to her back with a waking groan. She rubbed against him, catlike, and without speaking or turning her to face him, he stripped off her jeans, then her sweater and blouse. She felt the warmth of him, prodding against her, entering.

'If it's always like this,' she murmured, 'I want to wake up with you every morning.'

He grunted a laugh. His voice was muffled by her hair. 'I'm not sure I could manage it.'

Kristin watched from the bedroom window upstairs. She had imagined, she realised now, that the others would not stick it out all night; that they would wake and find their way indoors, as she had. The wide bed sat low against

144

unpainted eaves, its sheets barely rumpled because she had taken up only a corner of it.

She propped her elbows on the sill. She could see them perfectly. The intertwined, nearly naked bodies, framed by a rim of trees and the flatness of the water's edge, lithe and strangely small against the shingle.

Yet she felt less jealous than curious. So this was how other people made love. With their mouths, hands, whole bodies at once. So greedy.

She found that she did not want to stop them: to get in their way. Her time would come. She reached inside her overnight bag and found her camera.

The sun was already growing hot. Kristin could feel it as she stood on the wooden porch. It felt so warm, it almost invited her to slip out of her silk dressing-gown, even while she still held the camera.

She took a step further down the stairs to the beach; and another. The two bodies lay still now. Perhaps Peter was even dozing again. But Tasha heard Kristin moving: turned and saw her.

'Look!' She nudged Peter. He stirred and looked up.

Kristin took one last photograph, then gave an impish smile as she put the camera down.

'You didn't,' said Tasha.

And Kristin laughed now, high, gleefully, maniacally, almost; and she shed her robe in a flash and ran, a pale thin sprite, into the water.

It was very cold. She felt it right away, but she didn't want to give up. She also remembered that she couldn't really swim – that she had only ever paddled ineffectually in heated pools, before – and now she felt the cold grind into her bones, and wished she could make her way out. But not yet. Not so soon. She was not a coward.

So she stayed where she was, neck-deep, her feet grazing the sand below but not resting securely enough for comfort. She smiled at the other two to hide the chattering of her teeth.

Peter stood at the edge of the water. 'For fuck's sake, come out of there, Kristin. You'll freeze.'

'Come on,' pleaded Tasha. 'The water here's really cold.'

Kristin dived down, and bobbed to the surface. Salt stung her eyes. She could hear the other two talking, though not what they were saying, and now, just to keep warm, she paddled a little way towards shore, then back out again. Despite the warmth movement generated, she could feel her body beginning to tremble.

Peter let out another curse. 'For Christ's . . . Are you going to make me come and get you?'

She laughed and nodded, her teeth clattering together. Tasha, she noticed, had run inside.

Peter still hesitated. But then he did it. As she knew he would. He strode into the water, still naked, the black hairs on his chest slicked to his skin. But she could not seem to move towards him as she wanted to. She could not seem to locate her toes.

'You're crazy,' said Peter, gathering her up in his arms. 'Totally crazy.'

He sounded angry. But she clung around his neck and felt something throb inside her. He wasn't really angry. He wasn't. He was pretending. Pretending a harshness that wasn't there, because it turned her on. That was why she loved –

No, of course she didn't love him. But she wondered: would the sea water have washed the scent, the cells and sweat, of Tasha from him?

She hoped so. She smiled up at him. And then she could not stop smiling. Her teeth clenched; her mouth stuck in a grimace.

'You're mad,' he said. 'There's no way I'm going to let you do a crazy thing like that again.'

No, she thought. *Don't. Stay with me, stop me.* She felt a

146

slow warmth growing inside her, but then they reached the shore, and he let her down abruptly. She stumbled on the shingle. Tasha was running down the steps with a towel: wrapping her up.

Now, as they helped her into the house, they both chided her. *You're crazy, kid. Who goes skinnydipping in Maine?* That was Tasha. And Peter: *You crazy little show-off.*

They were making her scrambled eggs and coffee; bundling her into a shower, then bed. She didn't mind what they said now; she accepted their reprimands. Their warmth surrounded her. *Never leave me, don't leave me,* she thought; and when Peter moved towards the door of the bedroom, while she still lay in the bed, she called out – her first words in almost an hour – 'No. Don't go.'

So he came to join her: to keep her warm. Tasha came in and sat on her other side and talked – aimlessly, as she always could, about anything and nothing.

And Kristin felt their closeness, and knew that they would not leave her alone again. And that perhaps they would make love soon, all of them; and that she did not mind.

Tasha wondered if she actually wanted Kristin: desired her. She had not let herself think such thoughts before, and now they scared her. Of course, she had always been a little fascinated by that wispy cotton-soft hair, that nymphlike body: how could anything so close to her own height and size appear so fragile?

Kristin had always been bashful about showing herself naked, but now she lay bare, unaware in the noontime sun. Peter had just made love to her; with a whimper, an anxious look at Tasha, she had allowed it – clenching her legs around him for a brief moment, never kissing him, her gaze fierce and intent on something, apparently, in the distance behind him. Now she lay as if asleep, and Tasha leaned over Peter's body to touch her. Kristin's eyes were

147

closed, her nostrils flaring with each outward breath. The skin of her breast felt smooth and fine, the pink centre softer and larger than Tasha had thought.

Kristin started; looked up with wary eyes. Then Peter, nudged awake by their movements, glanced from one to the other, and smiled, and closed his eyes again.

'You look like the cat that got the cream,' said Tasha.

'So I am.' He opened his eyes again and took hold of her hand, leading it to Kristin's other breast.

Kristin squirmed.

He leaned over and kissed her forehead. 'Go with it,' he said. 'I want you to.'

She looked up at him, her gaze more studious than trusting.

He traced the line of her throat, then the bump of her collarbone. Tasha, who lay on his other side, watching, suddenly lifted herself up and fell down on him, kissing, covering his chest in a sweep of hair. She felt a hand creep towards her. Kristin's. Tentatively it touched her shoulder and retreated. Tasha felt a small tremor and was ashamed of herself.

Experimentation, she reminded herself. That was all. She had learnt things already, in these last few hours. She had seen the odd way Peter and Kristin made love: quickly, almost brutally, never kissing, as if there were wariness between them – even dislike. But Tasha knew that was not the case. Not the case at all.

Kristin seemed oddly passive. She was passive now, as Peter stroked her and Tasha, in turn, stroked and kissed his body. And then somehow they all began to move, to act together. Tasha couldn't have described, even a few minutes later, how it happened. But, very briefly, they were one. They looked at each other in the bright sunlight.

Kristin laughed, suddenly, and Peter smiled. Then he groaned. 'Christ, I can't go on,' he said. But somehow, late into the afternoon, he did.

148

Later, they took showers and cooked and ate and walked along the beach. Tasha wanted to ask the other two a thousand questions; she wanted to talk about what had happened, but she could tell that neither of them did. Only when they climbed between the sheets that night – all three, by unspoken agreement, together in the big bed again – did she venture to ask Peter, 'Have you ever done anything like this, before?'

'No.' He laughed and shook his head. 'No way. How about you, Tash?'

'No! Of course not.'

'Couldn't be sure. I thought you were the type.'

'Half of Elliott thinks we've been doing this all spring.'

He laughed. 'I wish.'

Kristin had stayed silent, and now they both looked at her.

'I think,' said Peter, suddenly serious, 'it's the kind of thing that only happens to you once in a lifetime. It's like an incredible fantasy. And you feel so lucky it's happened, but you've got to keep it to yourself.'

'Once in a lifetime,' repeated Tasha. 'Isn't that kind of sad?'

'Sad?' Kristin spoke suddenly. 'Why?'

'It sounds like – part of my life ending.' Tasha frowned and started to play with the ends of her hair. 'I hope we'll stay friends.'

Peter slid his arms round them both. 'Sure we will. All of us.'

'Do you think so?' Kristin sounded doubtful. But the other two ignored her.

Hours later, after she had dozed and woken, Tasha felt one of Peter's hands moving over her body.

She stretched to look over at Kristin. Her hands were moving, too. This time, the room was lit by moonlight, and what happened was briefer, wordless, more like a dream.

Nor did they speak of it in the morning.

*

Sunday afternoon came, and the drive back to Lawrence-town. They packed the car, and locked the door of the little house, and looked at each other, sad, bemused, resigned. It was over.

'Do you want to drive, Tash?' said Peter; and Tasha laughed because it was an old joke between them. She hadn't learnt to drive yet, but was desperate to.

They talked very little during the ride home. Just after five, Peter dropped Kristin and Tasha off, around the corner from Hobson House. They shouted their goodbyes and started carrying their bags up the block. Halfway to the house, they saw Sarah.

'All right,' she said. 'Where have you two really been?'

And all at once Tasha realised they were in for trouble.

11 The meetings, the discussions and reprimands, began that night and did not end until late the next day. Kristin and Tasha sat in front of Sarah, then in front of the Disciplinary Committee, then the Dean. The Dean, dour and long-faced, said she had considered calling in the Headmaster.

'However,' she said, 'that won't be necessary, as Mr Conaway has agreed to leave the Academy. Now you, Natasha –'

Tasha wanted to break in and ask what Peter had said, exactly: when he was leaving. Today? Tomorrow?

'You, Natasha, have been admitted to Yale. It would be unfortunate to jeopardise that.'

The Dean talked on. Tasha's mind wandered. She heard the words 'fine school record' and 'one small incident last year. If it weren't for that I might be able to overlook . . .'

Tasha tuned out again.

'. . . grounds for expulsion.'

'Sorry?' said Tasha.

'I said that being off campus for three days without permission, never mind in whose company, would normally be grounds for expulsion.'

Tasha felt her face growing warm. Her world was ending. She hated the Dean: hated her. Despite herself, she felt tears coming into her eyes; she looked at Kristin for reassurance. For hope.

Kristin said, 'Then expel me.'

'I'm sorry?' said the Dean.

'If you have to expel someone, expel me. It's not Tasha's fault.'

Tasha almost spoke up then, but somehow she couldn't.

151

And Kristin was talking on, quite calmly. 'Frankly, I don't see why any of this matters to you. We're both eighteen. Old enough to look after ourselves, I should think. But if this school's silly rules demand some sort of sacrifice, expel me. I really couldn't care less.'

Tasha drew in a shallow breath. She wanted to tell Kristin to stop before she made the Dean really angry – but it was too late for that. And perhaps Kristin really didn't care. All through Sarah's scoldings she had remained silently indifferent. Tasha had been the one apologising – fearful.

The Dean tapped her fountain pen on the leather top of her desk. 'Let me understand you.'

You can't do this, Kristin, Tasha wanted to say. But something silenced her.

Nothing was Kristin's fault, of course. It wasn't anybody's. They had simply forgotten: on Saturday night they should have phoned again. Tasha should have explained to Sarah that they had been delayed in New York. That was the way they had planned it.

But they had forgotten, and Sarah, naturally enough, had phoned the Seidelmans . . . .

Tasha forced her attention back to the voices of Kristin and the Dean.

'If that is the way you feel, Miss Ward . . . I will have to tell your parents exactly what has happened.'

'May I go now?' With a quick, balletic, almost contemptuous movement, Kristin spun and stood.

The Dean gave a quick nod, and Tasha was left alone, facing the wide mahogany desk.

'Well, Natasha. Do you think you can manage to obey our rules for the two weeks until you graduate?'

Tasha nodded, not quite believing what she heard. She was being let off. She was saved.

Kristin knew only that she had to find Peter, and learn whether what he had said yesterday morning, when they were alone on the beach outside the house in Maine – it seemed an age ago – was true.

She knew he wouldn't care that he was being forced to leave. He felt the same contempt for the Academy as she did. He had plans for the summer – a stay in Provincetown, a show in Chicago – so he could just start out early. Strike out on the road, with the money he had saved here. She envied him.

Foolishly, of course. Why should she envy him? When . . .

She made herself not think of it. She thought, instead, of Tasha, who by now might have been sprung by the Dean. Who should be grateful. Kristin felt a slight, momentary pity for them both: Tasha, with her ingrained respect for this place and its rules; the Dean, prepared to accept any excuse rather than jeopardise that Academy prize, a Yale admission . . .

It was all quite ridiculous. Borson would be angry, of course. Two years of fees down the drain. No diploma. Yet she suspected the American College in Paris wouldn't mind. She thought again of Peter, and his great, free-wheeling faith that something would always turn up. She would learn to be like him. She could do it.

She ran up the stairs of Quincy Adams, because the door was open.

'Peter?'

His sleeves were rolled up, and he was packing things with newspaper into boxes. He didn't speak, but grinned, looking bemused, almost surprised that she had made it out so quickly. For once she did not hesitate but threw herself into his arms.

Tasha tried to keep from running from the Dean's office to Quincy Adams. Luckily everyone must be at sports, for she met no one along the way, and when she caught sight of the long yellow house across the stretch of grass, she picked up speed. She was out of breath by the time she reached the open door.

It hadn't occurred to her that Kristin would be there. But now it came to her belatedly, because she heard the voices. Laughing: speaking rapidly, excitedly.

'But are you sure?' Kristin said. 'They're going to give you a studio?'

'Aye, it's too good to be true, isn't it? Over on the Left Bank. These numbers, these *arrondissements*, don't mean anything to me –'

'They go round in a spiral. They start on the Ile de la Cîté –'

'Christ, you're lucky. You speak the language. You're going to have to do my talking for me . . .'

Peter was laughing. Tasha stood stock-still, her heart pounding. She wanted to run away, but her legs felt weak. If they had heard her coming, they would find her down here.

They couldn't. She wouldn't let them. She thought she could bear any number of embarrassments, but not this. She was a fool: they had played her for a fool, and the only way she could possibly tolerate it was not to let them know.

Peter had talked about New York. He had never made any promises. But he had never mentioned Paris, either. *Never*.

Eventually she forced her feet to move. She could still hear the voices talking upstairs, but they had moved to a different, further room. She backed away over the threshold and then turned and jogged slowly across the lawn. She wished she could leave today, like Kristin. Kristin was lucky.

Kristin packed her bags that night. She had agreed to be off campus by noon the next day.

'I'm sorry,' she said to Tasha. 'It just – came up. I didn't make it happen. I didn't ask him to apply for the grant. Honestly. I swear it.'

Tasha, sitting on her bed and cradling her tattered copy of *The Hobbit*, ignored her.

'Look, I don't know if anything's going to work out between us. All right, to be honest, I'm glad he'll be there. Because it's scary starting out in a strange city.'

'You didn't have to go there.' Tasha still stared at her book.

'No. I suppose not.' Kristin sighed and refolded a jumper on the top of her suitcase. 'You said you're not really in love with him. If I'd thought you were . . .'

'Right.' Tasha gave a thin half-smile. 'Sure. You're right. I want to be free just now. No commitments.' Suddenly she picked herself up off her bed. 'Well, good luck. I'm going over to Lorenzo's.'

'Tasha?'

She gave no sign of hearing. Kristin watched her leave. She sighed and rubbed her head, which was throbbing. She had a train to catch tomorrow at eight.

I didn't want to do this to you. She had hoped she might get through to Tasha before she left, but now it didn't look like she would. Maybe she could write her, eventually, though. Or phone.

To be honest she couldn't blame Tasha for being hostile. Looking back over the last month or so, she supposed she had realised what Peter was hinting at. That when he told her, *I could fancy Paris*, he had meant it. She hadn't discouraged him. Rather the reverse. Every day she had wished it: fervently, though, she thought, pointlessly. She wished he would get the fellowship he had applied for. It seemed the chances were slim. She told herself that there would be no need to hurt Tasha by telling her – unless it happened. And then, when it had – when she learnt the news, two days ago in Maine – she had made herself all kinds of excuses. Tasha had had a string of boyfriends: she couldn't really care about Peter.

155

Yet perhaps she had suspected how Tasha felt, and had wanted to make it up to her. Perhaps that was why she had blurted out those words in the Dean's office. *Expel me.*

He's coming to Paris. He's coming with me. Because he was in love with her? No. She didn't go so far as to believe that. It was luck. Luck, that the fellowship had come his way. Luck, that they could be together a little longer, before . . .

Before their ways divided, she supposed. They were both unknown and poor: they would need other partners. She wished she could explain that to Tasha, too.

But Tasha, she thought, wouldn't understand. She would only be angry. Angry, because she was hurt. Kristin hadn't meant it all to come out this way. She wished, almost, that she could go back and undo everything since that last day in Maine. But she couldn't.

12 It took a moment to recognise the envelope. It was addressed in an unfamiliar type: *Katharine Skelton*. She glanced at the postmark as she always did: 5 October, Seattle. All the way across America. Could it have come so quickly?

She tore the letter open and scanned the pages, her heart beating, as always, with an unnatural heaviness. He said he had bought a new computer: that explained the type. Peter and his gadgets. He still had the Corvette, though. He had driven it to the West Coast, all the way from Boston.

I like this place, he wrote. *Its rainy and misty. A little like home.*

She felt a familiar surge of hope, reading the words. Then she damped it down. He was not tired of America yet. His enthusiasm shone from the pages. He had found some sort of patron, it seemed. He would even, he promised, be sending her a cheque.

She almost wished he wouldn't. It made her own achievements seem so small. She went over to the sink to wash her hands, kicking aside the studio's detritus: crumpled newspapers, a clay-specked jumper, a football. She imagined writing him her news tonight: getting out a fountain pen and a sheet of thick watercolour paper. She would give him the address of the new house, in Crail. A queer place, all up and down, with scarcely a garden. It was cheap, though. Up there, she could afford not to teach. She was growing tired of teaching – the back-and-forth, the need to concentrate on other people.

Artists, Peter said, must be selfish. And he was right. He might be right about something else, too. She had missed

157

Scotland. Even though she hadn't been born there, she supposed it had become home to her. Maybe, she thought, we all find the place that is home. Or come back to the place we never should have left.

1986

13 Lorenzo de Maas had everything worked out. Tasha couldn't help envying him a little as, sitting across from her at their favourite New Haven pizzeria, he rattled off his plans for the year after graduation: a month working for a theatrical agent, followed by two with the New England Rep, and then a temporary job – which could become permanent – with New York's Metropolitan Opera.

Small and lithe, with a nose too big for his face, Lorenzo would never be conventionally handsome, so he had adopted an arty look over the years, emergent in his days at Elliott Academy, more pronounced since he had come out of the closet at Yale: oversized Italian suits, ties in fluorescent colours, spiky haircuts that required the liberal use of styling gel.

Tasha knew that a lot of people at Yale didn't take to Lorenzo. But she had borne with him – after all, she had known him since they were both fourteen – and he had become, she supposed, her best friend during her years at university. They had their weekly lunches; they threw parties together and gossiped for hours on the phone. In the last four years, Tasha had had various roommates and boyfriends, but none of them had seemed to stick, the way Lorenzo had.

He had a big weakness for name-dropping, though: and for reminding her of the old days – of people from the Academy whose successes always seemed to dwarf hers.

'Courtney,' he was saying now, 'has got a Rhodes. She's going to Balliol College, Oxford. Rachel told me. Maybe you'll see her when you're over in Europe.'

'Yeah, maybe.' Tasha was unenthusiastic. She hadn't

161

kept up with many people from the Academy, and that included their brilliant blonde ex-Class President.

'So what're your plans?' Having scraped all the cheese off the top of his slice of pizza, Lorenzo was lighting up a cigarette.

'For next year? Well, basically, I'll travel till I run out of money.' Tasha's parents had given her a thousand dollars at graduation, and Grandma Natasha, astounding her, had done the same. Tasha had no idea where she got the money from. 'Never mind, *Taschulka*,' her grandmother told her. 'Take it, be happy. Only once you are young.' Grandma Natasha had been the only one in the family to regret the fact that Tasha had passed up her chance at art school. In the end, Tasha herself had regretted it less than she had expected to. She had majored in art history and spent satisfying hours in darkened lecture halls, studying the nuances of Tiepolos, Courbets, Canalettos. When she went to collect her senior essay, her professor had urged her to consider graduate school: hinted at available scholarships. Feeling almost embarrassed, she told her parents about it, knowing how they would feel – 'You could be a professor,' clucked her father mournfully, 'it's not a bad life' – and that, for once, she had to go against them. For years she had wanted to go to Europe, and now that it lay on the horizon she wasn't going to give it up, or set limits to her time there by making plans for her return.

'So what'll you do when you get back?' said Lorenzo, as if reading her mind.

'Renzo, I haven't even gone yet! I don't want to think about coming home.'

'You'll end up broke and living with your parents and going nuts.' Lorenzo put on his New York accent and patted her hand with one of his oversized ones. 'Mark my words.'

Tasha shrugged. 'I'm staying in Europe as long as I possibly can.' As she spoke, she felt an alluring breath of freedom. Lorenzo could have his plans: his endless talk of hype and PR and box office returns. For all that he was a theatrical, he wasn't that different from everyone else in their class at Yale, half of whom seemed destined for seventy-hour weeks at merchant banks. And all for money.

'So,' Lorenzo was saying now, 'are you going to look up Kristin in Paris?'

Startled, Tasha almost choked on a mouthful of crust. Since the beginning of her freshman year at Yale, when, sitting up late drinking, she had told Lorenzo – perhaps too much – about Kristin and Peter Conaway, neither of those names had passed his lips again. 'Well,' she said with a forced lightheartedness, 'we haven't exactly kept in touch.'

'I know.' Lorenzo spoke glibly. 'But it's just this coincidence. I was talking to Steve, and he told me he ran into Kristin in Paris. Last Christmas.'

'Last Christmas?' Tasha blinked. 'You never said.'

'He said she was looking good. They ran into each other in a park somewhere. She was out with her camera. I guess she's still doing photography.'

'Oh.'

'So why don't you look her up? She's probably still there.'

'Oh . . .' Tasha shrugged. 'I don't know. Water under the bridge.'

Lorenzo gave a broad shrug. 'If it is, what's the harm?'

'Well, I don't know what good it would do me, seeing her, either.' Tasha started to pick at her nails. Lorenzo hadn't mentioned Peter. She had to suppose Steve hadn't, either. So perhaps Kristin was on her own now? Although there could be no assuming.

God, how it still hurt to think about those two. Tasha thought she had grown quite skilled in the last four years at forgetting them: at putting them out of her mind. She remembered her first year at Yale as a numb, slow passage of time: time she knew she should be enjoying, but wasn't.

She went to all the parties; she danced; she slept with two boys from her art history class, experimentally. To her parents, and all of her brothers except Nat, she pretended that she was having fun. She told Nat the truth, though. He hadn't said she would get over it, for which she was thankful. He said, 'That sounds like just about the worst possible way to fall out of love.'

Which it was. The hurt, the anger, the feeling of betrayal – that, worst of all – had not gone away. But as time passed, she noticed them less. She studied and painted and took on odd jobs; in her second year she acquired a steady boyfriend, a law student, conventionally good-looking and just a shade too cool to talk about love or demand it of her. When Charlie left New Haven the next year, she had flings with a succession of men from her dormitory; this last year had been a quiet one. *I feel,* she remembered confiding in Lorenzo, *tired out by sex.* He had just laughed: 'Over the hill at twenty-two?'

She shook her head and recalled herself to the present.

'She *was* your best friend,' Lorenzo said.

'"Was" being the operative word. Adults don't have best friends.'

'Maybe not.' He shrugged. 'But you used to be, like, inseparable.'

'I don't even know what we had in common, Renz. There sure wouldn't be anything now. She's totally fastidious and you know what a slob I am. She keeps secrets, I talk all the time . . . . I'm amazed we even managed to share a room for two years.'

Lorenzo cocked his head knowingly as he took out a credit card to pay the bill that had appeared on their table. '*I* think you want to know what she's like now. Whether Conaway's there or not. Which I bet he isn't.'

'*Lorenzo.*' Tasha had had enough. It was bad enough that he should talk about Kristin. But to mention the other . . . .

Lorenzo only smiled. 'Water under the bridge. You said so.'

'Renz, I've got to go.' Heat rising to her face, Tasha stood up and threw a handful of notes on the table. 'And you're not paying my half of the bill.'

'What're you doing tonight?' he called after her as she left.

'Moving into my sublet. My summer job starts tomorrow.'

'The painting one?'

She threw him a mocking look from the doorway. 'Yeah. The painting one.' She gave him a wave, feeling more cheerful now that she was escaping, and almost avoided hearing his last words.

'Steve said she was living in the Marais –'

New Haven, Connecticut in the summer was grimy and hot. Every day of the next week, as she lugged heavy cans of paint up and down stairs and smeared the rollers in the trays, Tasha wished she had picked a different summer job, no matter how well this one paid.

It didn't help that her co-workers, all male, knew that she was a painter of a different kind.

'Hey, Seidelman,' they would tease her as she perched up on a ladder, spreading white across a ceiling, 'who do you feel like? Picasso?'

Every morning she woke up with her arms and legs aching; every night she had to wash flecks of emulsion out of her hair. They worked in graduate student territory, mainly: the apartment blocks and row houses out beyond Yale's Neo-Gothic quadrangles. At the end of every week, Tasha counted her pay, thinking to herself, *Paris, Vienna, Budapest*. At least every dollar she earned brought them closer.

By the last week in August, her arms and legs were no longer sore. She could see new cords of muscle in them; she felt lean and strong. That Wednesday, as she slid out of the back of the station wagon belonging to Student Painters, Inc., she realised that the house they were about to start – white clapboard like the others in the street, faded to a dingy grey – would be her last paint job. *The last*! She grinned at the thought.

The others had gone in ahead, and left her with the ladder. As ever, she thought. Selfish brutes. She hauled it out of the back of the car and, balancing it on her hip, started slowly up the street.

'Mind watching out? You're scraping my car there.'

She turned; something was holding the back of the ladder. Just before she could let out a flood of abuse, her eyes widened and her mouth opened, wordless.

'Oh, my God. Peter.'

'Tasha.' He smiled.

'You nearly gave me a heart attack. What are you doing here?'

'I could ask you the same thing.'

'No.' She shook her head. 'No.' Perhaps if she blinked again, it would clear her vision. For he looked just the same as she remembered him: too much the same, when he couldn't be. After all, it had been four years. A faint smile played around one corner of his mouth, the hollowed-out cheeks filling and creasing. 'You should be in Paris,' she said now.

'What?' he laughed.

'Paris.'

He only shook his head, looking perplexed. And then he nodded. 'Paris! Aye, all that. I'd forgotten. Jesus, you know what a shock it is to run into you right here, Tasha Seidelman?'

Tasha smiled and tilted her hip up under the ladder. 'Yeah, I should think so. Hope it's not a bad kind of surprise?'

'No way. The best.' He grinned and moved towards her. She let the ladder clatter down to the ground. She

remembered the hard, wiry feel of his arms around her;
the way his shoulders struck against her mouth.

'Hey.' She hugged him back. When she let go, he was
still holding on, relinquishing her only slowly. 'It was just
so weird to see you here. Are you –'

'*Seidelman*!' a voice bellowed from a window above.
'Where's the fucking ladder?'

Peter glanced up and smiled. He was still holding her
hands.

'My summer job,' Tasha explained. 'Those are the guys I
work with. Real gentlemen.'

'I'm living down the street,' said Peter. 'I've just flitted –'
'Just what?'

Peter only smiled. 'Come see me.'

'Seidelman! Move it,' the voice upstairs shouted, again.
Tasha shrugged apologetically.

'Number thirty-four,' said Peter. 'Come when you get
off work.' He had let go of her and was turning away: a
spare figure in jeans and a creased shirt.

'I don't know about just after work,' said Tasha. She
thought of herself sweaty and paint-stained.

'Whenever. Come whenever you like. All right, Tash?'
He watched her as she turned, with her ladder, towards
the doorway.

Tasha hitched a ride home with the paint wagon after
work. She knew she shouldn't mind what she looked like,
turning up at Peter's house, but she did. Questions had
played through her mind all day; they still hadn't stopped.
What was he doing here? What did he mean about Paris?
Had he ever seen Kristin?

Her heart was beating loudly as she combed out her wet
hair. She hated herself for feeling like this. It had been over
with Peter, over, four years ago, and she had never
expected to see him again. She had always known there
was no reason she should – the world was just too big for
that – and she had long resigned herself to that fact, while

playing, occasionally, with the fantasy of running into him, by accident of course, in some appropriate setting – MoMA, the Guggenheim, the opening party for her first proper show. Then, of course, she would be sleekly dressed, chic, successful. And he. . . .

It was odd, but she always imagined him just the same as he had been at Elliott. And he had looked the same today. Though of course he couldn't be. He had moved on. . . .

She walked across town from the flat where she was staying, to Peter's street. Deliberately, she had dressed in her most casual clothes, cut-off jeans and a cropped top which tied in the front and left her stomach bare. If her clothes happened to show off her current leanness and her tan, she told herself it was only accidental.

She pushed the buzzer at the edge of the battered screen door. For a few seconds no one appeared, and she backed off, scanning the house again. Had she heard the number right? Had she dreamed it all?

'Tasha.' Peter arrived at the door carrying a big mover's box. He kicked the door open. 'What do you think of the place, eh? Gorgeous. This morning I looked around and said to myself, why in God's name did you leave the west coast, Peter Conaway? Answer me that if you can.'

An hour later, they sat on opposite sides of the battered card table in his kitchen, still talking. The air conditioner in the next-door room flapped and hummed.

'I was totally mad to take up this job.'

Tasha smiled. 'Probably.'

'I mean, I had this terrific apartment in Seattle. Looked out over the sea. I got this letter from Yale – first instinct told me, chuck it in the bin. Don't know why I didn't. Maybe I had it in my head that Yale would be like – you know, New England. Like Lawrencetown all over again.'

She laughed.

'Well, was that so crazy?' Peter's skin was tawny, shadowy in the light of the streetlamps that glowed in

168

through the windows. They had sat here as dusk fell, not putting on lights. He had told her all about the last few years: the drive out across the country, via Chicago, ending in Seattle, where the owners of a gallery whom he knew vaguely, through Alexei, introduced him to a man who wanted Peter to build him a sculpture garden. He had planned to stay six months, just to complete the job, and ended up staying four years, travelling up to Vancouver and down to San Francisco and LA, getting into a few shows; making a name for himself, almost, or the beginnings of one. 'And, Jesus,' he said, 'you wouldn't believe the money that's out there. LA especially. It makes New York look skint. Those fantastic houses . . .'

Tasha had retorted, with her instinctive loyalty to her hometown, that LA was all glitz and tack. 'And you really thought,' she said now, 'that New Haven would be like Lawrencetown?'

'Well, you know.' He shrugged. 'Small town, I thought. Hard to pass up the name. You know, on the old c.v. "Yale College of Art".' He outlined the words with his hands, as if on paper. Then he shook his head and poured out the last of a bottle of red wine. 'Serves me right for getting above myself.'

'But Paris. You never went?' Tasha studied him.

He leaned forward, his elbows on the table, then looked down at the steeple of his fingertips. 'No.'

'How's that?'

His body gave a quick, convulsive movement – a shrug that stopped itself – and then he looked up at her almost coolly, through narrowed eyes. 'Couldn't. I thought about it – that fellowship and everything – and it just felt wrong. I got to Seattle, and I knew I didn't want to leave this country. And I thought about . . .'

Tasha supplied the name. 'Kristin.'

'Do you keep in touch?' he said suddenly.

'No, actually. We don't.'

'I'm sorry about that.'

'Why should you be?'

He shrugged and gave a faint smile. 'Because you two were friends. I shouldn't have got in the way. I shouldn't have made that promise to Kristin, anyway, about meeting her, because I'm not sure I meant to keep it. Something just carried me away.'

Tasha looked at him doubtfully.

'You never,' he said slowly, watching his fingers again, 'said goodbye. That day at Lawrencetown. I went looking for you.'

'Did you?'

'You were out. And I couldn't exactly hang around. Not with that cow Sarah watching me . . .'

'No. I guess not.' Tasha smiled.

'I felt bad that I never saw you before I went.'

'It doesn't matter. I hate goodbyes anyway.'

''Cause I knew I'd miss you.'

Tasha smiled down. Something in her chest felt sore and twisted. She knew that if she wasn't careful, she might cry. 'I said I don't like goodbyes.'

'So forget goodbye. That's all over now.'

Before she knew it, he had reached for her hand. One of his clasped around it, across the table, and seized it harder when she started to draw away, pulling it towards him, intertwining the fingers with his own and kissing each one.

'It's a long time,' she said, 'since – '

'Aye. Too long.' Suddenly he relinquished the hand and stood up, coming around the table to kneel behind her. Gently he gathered her long, heavy hair up off her neck, and traced a finger from the lobe of her ear down to the curve of her shoulder. 'Just seeing you at the door tonight, Tash,' he whispered, 'I felt like, "Hey, Peter, you've got lucky again. Fuck New Haven, so what if it's ugly, your luck's about to change."'

Tasha smiled and touched his hand. She didn't trust herself to speak.

'I was hating this place, but seeing you this morning, it lit everything up. You looked so gorgeous. You *are* gorgeous, Tash. You've got the most incredible body. And this.' He gathered up her hair in his hand. 'I'm glad you never cut it off. Remember when I said I was going to? I was crazy.' His hands moved suddenly down to the bare skin of her stomach. 'And then trust you to turn up tonight wearing hardly any clothes.'

Tasha said lightly, 'It's hot, Peter.'

'You bet it is.' His voice was low and caught in his throat. She turned, clasping his hand, and they stood up together. Their bodies just touched. It seemed important, suddenly, that she should tell him: it would make them equal, somehow.

'You know I'm going to Europe.'

'When?' He pulled her closer.

'Next week.'

He laughed. 'Next week! Christ. Serves me right, I guess.'

For what? she thought, with a little beat of triumph. She let herself slide up against him and felt the fit of their bodies, and knew at once that nothing had ended or changed, that June day in Lawrencetown. They were meant to be together.

Sun splashed in through the uncurtained window. Wakened, Tasha sat up to look down at Peter. His head lolled to one side, and his body lay flat, open and vulnerable beneath the single sheet. All she had to do was look, and think, and her heart beat faster.

She was not sure whether her memory had played tricks on her: whether Peter's face, in repose, had always had this hawkish hardness. Perhaps it was the effect of age – he would be twenty-nine now, after all. Yet he was as good-looking as ever: perhaps better, because boyish-looking men – it was Tasha's private theory – tended to age well.

She went away to shower, and when she came back, Peter was awake. 'So you're real,' he said and grinned.

'I could say the same for you.'

'So what do you make of it all?'

'All?' Tasha was determined to keep cautiously casual.

'Us. After all these years. You could have knocked me down with a feather.' He laughed. 'Hear what I'm coming out with. That's something my old mum used to say in Dornoch.'

'Do you go back to Scotland much?'

'I've been back twice – two Christmases – to see my family.' He gave a great yawn. 'Nothing's changed there. Never does. My sisters keep asking me when I'm settling down. All it makes me want to do is run back over here quick as I can.'

'I know! I –'

'So how long are you in Europe for?'

'I don't know. Six months, maybe longer. Maybe less' – Tasha heard herself sounding more eager – 'if my money runs out.'

'Just my luck,' he said.

'What do you mean?' Tasha studied her emulsion-specked fingers.

'I mean I find you, and off you go! Well, never mind. You'll be back, won't you? New York or somewhere –'

'Of course I will.' Tasha tossed back her hair. 'I'll write you. If I do, will you write me back?'

He looked amused. 'Sure.' He was reaching up towards her bare body.

'Would you write me real letters, like you used to write Katey?'

'If you want. Can't promise much excitement. You won't want to know about New Haven, Connecticut – you've been here for years.'

'Sure, I want to know.' Tasha beamed, and pulled his hand up to one bare breast. She had seen where he was looking.

'And for now?' he asked.

She bent down and let her hair brush his chest. 'I've got three whole days till I really have to leave for New York. Let's make the most of them.'

At noon that day it suddenly dawned on Tasha that she had forgotten to turn up for work. She told Peter that she was probably out of a job; he only laughed.

'Tell you what,' he said. 'Let's paint this place instead.'

'What? Are you out of your mind? I've been painting houses all summer.'

'Aye, but I don't mean that kind of painting. I mean the two of us, doing what we want. Trust me, it'll be different.'

So they took his car – not the old Corvette, which he said had given up the ghost back in Seattle, but a bulky black and white Chevrolet, with replacement parts of various vintages – and drove to one of the big home improvement warehouses out of town. It seemed a strange adventure to Tasha – the sort of thing suburbanites and married people did. Yet Peter was right: it was fun, because when they went back to his flat, they splashed all the bare walls with different colours. They used thick brushes and thin ones and made no attempt to cover the bare spaces evenly. Instead, they concentrated on one spiralling, gigantic mural: flowers and roots and trees; cubist fantasies; each other. Each other, over and over again, in the style of Holbein, of Manet, of Lichtenstein. When hunger struck, they went out and ate: sometimes it was midnight, sometimes six a.m., and all they could find open was a pancake house or an all-night diner.

'Is this what it's like,' Tasha asked him once, as they were splattering paint on each other and laughing, 'living with you?'

'You've got me. I've never lived with anyone before.' Peter threw down his brush on the newspaper-covered floor and crawled over to kiss her.

173

'Are you looking up Kristin when you're over there?' he asked, sometime in the middle of their last night together. The question took Tasha by surprise, and she answered guardedly, 'I don't think so.'

He turned over restlessly, running a hand through his hair.

'Why?' she said.

'Guess I just feel guilty about never turning up. If you saw her, maybe you could tell her from me –'

'Peter, I'm not going to tell her any messages from you.' Tasha was a little incredulous. 'What do you expect me to say? That you turned up in New Haven and we spent three days together? Besides, whatever's happened, she's probably moved on. People do.' *I didn't*, she thought. But she didn't want to admit that.

'I still think about that time. Maine,' he said.

'I'll bet you do.' Tasha gave him a teasing poke.

'Hey. I didn't mean anything –'

'Sure.' Tasha felt quite prickly; and to cover up the prickliness she reached over and, finding her hand had buried herself in the hairs of his chest, let her mouth follow it, nuzzling, burrowing, breathing him in.

He didn't mention Kristin again. On the last morning, a Saturday, Tasha left early. She preferred to clear out her flat herself; she didn't want any prolonged goodbyes.

Besides, she would be back soon. 'Promise,' she said half-solemnly on his doorstep, 'you won't fly off again before I'm back?'

He looked uneasy. 'Tash, I'm not so good at promises. And I'm not sure about this place –'

'Well, write me.' A smile flickered across her face. 'You won't be able to go without repainting that apartment. Leave it the way it is and your landlord'll have a cow.'

'Aye, you're right.' He grinned, and traced the curve of her cheek with his thumb. 'So take care.'

174

'You, too. *Write*.' Tasha went up on her tiptoes to kiss him quickly, then walked away. She looked back only once to wave before she turned the corner, carrying her backpack. She did not need to look again. She felt lighthearted. She knew he was there.

On her second day in Paris, Tasha looked in the phone book of the house where she was staying in Neuilly, with a friend of her grandmother's, to see if she could find any 'Wards'. She couldn't.

Well, never mind. She could try the school, eventually – the American College. For the meantime, Tasha forgot about her quest, and set about exploring the new world that laid itself out for her. She wrote Peter a very long letter, telling him how overwhelmed, overjoyed she felt by this city. No answer came during the two weeks that she stayed in Neuilly, but then she didn't really expect one to. She sent a postcard on the day she left.

> *Sur le pont d'Avignon* – me tomorrow, I hope.
> My French is totally failing me. I'll be
> thinking of Van G and those crazed swirly
> skies. Clichéd but I love them. Do you think
> the real thing can ever live up to them? Is
> Nouveau Havre redeeming itself?

> XXXXXXXX
> Tasha

She studied her message for a long time before mailing it. It shouldn't matter what she wrote, of course. Peter was only an old friend. Friend – and occasional lover. So why, two weeks after leaving him in New Haven, was she still thinking about him so much?

14 It was September: *la rentrée*. The return. Before, Kristin had always liked this time of year, when Parisians filtered back from their holidays towards the city, and the start of the school year. It had always made her feel that the loneliness of high summer was over: that life could return to normal.

Of course, what was normal? She was no longer sure. René was back, now, with his wife and sons: back in the Place des Vosges, a bare few blocks away, but it might as well be the other end of the earth. Already Corsica – their two weeks together – seemed to have fallen into the distant past. How René had freed himself, what he told his wife, Kristin never learned. When she asked him, he said only, *'Ne t'inquiète pas, petite souris.'* Don't worry, little mouse. He had always called her that, *souris*. Since the beginning.

The beginning. She had been at the start of her second year at the College. She had few friends. Not wanting roommates, she had rented a tiny, well-heated room high up a back staircase above the rue Vaneau. She had started, in her photographs, to experiment with colour. Which was how she met Thierry.

Thierry was an old man, at least sixty, a native of Lausanne: he ran the shop where she took her films for developing. In between appraising her efforts at framing, lighting, focusing, he used to talk to her. She found his Swiss accent easy to understand. He talked about his wife, his dogs, his niece Josephine. Especially his niece. 'You are so like her. She had hair like that, like gold. She became a model, but those were bad days, you know, the Sixties. She is dead now.'

Somehow it didn't surprise Kristin when, one day,

Thierry asked her to model for him. She had seen his photos of women around the shop: black and white, semi-nude, usually back-lit so that faces were rarely visible. She supposed she would be doing Thierry a friendly favour, and so didn't hesitate on that count; if she felt a momentary tremor at the thought of the last time she had been photographed in the nude, she suppressed it. She went along to Thierry's upstairs studio one Saturday morning, undressing while his wife Agathe bustled back and forth with cups of coffee; in the end, the three of them chose to concentrate on a pose by a window: Kristin perched on a bed with her back to the camera as the sunlight caught her hair. It caught the outline of a breast, too, in the final print. Kristin didn't think twice about it. She went along in a black jersey dress to the out-of-the-way gallery where, a few months later, Thierry's photos were being exhibited. She knew no one there except Thierry and Agathe; feeling conspicuous, she had been about to make her exit when a hand tapped her lightly on the shoulder.

'C'était toi, là-bas. Dans la photo.' The stranger smiled slightly. He was older: tall, six feet or so, with a heavy frame and broad shoulders. He had sleek short hair that would once have been quite dark, but extraordinarily light blue-grey eyes. She looked up at him, a little hostile, caught off-guard.

'Oui,' she said warily, extending the syllable in the way she had heard Parisians do. She had noticed the way he addressed her: *toi*, as one spoke to a child.

'You're a foreigner,' he said, still in French. *'Danoise? Norvège?'*

'Anglaise.' She drew herself up.

He laughed. 'You don't look in the least English.'

Kristin clung to her clutch bag and glass of wine, ready to turn away. She really couldn't care less how this stranger chose to pigeonhole her. Except . . . 'My mother's Danish,' she said coolly. 'If that answers your point.'

He smiled slightly then. 'How old are you?' he said. And then, before she answered, 'Come out to dinner with me.'

Kristin was never sure why she said yes, then. She was not even sure that she did say yes, but this man seemed to take her acceptance for granted, ushering her through the crowd and out towards the door. 'Did you bring a coat? A fur, perhaps? You should have a fur. You look cold.' He smiled, as if at the notion of a fur coat on one so young and impoverished; his eyes, though, Kristin noticed, showed no merriment.

Something in their coldness excited her. She wondered who this man was, and why she was beginning to feel she had seen him somewhere before. Certain people, wealthy people, carried that aura about them: like fame, except they weren't always famous. Kristin had observed it at the fashion shows she had managed to sneak into last year; she had noticed it, sometimes, in the boutiques where she scavenged for bargains. Glimpses of faces she thought she had seen in magazines, coming and going. Perhaps she *had* seen them? Perhaps she had seen this man, too?

A long dark car was waiting for them outside the front of the gallery.

'Where are we going?' said Kristin, suddenly wary.

'*Ne t'inquiète, pas, souris.*' The man ushered her in.

They drove. Or rather the driver did, silent, obedient in his chauffeur's cap, the city streets passing by, a blur of lights.

'Do you know what I like about you, *souris*?' said Kristin's companion. 'You wait. You wait for suggestions.'

She looked over warily: saw the square, symmetrical face. Thin lips smiling. 'What is your name?'

'René.'

'Do you have a last name?'

'Yes.' He picked up her hand: studied the blunt, clear-polished nails, then dropped it again. 'Why are you here, *souris*? Are you a student?'

Kristin answered all his questions, as briefly as she

178

could. She did not like to be quizzed; even less did she like René's implication that she was poor and therefore at his disposal. However true that was, at least in part. After she had come home from Elliott Academy in disgrace, Borson had announced that his inclination would be to wash his hands of her, there and then; however, for her mother's sake, he would pay for her first year in Paris. He made her the barest of allowances, just enough for rent and food, on which she skimped in order to haunt the boutiques and buy the occasional, precious new piece of clothing. When June came, she cashed in her return ticket to America and stayed in Paris over the summer. Since her grades had been good, Borson agreed to pay for her second year; however, she was perpetually counting change, scrimping even on taking the bus or the Metro because they cost money. She walked everywhere.

She prided herself, though, on the fact that her poverty didn't show. She didn't dress like a student; even in the cold, she preferred skirts and high heels to jeans. Like those older women at the fashion shows, she took trouble over her hair, her makeup, though she knew she could get away with less. *Start*, she thought, *as you mean to go on*.

The car had passed through a dark fringe of trees – a park – and pulled up in a quiet residential street. One of the chic, outlying *arrondissements*, thought Kristin: the sixteenth, perhaps. Though she couldn't be sure.

A door opened; a man in waiter's uniform bowed and ushered them indoors; Kristin felt René's hand on her elbow, propelling her down a dark lamplit hallway and into a small room. They were alone here. She saw a banquette and two chairs around a table: a starched white cloth and sconces on the wall. 'Where are we?' she said.

René's mouth curled. 'A restaurant. You might have heard of it.' But he never answered her question, and proceeded, instead, to scan the wine list and confer with the waiter, who came and went. And then, when at last it

179

seemed their order was taken, René pushed the door shut with a click. 'Now,' he said, and filled their glasses, 'to us.'

Kristin sipped, and could tell at once that the wine was good, expensive. For a moment she closed her eyes and let herself savour it.

'Don't get drunk, *souris*. I didn't bring you here for that.'

Kristin opened her eyes, and was instantly clear-headed. 'So what did you bring me here for?'

'I think you know, as I know. We are adults.'

'So say it.'

René looked amused. 'You want the pretty words? I should warn you, you won't get them from me.'

Kristin traced the stem of her glass, carefully, with one finger. 'No, not the pretty words.' She looked up.

'Then take off your clothes.' René's face was impassive. '*On va baiser avant de diner*. It's better that way.'

Kristin's mouth curled into a slow smile. Once, she knew, the flush that spread all over her skin would have discomfited her; now, she allowed it to give her pleasure. 'Here?' she said. She was waiting for him to command her.

'Here,' he said. 'Now.' He glanced at his watch. 'We should have twenty minutes.'

'Does the door lock?'

He looked amused. 'No, *souris*.'

Kristin undressed then, quickly. Outside, she heard footsteps, muted voices, doors opening and closing. *Twenty minutes*. Then their food would come. Maybe sooner. She tugged her dress over her head and unclasped the wisp of lace that served her for a bra; René made no move, except to loosen the tie beneath his evening clothes. Kristin shivered slightly, for the room was not so very warm.

'*Monte-moi, souris. Vite.*'

Looking away, suddenly shy of his gaze, she climbed above him, and felt his fingers give a cursory probe, followed by something large, almost painful. He leaned back beneath her, smiling slightly, his hands tracing her outlines. 'Make me come,' he said. 'I feel lazy. Slow. We may not have enough time.'

'How?' Her heart was beating fast, with fear. The footsteps and voices outside seemed to grow louder.

'How do you come, *souris*?' He was mocking her.

'Not so often. Hardly – ever.' But she was moving above him, thrilling to his words, the calm authority of his voice. The fear of discovery.

'Vite,' he said, and moved against her, within her, eyes glistening. 'You are tight. Good.'

It did not go on long. It could not, Kristin knew; and so the encounter left her feeling frustrated as well as strangely high. She pulled her dress down over her head just before the waiter's knock sounded on the door. And then she and René ate slowly, talked politely. Four courses. The swelling of her stomach seemed to match that other swelling she felt, unsatisfied, below. She felt a curious regard for René, though everything he told her – he mentioned a wife, two sons – she knew would have made most other women – *normal* women, she told herself – distrust, or even dislike him. Yet he was telling the truth, and she had a certain respect for that.

Then, suddenly, he was holding out his hand to her. An offering, she thought. A gift. *Why?* Her head was swimming with wine.

And then she looked more closely, and felt dizzy.

Money. A handful of bills, the number 500 visible on the uppermost one.

'Go on,' he said. 'For you.'

'What? No.' She drew back from the table.

'But you earned it. You did what I asked. You are charming company, too.'

'No. You have me wrong.' She was fumbling for her purse. Her coat, she realised with a rising feeling of panic, was somewhere else. The maître d' had taken it.

'If I may ask, what did you think we were doing?'

181

Smoothly, René had slid the bills back into a pocket, and now he just looked at her.

'Not what you thought, in any case.' She started to slide away down the long soft seat, but he caught her arm.

'I have an apartment in the Marais. I'll give you the address. Come there and meet me on Friday.'

She watched him through narrowed eyes. He let go, and shrugged.

'I wouldn't have said that to another girl. But you are different, evidently. Will you come?'

He looked up, and her eyes found his: cool, oblique blue-grey. 'No more money,' she said.

'No.' He smiled. 'No more money, I promise. I should tell you, I prefer stockings to tights.'

She moved into the apartment in the Marais, on the rue de Jouy, at the end of her second year at the College. And, as it turned out, her last. René did not like the fact that she attended school: 'I never know who you might be meeting,' he said, 'and whom they might tell. We need our privacy, *souris*.' Much as she tried to reassure him that she had no close friends, no boyfriends – rarely even went out to cafés with her classmates – he would not be convinced. So in the end, she gave up the College. It meant less and less to her. René's free time was limited. He was the chairman, she eventually found out, of a large pharmaceutical firm, one of the biggest in Europe. His grandfather had founded it. For his work, he had to travel; he had frequent meetings with government ministers though he often professed a disdain for politics. 'They get nothing done,' he said, but still he socialised, it seemed, with politicians. With his brown-haired wife Hélène, he went to opera and film openings. Kristin had spotted their picture in *Paris Match*: he in evening dress, Hélène in Chanel or Yves St Laurent. Oddly, when she looked at the photo she did not feel jealousy but a mingling of curiosity and sympathy. Hélène's position was more secure: Kristin

182

envied her that. But René needed something else. Even with all his wealth, the Paris house and the ski chalet and the villa near Cannes – even with Hélène herself, no more than forty – René still needed her. Still wanted her. Kristin.

She never saw the bills for the clothes she bought, or the antiques with which she furnished the flat, sparsely and carefully; she subscribed to and read a dozen fashion magazines, French and English and American. Twice a week she visited the hairdresser, the manicurist, the masseuse; she joined a health club where languid Parisiennes performed slow series of movements without sweating. She had her insides irrigated because, so the magazines had it, that would help her to stay thin. And René liked her thin, and she had to make up, somehow, for the enormous meals he insisted on sharing, at his favourite discreet restaurants or out of cartons from Fauchon, at home on the rue de Jouy.

She lived a well-regulated life. She took photographs when she got the chance, but attending to her body seemed to take up more and more of her time. Her appearance never satisfied her; she had a tendency, she knew, to put on fat. She had to be careful with herself: at times, severe.

She tried to avoid the old neighbourhoods around the College, where she might run into acquaintances who would pry. Luckily, by now, most of her contemporaries had graduated and wandered home to New York or the Hague or Jeddah. 'What are you doing these days?' they would ask her. 'Just hanging around?'

What a silly question, Kristin thought. She couldn't leave René. When she so much as mentioned it, he would clasp both her hands very tight. Promise,' he said, 'you'll stay here for me, *petite*. Promise.'

He used to talk jokingly, when they first met, about how one day she would run off and leave him and find a rich husband. She had noticed that he didn't do that anymore. And how any hint from her that she had met or talked to a man who was anything other than a homosexual or in some servile capacity, sent him into fits of jealous sulking. And yet, jealous, he wanted her more. He wanted to possess her entirely, and the power of his desire for her drew her, again and again. He loved her. He said so. He had taught her so much. She knew, now, how to belong to his world.

Sometimes, very vaguely, she imagined taking that knowledge away, back to England. But that would mean losing him: being alone. The fear and dread of it stopped her.

Two days after coming back to Paris from Corsica, she saw a picture of Peter Conaway in her copy of American *Vogue*. For a minute or two all she could do was stare, arrested in her nervy, habitual pacing around her living room.

Peter Conaway. Of all people. She didn't mind, she told herself. She didn't mind coming across him this way. He was nothing to her now.

Was he becoming famous? she wondered. Artists would kill for a mention in *Vogue*. All the others in the feature were older, established. Peter only got a few sentences: 'Conaway, a working-class Scot whose compositions in plaster and metal owe a great deal to an *épater-les-bourgeois* bravado . . .' It mentioned his age: thirty. Goodness, was he as old as that now?

Her stomach felt hollow – empty – and she decided to make a *tisane* to calm it down. Watching the water boil in her bare kitchen, she allowed herself to think again of Peter.

He hadn't turned up, of course. She told herself now that she had never really expected him to. And yet, the whole of that first year she had seemed to spend in waiting. She had tried the complex of artists' studios where he was supposed to be staying, but they knew no more of his whereabouts than she did. The months went by. She heard nothing: not a single letter. Not even a postcard.

Never mind. She had known pleasure with him, and happiness, of a kind she had not experienced before or since. Not even with René. She had no regrets, except that Tasha had come out of it all so hurt – as it turned out, for nothing. She missed Tasha. She had not found such a friend again.

When the water boiled, Kristin had not done thinking. She found she could not stop, this time, and put it all away. Peter's eyes stared at her from the magazine photograph, shadow-hooded, mysterious. Something nagged her about him and the memories: 'a working-class Scot . . .' Why did the neat summing-up not quite ring true?

But then, magazine phrases never did. She poured hot water into a glass jug over a handful of mint leaves, and just then, like a sign, heard the phone ringing. It would be René: no one else knew this number. He would want to come over, and she would dress – or undress – as he told her, and wait for him. And stop thinking about Peter and Tasha and the past, because there was no point in it. None whatsoever.

15 Tasha moved down the rue de Fourcy, huddled against the January wind. Though she was in Paris again, her spirits were not at their highest. She had just left London, and a comfortable bed with some cousins of her father's, the Sebergs, in Hampstead; over Christmas, it had been good to be part of a family again, which perhaps explained the slight letdown she felt on leaving them.

And she had liked London, too. She could imagine settling down there. Every other city she had visited had felt quite foreign: London, too, but there was just enough there to remind her of home that she forgot, sometimes, that she was abroad . . . Perhaps she was starting to get homesick. That was the problem.

She had not left London, except to catch the overnight train to Glasgow. There she had wandered the streets and searched out the College of Art, thinking to herself in amazement, almost awe, that ten years ago Peter must have stood here in front of Rennie Mackintosh's tall windows, and walked through these doors. Yet she had no sense of his presence. Glasgow was rather different from the way she had imagined it: neater, less sprawling, less swathed in industrial gloom. She tried, at the railway station, to buy a ticket to Dornoch, but she could not seem to make herself understood. She finally gave up. Maybe it wasn't on the railway lines.

But then, returning to the Sebergs', she found a letter from Peter waiting on her bed. As if he had read her mind. It was the first, since she had left him in September.

Darling Tash,

> *This is me pleading guilty – every time Ive sat*
> *down to write Ive realised Im too late for the last*
> *address I have & too early for the next. So there it*
> *is. A feeble excuse but my own. Yale has a lot to*
> *answer for. My boilers broken down & Im sitting at*
> *this kitchen table wearing gloves*

He went on for some time about his tribulations; but
Tasha, reading the letter, laughed. She wanted to know
everything: the smallest details. He wrote about his
teaching, about his pupils, from talented to mediocre to
hopeless, and finally, about the two of them. About
September. What Tasha had been waiting for.

> *Id say I wish you were here, Tash, but I know I*
> *shouldnt, youre having too good a time Im sure. &*
> *so I wont say that, Ill say live it up for me, even*
> *have a few flings. & then you can come home & tell*
> *me all about them. But seriously, Im not sure how*
> *much longer I can stick this place. Finding you in*
> *Sept. made it OK. Im glad we did that –*
> *everything. You know my landlord came & saw*
> *this place & wants to charge me $500 damages?*
> **&%$$! He doesnt know you & I will be famous*
> *someday.*

And then, after a few more lines, the letter came abruptly
to an end. He signed it, 'Love'. Tasha studied the word, as if
for hidden meanings. And then she heaved a deep sigh.
Her skin was flushed, her heart pounding.

That night, which was New Year's Eve, the Sebergs held
a party, at which Tasha met a freelance film director called
Anthony with whom she made love at six a.m. in his flat,
after they had stayed up all night. She was glad the Sebergs
were open-minded people, and not nosy. They had
already murmured about introducing her to a cousin of
theirs, a medical student, but when Tasha showed, all too

clearly, her horror at the idea of being matched up with some all-too-appropriate Jewish doctor, the Sebergs let it drop. If they had any opinion of Anthony, they didn't show it. He was, Tasha told herself defensively, attractive: tall, rangy, bearded. She had resisted quite a few men who had approached her during her travels but had begun to feel the need of one, and here she was safe, on home ground.

And she could write back to Peter and say that, after all, she had had a fling. She was free to do as she liked. They were not exclusive lovers.

They were friends: she could tell him anything, and the thought made her happy. Though, for some reason or other, she did not write about her trip to Glasgow. It might seem clingy of her, to go spying on his past that way. Not that he'd mind: of course he wouldn't. But she didn't want to be clingy: demanding. She hated the thought.

When, finally, she bade the Sebergs farewell, she knew she was on the last leg of her journey. She had already been to the south of France, Florence, Venice, Vienna. Now she would spend a few more weeks in Paris, this time at the youth hostel because her grandmother's cousins in Neuilly were away from home; she would count her money and see whether she could afford to travel further before heading back to New York. Perhaps she was growing just a little tired of the road.

Today, as she deposited her backpack on a bunk at the hostel in the rue de Fourcy, she wished it were summer. This place was half-deserted and she could do without the cold. She decided to lie down, just for a minute; she hadn't slept much on the overnight bus from London.

Twelve hours later, she woke up. It was six a.m. She felt much better. After showering and drinking the hostel's *café au lait*, she wandered out into the street. She had not explored the Marais before; that, she told herself, was why she had chosen this particular hostel. For nearly an hour she meandered amongst the vast old houses; peered in through high windows, gates and grilles. She knew that, striding along in her jeans and cowboy boots, she must stick out a mile in this neighbourhood. She didn't care. A woman in a short skirt and black fur hat, carrying a Guy Laroche bag, crossed the street in front of her, and Tasha prepared for the look of bemused contempt that was bound to come her way. Then she squinted and stood still.

'Kristin?' She shouted louder. '*Kristin?*'

It was impossible; she couldn't see her properly at this distance. She was probably wrong. And yet, now, the woman turned; she held up a hand to shield her eyes from the sun.

'Tasha!'

The other woman – girl – was walking quickly, then running towards her. Her high heels clicked on the pavement. Tasha wanted to tell her to stop before she fell, but instead she ran forward, too. 'I can't believe it's you,' she said.

Now they stood facing each other. Kristin's eyes were wide, staring, surrounded by blue kohl. Her face looked thinner than Tasha remembered. She started to speak again, and so did Tasha, at the same time.

'I heard you were living here, but –'

'What are you *doing* here?'

They both looked down, away, and laughed. Kristin was the first to try again. 'How long have you been in Paris?'

'Just since yesterday. I've been all over Europe. You know, on the road. I heard Steve ran into you here last year . . .'

Kristin looked blank.

'You know! Steve Steifel?'

'Oh, yes. Of course.' Kristin rubbed one red-leather-gloved hand against the other. Her gloves matched her shoes, and the short herringbone suit she was wearing. She seemed to draw back for a moment; then she spoke with a sudden eagerness. 'So where are you staying?' When Tasha answered, Kristin said in a rush, 'But that's silly. I live round the corner, I have loads of room. You could stay. At least come for coffee.'

'Sure. Okay.' Tasha was unsure which invitation she was accepting. But she was glad of the warmth when, barely a minute later, Kristin unlocked the tall creaking door of her flat, which ran off the first-floor landing of what looked like an eighteenth-century mansion.

'I'll open the shutters. You can sit here while I make coffee.' Kristin unhooked a pair of panels, and light filled the room, revealing bare walls washed in a pale shade of blue, high white cornices, a chandelier. A few pieces of furniture lined the walls: a carved chest, a crescent-shaped table, a long nineteenth-century-looking sofa with a curved mahogany back.

'Some place you've got here,' said Tasha. Kristin smiled briefly, and left the room. When she returned from the kitchen a few minutes later, Tasha was still staring around her. 'So how'd you find this place? This is like, fantastic. Do you share it with someone?'

'No. It's not really as big as it looks.'

Tasha opened her mouth, as if to ask another question, then, on second thoughts, closed it, and forced herself to take another sip of the sour-bitter potion Kristin had presented as coffee. 'Sorry, but, um, do you have any milk and sugar?' There were no biscuits on the tray Kristin had brought out.

'Oh.' Kristin looked flustered. 'I don't think I do. I should have thought . . .'

'Oh, no, never mind.' There was an awkward silence. 'So have you graduated?' said Tasha. 'You know. From the American College.'

'Actually, I left.'

'How come?'

Kristin looked away. 'Oh, various reasons. I didn't feel I was learning a great deal.'

'Don't you want to finish your degree?'

Kristin refilled her tiny coffee cup and stood up, leaving

Tasha alone on the curly-backed sofa. 'So what have you seen of Paris?' She paced to the window. 'And where have you been on your travels? You must tell me all about it.'

Tasha, recognising a rebuff, and feeling increasingly perplexed, obliged. She told Kristin about Avignon and Italy and London and the Sebergs; she left out Scotland. At least, now that she was no longer doing the talking, Kristin seemed to relax. She was full of questions.

'I know it's odd,' she said, 'but all this time I've been in Paris, I've hardly travelled. I wish I had, now I hear you talk about it. Tell me, what are your arrangements at the hostel? Can you just sign out when you like?'

Tasha nodded. 'Sure.'

'Then you must come here. Oh, no,' Kristin went on, almost insistently, when Tasha looked about to speak. 'It's no trouble, and I'm all by myself here. There's only the one big bed, but you won't mind, will you? There's lots of room in my wardrobe . . .'

So Tasha moved her luggage over from the hostel that afternoon. She had no idea what had prompted such a warm welcome from Kristin, but she found, all of a sudden, that she enjoyed the prospect of the rest of her stay in Paris a whole lot more.

That night, over dinner at a crêperie, she filled Kristin in on her family's doings: Grandma Natasha's health, Zeke's career at medical school and Nat's in journalism. Kristin seemed most insistent to know.

'I'll have to tell them I saw you,' Tasha said eagerly. 'They'll be psyched to hear you remember them.'

Kristin laughed. '"Psyched"! Goodness, I haven't heard that word in years.' Then her face flushed pink, and she looked down. 'Anyway, of course I want to know about your family. They were always so nice to me.' She scraped at the last traces of chocolate sauce on her plate.

'I'm sorry,' said Tasha suddenly. 'I was horrible to you at the end of school. When you left. I was just – jealous.'

Kristin shrugged jerkily. 'I quite understand. Anyway. You ought to know. Peter never turned up.'

'Didn't he?' Tasha's heart pounded. *Liar*, the beat of it told her. *Liar*. She knew the truth: she had seen Peter. She ought to say so. But at the same time she knew it was impossible.

Kristin shrugged again: a repeat, almost a tic. 'I don't know how much he really meant to come. He was such a fly-by-night, always so full of schemes.' She laughed. 'It's funny, I'm not angry at him, really. I gather he's getting a bit famous.'

'Is he?' Tasha's ignorance, this time, was genuine.

'I saw a mention of him in *Vogue*.'

'You're kidding.'

'The American edition. By which I gather he must have stayed in the States.'

'I guess so.'

'But you haven't heard from him?'

Tasha looked straight into Kristin's eyes, and shook her head.

That night, lying in bed and waiting for Kristin to finish in the bathroom, she heard an odd coughing. It was a wretched, racking sound, which was strange, because Kristin hadn't shown any signs of having a cold earlier.

And then, listening more carefully, Tasha recognised the sounds for what they were. She jumped up out of bed and went into the corridor. 'Kristin? Are you okay?'

Kristin stammered, after a moment, 'Fine.'

'Do you think you've, um, got food poisoning or something?'

'What? Oh, no. No. I'm all right.' There was a sound of flushing and Kristin reappeared in the bedroom. Her face looked bleached.

Tasha decided not to ask any more questions.

Several things struck her as strange in the next few days. Kristin did not seem to have much to do with her time. She had no visible source of money, and Tasha's tentative queries about her mother and stepfather received clipped answers.

'Oh, we don't see much of each other,' Kristin said.

'Do you see them at all?' asked Tasha bluntly.

'Not lately. No. They visited here a couple of years ago.'

'So how'd it go?'

'Oh, fine, I suppose,' said Kristin.

It made less and less sense, and the only conclusions Tasha could draw from what she saw – the enormous apartment, the wardrobe of designer clothes – seemed too outlandish and appalling to contemplate. She hated to act like a spy, but she was beginning to feel like one. Every time the phone rang – which was not often – she found herself listening in. She never could make out much. Kristin always spoke in murmured French behind the closed door of her bedroom.

On Tasha's third day at the apartment, there was a longer call than usual. Emerging, Kristin said, 'Are you thinking of going out this afternoon?'

Tasha hadn't been. 'Do you, like, want me to be out?'

Kristin picked at the sleeve of the cashmere dress she was wearing. 'It might be handy. Just this once.'

'Do you have a boyfriend?' said Tasha curiously.

'Well, yes. I do see someone.' And then Kristin disappeared into the kitchen. A few minutes later, Tasha heard the sound of boiling water. Kristin seemed to do two things in her kitchen: make coffee and wash cups. She seemed unacquainted with the idea of cooking; when Tasha, on her second day at the flat, went out to a street market for cheese and vegetables and suggested that she cook lunch, Kristin had acted politely interested, but ate little. A bowlful of broth, as Tasha remembered. Most days, she seemed to have coffee for breakfast, and an impossibly scanty lunch and dinner. That outing to the crêperie had been the one exception. When Tasha asked once, 'Shouldn't you be eating more?' Kristin had laughed

193

wearily and waved a cigarette in the air. 'Oh, I daresay I should. It's because I'm smoking again. It takes away the appetite.'

In an odd way, it relieved Tasha to think that Kristin had a boyfriend: at least there was someone else who might take an interest in how she looked after herself. When Tasha came back at ten the night after the phone call, the boyfriend, whoever he was, had gone. Tasha's pillow smelt of an unfamiliar aftershave, and her backpack, she noticed, had been shoved into the back of a wardrobe.

The next morning, she half-woke as Kristin was getting dressed. For some reason, perhaps lethargy, she did not speak at once. She saw Kristin flitting back and forth from the wardrobes.

A skeleton.

Tasha blinked, but could not erase that first image from her mind. Even when she stared harder and saw the skin above the nest of bones; realised that perhaps the light had deceived her. Kristin had always been thin. It was crazy, the way she tried so hard to be; still, she had never seemed in danger . . .

Catching sight of Tasha's wide-awake eyes, Kristin gasped and moved jerkily away behind a wardrobe door.

'Morning,' Tasha mumbled. *Act like everything's normal,* she told herself.

Kristin let out a strange sigh, but did not emerge until she was dressed, a few minutes later.

After that, Tasha couldn't stop thinking about Kristin and food, food and Kristin. In clothes, she might pass for normal; without them, she did not. And perhaps she knew it.

Tasha had read all about eating disorders – anorexia, bulimia. Magazines were full of them. She wondered if Kristin had one of these problems, and, if so, what on earth she, Tasha, could do. There must be something. But then, it seemed to her that food wasn't the whole problem. The

194

whole life Kristin led was almost too weird, too depressing, to contemplate.

She didn't sleep well that night. Kristin seemed edgy around her; neither of them seemed able to come out with what was on her mind. In the morning, Tasha went out for a walk to clear her head. When she came back, she heard voices shouting as soon as she reached Kristin's door.

She stood on the landing outside, and listened. It was hopeless, of course. Her French was not good enough for her to make out anything that was being said. But she could pick out the male voice, haughty and accusatory, from amongst Kristin's muted objections.

Tasha opened the door. She could hear, now, that the voices came from the living room.

'Well, there he is,' said the man, in French. 'Your friend. Let us ask him.'

'It's not a *him*, René, it's a girl.' Kristin sounded resigned.

But the man had already left her behind. He charged out into the hallway and came face-to-face with Tasha.

For a second they measured each other up. Tasha saw an expensive suit, wrinkled jowls, and humourless grey eyes.

'*Et bien, c'est toi, la copine,*' he mumbled, and backed away again and slammed the door.

'Wait a sec,' said Tasha, and followed him in.

'Tasha —' Kristin was looking at her, worried.

'Aren't you going to introduce me?'

'Tasha, this is René . . .'

The man turned his back on Tasha, and spoke to Kristin. Tasha understood the words well enough, this time. 'Tell your friend to go away. We have business to discuss.'

Tasha waited. Looking down, Kristin started to speak. 'Tasha, maybe he's right. Just for a minute . . .'

'Kristin, what's going on?'

'*Christine,*' said the man. 'Now.'

'*Tu es un vrai salaud, parfois, René.*'

Tasha understood enough, again. *A real bastard.* She saw

195

the man smile as if it were a joke. Then he stepped forward and slapped Kristin across the face.

Tasha moved, then, quickly and without thinking. She grabbed René's wrist and hauled him back and, while he was off-balance, socked him in the jaw with her fist.

He staggered back. Then, shaking Tasha off – for he was big, big enough that Tasha realised at once that he could easily overpower her if he wanted to – he gave a thin smile. 'I don't,' he said, in accented English, 'hit women. So, out, *copine*. Go.' As Tasha was backing away, playing for time, she heard him murmur, in French, to Kristin, 'So this is what you decide to share my bed with when I'm gone. A fat lesbian.'

The words stung. 'Asshole,' Tasha shouted.

'René, don't be ridiculous.' Kristin's voice was small.

'I told you, no visitors,' he said. 'No little schoolfriends. In my position I can trust no one. Besides, I don't want to share you. I want you here for me when I want you.'

Kristin was silent.

'Get her out. I'll give you two days. Then I'll call you.' René strode out past Tasha, without looking at her again.

That afternoon, over coffee and endless cigarettes, Kristin explained.

'He has a wife?' said Tasha, incredulous. 'So what's in it for you? What's ever going to come of it?'

Kristin shrugged helplessly. 'I love him.'

'I don't believe you. That's impossible.'

'How should you know?'

'Kristin, all over the world, this very minute, married men are screwing single girls and telling them they love them. And if you're stupid enough to think this one's any different . . .'

'Stop it, Tasha. Just stop.'

She drew back, sighing, and batted the smoke-filled air. She wanted to open a window, but she was afraid Kristin would start shivering. 'All right,' she said. 'So he buys you nice presents.'

'It's not just that.' Kristin waved her cigarette in the air. 'He pays for everything. He's very generous, but . . . I don't *have* any other money.'

'What about your parents?'

'My mother and Borson? We had a fight when they came to visit. They were angry that I'd quit school, and then they found out about René. Borson cut me off.'

'Oh.' Tasha thought for a moment. 'But what are your *plans*? Don't you have any?'

'I don't know.'

'You used to want to go back to England.'

'I still do.'

'So!' Tasha waved a hand, triumphant. 'Do it! You can sell an antique or two. That'd pay for your ticket.'

'Tasha, I couldn't.' Kristin pressed one hand to her forehead. 'You don't see. You don't know, but he's given me so much. I can't use his gifts to deceive him.'

'Kristin!' Tasha exploded, exasperated. 'You're sleeping with a married guy and you think he isn't deceiving *you*? Well, he's deceiving his wife, at the very least.'

'René and Hélène . . . go their own ways.'

'Oh. Except that she gets to live with him. While you're stuck on your own over here. Why do you put up with it?'

'Don't tell me what I should put up with until you've been there yourself!'

At the blue flash of Kristin's eyes, Tasha fell silent. But only for a moment. She looked up, truculent. 'One thing I've always sworn I'd *never* do is sleep with a married man.'

'Oh. I'm glad to hear you have such hard and fast rules.'

'So I bet it's the sex that keeps you hooked, right? With this fifty-year-old guy.' Tasha's tone was heavily sarcastic.

'As a matter of fact, yes, it is.'

That stunned them both into silence. Finally, stubbing out her last cigarette, Kristin stood up and walked out.

Kristin didn't want Tasha to leave. Eventually, that night, she told her so. She spoke in the dark, under the sheets.

'You're right, Tasha. I do need to change . . . things. This situation.'

Tasha blinked in the darkness. She hadn't been asleep, but she wanted to be careful what she said, this time.

'René wants to own me. He's jealous, he wants to control me. But he won't divorce Hélène, either. Nothing's going to change.'

Tasha found that she didn't have to talk. Kristin talked. On and on – about how she *must* leave; how she still wanted to get back to England but despaired sometimes of making herself actually do it. What would she do there, on her own? How could she earn money?

When, abruptly, she stopped talking and fell asleep, Tasha glanced at the clock and saw that it was four a.m.

Over their breakfast coffee, Tasha asked if Kristin had a portfolio she could see.

'Of photographs?' said Kristin.

'No, of Rembrandt etchings. What do you think, silly? What have you been doing all these years?'

Kristin weathered Tasha's sarcasm with unexpected meekness. She got out boxes and albums of her photographs, and then they both started making lists.

'So,' Tasha said. 'Potential employers. What kind of work do you want to do? Studios? Photojournalism? Magazines?'

'Magazines,' said Kristin suddenly, looking up from the pile of contact sheets she was idly scanning. 'I'd like to go into magazines.'

'What, as an art department assistant or something?'

'Oh, anything. I'd fancy . . . layout. On a fashion magazine, or maybe an interior design one. I'd quite fancy running one, come to think of it!' Kristin laughed. 'Think they'll hire me as editor? No experience, no degree . . .'

Tasha smiled, encouraged by Kristin's laughter. 'Well, first things first. How about this?' She held up a print of legs and caped arms, taken outside a fashion show. 'This is excellent.'

'You think so? I've got more.'

But at other times, Tasha nearly despaired. Every time René called, Kristin's resolve seemed to weaken. Tasha wished she could just unplug the phone. Two days came and went; at the end of them, coming into the living room after what had sounded to Tasha like yet another long argument, Kristin slumped on to the sofa, looking defeated.

'He's angry,' she said in a small voice. 'He keeps asking if you're still here, so I had to tell him.'

'Kristin, do you *want* me to go?'

Kristin stared at her fingers for a moment, then shook her head.

'So. He'll have to lump it. Anyway, it doesn't matter, because you're going to be leaving.'

'Tasha, I'm not sure I can. Just yet. I could tell from his voice . . . it would really hurt him.'

'He'll recover,' said Tasha shortly.

'I suppose he will.' Kristin sighed. 'Sometimes I'm not sure about me.'

Tasha held her friend; hugged her, comforted her. That afternoon she went out to the market and bought all the ingredients to make Grandma Natasha's chicken soup. 'Always use the *whole* chicken,' her grandmother said. So Tasha bought a chicken, and carrots and potatoes and leeks; she was rather proud of the finished result.

'Gosh.' Kristin lifted the lid of the pot. 'That smells good.' But when Tasha ladled out bowlfuls, she said, 'Only broth for me.'

'You haven't eaten today –'

'I know. I don't feel well.'

There were always excuses. Tasha was beginning to despair. Kristin seemed to be starting to take charge of her life in every way but this one; and Tasha just couldn't see how she was going to get herself to London on cigarettes and thin air. She would collapse. She tried to tell Kristin so.

'I don't tell you what to eat and what to do,' Kristin retorted. 'I've had enough sermons from you about René. Can't you just leave it?'

Tasha retreated, feeling hurt. Finally, one afternoon when Kristin was out, she called her father. Maybe she was making too much of this, about the food.

'Maybe.' Maurice sounded sceptical. 'A lot of girls have these problems, in varying degrees. Tell you what, let me talk to her.'

'She's not here right now –'

But Maurice said he would phone back later. This, Tasha thought, could get her in deep trouble. But it had to be worth trying.

Kristin looked perplexed when, that night, Tasha called her through to the telephone. But then she smiled at the sound of Maurice's voice. After a few minutes' chat, she frowned slightly and closed the bedroom door behind her. It stayed closed for nearly an hour.

When Kristin came back into the living room, Tasha avoided her eyes.

'Tasha.' Kristin sounded almost stern. 'Your father was sweet to call, but what have you been telling him?'

Tasha looked up. 'That you don't eat. Well' – she cut off Kristin, who looked about to protest – 'it's true, isn't it? No breakfast, no lunch, no dinner, except if we go out, and then –'

'It's none of your business.'

'It is too my business. You're going to ruin your health, you can't go on –'

'For your information I've gone on for years,' said Kristin sharply, 'and, for that matter, without your interference. Leave me alone, Tasha.'

'I won't.' Tasha stood up and went to the window. 'I'm not going to leave you here. Stuck all on your own, taking money from that sadist –'

'Just stop it, all right, Tasha? You don't know anything about René.'

Tasha threw back her hair and turned to look at Kristin again. 'I know enough. I know you need out of here. I know you used to have plans, ambitions, and God knows where they've all gone –'

'I still do.'

'What plans?'

Kristin was silent.

'What plans? Go on, tell me! What?'

It was Kristin's turn to face the window. 'The same as ever. To go back home.'

'And you're going to do it in this state? Falling to pieces over some guy –'

'I can eat if I want to.' Kristin spoke quietly. 'Since that's what seems to concern you and your father so much.'

Tasha shrugged. She felt worn out. 'Then do it.'

Kristin traced a wavy line down the window glass. 'I didn't need your father's scare stories. Hospitals and tubes. Don't you think I don't know all that already?'

Tasha shrugged. '*I* don't know. I don't know what he said to you.'

'To tell the truth, there was only one thing that alarmed me.' Kristin's mouth curled slightly. 'He said if I wasn't careful, I might have trouble having babies.'

Tasha stared at Kristin. She could hardly think of anything so utterly irrelevant. 'Oh. Well, yeah. I guess that might be true.'

'He said they've done – studies. Things – shrink. It's not definite.'

Tasha nodded.

'I haven't had a period in years. I hadn't missed it. I didn't really think . . .'

Tasha looked over at Kristin's thin silhouette. 'Um, this may be beside the point, but – if you don't have periods, how do you know you aren't . . .'

'Oh, René had a vasectomy years ago.' Kristin shrugged.

Tasha could only stare. 'Kristin?' she said. 'You're telling me you want children, and here you are staying with a guy who can't give you any? Ever?'

Slowly Kristin nodded.

'That makes no sense, Kris. That is beyond crazy.'

Kristin gave a sharp, sudden laugh. 'Of course it is. What else do you expect of me?'

Kristin started to eat. At least apparently she did. She bought eggs and vegetables and boiled them and chewed on crispbreads and carrots. It all looked quite tasteless. Occasionally she would share something Tasha cooked. Tasha supposed she couldn't hope for miracles. She suspected, also, that Kristin was putting on a show for her, but she could only hope that, removed from Paris and René, which she suspected of being the root causes of Kristin's problems, she would carry on feeding herself. It was easier than not to, wasn't it?

One day, Kristin came home carrying a bag full of vitamins and calcium supplements. Tasha wondered at first whether a new obsession had merely eclipsed the old one. But that, her father told her later, over the phone, mattered less than the fact that Kristin had set her mind on changing. 'I read an article or two about all this after you called,' he told her. 'She probably ought to see some kind of a therapist in London, if you can convince her to.'

Tasha was hesitant to raise the subject, but when she did, Kristin resisted less than she expected. 'All right,' she said. 'But, gosh. London seems an awfully long way away.'

'You'll get there,' Tasha urged her. Surely Kristin couldn't be weakening, after all this time: missing René? The phone calls had ceased; with any luck, René himself might just give up soon.

But then one morning, on her way out, Tasha ran into him coming up the building's stairs. His eyes flicked over her, contemptuous.

'She doesn't want to see you,' Tasha said loudly, in English, but he ignored her and brushed past.

She lingered halfway down the stairs as René opened the door with his key. She listened. She could hear the raised, tense voices, but not make out what they were saying.

A few minutes later, the door opened and René brushed past her. Tasha ran up the stairs and inside. She found Kristin huddled on the sofa, dry-eyed, her hands clasping her knees.

Kristin said, 'He offered to marry me.'

'He wouldn't. You know he wouldn't.'

'He said he would leave Hélène. Everything.'

'But, Kristin, you know that's just talk.'

'But what if it wasn't?' Kristin turned round, looking suddenly fierce. 'What if he meant it? I could have been his wife. Have you any idea what I would have been giving up?'

Tasha looked at her hard. 'Yeah. Money.'

'Don't sneer at it. You don't know what it's like not to have it.'

'Kristin, there've got to be prices that aren't worth paying –'

'I don't know about that.' Kristin sighed.

'Look, you'll be going back home soon. Like you've always wanted to.'

'Mm. Alone.' Kristin sniffed.

'There'll be other guys.'

'That's what I thought, after Peter. And there weren't for a long time. I got used to being alone. But I don't like it.'

Tasha felt a vague stabbing sensation: it passed. There was no point in telling her about Peter – about last August. Not now.

'I wish,' Kristin said, 'I felt braver about all this.'

'You *are* brave.' Tasha put both arms round her.

At the end of February Kristin moved to London. She

locked up the flat on the rue de Jouy for the last time, dropping the key through the letterbox. Last week she had gone to the second-hand clothes shop Tasha had found, and traded in half her wardrobe for fifteen thousand francs. She felt uprooted.

Paris wasn't her home: Tasha was right. Did she want to live the rest of her life as a foreigner, always speaking the language imperfectly – always having to try? Her father had fought that battle already. She owed it to him . . . .

Yes. To go home.

For a moment Kristin felt queasy as she stood beside Tasha in the Gâre du Nord. Tasha had arranged things for her, in London: she felt deeply grateful. She was to go and stay in Hampstead with some people called Seberg. Perhaps, after a few days, she would find her feet again. Find a job.

Well, she didn't have much choice about that.

'There!' Tasha pointed suddenly. 'It's up. Your plat-form.' And she picked up Kristin's two heavier bags and led the way.

'Wait,' Kristin called. For, again, she had the feeling that it was all happening too soon. In a few minutes she would be leaving Paris. Or was it really Tasha she minded leaving? Funny, how she could have done without her for all these years: and then suddenly, parting from her seemed unbearable.

They would see each other again, of course. They had to. Years might go by before they did, though. She didn't like to think of it.

Tasha arrived back in New York on a day as cold and blustery as the one she had left Paris. That night, as she lay in her bed at her parents' apartment, she realised that she had no idea what she was going to do next.

Unable to sleep, she decided to go ahead and phone Peter, even though it was after midnight. She dug out the vital scrap of paper from her address book; downstairs, in her father's study, she dialled and heard the empty, repetitive ringing.

Well, never mind. She was about to give up when, at last, a voice answered. A male voice, but it didn't sound like Peter's. American, groggy and annoyed, in fact, so that it seemed to take some time to explain who she was and what she wanted.

Then, abruptly, she heard a clunk. She almost thought she had been hung up on. There was a shuffling sound, and the voice returned.

'Peter left two months ago. I sublet this place. You sure you're Tasha Seidelman? He gave me his address, but said he didn't want anyone else to have it. Only you.'

'Yeah, I'm the right person,' said Tasha, bewildered. Her heart was thumping. The disappointment of finding that Peter had gone had eased slightly, when she heard those last words. *Only me.* She clicked her pen in readiness.

The man read out a succession of numbers. God, this sounded foreign. Tasha had hoped it wouldn't be: she had no money left for travelling. With each line she read back to the man on the phone, Tasha's heart sank, until finally she heard the last word: 'Japan.'

'Japan,' she repeated. Her voice was so dolorous as to be almost inaudible.

'Yeah, Japan,' said the man. 'That okay?'

'Sure. I guess. Thanks.' Tasha put the phone down and stared at the notepad where she had written the address. Like all of her father's, it had been supplied as a promotion by a drug company. SINALGESE. FOR DEEP PAIN, it said.

Tasha looked at it. 'Christ. Japan,' she said, and let out a single, bleak laugh.

16   Kristin stepped into the Art Deco lift of the Josef Prost Building, and pushed the button for the fifteenth floor. A man was sharing the lift with her, but she did not notice him until he spoke.

'Excuse me. I'm looking for Advertising Sales. Is that up on eighteen?'

She turned. The man was youngish, bespectacled, conservatively dressed.

'Sorry. I don't really know my way around. I'm only here for an interview.' The lift stopped and opened, admitting a group of passengers who crowded Kristin to the back, closer to her questioner.

'Oh, are you? Which magazine?' The man looked down at her. He was a head taller than she, which, perhaps combined with the reflection of his glasses, gave his smile a slightly aloof air.

'*Weekend*,' she said.

'Oh.' He gave a slight cough. 'I . . . .'

'Yes?'

'Are you getting off on this floor? I'll get out with you.'

Kristin made her way, puzzled, out of the lift. The man glanced round, as if to check that their surroundings were free from listeners. 'I'm not sure,' he said hesitantly, 'that you ought to take a job here.'

'Why on earth not?'

'I shouldn't explain. Not here, just now. But ring me.' The stranger reached into an inner pocket, and offered her his card.

Kristin glanced down at it. *Alexander Renfrew. Assistant Director. Chappell Chase Matthews*. 'Thank you,' she said, unenlightened. Just then a lift door opened, and her companion moved into it, nodding goodbye.

Kristin shook her head and stowed the card in her handbag, then moved towards the receptionist's desk down the corridor. She hadn't the faintest idea what *that* was all about.

In fact, when the art director of *Weekend* offered Kristin a job thirty minutes later, she was slightly nonplussed. She wasn't at all sure she would hire *herself*, on the basis of half a degree and four months in her current job, as assistant – general dogsbody, really – in a photographic studio on the edge of Soho. Remembering Alexander Renfrew and his card, and his warning, she asked the art director if she could have a day to think the offer over. The other woman looked surprised, but said, 'Of course. Yes.'

Alex Renfrew wove his way back to her carrying two glasses, and shouted over the background noise of the wine bar: 'Sorry I had to drag you down to my part of town. I'm afraid –'

'No, it's my fault.' Kristin found she had to shout, too, to be heard above the noise. Young men in striped shirts and women in dark suits with padded shoulders were drinking and shouting in each other's ears, all around them. 'I'm afraid,' Kristin said, 'I couldn't give you much notice, because they want a decision by tomorrow.'

'Then you'd better say no.'

'No?'

Alex seemed to flush slightly. His eyes, Kristin noted, were a pale blue behind his squarish spectacle frames; his hair was wavy and thinning on top. 'Actually,' he said, 'I oughtn't to be telling you any of this.'

'Any of what?'

'About Prost's. The takeover bid.'

'The what?'

'They're trying to defend themselves. It usually means

staff cuts. Their best people drop out – deserting a sinking ship.'

'I see.'

'There's been talk about closing down *Weekend*.'

'Oh.' Kristin looked down, disappointed.

In a quiet voice, Alex Renfrew said, 'I'm sorry.'

'No. It was kind of you to warn me. Especially since you don't know me.'

'I suppose I'd hoped I might' – Alex hesitated – 'get to know you.'

Kristin wasn't sure how to answer that. She smiled. 'Will you be in trouble for giving away state secrets?'

Alex gave one of his thin smiles. 'I rather hope not.' He looked down.

Kristin decided then that either he had never been making a pass – he did not look a pass-making sort of man – and now found himself in an awkward position; or else he had, for whatever reason, made an overture, but that that was not his usual way of going about things. Either way, she felt like being kind to Alexander Renfrew. 'What do you do, exactly?' she said.

'Corporate finance.' Alex reached towards his inner pocket, as if for an explanation.

'I've already got your card. Remember?' Kristin smiled, and Alex flushed slightly.

'Sorry. It becomes sort of a nervous tic.'

'Do you order the cards by the hundredweight?'

For the first time, Kristin heard Alex Renfrew laugh.

They didn't go on to dinner, because, he explained, he was waiting for some papers to be delivered to his office. 'But would you be free on Friday?' he said, holding the door of the wine bar open for her.

'Yes. I suppose. More state secrets to give away?'

Alex looked away, towards the still-light evening street. 'I have to hope that more won't come into my keeping.'

It was, she reflected later, a typical answer for a man of Alex's type: smooth, yet bashful. English manners, she supposed. Though, as he had explained, he was half-Scottish, having grown up in Aberdeenshire and Edinburgh, then gone to school at Glenalmond, before Cambridge. Kristin wasn't sure why she had felt a momentary nervous tremor when he explained all this: a fear of being found out. Alex knew nothing about her; he hadn't asked. He must have liked her, or else he wouldn't have told her about Prost's.

She supposed she liked him, too. Though liking had hardly come into her relations with men before. Perhaps it was time it did.

He was, she had to admit, not wildly attractive; but not unattractive either. He seemed polite and careful and considerate. He came from a good background and must be making a fair amount of money. Dinner . . . one dinner . . . should he happen to ask her, what was the harm?

She needed new friends, anyway. Aside from her Aunt Poppy, and the Sebergs, and of course Adrian, who was up at the Edinburgh Festival just now, she still knew no one in London. After a month with the Sebergs, she had moved into a bedsit off the Finchley Road. She tried not to compare it too often with Paris. She felt safe there, she told herself. The room's bare walls resembled the tasteless, spiceless food she cooked on her gas ring. Safe. She wasn't sure yet how to progress, to move on. Perhaps Alex was as good a way as any. Yes, she decided. If he asked, she would go out with him.

It was a warm September night; the restaurant was in a converted warehouse, sprawling out on to a pier overlooking the Thames. Kristin shivered.

'I'm sorry. I should have asked for a table indoors. Are you cold?'

'Never mind. I always feel the cold.' She rubbed her arms. She was wearing a sleeveless peacock-blue silk shift.

'It's because you're so thin,' Alex remarked.

'Oh, no, not really.' Kristin felt suddenly threatened. But then she heard Alex going on, unperturbed.

'Actually, we're all thin in my family, too. My brother Angus in particular. Our poor nanny used to try everything to make him fatter. Extra cream in his milk, lumps of butter in his custard . . .'

'How horrid. My nanny never did that, but she made that powdered kind with milk. She was a hopeless cook. Her mashed potatoes, too. Do you remember those hard bits –'

Together, they laughed. Kristin felt momentarily glad: she had been able to talk of her childhood, without explaining. Alex's next question brought her up short.

'Where are your family living now?'

'My mother,' she said guardedly, 'is in America.' She did not much relish talking about the more recent past, but it was bound to come. Briefly she sketched out her parents' divorce, Elliott Academy, Paris. It all sounded respectable enough.

'So are you still looking for a new job?' he said. 'If they get on their feet at Prost's, I shall feel awfully guilty.'

Kristin had turned down the job at *Weekend*, finally, trusting his advice. 'I've got an interview next week at *Venue*.'

Alex looked quizzical.

'You know. The music and fashion magazine?'

'I'm afraid I don't follow these things. What is it you want to do, eventually? Layout? Art direction?'

Kristin laughed. 'That's a long way off. I'm hardly qualified.'

'Is it what you'd want?'

'I'd prefer to be taking photographs, actually. But I don't have the experience to set up on my own. Or the connections. What one wants and what one's able to do turn out to be rather different things.'

'I don't know.' Alex swirled his wine around in his glass, considering. 'I tend to hope I'll be able to bail out of

210

Chappell's in ten years or so. Say, by the time I'm forty-five. Then there'd still be time for something else. Consultancy, politics . . . It helps not to be entirely dependent on an MP's salary.'

'You'd like to be an MP?'

'One would hope for a safe seat, of course.' Alex gave a wry smile. 'Preferably in the country. A good excuse for a country house. Though I'd like to have one anyway.'

'Oh, I would, too. I don't care for London, really. I grew up in Oxfordshire. I'd love to go back there.'

'I'd go back to Scotland, but it's too far. I like the West Country. But it'll have to wait till I can do it properly. I don't want one of those poky little cottages where I'd be hitting my head on the rafters.'

'Oh, no.'

'And there are other things one has to consider, too. Education – if one has children . . .'

Privately Kristin thought that, for an unmarried man, Alex was looking rather far into the future. But she smiled and nodded. 'Of course.'

Suddenly Alex seemed to change tack. 'A lot of people think wealth is irrelevant. Well, that might be true. But I wouldn't feel I had the right to impose such views on my children. I feel they'd deserve what I've had myself. A degree of security.'

'I know,' said Kristin slowly, 'what you mean.'

'After all, one makes more money, a lot more quickly, on the trading floor. It's absurd. There are traders my own age driving Porsches . . . Ah. Our food.' Alex glanced up at the waiter bearing down towards them. 'Here we are. My venison, your . . . vegetables.' He gave her a quick, puzzled smile. 'Are you quite *sure* you don't eat meat?'

Over the next few weeks, that seemed to be the only area of disagreement between them. Alex was a die-hard carnivore and perplexed by Kristin's meagre and picky appetites. He prodded and teased and questioned her

211

about them every time they met. Kristin preferred to think of their dinners together as 'meetings', because it sounded more professional: as if Alex were still handing out advice about companies she might want to work for.

Though of course he was not, and the only excuse for continuing to see him must be that she enjoyed his company. Which she did, because they agreed about so much, though she didn't think Adrian or Poppy would like him. For the meantime, she kept old friends and new apart. She enjoyed her Aunt Poppy's mad costumes and Adrian's theatrical anecdotes, but somehow she didn't think Alex would. At the same time, Adrian was her oldest friend, and Poppy – not an aunt, really, but a devoted ex-secretary of her father's – was a reliable confidante, and had helped her to her current job. As for Alex, it was early days. They went out to dinner; they talked, planned, occasionally laughed. She ought not, prematurely, to make more of it.

At the beginning of October, Alex invited her up for a weekend at his parents' house in Scotland. They would fly up to Aberdeen on Friday night, back south on Sunday. Kristin found her nervousness mounting as he told her.

She didn't know what to expect, really, of the Renfrews. They might live in a castle, for all she knew. There might be shooting. She didn't have the right clothes. Would there be other guests? Alex laughed away her questions. 'Just us,' he said. 'A quiet weekend.' But she didn't believe him.

When Alex's mother, Margaret, who had fetched them at the airport, drove them up through the gates of the house, Kristin saw to her relief that, though it possessed a turret, it was long and low, white-harled and unpretentious. It sat halfway up a green valley, rather than amongst the raw Highland hills she had expected.

'Oh, it's neither here nor there,' said Margaret airily, when Kristin, complimenting her on her home, asked its age. 'Bit of seventeenth century, bit of nineteenth, even twentieth, eh, Geordie?'

Margaret's husband, Alex's father, had appeared at the gate as they drove up, an Irish setter on either side of him. He had a lean, weatherbeaten face, and, in the cold rain, wore gumboots and shirtsleeves.

Kristin wondered momentarily if the Scots chilled less easily than other people. She could not help thinking, however briefly, of the only other Scot she had known. Then she forced herself to focus on Geordie Renfrew, who was extending an arm towards her: welcoming her. There were no other cars in the drive, she noticed. A quiet weekend . . . perhaps it really would be.

It went more easily, on the whole, than she had expected. On the first night there were dinner guests, elderly neighbours; the next day Geordie took Alex and Kristin out for the obligatory, rain-soaked tour of his estate and the nearby village of Dunnochar. Here and there he talked disparagingly of neighbours who were absentees, who sold off all their fishing rights or planted the wrong new trees. Now and then he punctuated his comments with an, 'Eh, Kristin?' or 'Kristin will know what I mean.' But he seemed to take no very personal interest in her. Kristin had almost begun to feel quite safe when, over tea that afternoon, his watery blue eyes settled on her.

'So, Kristin. Was your father that Hungarian chap? Ward Construction?'

'Why, yes,' she said, startled.

'What was the first name? Leonard? Leslie?'

'Geordie,' said Margaret reproachfully, 'for heaven's sake . . . Kristin, dear' – she turned with an apologetic smile – 'I'm afraid Geordie makes an absolute fetish of looking everyone up in *Who's Who*, now he's retired. I'm sure there are dozens of Wards. You must forgive him . . .'

'No, no, you're right,' said Kristin, looking Geordie in the eye. 'My father was the one you're talking about.'

'So what happened –' Margaret Renfrew began.

'Topped himself, didn't he?' Geordie glanced around him, untroubled. The room fell silent.

'Geordie!' said Margaret.

Kristin looked down at her cup. She heard someone – was it Alex? – draw in a deep breath.

'Now, Geordie, honestly, I'm sure –' said Margaret. At the same time Alex spoke.

'Mother, I'm thinking I ought to change clothes after all. I got drenched outside. I expect Kristin did, too . . .'

With a flurry of apologetic mumblings, Kristin was ushered out of the room. She rather wished she had had the guts to stay. To look Geordie Renfrew in the eye and say, *So what? It was your fault. People like you. You ditched him* . . .

Though of course she never would. It would ruin everything. Alex took her hand, upstairs in the hallway.

'I'm sorry,' he said. 'My father can be frightfully blunt. I'm sure it's not true. There are so many rumours . . .'

'But it is true, actually.' Kristin looked up at him. She felt strangely calm. 'I don't know how your father knew about it, though. It was never – generally talked about. My father was buried in a churchyard.'

Alex seemed to frown. 'Is that why – all those years in America?'

She shrugged and nodded.

'It must have been awful for you.' He laid a hand on her shoulder. 'Well. We should get changed.'

'Alex?' Kristin looked back from her own door.

He met her gaze.

'Thank you.'

'For what?'

'For understanding. For not expecting me to talk.'

Alex shrugged, smiling slightly, then went into his room.

By dinner, it was as if the whole matter had never been mentioned: which was how Kristin had guessed it would be. Afterwards, she and Alex went up to their own rooms

214

again. Out in the hallway, they exchanged a chaste kiss on the cheek. Kristin didn't suppose there would be more than that here: not that there had been in London, either. Once, after dinner, they had kissed briefly on the lips; she guessed that Alex was not so much reluctant as courtly, and she liked that.

On Sunday, Alex's parents went to church, then gave them lunch before driving them back to the airport. Margaret Renfrew murmured something to Kristin about meeting when she was down in London. 'I do get down sometimes,' she said wistfully, 'for a bit of shopping. Or a party.' She looked a good ten years younger than Geordie, and besides being English and a stranger here, would have liked, Kristin guessed, a more sociable life. Kristin felt reassured by her approval. She could not begin to guess whether she had Alex's father's.

'Of course you do,' said Alex, when, in the cab just outside her door, she hinted at her fears. 'He's just blunt. If he'd thought you were boring or ordinary, he wouldn't have talked to you at all.'

'Oh. I should feel flattered, then.' Kristin smiled.

'Can I see you sometime this week?' he said.

So if Dunnochar was a test, she reflected, she had passed it. After dinner that Wednesday, Alex asked her back to his flat.

'Why not?' said Kristin, smiling up with, she hoped, the right mixture of caution and enthusiasm. Their cab dropped them off in front of a large house in South Kensington, evidently converted, with a column of buzzers by the door. The hall was thickly carpeted and quiet, the interior of Alex's flat much the same. While he went into the kitchen to fetch them drinks, Kristin studied the room around her. It had the clean but unloved look of bachelor quarters: no pictures, books piled haphazardly on the mantelpiece. As Alex returned with her drink and sat down on the sofa beside her, Kristin asked, 'Have you always lived alone?'

'Except after university. I lived with a couple of friends for a year. *Male* friends,' he clarified, and coughed.

Kristin sipped, then eased back against the cushions. Before she had thought what to say next, Alex's arms were around her. Startled by his speed, she turned her face towards him. His kiss was long, and more skilful than she had expected. He stroked her cheek and the lobe of her ear with smooth fingers. 'Gosh, I hope,' he said, retreating, 'that wasn't rude of me. I've wanted to do it for the longest time.'

He sounded strangely youthful and flustered. Kristin laughed, she hoped kindly. 'Why should I mind?'

He smiled then, and removed his glasses, and again drew her towards him.

It was the first time, Kristin realised later, that she had slept with a man she did not love. Though love was, perhaps, a strange way of describing it, as she doubted now that she had ever loved René, in the usual sense of the word; and if she had loved Peter Conaway, well, that was long ago. She felt a certain tenderness towards Alex; as a lover he was gentle and sweet, perhaps even a little naïve. He did not even ask her about contraception – although, expecting this to happen sometime, she had stowed her rather ancient diaphragm in her purse. Alex's lips were smooth, his touch was gentle; his almost hairless body had the clean smell of shampoo and talc.

And if she liked her sex violently other than it had been tonight, who was he to know? She was not inclined to tell him. She preferred to think that she was making a new start: that the dirty talk, the mind games, the perversities of the past were behind her. They were not part of her: not as she wanted to be.

So when Alex said, 'I hope that was – all right?' she answered, 'Yes, of course. I don't know why we waited.'

'I wanted to wait till it seemed right.' His face, on the pillow beside hers, had gone serious. 'You know – I ought to tell you. There has been someone else before you. I was engaged once.'

'You were?'

'Her name was Caroline. We'd met at university. It was probably best that we didn't get married in the end. She wanted to see the world. I didn't.' For a second Alex's eyes lit: he had made a joke. 'Well. Actually what happened was, she got a travelling scholarship to Korea. I had my job at Chappell's by then. I couldn't leave. By the time she came back . . .' He shrugged.

'How long ago now?'

'Six years.'

'Oh.'

'I suppose this is the sort of time that – one talks about one's past.' Alex gave a sort of cough.

Kristin turned on her side. 'You don't have to, you know.' She traced a hand over his shoulder. She would much rather they didn't pursue this line of talk.

'But then,' he said briskly, 'apart from Caroline, there's never really been anyone else.' He touched her hair, and his voice slowed. 'I suppose you've had other lovers? You must have.'

'Yes.'

'Do you want to tell me about them?'

'Not really.'

'Darling, I'm sorry . . .'

Kristin looked up and met his eyes. If she was careful now, she thought, perhaps this would never need to come up again. 'No!' She heard a throb of emotion in her voice. 'There's nothing ghastly. Nothing to hide. I'm not particularly proud of myself, is all. I . . . had a boyfriend at high school in America, who more or less ditched me. And a lover in France. Who turned out to be married.'

'Oh, darling.'

'Well, yes, I was a fool. I grew . . . far too attached to him before I realised the mistake I was making. Anyway –' It was Kristin's turn to speak briskly now. 'I couldn't have

217

lived in France. Not forever.' Leaning her head on Alex's shoulder, she spoke a little longer about France in a general sense; then somehow they came back to London, to themselves and their everyday lives. To safety.

Safety. That was exactly how she felt with Alex: safe. At ease. It was a new feeling for her, with a man.

'You smile' – Alex glanced down at her and touched her nose – 'like an elf.'

It was one of his few pieces of whimsy, and one of the few times, she reflected, that he had ever remarked on her appearance at all. She rather liked that.

Later, he did tell her he found her beautiful. He had almost lost his nerve, before he even started to speak to her in the lift. 'And then I thought,' he said, 'that after we met that one time, you'd certainly not want to see me again.'

'Whyever not?'

'Because I knew you were way out of my league.' Alex gave a wry grin. 'I only seem to fall for beautiful women. Caroline was, too. Different from you. Darker.'

'I expect – most people seem beautiful, if you care about them.'

'Maybe. I don't know.' He turned to her suddenly. 'Would you be willing to think about – getting engaged?'

She stroked his hair. 'Isn't it a bit soon?'

'I mean it.' He leaned up above her and kissed her forehead, very gently. 'I love you, Kristin.'

'Are you sure you know me well enough to love me?' Kristin thought that she was teasing him. Perhaps.

'Fairly.' He stroked her cheek. 'So do you have an answer for me?'

'Can we stay as we are? For just a little while longer. I don't like to change things.'

Satisfied with that, he got up and made them both tea.

They went on seeing each other: mainly at weekends, except when Alex was away. Sometimes his business trips, to Frankfurt or Zurich or Milan, intruded on his Saturdays

218

and Sundays. Kristin knew, without his needing to tell her, that work ruled much of his life. She supposed the demands of his schedule gave her the breathing space she needed – the time to think about his proposal. The more she thought, the more it began to seem like a good idea.

She liked his family; she liked the feeling of security he gave her. He was cool, even-tempered except for his occasional diatribes against street buskers or hardline feminists or left-wing London councils; all of which Kristin could dismiss as mere political rant. An irrelevance. Basically, she wanted the same things from life that he did. He encouraged her in her work, but did not seem to expect her to be a driven career woman; if he ever had children, he had once mentioned in passing, he rather hoped that his wife would stay at home to bring them up.

She began to contemplate his flat. It had good light, good high ceilings; given time, she thought, and a little money, she could make it extremely comfortable.

At the end of November, Alex went away on an extended trip to the Far East; it meant he was gone for two weekends in a row, and she began to miss him. Still, she could always occupy herself. On weekend afternoons she liked to go out with her camera, often to museums, where she could catch people's expressions – their rapt or cynical or bored reactions to the works on display – hopefully without their noticing.

The second Sunday Alex was away, she went to the Tate. She meandered the first-floor corridors, looking for shots; she didn't really understand modern art, but she knew from experience that it made for good photographs. Today, unfortunately, there were few interesting-looking people to work into her pictures. So she started looking more carefully at the sculptures. Along one wall there was a special exhibition of some sort. She looked at the sign above. *Man & Machine*, it said, and in smaller print, *Recent Acquisitions*. There was a long, bent tube of something that looked like corrugated cardboard, or a giant pipe cleaner. Then a complex, half-molten construction: a heat-warped adding machine. The next one made her laugh: a computer monitor out of which a larger-than-life hand reached, through broken glass, to tap the keyboard. The machine was painted a flesh colour, the hand slate blue. *Intimations*, the tag behind it on the wall read, *Peter Conaway, 1986*.

She blinked and stepped back. Good God, Peter Conaway.

She looked again at the tag, just to be sure she was right. But the words had not changed. She had not imagined it. *In the Tate, of all places*. Had they really bought one of his works? It was hard to believe. If they had, then he had certainly hit the big time. But then, maybe he had. He had been in *Vogue* last year . . .

Stepping back again, she caught the eye of an attendant patrolling the corridor. She spoke quickly, before she could lose her nerve.

'Excuse me, I was wondering. That piece over there – the computer. Do you know when the museum acquired it?'

The guard grinned suddenly, unexpectedly, and answered in a West Indian accent. 'Funny you should ask that. I don't know, to tell you the truth. But the fellow who did it, he's here. Behind that screen.' He twitched his head. 'Why don't you go and ask him?'

'Well, thank you. I . . .' Kristin backed off.

'Nice bloke he is. Friendly. Not like some of them. He won't mind.'

Kristin felt the guard's encouraging gaze on her. She saw the screen he was pointing to, blocking a doorway, behind which, she supposed, some exhibit was being prepared.

Chances were, she told herself, Peter wouldn't be here. Or it would be someone else. A mix-up. It was just too unlikely . . .

She smiled at the guard. 'Thank you,' she said again, and walked slowly towards the screen.

17 'Good God, that's Kristin Ward. I know it is. No, hold on Kristin, don't go. What are you doing here?'

Kristin balanced on one heel. It was too late to flee now. Peter was moving quickly across the empty exhibition room, small, then growing larger, arms outstretched. Kristin answered in an unsteady voice. 'Funny. That's exactly what I thought. I saw the sculpture outside –'

'Sweet Jesus.' Suddenly he was taking her hand and kissing her – pine-scented, stubble-cheeked. 'Let me take a look at you. How many years has it been?'

For a second, they stood back, examining each other; Kristin took in only the fact that Peter's face seemed browner, his hair shorter than she remembered. Then he pulled her into his arms and hugged her, spinning, lifting her off her feet. She laughed and said, 'I never would have believed it. We have that man out there to thank. He must be your friend.'

'Aye, Terence. He's great. Brings me coffee here in the mornings. Sometimes cake from his mum –' Suddenly Peter let Kristin go, wheeling around with a sweep of his arm. 'So what do you think?'

'Of what?' Kristin laughed.

'My installation.'

She looked harder at the room around her and saw bare walls and a wooden floor. 'It's, um . . .'

'You see it, don't you?'

'Um . . .'

He burst into laughter. 'Here, that was me having you on. I haven't brought it in yet. I've been working on the floor, sanding it. Got to get the floor right.'

'So what are you installing?'

He glanced up and down her, digging his hands into his jeans pockets. 'Ach, the usual. Few bricks, bits of joinery, plumbing. An old sink or two.'

'You're having me on again.'

'I kid you not.'

'So your style hasn't changed.' Kristin allowed herself a wry smile. 'I came across your piece out there in the corridor.'

'You mean *Intimations*?' Peter looked excited again: bright-eyed. 'I'll tell you, Kris, that thing's made me a packet. You know somebody's made a poster of it and they tell me it's selling around the world.'

'Eye on the main chance as ever, I see.' Kristin spoke tartly.

'Aye, what else? So how long are you here for?'

'In London? I live here.'

'So you do. You always said you would, didn't you? I'm only here three, four more days. Staying with friends. Then I'm away up to Scotland and back to Kyoto.'

'Kyoto?'

'Aye. Are you hungry at all, Kristin? I'm starving. There's a café in this place –'

So somehow he was hooking his arm through hers; they sidled round the barrier and waved to Terence, who waved back. A few minutes later they were facing each other across a table, still talking. All the way to the café, they had not stopped: not for a second. The harsh, functional light overhead cast dark grooves at the corners of Peter's mouth; Kristin wondered if it did the same to hers, and found herself rubbing her cheeks to erase them.

She wanted to ask him a dozen things that seemed more important than what she was actually saying. She wanted to ask him why he had never shown up in Paris, though she guessed that she knew the answer. She wanted to ask him if he ever thought about Tasha. But she suspected that she knew the answer. Peter was the sort of person who lived in the present. What had happened at Elliott – he

223

could not have forgotten it, but at the same time, Kristin doubted that he thought back to it terribly often.

Peter was glancing pointedly at the slice of cake he had picked up for her when they got their coffees; he had already polished off two of his own.

'Have it,' she said, smiling, and shoved the plate over.

'No lunch,' he explained. For a few seconds – no more – his mouth was too full for talking.

'Same healthy eating habits as ever, I see.'

He nodded and wiped the chocolate off his mouth. 'Anything else wouldn't agree with me. It's in my blood. Hey, are you doing anything for dinner?'

She spluttered a laugh. 'You're thinking about dinner already?'

'By the time we get there I will be. So.' He sat back: watched her with knowing dark eyes. 'You didn't answer my question. Are you?'

'What?'

'Free. Tonight.'

'I suppose –'

'Good.' He whirled round the table and took her arm again, and a minute later they were outside the museum, walking along the embankment.

'Don't you have to go back to work?' Kristin said.

He shook his head. 'I'll go in early tomorrow. It's not every day I run into Kristin Ward.'

She felt the skin of her neck tingle. 'Nothing special, I assure you. A few hundred Londoners on the Tube seem to do it every morning.'

He smiled over at her and didn't answer.

The further they walked, the more certain Kristin grew that she ought to back out of dinner. Alex would probably phone tonight. Not that a ten-minute phone call would exactly fill her evening. But perhaps, since she was nearly engaged, she ought to tell Peter . . .

She couldn't seem to do it, though. Beside her, he let out a long, deep breath. 'You know, sometimes there are these

224

nights that remind me of Elliott. When there seem to be, like, thousands of stars up in the sky. You could always see so many at Elliott. Do you ever think about that place?'

She gave a brusque laugh. 'Not much.'

'I do. I think how lucky I was. How I had all this time. How I had both of you – you and Tasha –' He glanced at her, as if for permission to go on.

'And?' she said easily.

He laughed. 'I think I should have known at the time, I'd never be as lucky again. It's funny, I've had shows and things since then. I've started to make some money, which is what I wanted all along, right? But I've never been as happy.'

'Do you ever,' said Kristin carefully, 'hear from Tasha?'

'No-o.' He shook his head.

Kristin was not sure why, but she doubted his answer. She had not thought much, before, about the possibility that he and Tasha might have met, perhaps by accident, just as he and she just had, sometime in the last five years. But she wondered, now.

'Have you?' he said.

'What?'

'Seen Tasha.'

'Mm. I did. In Paris. I was in a bit of a mess. I'd quit my art course and I wanted to leave and come back here, but I couldn't seem to get my act together to do it. She helped me out.'

'She's a good girl. A good person.'

Kristin nodded.

'Hey, have you ever tried hitching a lift in London?'

'What?'

'Well, I've been looking for the past ten minutes for a bloody cab. Have we decided where we're going, anyway? I'm staying in Fulham. If it's okay with you, there's an Italian place . . . What do you say we run out in the street and stick out our thumbs?'

'Peter – 'Kristin shrank back, laughing; but already he

225

had sprung out to the edge of the pavement, and was walking serenely along, backwards, thumb in the air.

'Some mad person'll slow down for us. They always do.'

But just then, as if by a miracle, a cab appeared from round a corner and pulled up. Peter pulled Kristin by the hand into its large, black depths. He kept hold of her hand as the cab drove off, and she didn't object. Suddenly, he was talking with a manic earnestness about his project for the Tate: about Kyoto. 'You see,' he said, 'it's all about harmony. With nature. The thing is, Kris . . .'

What had come over him, she didn't know, but she felt herself being pulled along as if by some inexorable force. It had been this way, she remembered, at Elliott. As he spoke, he pounded the back of her hand against his knee; his thumb bumped back and forth across her fingertips. *Wait*, she wanted to say, *stop, I might want to get off*. As if this were a carnival ride that threatened to spin out of control.

And then she took a deep breath. *Why the hell not?* she thought. This might be the last time, ever, in her life. She knew that she was going to sleep with Peter that night. She would make it happen, if she had to. Before she married Alex. *One last time.*

The restaurant was in one of the less trendy bits of Fulham; its decor couldn't have changed in twenty years. There were wobbly tables with red-checked cloths and walls covered with posters of Pisa and Siena. Peter was talking, now, about the day he had first arrived in Japan: his first run-in with Tokyo's ever-changing addresses. As far as Kristin could make out, some Japanese school or foundation was paying him generously to live and work in Kyoto, which, besides its being a beautiful city, seemed good enough reason to be based there.

'So do you speak Japanese now?'

He shook his head no, then laughed and came out with a mouthful of syllables.

'You do.'

He laughed again, and spoke again.

'Don't you miss home?'

He shook his head; more words came out.

'Stop, Peter! Stop it. Stop.'

His fingers had crept across the space under the table, and now rested on her knee. 'I've got too many people,' he said slowly, 'after me.' He spoke with the slow, exaggerated pronunciation of a Scot on the verge of drunkenness.

'Like who?' she said.

'My wife?' He raised his eyebrows hopefully.

'Don't be silly. You don't have a wife.'

'No?' He blinked and smiled. 'Couldn't catch you there.'

'I might be about to have a husband.'

He blinked again, in genuine surprise. 'No. You're not. You're kidding.'

'Someone wants to marry me.'

'Well, I'm not surprised at that.'

'So I might.'

'Are you in love with him?' His index finger moved up the inside of her leg with surprisingly delicate precision, and then stopped. 'Christ. Stockings. I didn't know any girls wore them anymore.'

Kristin felt her face flush, deeply and instantly.

'Lucky bugger. Your fiancé, I mean. Who is he?'

'Oh – just someone I met when I was looking for work.'

Peter didn't seem terribly interested. His fingers had roved up the inside of her thigh, and latched round the satin crotch of her panties.

'Not here –'

But they were sitting near the wall, and the checked tablecloth draped down below their knees on the visible side of the table. 'How far could we go right here, do you think?' he murmured.

She glanced around. Only two other tables in the restaurant were occupied, both by customers who looked half asleep. 'Don't be silly.'

'Take off your panties.'

'I can't. Not here.'

'Then go away and come back.' He nodded impatiently in the direction of the ladies' room. 'Go on. Do it.' He gave a hint of a smile. 'You know you want to, Kristin.'

He was right, she knew. She felt weightless, magically tall as she walked away to the bathroom and did his bidding. Coming back, she felt the air rush up between her legs. It seemed to her impossible that the other, drowsy people in this restaurant could have no inkling what was going on. They could only be half-alive. She felt alive in every cell, every pore.

His fingers slid slowly up the inside of her leg again. 'You've had someone else,' he said, 'since Elliott. I can tell. Of course, you would.' He looked down, then up at her. 'How many? Were there lots of them?'

'No.' Her face warmed. 'Just one, really.'

He smiled slightly. 'And you're not over it, are you?'

'How do you know these things? It's really none of your business.'

'Does your husband know?'

'He's not my husband yet.'

'Something tells me he doesn't know much about you. Not what you're really like.'

Kristin felt too uncomfortable to answer. Peter only smiled. His fingers twitched and buried themselves, hard, slightly cold, inside her.

They took a cab back to the house where she lived. As if by mutual consent, they didn't speak, and didn't touch, and scarcely looked at each other during the journey there. Kristin wondered why she did not mind that Peter was going to see her dingy room, when Alex never had. Perhaps because, in an odd way, she had nothing to hide from him. He knew her.

The cab moved off, and silently she unlocked the front door of her building. Peter, leaning against the wall, slid a hand along the curve of her waist, underneath her coat.

'So who bought you that?' He nodded at the coat. 'The one in Paris? Or the one you're marrying.'

She tossed her head. The door fell open. 'The one I'm marrying.' She walked ahead of him up the stairs.

'So he's loaded. I should have known.'

'He's a banker.'

Peter laughed. 'I always knew you'd end up being kept by a rich man.'

'Very funny.' Kristin spoke tersely as she fiddled with the lock on her door, at the top of the stairs.

'Well, why shouldn't you? We're two of a kind, you know.' He had come up behind her, and she flattened her back against the still-closed door.

'I don't know any such thing. Sometimes I'm not sure I really know anything about you.'

'There was a rich woman once, wanted to keep me,' he said.

'Was there? When?' Their eyes met and locked.

'Back when I was still at school. I couldn't hack it.' He shook his head. 'I'm not much use at being kept.'

'I'm sure,' said Kristin sharply, 'you gave good value.' Then she spoke more quietly. 'Why didn't you ever tell me this before?'

He shrugged. 'You were young. Back at Elliott. Maybe I glossed things over.' Then he smiled and peeled back the lapels of her coat, which he dropped, like so much rubbish, on the hallway floor. She turned the knob and led him into her room, opening the curtains to let in the glow of the streetlamps. Then she started to peel off her clothes. He leaned back against the washbasin, watching her.

'So,' she said defiantly. 'Show me.'

'Show you what?'

'What you did for this rich woman of yours.' She half-expected him to laugh, but he only walked towards her silently, then pushed her down on to the bed.

'All right,' he said, and tugged his trousers away and threw off his sweater and shirt. In a few seconds he was as naked as she. 'You like that, don't you?' he said. 'Having me tell you what to do. But you're in control all the time, aren't you?'

'What?' She fell back, surprised.

'Like I'm here to service you.' His thumb traced the line of her neck.

'I don't think that.'

'Oh, no?' He grinned suddenly. 'What do you think, then?'

'I don't know.'

He studied her for a moment. 'No, maybe you don't.' His voice softened. 'Were you angry when I never turned up in Paris?'

She gave a quick, harsh laugh. 'I never expected you to.'

'You weren't in love with me then?'

'No,' she hissed. 'Why ever should I be?'

He shrugged. 'Because.' And she thought she saw his eyes glitter in the dark, before his body penetrated her own: hard, ruthless, rhythmical.

She turned her overheated face towards the window, and brushed back the crinkly hair that had stuck to her forehead. 'Why did you ask all that?' she said. 'About love.'

'What?' he laughed. He lay relaxed, now, with his head on her shoulder. 'What did I say?'

'You know.'

'Honest, I'm not sure, Kristin. I make it up as I go along.'

She laughed, bewildered.

'You don't mean to tell me you always tell the truth.'

'I feel somehow as if I ought to try.'

'So you're going to tell this fellow you're marrying that you've been screwing an old friend over the weekend?'

'Don't be silly. Of course I couldn't.'

'I rest my case.' Peter shifted, and ran a hand through her hair. 'So what's he like in bed?'

'Alex?' Kristin laughed. 'It seems rather . . . beside the

230

point somehow. There are things I couldn't say to him. About . . . me. He's very *proper*.'

Peter ran a hand down her bare stomach. 'So I guess that's his loss.'

She dozed off and woke with the light. Something was tugging at her: working, antlike, between her legs, and it took her a moment to recognise Peter's head, above her, and remember what had happened last night. Then, when she started to move, he pressed her legs down. 'No. Hold still, just another second. It's got to dry.'

'What?'

'You sleep like a baby.' He blew gently on her pubic hair.

'Not usually. Peter, what the hell are you doing?'

'Here.' He held her hand mirror up over the place where he had been at work, and she let out a gasp. And then an oath. Under the blonde curls, she saw a fine network of wavy black lines, like shadows. It was, she thought, a surprisingly beautiful artwork, and unlike anything Peter usually produced. Then her heart sank. 'Peter, that pen's indelible. I use it for marking prints.'

He shrugged. 'Sorry. I didn't want to wake you.'

'Peter Conaway, you are a complete . . .' No word seemed to suffice. She wanted to throw something at him. 'It'll take ages to wear off. What the hell do I tell Alex in the meantime?'

He backed off, grinning, an arm raised in self-defence. 'That all of a sudden you like to make love in the dark?'

'No.' She laughed. 'But he does, actually.'

'So you're all right, then. When's he come back?'

'The day after tomorrow.'

'Good. Two more nights for us.'

She was glad the same thought had run through both their minds. She smiled, and knew that if her eyes ever took on a wicked sheen, as Peter's did, they must be doing so now.

He kissed her lightly on the lips. 'Do me a favour. Don't wear any panties. Ruins the artwork.'

Later, when he had gone, she studied herself in the bathroom mirror and noticed that, very small, along the inside line of her thigh, he had left his signature. The two Greek 'e's glistened slightly. She breathed out another swearword – why was it, she wondered, that her language seemed to go straight into the sewer when Peter was around? – and then tugged her dress straight and put on her coat to go to work. Only eight hours, she thought, and then she would see him again. For some reason she felt happier than she had since coming to London: since before Paris, in fact. And she didn't want to ask herself why.

That night as she was on her way into her room, he grabbed her, outside in the corridor. For just a moment, she was afraid. Not, she realised later, because she had thought she was a stranger – but because, for a fleeting second, she wondered if he might be Alex.

Peter's hand worked a path up under her short skirt. 'Good. You didn't,' he said.

'It was bloody cold today for these sorts of games.'

'You're wet already. Did you miss me?' He grinned.

'Conceited git. Well, yes. I did.' She turned and unlocked her door. 'Most of the day, actually. Perhaps more to do with my rubbishy job than anything else.' She threw off her coat and began to undo the zip that ran down the front of her short black dress.

Peter looked bemused. 'Not so fast. What about dinner?'

'Later.' Kristin gave him a possessive look, up and down. 'First things first.'

'You're lucky I'm easily led. Another fellow might feel used.'

'If you do,' Kristin said, her eyes measuring him, 'then you must like it.' They were on top of her bed a few minutes later, entangled, when the phone rang. Peter tried to stop her reaching for it, but she twisted past him.

'No machine,' she murmured. Then she shook her head and blurted a 'Hallo?' into the receiver.

'Kristin. Tried you last night.'

Alex's crisp tones drew her instantly to attention. 'When? Late?'

'No. Sevenish. Were you out with that chap Adrian or something?'

Alex could be absurdly jealous of Adrian. 'Just doing a bit of window shopping. My tube got held up. You know, I found one of those table lamps we were looking for . . .'

She knew that talk of her latest project – redecorating his flat – would divert him. And it did. So well, in fact, that she found herself nodding into the phone for several long minutes while Alex described his meetings and his flight delays. 'But I should be home Wednesday,' he said.

'Oh? Good.' Kristin watched Peter lean back against her pillows, smiling, hands locked behind his head. The hair in his armpits was long and dense and dark.

'So I thought on Wednesday night, if you could manage to meet me at Gatwick . . .'

'What?' The words caught Kristin by surprise.

'Darling, we've discussed this. Don't you remember? We'll pick up my car, and then we can go out somewhere in the country. Molyneux said that there was quite a good place near Brighton . . .'

'Oh, that. Yes.'

'Well, I thought it would make a change.' Alex sounded peevish.

'Yes. It sounds lovely.'

'Well, then.' Alex made a kissy noise into the phone. Kristin felt her face reddening, and couldn't bring herself to return the sound.

Putting down the phone, she crawled back up the bed, but Peter made no move to meet her.

'I think,' he said, 'it's time for dinner.' He swung his feet down and started reaching for his clothes.

'Are you angry?'

He gave a slight smile. 'No. Just a wee bit put off.'

'Alex doesn't know. It doesn't matter –'

'Kristin, that's your business. I'll keep my nose out of it, okay?'

'But if you do care. If you really do mind . . .'

He shrugged, almost insistently, and shook his head. 'I could fair go a bag of chips just now. I guess you wouldn't let them in here.'

'I'd be smelling them for weeks.'

'So would someone else.'

'No. He doesn't come here.'

Peter raised his eyebrows at that; and then they compromised, and went to an Indian place down the road, where Kristin started to pay for the meal, which seemed to amuse Peter. 'I'm not skint anymore,' he said.

'But still –'

He shoved her money back at her. 'Couple of posters of *Intimations*'ll cover this. Trust me.' And then, finally, back in her room, they made up for the phone's interruption. When Peter drowsed off against her pillows, afterwards, Kristin snuggled against him. *Damn*. They had only one more night till Wednesday.

Reluctantly she stirred him from sleep the next morning. She was supposed to be at work by nine.

'Will I see you here tonight?' she said, watching him sleepily run his fingers through his hair, in front of her mirror. She liked the sight of him here, in her room. In fact, she had toyed, in the hour or so it had taken her to get to sleep, with the idea of telling him how much she liked having him back: that she didn't want him to go. That she would solve the problem of Alex, somehow. She wondered if she could get a few days off to join Peter on his trip up to Scotland – if he should invite her. Perhaps, though, he was going to see his family. If they lived in a council house in that depressed-sounding town on the Clyde, perhaps they wouldn't exactly welcome her with open arms. Oh, well. And where was he off to next? Japan . . .

All the same, she found herself humming on the Underground on her way to work, and walking home faster that night than she ever normally did, carrying a bag full of cheese and bread and wine that she had picked up during her lunch hour. This time, Peter wasn't waiting for her in the corridor, but then she was a bit early.

She was sifting through the morning's post, shoved under her door by the landlady, when she realised that one of the letters was unstamped, with her first name written on it in an all-too-familiar hand.

She bit her lip and tore it open.

> *Dear Kristin*
> *By the time you get this Ill be up north. I decided to fly tonight. I couldn't tell you this morning but I thought I ought to go before it was too late. Its none of my business really mixing myself up in your plans – especially as youll have guessed by now I'm not much of a one for marriage. I can tell you are though – and so I'll just wish you the best of luck for the future – and I do mean that.*
>
> > *P.*

She told herself that every word was true. That it didn't matter. She would forget all about him and get on with her life and remember these few days – if she were forced to remember them at all – as an interlude. For a moment, she even felt a pang of conscience towards Alex. But then she remembered that he expected her to get herself out to Gatwick tomorrow evening, which was surely enough of a nuisance. She had lost track, already, of the number of times she had gone out of her way to meet him, or do errands for him: enough, perhaps, to excuse her a small deception.

But it's a big deception, she thought suddenly; and then

quashed the thought. *Never mind.* Alex would never know, or have any cause to reproach her. Because from now on, she was going to be good. No, more than that. She would be perfect.

In the restaurant where he took her, as planned, outside Brighton, Alex asked Kristin to marry him. He opened up a box which contained an engagement ring complete with a large, pear-shaped diamond. It fitted her perfectly. He had, he told her with some pride, measured one of her rings from the bedside table while she was sleeping.

'Oh, Alex.' She felt genuinely touched.

'It is yes, then?'

'Oh, yes.' Their eyes met, and Kristin's felt misty with unaccustomed tears. She remembered her promise to herself. *Good,* she reminded herself. *Perfect.*

That night, uncharacteristically, Alex wanted to keep the lights on when they made love; but she insisted with some force that they turn them off.

18 The snow was piled high in white, sodden banks, and from all around came the sound of shovels scraping.

'Tash?' A thin blonde girl with a flushed face tugged at Tasha's sleeve. 'Can I quit? I feel really horrible. I would have gone to the infirmary except I had a History 42 paper.'

Some things, Tasha reflected, never changed. 'Right, Albrey. Okay.' She doubted Albrey Tenier had anything worse than a hangover – but she could remember many a time she had fled snow-shovelling duty, pleading some hideous malady. If only she could do so now. That was the trouble with being a teacher.

When she had told Lorenzo, last summer, about her new job, he had been astounded. 'The Academy? You're going back? You're crazy.'

'Renzo, man, I've been kicking my heels since Easter. The job offers aren't exactly thick on the ground.'

'You need your head examined.'

'I'll have lots of free time to paint there.'

That, Tasha thought now, had turned out not to be so true. 'Her' girls, the inhabitants of Bennett House, came to her at all hours with their problems: parents, boyfriends, lack of money. She had all three of those herself. If Maurice and Rona had not exactly kicked her out of their apartment, they had seemed to be getting pretty fed up with her indefinite presence there. Now, thanks to the Academy, she had a free roof over her head, but, on their tiny salary, she was perpetually broke. And as for boyfriends . . . *Ha!* She could only give a grim laugh at the thought. Leaving out students – as she supposed she ought

237

to – and the predominantly married, aged faculty, where on earth was she supposed to find them?

There was, perhaps, Peter. Though he wrote only every few months, and always more about art and life in general than anything particular, personal, that might smack of commitment – at least he did write. He had spent a few months in Britain preparing an installation at the Tate, and Tasha knew that was big-time. He might be in New York next summer: he said he would see her then.

She tried not to think too much about it – not to count on it. But she couldn't help it. She did occasionally meet a man who seemed a plausible sort of prospect. Her friend Natalie, one of the English teachers here, had introduced her to a friend of hers who was doing a PhD at Harvard. He had seemed sort of cute – though Tasha tended to grow impatient with the academic type. She liked *real* men, who took on life, who did things: who wrestled with what they were good at. Like art. Like Peter.

Though she would certainly not admit to him, if she did see him next summer, how often she thought about him. It was better that he shouldn't know – that they should both be free.

Which left her, exactly . . . where?

Preferring not to think about that, Tasha gave the banked snow one more desultory scrape, then stood up and looked around. Amazingly, the path from Hy El to Commons was clear. She gave a brief blast on her school-provided whistle. The few diligent shovellers ahead of her raised their heads. 'Hey!' she shouted. 'I think we've done it! Time to go home.' She swung her own shovel over her shoulder and took off down the path towards Bennett.

Back home, she was just stepping out of her snow-caked jeans when the phone rang.

'Tasha? Is that you?' The voice on the other end sounded bright and energetic. 'I hope I didn't wake you. We're in Boston.'

'Kristin! My God. "We"? Who's "we"?'

238

'Alex and I! We were thinking of driving up your way. Are you free for dinner tonight?'

'Well, I . . . sure. The snow's pretty heavy.'

'Oh, we'll make it.'

A few seconds later, Kristin rang off, still sounding as chirpy as before. Something, Tasha guessed, had gone awfully right in her life. Maybe this Alex person. She had mentioned him a few months ago on the phone, but Tasha had no idea he and Kristin had reached the travelling-together stage.

As she put *Abbey Road* on her record player and sank into a bath – cleaning up her chaotic flat, she decided, could wait – Tasha's spirits rose several notches. Kristin! It had been almost a year. So who was this Alex? she wondered again. Was he English? Would he be stinking rich? Tasha wasn't sure why, but she suspected so. Not that it mattered. For Kristin's sake, she just hoped that he was single, and halfway normal.

Alex hit his head climbing the stairs to Tasha's flat. It was not an auspicious beginning. As he rubbed, gingerly, among his thinning hair, Kristin hung on his arm looking solicitous.

'I'm sure you'll be fine, darling,' she said at last, and ran up, opening her arms to hug Tasha.

'The car,' said Alex now, 'is parked outside in the street. I hope it'll be all right there.'

'Oh, sure.' Tasha was jolly. 'If you get snowbound, we'll dig you out.' She led Kristin through to the living room and took her jacket. 'Gee, is this fur?'

Kristin smiled, abashed, then looked over, starry-eyed, at Alex. 'Just the lining. Alex bought it for me.'

'Kristin feels the cold so.' He moved closer and laid a protective hand on Kristin's arm. 'Tasha, by the way, I noticed there's a sort of hotel up the road. Do you think they'd be able to take us? We'd been counting on driving back tonight, but now it's starting to snow again –'

'You mean the Elliott Inn?' said Tasha. 'You don't need to do that. It costs a fortune. You can spend the night here. I've got a futon.'

Alex looked uncertain. Kristin glanced back and forth. 'Gosh,' she said, 'that's awfully kind, Tasha . . .'

'It's no problem,' said Tasha breezily, moving past him into the kitchen. 'What do you guys want to drink now? Tea? Coffee? Vino?' She heard a murmuring in the other room. When she poked her head out for orders, Alex seemed to look up suddenly.

'Actually, Tasha,' he began, 'it's frightfully nice of you to offer to put us up, but . . .'

'No problem!' Tasha gave an expansive shrug. 'And I've made us dinner already. So it's settled, right? You'll stay.'

The bean casserole, unfortunately, had cooked too long and came out mushy, and Alex was not fond of salad.

'This is delicious,' said Kristin politely, taking over the remains on Alex's plate. 'It was so nice of you to cook for us, when I gave you no warning –'

'Would you mind awfully,' broke in Alex, to Tasha, 'if I made another call?'

'What exactly does he do?' whispered Tasha when he had left the room.

'Don't bother whispering,' said Kristin briskly, 'he can't hear us. He's with a merchant bank, Chappell Chase Matthews, in London. They do mergers and things. Privatisations.'

'Oh,' said Tasha, nonplussed.

'We haven't had the chance to tell you.' Kristin gave a sudden, confiding smile. 'We're getting married in March.'

'*What?*'

Tasha had several minutes, while Kristin filled in the details, to recover her composure before Alex came back into the room.

'I've told Tasha our news.' Kristin beamed up at him.

'Ah, yes.' Alex adjusted the lapels of his dark jacket, which, despite Tasha's repeated urging and the heat of the flat, he had persistently declined to shed. He wore a white shirt beneath it, and a red silk tie, discreetly patterned, which was the only dash of colour the two visitors shared between them. Kristin was wearing a long soft black sweater of the kind Tasha instinctively knew was cashmere, together with pearls, grey flannel slacks and slim black loafers. Her hair was trimmed to shoulder length, airy and swinging; her careful makeup played off the pink tones of her skin, and her manicured hands showed off a large diamond. She looked well, Tasha had to admit. And expensively kitted out, Tasha suspected with Alex's money. Kristin had admitted that they were already living together. And then, here she was, along on what appeared to be one of his business trips; they had flown to New York and stayed for five nights at the Helmsley Palace. Now Kristin and Alex were talking in turn about the wedding . . .

'It's on an island called St Fortt's, maybe you've heard of it?' said Alex. 'There are no direct flights, I'm afraid, but there's a local one from Aruba. Or the boat from Nevis.'

'We do hope you'll come,' said Kristin.

'Yes, of course,' said Alex, more mutedly.

'Well, I don't know,' said Tasha, dumbfounded. 'I'm not sure I have the money . . .' In fact, she was sure she didn't. What did Kristin want with getting married on some island, anyway?

'Oh, well,' said Kristin. 'We do hope you'll come. But if you can't make it, you'll have to visit us in London. Won't she, Alex?'

'Mmf,' was all Alex said.

'Just out of curiosity,' said Tasha, 'why are you guys getting married in the Caribbean? I mean, don't your parents want the wedding near home?'

Kristin gave a sparkling laugh. 'Oh, they could never agree about the church. Alex's father's a Presbyterian, but

241

his mother's C. of E. Actually St Fortt's was Alex's idea. Lots of his friends have had Caribbean weddings.'

'Are *your* parents going to come?' said Tasha, looking at Kristin.

She looked uncomfortable. 'My mother might. We have pictures of the hotel on St Fortt's, don't we, Alex?'

To change the subject, Tasha offered her guests tea. She brought it out in mismatched mugs and removed the bags, one by one, with a spoon.

'So how *do* you like teaching?' said Kristin, and Tasha wondered, even as she launched into an answer, whether she hadn't detected a note of artifice in her friend's interest.

The next morning, she woke up and found Alex fully dressed, locking up his briefcase. 'Just thought,' he said, flashing keys, 'I'd check the car.'

'What does he think is going to have happened to it overnight on the Old Bennett Road?' said Tasha, shuffling towards the kitchen after Alex had gone.

'Oh, he's just that way.'

'Kind of uptight, isn't he?' Tasha said, returning after putting the kettle on the hob to boil. She felt like a wreck – her usual morning state – and yet here was Kristin, all made up and ready to go. She was wearing another cashmere sweater, and brown suede trousers and boots. 'Those'll get ruined,' said Tasha, nodding down at them, 'in the snow.'

'Oh, if we go anywhere, Alex will drive me.' Kristin smiled. 'I do hope you'll get to know him a little better.'

'That seems kind of hard to do. He doesn't say much.'

Kristin's eyes flashed. 'Not everyone is a chatterbox in the first half-hour you spend with them.'

'Sorry.' Tasha wondered what she had said wrong. She could hear the kettle starting to hiss in the kitchen. 'Just, are you sure you're doing the right thing, getting married? We're still pretty young. And it seems so sudden.'

Kristin rolled her eyes. 'For heaven's sake! I'm twenty-four.'

'Well, I wouldn't get married until I'm at least thirty. If I ever do.' From the kitchen there came a fizzling, spluttering sound. Tasha ran out to rescue the kettle. 'Couldn't you just live together for a while,' she shouted, 'to be sure?'

'But I *am* sure!' A minute later, Kristin accepted the mug of coffee Tasha handed her. 'Oh. Thanks. I should tell you, Alex prefers tea in the morning.'

'No problem.'

'You sound annoyed. Are you annoyed, Tash?'

'No, no.' Tasha shook her head distractedly. Alex sure was taking a long time over that car.

'He's one of the nicest people I know,' Kristin said in a quiet voice. 'Really. I know he may seem a bit stuffy to you, but –'

'No. No, he doesn't. Not at all.'

Kristin looked up warily. 'I do want you two to like each other.'

Tasha sipped her coffee, took a deep breath, and gave her broadest smile. 'I'm sure we will. And – I'm sorry I stuck my oar in about the wedding. Really, I'm happy for you. Congratulations.'

Alex and Kristin bought Tasha a thank-you present while they were out that morning in Lawrencetown: a Royal Worcester tea set, in fluted white bone china with gold trim.

'Hey, that's great.' Tasha's eyes widened as she opened the boxes. This must have cost a fortune. And what on earth was she going to do with it?

'We thought you should have a proper pot for your tea,' said Kristin.

'Oh. Yeah, right.' Tasha grinned.

Kristin flushed slightly. 'We wanted to say thank you.

We've had a lovely time, haven't we, darling?' She looked up at Alex.

'Are you guys going already?' said Tasha. 'Did you get a chance to look around the school? See all the old haunts? Commons, the art block . . .'

'No, not really,' said Kristin. 'Maybe another time. But we need to get back to New York tonight.'

A few minutes later, Kristin and Alex's rented sedan moved off down the Old Bennett Road. Tasha waved until they were out of sight. Back indoors, she studied the gold-trimmed teapot and cups, before wrapping them up again. She didn't know why, but she felt vaguely insulted by their presence.

Alex turned on to Lawrencetown Main Street, scanning the road for signs to Boston. 'What on earth was that stuff she gave us to eat for dinner?'

Kristin glanced to the right and left, also looking for signs. It was queer, she thought, how unfamiliar the Elliott campus had become after six years away. 'I think,' she said distractedly, 'it was some sort of cassoulet. She probably made it for me, since I don't like meat.'

'Hmf,' said Alex. In the two months they had lived together, he had still not come to accept that particular difference between them.

Still, thought Kristin, sighing, that was only a small discrepancy. They agreed about almost everything else. Though she had had some misgivings about introducing Alex to Tasha. And vice versa. Her only other old friends, Poppy and Adrian, had reacted to him almost exactly as Tasha had. *Why?* she wondered.

'I don't suppose she'll come to St Fortt's,' said Alex now.

'No,' agreed Kristin regretfully.

'Well, I don't exactly see her fitting in.'

'I don't know about that. I imagine some of your banker friends might rather take to her.'

Alex maintained a silent dissent as he drove on. Kristin

244

had learnt to distinguish this from his silent agreement: he held his head more stiffly, and did not look her way.

'How did you two ever get to be such pals?' he said eventually. 'I can't see that you have much in common.'

'Oh –' Kristin let out a slow breath. 'You know. We go back a long way.' She left it at that.

'Kristin's getting married,' Tasha told Lorenzo. They walked underneath the shadow of Hy El and across the great lawn, recently turned to mud by the spring thaws. 'Well,' Tasha corrected herself, 'I guess she's already married, by now. The wedding was in March, out on some island in the Caribbean.'

Lorenzo kicked at the mud and watched a clod fly towards the tower. 'So who's the lucky dude?'

'He's called Alex Renfrew. He's, like, this rich banker. Totally uptight and conservative.'

'Come on, you've just got a chip on your shoulder when it comes to people who make money.'

'I do not!' Tasha dug an angry toe into the mud. 'Anyway, he must be at least ten years older than us. If not more. I just wouldn't put it past Kristin to marry for money.'

'Did you tell her your little theory about her motives?'

'Of course not. She would have been insulted. And it was hard enough to talk, anyway. They were only here overnight.'

They walked on silently for a while; then Lorenzo turned his head to scan Tasha's face. His eyes, so reptilian and acute, had, she reflected, a way of seeing right through her, sometimes.

'You're just bummed,' he said, 'because you didn't get to go to the wedding.'

'It's not just that. I wouldn't have known anyone. They'd all be English. It'd be too weird a scene.' Tasha chewed her lip. 'It's like – Kristin's moved into this whole

245

different world from me. Kind of a stuffy world, full of rich people.'

'So?'

'So – I don't know. We're going to lose touch.'

'Are you jealous of her?'

'Of course not.' Tasha spoke instantly, instinctively. Why was everyone in her generation so hung up on money? Lorenzo was no exception. He had whirled up to Bennett House this morning in a black two-seater car whose make, she suspected, would have meant something to her had she known anything at all about cars; ditto for his fuchsia-coloured silk tie and drainpipe-trousered suit. Whatever Lorenzo was earning at the Metropolitan Opera, his wardrobe wasn't suffering. Just for once, Tasha realised, she wished she could appear as something other than what she was – an impoverished teacher. She still dressed like a student, in beat-up jeans and sweaters, and cut her own hair in front of the mirror. Her secondhand Ford got her around Lawrencetown, and down to New York occasionally, which was all that she needed it for. Screw status symbols, though. They didn't matter, did they?

'This place getting you down?' said Lorenzo.

A chill wind blew across the great lawn. Tasha shrugged. 'You know, I'm still thinking about getting a show together off-Broadway. Working up a few ideas.'

'Really?' Tasha couldn't help taking a vicarious interest.

'Like I'm into this one at the moment, about Freud. I mean, there've been plays about him before, but what I'm really interested in is his patients. The women especially. I wonder how *they* saw him. Did they look up to him? Were they brainwashed? Were their problems real in the first place?'

'Nah. Vienna was just a totally oppressive society. Plus, for Jews, it stank. Karl Lueger and all that.'

'You've read up on this?'

'A little.' Tasha shrugged.

'So, what I was thinking is, we need to make this thing, like, totally minimalist, or else go for it and give it the whole nineteenth-century look.'

'Hey, that's what I'd do if I were you. You could do some amazing things with those dark rooms and the big heavy furniture. Use the right lighting and you could make them change. Turn them into dreamscapes.' Tasha was warming up, walking faster and waving her hands.

'Hey, do you think so, too? I just don't know who . . . Hey, Tasha.' Lorenzo had stopped walking, and went suddenly silent. 'I never thought of it before. But, you! You're the answer. Obviously. You're the one. I've seen your paintings. *You* could do the sets.'

Tasha only laughed.

'Tash, I mean it. If you're interested . . .'

She looked back at him and grinned. 'Sure, I'm interested. I have to tell you I don't know a thing about set design. And the last time I ever built anything was when I was thirteen, in woodwork class.'

'Well, you've got a while to learn. I'll have to get my finance together. Want to shake on it?' Lorenzo beamed.

Tasha held out a hand; then he slung an arm over her shoulder, and they ambled back towards Bennett House.

'Hey, what are we doing for dinner?' said Lorenzo. 'You got any food in?'

'My fridge is as empty as my love life.'

'You're kidding. I can hardly believe that's the Tasha I know talking.'

'Well, it's true. You should try living out here where the only straight men are married or under eighteen.'

'I wouldn't have guessed that'd stop you.'

'Well, I've got this one rule about not going for married men. Not that anyone here tempts me.'

'And the under-eighteens?'

Tasha rolled her eyes. 'Don't ask.' She thought for a second of Basil deAngelis, from her painting class. *Basil the angel*, she thought. Black curly hair, long lean body, green eyes . . .

Lorenzo looked at her evenly. 'You're tempted.' They were back at the front door of Bennett House now. 'So,' he said, 'why not?'

Lorenzo's reaction, Tasha reflected, was strangely similar to Peter's. *I seem to remember*, he had written in his last letter, *when it came to students & teachers, in the old days, no one batted an eye. Wouldn't you like to be on the other side of it? Why not?*

She remembered reading that, and wishing, with a momentary pang, that he *minded*: that he might be just a little jealous. Though of course their relationship didn't work that way. Now, since she had no intention of confiding all about Peter to Lorenzo, she decided to put him out of her mind. She wondered if Lorenzo really meant that, about the off-Broadway show.

As if he had read her mind, Lorenzo grabbed her arm and pulled her up the stairs of Bennett House. 'Come on. I've got an idea. You're going to dress up in your wildest clothes and I'm going to call the Elliott Inn for a reservation.'

'The Elliott Inn?' Tasha spluttered. She couldn't in a million years imagine Lorenzo in those staid surroundings. 'Why?'

'There's got to be a first time for everything.' He shrugged. 'And I think we should celebrate. Our show, that we're going to do together.'

'Sure,' said Tasha, sarcastic.

'Come on,' he said. 'You've got to believe. There's going to be a show. Maybe not immediately, but it's going to happen. So the question is, are you in with me or not, Tash?'

'Well, yeah. I am,' said Tasha, with renewed conviction. Then she ran into her bedroom to look for Grandma Natasha's black lace flapper dress. And the string of jet beads. Off-Broadway. She was there.

Spring break started a week after Lorenzo's visit. Despite her parents' regular phone calls, wheedling for a visit, Tasha stayed in Lawrencetown, putting the finishing touches to four small new paintings: all of them interiors, rooms looking outdoors at different stages of the day. The rooms were all parts of Bennett House; empty, the place seemed eerily quiet. Tasha found herself beginning to miss the girls – even wheedling, whining Albrey Tenier. When the first few of her charges trickled in on the Sunday night before term, she felt like welcoming them with open arms. She served them all pancakes and maple syrup in her flat, and when the pancakes ran out she started popping corn. Somehow word that there was a party on trickled out, as it always did. A few of her painting students dropped by, too, and Basil deAngelis turned up just before curfew.

She grinned, startled, at this sudden apparition. Such green eyes, she thought. He really did look like an angel. And he was a good painter, too. Wouldn't take it seriously, of course; he refused to be serious about anything.

'Hi, Tasha,' he said. 'Hope you don't mind me crashing in. I've heard all about your parties.'

'Really?' As she moved through to the kitchen to make more coffee, it occurred to her that she might offer him the leftovers of her wine. After all, there wasn't enough for everybody. She pulled a bottle out of a cupboard. 'This is nothing great, but . . .' She raised her eyebrows in question.

'I'll try it. My tastebuds are dead these days.'

'How was LA?' Tasha threw back her hair, feeling suddenly hot.

Basil rolled his eyes. 'Oppressive.'

'Hey. That's a big word for a Californian.'

'You East Coasters are such know-it-alls.' Basil glugged back his glass of wine and smiled. 'Any more where that came from?'

'Just about.' Tasha poured again. 'So why was it oppressive?'

'Oh, you know. The 'rents.'

'What do your parents do?'

'Produce movies.' He shrugged. 'I got some heavy-duty lectures about college. You know how I want to take a year off to travel first? They're not into that.'

'You've still got a while to convince them. Where are you thinking of travelling?'

Basil was about to answer when Albrey barged in.

'Tash? Can we borrow your downstairs keys? Thanks.'

'Popular party,' observed Basil.

'It'll thin out.'

'Yeah.' He shrugged. 'Too bad. In ten minutes it's curfew.'

'So do you ever manage to get out of your house *after* curfew?' Tasha's heart was pounding. She knew she would be drummed out of the school in seconds flat if any member of faculty had heard her say that. Luckily, all the students around were her friends.

Basil smiled down and seemed to flush, just a little. For a moment, Tasha realised just how young he was: how, just possibly, inexperienced, despite the blasé Beverly Hills attitudes. 'If you've got a way out,' she said, 'why don't you come back when the coast is clear? In the old days we used to use the fire escapes.'

What am I doing? she thought. *This guy is seventeen. Here I am telling him to break the rules* . . . Maybe she had gone too long without a man. She was getting a little crazy.

Basil reached forward, touched her shoulder: swung his hips forward and into hers. She could feel his erection: see his knowing smile. *He's no innocent*, she registered, as, outside, she heard the dying clamour of girls' voices. 'Hey,' she protested, 'Bas. Later . . .'

He shook his head and wedged a foot against the kitchen door. His kiss was aggressive, rough – perhaps, thought Tasha, she had forgotten the techniques of teenagers – but the gentle pressure of his thumbs at the nape of her neck was assured and assuring. She relaxed against him. She imagined him naked: long, lean, slim-hipped as a faun.

Someone pounded at the door. 'Shoot,' he said, as he pulled away, and smiled. 'Can't anyone leave us alone?'

'They're going to have to learn,' said Tasha happily. This might not last, she thought – in fact she knew it wouldn't – but she was sure as heck going to enjoy it.

19 In the summer of 1989, Kristin and Alex Renfrew found the perfect country house. It was late-Georgian, built of sun-mellowed bricks, set sideways against the main road through the Wiltshire village of Tewne Abbot. A high brick wall surrounded its front garden, which housed a neglected orchard, and the interior – a large parlour, a dining room, a study, four bedrooms and innumerable cubbyholes – gave off a smell of mildew and dust.

Kristin wanted it.

They talked it over long and late in bed, the Sunday night after they had driven back to Tewne Abbot to meet the estate agent for a proper viewing.

'We've hardly considered other places. We weren't thinking of buying a country house for a few years yet,' said Alex.

'But we might never see one like this again.'

'It's right on the road.'

'It's not a very *busy* road.'

'It's not got much land.'

'But don't you see, that's the best thing for us? We'll only be there at weekends. This way there's less to maintain.'

Alex sat up and turned on his bedside lamp, and reached for a notepad and a pen. Kristin, watching him, did not venture to speak. He was scribbling. 'It's really too far from London,' he said.

'But we like Wiltshire.'

'Hmm.'

Kristin watched him, still scribbling. 'What are you doing?'

'They're asking a fortune. Considering the place has been empty for a year. I'm trying to figure out what it'd cost us.'

'Oh, Alex . . .' Kristin beamed over at him. She thought the smile would overflow from her face.

'I suppose,' he said drily, 'I'm not taking full advantage of the mortgage rates the bank offers us. Still, we might be stretched. Or rather, I would.'

Kristin overlooked his allusion to the fact that since she gave up her job to get ready for the wedding, she hadn't taken up another. He hadn't exactly encouraged her to. Not working, she was free to do all the things his job kept him too busy for: picking up his shirts and suits at the cleaner's, keeping the flat in order, providing food, entertaining . . . 'Of course,' she said gently, 'house prices are rocketing up so. The way they're going, I don't suppose we could *afford* this place next year, or the year after.' She let out a quiet sigh.

'I know.' He laid down his pen and reached for her hand. 'We'd have to cut back, you know. Not so many meals out, fewer new clothes . . .'

'Oh, Alex. I'd be careful, I promise.' Kristin took a deep breath. Was it necessary, she wondered, to say more?

Then she saw him nod, once, twice, and knew from the resigned way he laid back his head that she had won.

The surveyor's report was equivocal. 'They ought,' said Alex, 'to knock twenty thousand off the asking price, given the work we'll have to do.'

The sellers knocked off eight thousand. Alex grumbled and acceded. As soon as the contracts were exchanged, Kristin started phoning builders. By October, she was up to her neck in estimates.

'We'll go up next weekend,' she said, lifting her glass of champagne to meet Alex's. She had laid out a celebratory feast of tiny hors d'oeuvres on the kitchen table in South Kensington.

'Where'd you get all this?' Alex glanced down at the food, and over at the half-bottle of champagne.

'Fortnum's.'

'Darling.' He sighed. 'This is exactly the kind of thing we're going to have to –'

'Oh, Alex. Just this once.' Kristin speared an artichoke heart. 'Anyway, I thought if I stayed down in Tewne Abbot next week . . .'

'Next week? I don't remember agreeing anything about your staying down there without me. And I'm at work.'

'Well, we're hardly going to get builders in at weekends, are we? I'll have to spend some time on my own down there. Just till things are finished.'

Alex frowned, and Kristin knew what he was thinking. He was weighing his options, visibly, as he often did: imagining the house decorated and complete, soon enough to invite his friends from Glenalmond, Cambridge and Chappell's – perhaps by next summer. He was foreseeing his parents' admiration – his brother's envy. Calculating the inevitable, rapid rise in the house's value; his net worth in a few years' time.

'Well,' he said, 'all right.' And, after a moment's further silence, 'What's for dinner?'

Kristin gestured at the spread in front of them. 'I thought this.'

'Hm. I didn't have much lunch, you know.'

'More champagne?' Kristin knew that it should be possible to distract him. She poured and smiled, and reached out to take his hand, tossing her head so her hair fell loose and thick around her shoulders.

And he responded. Slowly but surely. 'That's a pretty dress you're wearing.'

'Oh, do you think so?' Kristin stood and turned, to show it off. 'I picked it up at Nicole Farhi's the other day.'

She could see him bite off the question on the tip of his tongue – *how much?* – as his lips worked into a smile. 'Very

254

nice indeed,' he said again, and stood, and slowly, with heavy steps and hands reaching out, approached her.

The antique four-poster bed faced Kristin from the back of a shop full of bric-à-brac in Devizes, and she knew, even though she had never thought before of owning such a piece of furniture, that she had to have it.

It was made of dark wood – oak, she supposed – with heavy panelled sides and posts like Corinthian columns. These ended abruptly: they would once, she suspected, have supported a canopy.

'What a splendid bed,' she said to the owner of the antique shop. 'What period is it?'

'Ooh, now that'd be hard to say. Bit of Jacobean, bit of Georgian maybe. It's been sitting there so long I almost think of it as part of the place.'

'It is for sale, though?'

'Ooh, I suppose.'

Kristin went home, mulling over the figure the man had quoted her, which seemed impossibly high. Alex, of course, would be able to bargain it down; he was good at that sort of thing.

Her initial week at Tewne Abbot had lengthened into two, then three; Alex came down from London at the weekends. 'After all,' as Kristin put it, 'it'll be getting cold soon, and I shan't want to be staying out here then, with the heating in its present state. Better to get as much as we can done now.'

The roofers had come, then the dry rot men, the plumbers and the joiners. One set of works led into another, and though they had initially planned no major changes to the house, Alex and Kristin found themselves reconsidering. So long as things were already in upheaval, wouldn't it be just as well to add an extra bathroom, and perhaps widen one of the spare bedrooms to make a nursery?

Kristin never felt lonely, by herself at the house, even in

the evenings. She found each room endlessly fascinating; instead of reading or watching television she would wander from the kitchen to the parlour to the dining room, and then upstairs, observing each day's changes. She could easily see how a house could become an obsession. As Littledene, she supposed, had become for her father. She wanted every detail right, every piece of furniture at home here and appropriate.

As the works progressed, she began to take pictures. She wanted a record of the house as it was now, unfinished, so that she and Alex could look back proudly when it was done. When he came out at weekends, they scoured antiques shops and fairs and auctions: it would not be right, they agreed, to fill such a house with reproductions. Which was why, in the end, Alex came round about the four-poster bed. He raised the predictable objections: the canopy was gone, the mattress sagging.

'We'll get new ones.' Kristin hung on his arm in the little antiques shop, gazing at the object of her desire. 'Think of us in it. So cosy. We'll draw the curtains at night.'

'And have the children climb in to wake us up in the mornings.' Alex smiled and put his arm around her waist. 'All right. I'll go and ask the man how much.'

The bed came, in pieces, into the master bedroom before the rest of the house was even completed: for that, in the end, took more than a year. With the heating still not working, Kristin and Alex were unable to spend Christmas at Tewne Abbot as they had planned; they went up to Scotland instead. Kristin showed Alex's mother her pictures.

'I'll tell you,' said Margaret Renfrew, 'who should see this house of yours. Diana MacLeish – no! Silly me. Diana *Barbour*. She's had so many husbands I can't keep track. But she's an old, old friend of mine. She edits *Décor* magazine.'

Kristin smiled, taking the remark as the compliment it

was meant to be, and forgot all about it until, six months later, the same Diana Barbour rang her in London. It took a moment for Kristin to register the name.

'Oh! Yes,' she said, after a moment's pause.

'Margaret's told me all about this lovely house you two are doing up. I think young people are so brave to take an old place on. So much else you must have to do.'

'Oh –' Kristin had been about to say 'not really', but changed tack. 'We enjoy it.'

'Sometimes they just cry out for attention, don't they? I was wondering, Kristin, if I might come out? Just for a look round.'

'Oh, of course,' said Kristin, absurdly pleased. She dug out her diary from the bottom of a pile of sketches, and they fixed a date for later in the week.

The older woman's voice did not prepare Kristin for her appearance. She had expected someone flat-soled and tweedy, which Diana Barbour was not at all. She was in Chanel, or a good imitation, and somehow got away with wearing her hair long, though it was the colour of mother-of-pearl. She took in each room in a series of quick glances.

'Do you mean you planned all this yourself? You must have had a decorator. No? Perhaps you're a designer yourself?'

'Not exactly,' said Kristin.

'A hall of mirrors!' Diana burbled as she burst into the corridor which opened out on to the garden. Kristin, reading that the Georgians had favoured brilliant colours, had had it painted canary yellow and filled both facing walls with antique mirrors. 'We shall have to have a picture of *this*,' said Diana. 'It's only too bad we don't have any of *before*.'

'But I do, actually.'

'Oh, then you must show me.'

When Diana sat down to lunch, Kristin fetched out her photographs of the work in progress on the house.

'But these are quite good,' said Diana. 'You really could be a professional.'

'Well, I am, sort of,' said Kristin, abashed.

The soup-and-salad lunch she had prepared spun out into coffee and biscuits; Kristin was surprised to find that once she had adjusted to the older woman's unmatronly glamour, she quite liked her. She hardly ever saw her Aunt Poppy these days, and didn't have any other women friends in London. Most of Alex's friends' wives, and the women of Tewne Abbot, either worked full-time or were busy with babies.

'I almost wonder,' said Diana Barbour, over her third cup of coffee, 'whether you mightn't like to do a bit of work for us at the magazine? Freelance, of course. I know you're busy.'

Kristin felt a pleased flush rise to her face. 'Do you really think I'm good enough?'

'Well, evidently you have a feel for our sort of picture. I'd like to use some of yours for the piece on this house, if you don't mind. And – you know, I can think of just the project for you to start off with . . . . Could you possibly come in and see us next week?'

Taken aback, Kristin heard her voice rise hopefully. 'Next week?' Then she remembered. She was giving a party on Friday: a large and formal one, for a dozen of Alex's bank colleagues and their wives. Not being a natural chef, she had gone on a cookery course last year; she and Alex both firmly preferred *real* food to hiring caterers, but the only way she could do a party successfully, she found, was by giving several days over to preparations. 'Could we possibly make it the week after?' she said; and then remembered another thing. Next Monday she was supposed to be here in the country, for the bricklayer who was patching the garden wall; then the man from English Heritage was visiting, since the house was a listed building . . . 'Actually, that week's not much good either. I don't know how I seem to get so busy,' she said helplessly.

258

'Oh, well, never mind, dear,' Diana said. 'I'll tell you what. Ring me when you *are* free, and we can set something up.' She paused to light a cigarette, offering the pack to Kristin.

'Oh, no, thanks,' said Kristin quickly. 'I've stopped.'

'Must be recent, dear. You looked awfully tempted.' Diana smiled knowingly.

'Well . . . health reasons, I suppose. All these warnings about . . . if you're having a baby.'

'Are you!' Diana's eyebrows lifted.

'Well, not yet.' Kristin smiled bashfully. 'But soon, I hope.'

'You'll have your hands full.'

Too full, Kristin reflected in passing, to take up freelance photography. Though for a moment the idea had tempted her.

'Anyway,' the older woman smiled reassuringly, 'I imagine the art director will like the idea of using your photos in this piece. We'll keep in touch.'

Kristin wondered, after Diana went, whether the decision to try for a baby was as definite as she had made it sound. She and Alex had never discussed it, exactly; though before their wedding they had decided on two names: Iain George for a boy and Catriona Margaret for a girl. Kristin didn't mind that the names were Scottish, and reflected Alex's parents': she had no particular wish to honour her mother, and 'Leslie', it seemed to her, could belong only to her father.

Still, they had never taken the subject further, and time was, after all, getting on. She was twenty-six now. So, on the Saturday night following Diana Barbour's visit, under the newly built canopy and ivory silk curtains of the great bed, Kristin raised the subject of babies.

'I've been thinking,' she said, 'of going off the Pill.'

Alex blinked. 'Are you sure that's wise?'

'Well, we've always talked about children.'

'I suppose so.'

'You don't sound very enthusiastic.' Kristin bit her lip and glanced over; this conversation was not going exactly as she had expected it to. Alex was looking reflective, his head propped back against a stack of pillows. 'It isn't,' she went on lightly, 'as if we'd be presented with a baby all at once. It would take at least nine months!'

'But . . . isn't there plenty of time?' He raised his head.

'Well, yes, of course. But if we have two or three, I don't want to wear myself out having them too close together!' Kristin gave a high laugh.

'*Three?*' Alex looked alarmed.

'You know me, I'm an only child. I hate to think of my family dwindling to nothing.' For a second the image of her father's grave at Littledene flashed into Kristin's mind. How he would have liked to have grandchildren . . .

'Darling.' Alex squeezed her hand now. 'If you want three, or, heaven knows, even *four* children, I shall do my best to support them. Just give me a bit of time to get used to the idea. I do rather like just us, you know. It's strange, but – I think sometimes that I shouldn't mind if we never had children.'

'Oh, don't say that. We will. I know we will.'

'Then, if you like, darling, shall we take it one step at a time?' Alex leaned up on one elbow, unbuttoning the top of her white nightdress.

Relaxing as best she could beneath him, Kristin thought to herself that it was too bad, really, that she had taken a pill this very morning; tonight's endeavours would be to no purpose.

However, in a mood of celebration, she threw the remainder of the month's packet into the wastepaper basket the next morning.

She rang up Tasha to tell her the good news.

'You *what*?' said Tasha.

'That's hardly the delighted reaction I'd expected.'

'But what do you want a baby for? I mean *now*. What's the hurry? There's lots of time for all that – the crying and throwing up and getting woken up in the middle of the night, and your stomach going all flabby . . .'

Kristin laughed. 'Honestly! I don't think it has to be like that.'

'Oh, no? When people have babies, they age about ten years. They turn into baby bores. I'm telling you, if I ever have one, I'm going to wait until I'm at least forty.'

'By the time you're forty the risk of birth defects is ten times higher than it is now,' said Kristin in a superior tone.

'That's exactly what I mean.'

'Mean by what?'

Tasha sighed. 'Never mind. Let's agree to differ.'

'Tasha, this is really important to me.'

'Right. So how's Alex?'

'Fine.' Kristin answered warily. 'And . . .' She realised that she had no idea of the name of the latest man in Tasha's life – if there was a latest. She remembered something about a student called Basil, but he must have graduated and gone by now.

'Ryan? Oh, he quit his job in Boston two months ago. Flew back to Australia. Never mind. It wasn't serious.'

'Oh.' Kristin had a hard time telling whether Tasha meant what she said, when she sounded so dismissive.

'Anyway, I'm getting itchy feet, too. Itching to get out of here.'

That, thought Kristin, was nothing new. Tasha had been talking that way for the last two years: this was her third of teaching at the Academy.

'Yep, but I'll probably have to stick it out another term. Seeing as how I've got nothing else lined up.'

'Mm.' Kristin didn't like to sympathise too much. To her, Tasha's sounded like an insecure, shiftless existence; but presumably she had chosen it. Give her half a chance and she would start to wax lyrical about the bohemian, artistic life: shades of her Grandma Natasha.

261

'Oh, I don't think I told you. Grandma Natasha died about a month ago. She had a stroke.'

Kristin fumbled for a response. Every now and then, something like this would happen to her and Tasha on the telephone. One of them would mention something just as the other was thinking of it. 'Gosh, I'm sorry.'

'That's okay, she was ninety-three. It was a good way to go. She even left us all a little money.'

'Oh?'

'So I'm thinking of using it to go travelling. Maybe to Japan.'

'Japan?' Kristin heard the edge in her voice. She could not, she must not betray what she was thinking now. Good Lord, she had no idea whether Peter was still there: chances were, he had moved on.

'Yeah, I'd really love to hit the Far East. But I won't get the money for a while. We'll have to see. Hey, you know what I said about babies . . .'

'Mm?'

'Sorry if I sounded, like, totally negative. Hey, you guys are probably ready for it. Good luck, okay? Pregnancy must be a pretty cool experience. You'll have to tell me what it feels like.'

Kristin laughed. 'Like carrying a rugby ball around for nine months, I've always imagined. But I've no idea.'

When, a minute or two later, they signed off, Kristin hesitated for a moment over a stack of bills, then, deciding she hadn't the heart for them just now, decided she would call a cab to the station and surprise Alex in London. This might just be the right time of the month.

Tasha put the phone down and walked to the window. She felt exceptionally restless. Decisions, she thought: resolutions. It was time for making plans.

If she didn't hear from Peter by the time the money came through, she would just go. She wouldn't write him again – twice was enough, without getting an answer

262

back. Any more would seem like pestering. Anyway, she wanted to see the Far East. It didn't matter whether he was there or not. The Academy had just started up a Japanese course; she could sit in on it, and learn a little of the language, so she could manage on her own.

After that, she felt better. She had made up her mind.

Two weeks later, she got a phone call which turned everything upside down again.

'Tasha?'

She heard the old, familiar cackle at the other end of the line. 'Are you asleep or what? Don't you know me? It's Renzo.'

'Lorenzo!' It must have been a year since she had heard from him.

'I'm calling to tell you, we've got some serious dealing to do. I've just got some of the money for my show – it's going to be called *The Interpretation of Dreams*.'

'The Freud show?' said Tasha.

'Yeah, I'm producing it and writing the script. So can you come to New York? Like, tomorrow? Are you doing anything? School's not started yet, right?'

Tasha took a deep breath. Things were happening all at once.

'Tash? You there?'

'Yeah.'

'So why not? Come down!'

Two weeks later, Tasha had handed in her resignation to the Academy, and taken on a new job with Lorenzo de Maas's fledgling production, to start in October. She was going to be the set and costume designer for the new play, as well as what Lorenzo loosely termed a 'creative director'. That meant she would contribute her own ideas to the script and the final production.

'Teamwork.' Lorenzo had grinned at her, handing over the pen to sign the contract. 'That's my middle name.'

Having made one leap of faith, Tasha took another. She invested the whole of her inheritance from Grandma

263

Natasha – six thousand dollars – in the production. She knew her parents would never let her hear the end of her folly. So she didn't tell them.

She tried to forget about Japan. When doubts nagged at her, she reminded herself that she was doing just what Peter would: seizing an opportunity.

At the beginning of September, she packed up her Ford Mustang and moved, temporarily, down to Lorenzo's loft in the East Village. She forgot about forwarding her mail. When, two months later, a big envelope of stray correspondence, sent along by the Academy, finally reached her, she was startled to find an envelope inside it marked 'Express Mail' and covered with British stamps.

She tore it open. There was only a postcard inside.

15/9/90

Tash,
    Sorry lost touch so long. Im in Boston believe it or not for 2 days next week. Cant wait to see you. Are you still at same #? If not, will try Academy switchboard. SEE YOU SOON.

P.

Tasha stared for a moment, desolate, at the date. There was no mistaking it. The fifteenth of last month. He had come and gone. And there was no return address on the card. No explanation of where he was going next – nothing. *Damn.*

A few more select swearwords crossed her mind; then she forced herself to shrug, and smile. There would be other chances. She would see Peter again. You couldn't have absolutely everything.

20 Kristin stared down at the tray of neat, triangular smoked salmon sandwiches, and for a moment could not possibly remember what she was supposed to be doing with them: why they were here in front of her; why *she* was here.

'Christ,' she said, and felt tears warble up in her voice and start to sting her eyes. *Why?* She couldn't let her guests see her like this. She fled to the cloakroom off the kitchen.

Well, that explained everything. Sort of. Her period had started. Not that that was much of a comfort. It was only her third period in a little over a year since quitting the Pill, which surely wasn't quite right; but her GP had brushed aside her apprehensions when she had consulted him. 'Post-Pill amenorrhoea,' he told her. 'Quite common. Sorts itself out in a year or so.' *A year?* Kristin had almost echoed, aghast, but knew that sounded absurdly impatient. So she had resolved to wait, and to keep busy. The works at Tewne Abbot, hard as it was to believe, were nearly finished now.

'Everything all right, dear?' A welcome, familiar voice drifted into the kitchen. Kristin gave her eyes a quick wipe.

'Diana.' She turned. 'Is everyone all right out there? I've been a frightfully long time. Sort of lost track of what I was doing. Are the drinks holding up?'

Diana gave her a quick update. Kristin was eternally amazed by her friend's ability to take in the doings of the thirty other people around her at a drinks party while apparently playing full part in a conversation.

A silence fell and Kristin realised Diana had stopped talking.

'Kristin. Are you sure you're all right?'

'Oh, yes. Well, more or less. I've got the curse, I never feel exactly at my best when . . .' To Kristin's discomfiture, the tears had started to rise again.

'Kristin. Darling.' Diana gathered her in till Kristin's head rested on her shoulder. 'It's no fun, is it? I've always thought it's a terrible way to put things: *trying* for a baby. That makes it sound so stressful. I know, darling. You've given it a little while now, haven't you?' She stroked Kristin's back for a moment. 'Perhaps you might feel better if you spoke to a doctor? At least it might reassure you.'

'I've been to my GP, but he says it's nothing.'

'I don't mean your GP, my dear. I mean a specialist.'

'I've thought of that, but Alex won't . . . I mean, he thinks we should wait longer. He doesn't want – to be dragged in for tests.'

'Well, he wouldn't have to be! Not if you went privately. These specialists understand. Look, I know a man in town – you could go for a consultation on your own.'

'Maybe I should.' Kristin had felt, and sounded, so hopeful at that that Diana was able to detach herself and scribble a Harley Street address on a bit of notepaper, which she folded small and deposited in Kristin's hand.

'I'll bet,' said Diana, 'within a year from now – at *most* – you'll be standing here with a great big bump, and wondering what you were ever so worried about.'

'Do you think so?' Kristin sniffed.

'I'll take over those canapés, and you go mend your face, and we'll see you out there in a minute or two. All right?'

Thank God, thought Kristin, that someone understood. Alex didn't seem to, and Tasha certainly didn't. And beyond them, there was really no one else in the world in whom Kristin confided. Thank God for Diana.

The specialist was called Jenkyns, and his consultation, in sharp contrast to the GP's quick in-and-out, took about an hour. He talked in great detail about ovulation and hormones; he examined her and took a sample of blood for

266

tests and told her to stop worrying. 'By the next time you come to me,' he said, 'you might already be pregnant. It's hardly unknown.'

So Kristin wandered back to the flat, via Harrod's, feeling happier, and phoned Diana to thank her. That night she laid out a feast from her local health food shop on a plate in front of her, reminding herself that Mr Jenkyns had said she was to eat more: even to gain weight if she could. Then, feeling restless, she dialled Tasha's new number.

'Hey,' said Tasha, 'I've been meaning to call you. Things are great here. The show's really taking off. We've got a rehearsal space.'

'That's great,' said Kristin. 'I've been busy too. Actually, I've, um . . .'

'We're starting auditions next week. Renzo's negotiating with the theatre people. I'm hardly ever at home, but that's okay because this apartment is a total pit and it's freezing. My parents about died when they saw it, it's in Tribeca and there're bums out on the street, but it's all right really. Some of them are pretty funny guys. You know who Lorenzo's auditioning for the lead?' Tasha rattled off a list of names.

Kristin, who hadn't heard of a single one of them, said, 'Really? That's great.'

'You sound pretty mellow. So what's up with you?'

'Oh, nothing much.' Suddenly eating wheat germ and trying to ovulate seemed, indeed, like nothing much. Kristin knew that, given half a chance, Tasha would rabbit on about her show; Kristin was glad, truly glad, that Tasha had so much to talk about.

Yet somehow she didn't connect. A few minutes later, Tasha announced that she had a call on her other line, and Kristin made that her excuse to sign off. She would tell Tasha, she decided, when she was actually pregnant. Tasha was obviously not counting the months or noticing how long it was taking.

*

Just before Christmas, Mr Jenkyns got the results of Kristin's blood tests back. She bordered on anaemic, he said, and then began a long speech about hormones which she only partially understood.

'You're probably not ovulating. It's quite treatable. Now, normally, I would ask you and your husband . . . .'

'I'd really rather he wasn't involved.'

'Well, if you're certain that's the best way, we could probably manage your treatment without bringing him in on the consultation. But are you quite sure, Mrs Renfrew?'

Kristin thought of Alex: of his repeated refusal even to discuss her worries; his disapproval of the idea of fertility treatment, even when she mentioned it in passing. He seemed to think people should accept what nature gave them, in the way of children. Which might be fair enough, but . . . . 'Yes,' Kristin said now. 'I am quite sure.'

For Christmas, Alex's parents and brothers came to Tewne Abbot. On 6 January, Kristin went into London for a second consultation with Mr Jenkyns, which if all went well would mean the start of her course of hormones.

'Keeping me company?' Alex looked over, bemused, at her beside him in the car. 'Or have you got a busy day planned at the January sales?'

'Oh, no.' Kristin's gaze wandered. 'I just fancied being in town. Are you . . . going to be around? You haven't got any trips coming up, have you?'

'Ever since that New Zealand thing fell through, no. More's the pity.' Alex looked grim. 'I heard a rumour from Molyneux. Didn't want to mention it at Christmas. Apparently they're going to be letting some directors go.'

'Oh, no.'

'You know, it's all well and good how the media go on about the unemployed. The miners and all that. At least they've got their unions to look after them, and their council houses. The rest of us, at the enterprise end of the economy – when the recession bites, it hits us first.'

'Mm-hm,' said Kristin, half-listening.

'At least we got bonuses this year. Can't be sure about next.'

'Mm.'

When Alex dropped her off at the flat, Kristin went first to Mr Jenkyns, and then, in a celebratory mood, to Harvey Nichols. When Alex asked her sharply that night how much she had spent on her new cashmere coat, she lied. He was still fretting about work, and seemed too distracted to be interested in making love. Kristin didn't mind. The pills were designed to coincide with her cycle, so next week was the time to concentrate on, not this.

Unfortunately, when the first of the key evenings came, Alex was out to dinner and didn't get home till three a.m. Then he had an overnight trip to Edinburgh, and on the last of what Kristin thought of as the 'possible' nights, he was late home again. Curled up on the sofa to wait for him, Kristin blinked as the light came on a little after midnight.

'Darling, I hope you weren't waiting up for me.' Alex sounded impatient.

'I must just have fallen asleep here. Would you like a drink? I bought some of that red wine you like.'

'You must be joking. I've got to be back in the office at eight.' Switching the light off again, Alex shuffled through to the bedroom, brushed his teeth and fell into bed.

Kristin shed her clothes quietly and slid under the sheets beside him. She touched his cheek gently. 'Alex? Darling?'

He was fast asleep. Two weeks later, her period came.

She tried not to feel frustrated that just as her body had been jolted into action – producing eggs, having periods – Alex seemed to lose all interest in sex. Occasionally, on a Saturday night in the big canopied bed at Tewne Abbot, they made love. The rest of the week, he was either working late or coming home early – at seven or eight – and depressed. The buzz of elation, expenditure, and frequently lust, that had once accompanied late-working nights and the closure of a deal, never seemed to accompany him home now.

'It's all work,' he told her bitterly one evening, 'and precious little reward.'

'But they promoted you last year. You told me yourself that you're their most productive director.'

'Well, damn it, I'd like to know what I've got to show for it. I was better off five years ago. We're up to our necks in debt. I watch the traders driving off in their flash cars and spending Christmas in Majorca . . .'

'But we've got Tewne Abbot. And they don't have anything like that.' Kristin looked earnestly at Alex, across the dinner table.

'Well, what's the use, really? I wonder sometimes. You know, when I went to use the cash machine the other day, our account came up in debit. I must have been miscalculating somewhere, or else . . .'

'Oh, dear.' All at once Kristin remembered the price of her cashmere coat, and Mr Jenkyns's last bill. She had written cheques for both of them that Alex had never seen. 'I'm afraid I may have, um . . .'

But Alex didn't seem to expect an explanation from her. 'It's that house. Those sodding builders, bleeding us dry. We *would* buy just before the market sank. You know, if we had to sell now, we wouldn't even get our money back.'

'But we're not selling.'

Alex looked bleak. 'If something doesn't give, we may be forced to.'

'Oh, darling, don't say that.'

'I get a bit fed up, sometimes, feeling pinched for cash. It doesn't look good at work, worrying about whether I can pay my round or afford to hop in a cab. I could use a couple of new suits and some shoes. And in two years we haven't had any kind of proper holiday.'

'I thought we agreed we didn't mind about going abroad.'

'I might like to have the choice.' For a moment, Alex looked at her almost coldly. As if, she thought, he were appraising her and finding her wanting. His expression made her uneasy. She imagined, for a second or two, that it might change, and that Alex might explain, by way of apology, *It's not that I mind for my sake. But for yours . . .*

He didn't.

In the end, she didn't know exactly when their baby was conceived. In an uncharacteristic burst of energy, Alex took her to bed both before and after a business trip to Munich. Neither encounter coincided exactly with the day her home urine test told her she was ovulating, but the expected, dreaded period two weeks later did not come.

Superstitiously afraid of disappointment, she waited another full week before trying a pregnancy test. She watched the windows in the plastic wand fill up: one thin blue line, then another. 'Oh, my goodness,' were the words that came out when she spoke aloud for the first time, then she giggled. She could hear Mrs Digby, their daily woman at Tewne Abbot, hoovering in the next room; Kristin wanted to run through and tell her. But she held back.

Instead, she made an appointment for the next day with Mr Jenkyns, who confirmed what she had found.

'Darling?' She hovered around Alex that night as he took off his coat and jacket. 'I've been waiting to tell you all day, I simply can't wait anymore. I'm pregnant!'

He turned from the hall closet. 'Really? How clever of you. Is it definite?'

She nodded.

'Funny. I'd almost forgotten we were trying.'

'Forgotten?' Kristin couldn't believe it.

'What with everything at work . . .'

'Don't you want to know when it's due?'

'Of course, darling.'

His interest sounded almost more polite than genuine, Kristin thought. Then she scolded herself. Of course he cared. 'Christmas Day! Exactly. On the twenty-fifth. Though of course they're hardly ever born on their due dates.' She paused. She supposed this was the time – now that Alex was in a good mood – to bring up the fact that she had been seeing an expensive consultant. 'Darling, I've been seeing a new doctor lately.'

'Oh. Do you like him better than Halloway?' Alex was changing into his pyjamas and bathrobe.

'I . . . thought I might try a second opinion. Just to see if everything really was working, inside me.'

'So it seems it was.' Alex gave her a brief smile.

'Well, yes.' Kristin moved nervously towards the dressing-table. She had meant to tell Alex the truth, now, about the tests and hormones. But she couldn't see exactly how.

'So.' On his way to the bathroom, he planted a kiss on the back of her head, with a jocular smile. 'It looks as though by next Christmas we're going to need a nanny. Unless you plan on doing it all yourself.'

That Friday night, as they sat down to dinner at Tewne Abbot, he started to talk about school fees.

Kristin almost laughed. 'Isn't this a bit early?'

'Darling, five years goes quickly. It's unfortunate, now I think about it, that we sank so much into this house in '89. The money would have done better on the stock market, and we'd have had a bit of cash in hand.'

'Well, as it is, our child will have this house to grow up in. And there's always the village school.'

'If one can trust the state sector these days.'

'Well, I'm sure we'll be better able to decide when the time comes.'

'When the time comes, darling, it will be too late,' said Alex shortly, and swallowed the last of his red wine.

'I realise now,' he said later, in bed, 'that we hadn't thought through all the expenses. If we had, it might have seemed wiser to wait another couple of years.'

Kristin lay still beside him, the bedclothes drawn up to

her chin. She felt defensive of the microscopic being inside her: it seemed to be coming under attack. 'How do you mean, "wiser"? I *want* this baby. I thought you did, too.'

'Well, there's nothing we can do about it now.'

'What are you implying?' Kristin's voice shook.

'Nothing. Just that we'll have to start saving. We may be a bit stretched.'

For a time they both lay in bed, silent; then Kristin curled up on her side, sheltering her baby, away from him.

Over the next few weeks, Alex seemed to grow used to the idea of her pregnancy. After consulting with Mr Jenkyns, Kristin decided to install herself in the country for the first few months. Why expose the baby to London pollution at this crucial stage? She kept off caffeine and cigarettes, too, and of course alcohol was out of the question.

'Jeez, you're taking this awfully seriously,' Tasha said when she told her. 'I'm sure lots of women breathe in tons of pollution, and still their babies get born.'

But Kristin stuck to her resolutions. Though she had no real morning sickness, she found she had gone off the idea of cooking, so she and Alex postponed any more dinner parties. On the weekends, they kept to themselves now, and stuck to their usual recreations: gardening, going to antiques sales, walking the lanes around Tewne Abbot. Near the end of Kristin's third month of pregnancy, they drove to an auction at a country house two villages away.

'Oh, look,' said Kristin, as they walked past a line of clocks in a hallway. 'That grandfather clock there. I've always wanted one just like it. I wonder what they'll be expecting to get.'

'Well, in any case,' said Alex, 'we're not bidding.' He sounded tense. Kristin wondered whether work was on his mind again. Or money. He had insisted before they came out today that they couldn't even think of buying anything.

273

Still, she thought, he might be brought round. 'It might go for only a few hundred,' she said hopefully.

Alex snorted. 'What? A few hundred short of a thousand?'

'We could at least see.' Kristin moved closer to the clock; it had a window below the number XII, filled by a revolving panel that just now showed a smiling, descending sun. Leaving Alex behind for a moment, she went to enquire the price from a man at the back; she knew him from other auctions, and recognised a few other people along the way. When she came back, she found Alex chatting with a neighbour from Tewne Abbot. 'This is fun,' she said, when the neighbour had gone. 'I'm glad we came. Do you know, George Andrews thinks they'll only get about six hundred for the clock?'

'Hm,' said Alex.

'Well, we could manage that. Couldn't we?'

Alex ignored the question and started to walk back down the corridor.

'Alex. For heaven's sake, at least answer me.' Kristin had to keep her voice down, since she knew half the people here. 'It's not so awfully much.'

Alex walked out into the yard, which had filled up with cars. 'That's not the point.'

'Well, what is? We've always wanted a clock like that.'

'Correction. *You've* always wanted one.'

'Oh, well, that's very good. How convenient for you that whenever you don't want to be responsible for spending money, you blame it on me! What about all those suits of yours, and the shoes, and the cab fares in London? And the car.'

'Chappell's pays for the car, you know that perfectly well. And what about *your* cabs, from the station to Tewne Abbot? If you'd only learn to drive . . . .'

'*You* have the car all week in London! How am I supposed to?'

'That's beside the point.' Alex lowered his voice as a couple from the village passed by them.

'You're getting to be completely neurotic about money! Just because of the baby.'

'Well, if *you* were the one who had to go out and earn it . . .'

'Fine! If that's what it's all about, then –'

Alex glanced around at the people milling around them. 'Not here, Kristin.'

'Why not here? You'll hardly talk to me at home.'

'I'm not in the mood for this. I'm leaving.' Alex reached in his pocket for keys and half-turned.

'Go, then! Fine. I'm staying to see what that clock sells for.'

Abruptly he turned and walked away through the rows of cars. Kristin stayed rooted to the spot, staring after him. He would turn, and look back, and wait: she knew he would.

But he didn't. A minute later, she heard the low rumble of Alex's BMW revving up. *Fine*, she thought. *Fine*. Then she saw its maroon, shiny body lurch and move out of sight.

For a minute or two, she stood in the drive, considering her situation. She couldn't believe Alex had actually gone. They had argued before, but he had never just walked away like that. Most of the crowd had gone into the house now; the bidding would start soon. She could go back in, too, and phone for a cab when she felt like leaving, or cadge a lift from a neighbour. Yet somehow she didn't like the thought. Wouldn't people wonder where Alex was?

She found, besides, that she no longer much cared what happened at the auction – even to her prize clock. What mattered was making Alex repent.

Oblivious of the darkening sky overhead, she started to walk.

She had only a vague idea of the distance to Tewne Abbot – six, seven miles perhaps? – but she knew the way.

She could cross a few fields to cut it short. Walking might burn off her anger.

Halfway home, it started to rain. Her feet were sore by now, and she thought about ducking into a pub and ringing for a cab; but that would be like admitting defeat, so she kept on going. Occasionally she stumbled. She felt empty and a little queasy and her hair was wet by now.

By the time she came to the road through Tewne Abbot, her hair and clothes were soaked through. Her teeth were chattering. *Only a few more steps.* She noticed as she unlocked the door to the garden wall that all the house's windows were dark: wasn't Alex home? She walked round the back, to the garage.

Alex's car wasn't there.

Well, maybe he had gone out again to look for her. He wouldn't be able to find her; he'd be frantic. *Serve him right.* Upstairs, she turned up the heat and tore off her clothes and climbed into bed. For some reason she was letting out dry, heaving sobs. *Serve him right.* She thought of her baby, forgotten for three or four hours now, and stroked her stomach as if to comfort it. *I'll take better care of you now,* she thought, *I promise. I won't forget you again.* Her belly still felt flat, but by next week, Mr Jenkyns had told her, she would be able to feel a small lump above the pubic bone. Then it would just steadily grow. She fell asleep stroking its imaginary roundness.

When a light came on in the room, she jolted upright and felt a low, cramplike pain in her belly.

'Kristin?' He glanced around as if the light blinded him. 'God almighty, where have you –'

'Alex?' Kristin clutched at her stomach and doubled forward. 'I don't feel well. I'm not sure what's happening. I . . . No, it's gone now.' She breathed.

But it came again, only a few minutes later.

In the middle of that morning, the doctors at the local hospital told her she was miscarrying.

'What? Can't you stop it?' she said, incredulous. The cramps were regular and quite painful. And now the doctors seemed to be giving her – or rather Alex – instructions, as if it were all quite routine. '*No,*' she said. 'You don't understand. I had trouble getting pregnant, I had to have treatment, you should talk to my specialist . . .'

But they only reassured her again, and now Alex was leading her out, down the corridor, the blood that trickled out of her slowly soaking the pad between her legs.

'There'll be another,' he said, almost gently, 'sometime. I – shouldn't have left you like that. I feel as if somehow it's my fault.'

'Don't be silly.' She spoke slowly, feeling dizzy. 'It's not.'

'What did you mean, just there? What you said to the doctors.'

'Never mind. Nothing,' said Kristin abruptly. But she knew Alex would not believe her.

21 In May 1992, *The Interpretation of Dreams* opened off-Broadway. Lorenzo, as ever, had secured good publicity. He almost *was* good publicity, having already made *New York* magazine for his work at the Met followed up by his successes at an arts theatre in Greenwich Village. 'The wunderkind of Broadway', the cover story had titled him, not entirely accurately, since he had never yet worked on Broadway; but he wasn't complaining. Tasha knew she was lucky to be working for him – *with* him, she sometimes had to remind herself. When, within days of the rave review in the *New York Times*, the first month's tickets had sold out at the little theatre on West 43rd Street, she felt not only lucky but positively blessed. So many more plays failed than succeeded.

'Couldn't have done it without you, Tash,' Lorenzo told her magnanimously. They were sitting in an upstairs corner of his loft, drinking Kir and watching a group of cast members cavort down below, in the living room. 'All you've got to think about is, what next?'

'Yeah.' Tasha grinned sheepishly. That was exactly the question on her own mind.

'More stage design? It looks to me like you're pretty well cut out for it. Or, what the heck, you could go back to painting for a while. You'll have the money to, from your share of this shindig.'

'I could maybe travel.'

Lorenzo gave her a look of mild incomprehension. 'Yeah, you could, but if I were you I'd strike while the iron is hot. Publicity-wise.'

'Yeah, I guess you're right,' said Tasha, feeling foolish. How, exactly, was she supposed to go about that?

'Anyway, I want to take this babe to Broadway. To a bigger stage. We'll need to rejig the sets. So you'll stick with us for that long, won't you?'

'Sure.' Tasha wondered for a moment how she could point out that this 'us' Lorenzo talked about had included her from the very beginning: that she had studied his original script, rewritten lines for him, rewritten other lines for the writers Lorenzo had eventually called in to do the job when he got bored with what he called 'typewriter work'. She had vetted his decisions on casting, she had hired and fired, and she owned a share of the show, a fact of which he had not needed to remind her: though the realisation that it might actually earn her real money was a new one.

For most of a year, this show had been her life, and it had surprised her how she needed no other. She spent all day painting flats and supervising the building of the three-dimensional, moving parts of the set; after a rushed dinner she would talk scripts and lines with Lorenzo into the small hours of the morning. Any free time they had, they spent seeing other shows. These days, she saw more of Lorenzo than she did of her parents or brothers. If he had a lover, or lovers, she didn't know how he found time for them, because she certainly had none. A long-distance relationship was all she could possibly manage. She had written to Peter in Scotland after his postcard found her, and was ecstatic when he wrote her back within a week. He was back in Glasgow now, but spending time also in some village called Crail, out to the east; he felt, he said, like the prodigal son returned home. Though, as ever, he wasn't sure how long he'd stay. *Will you visit?* he wrote. *I dont know when Ill be in NY again – to tell the truth Im shagged out with travelling . . .*

Tasha had hinted to Lorenzo, when he started needling her about her lack of a love-life, that in fact there was someone who just happened to live far away. That seemed to satisfy him – though her mother, lately, was growing impatient. *Natasha, you're twenty-eight now, soon you'll be thirty. Did you read that article in* Time *magazine about how girls who get left on the shelf by thirty-five have about a zero percent chance of marrying?*

Life was too short, thought Tasha now, to start letting in *that* kind of worry. She had everything else but a steady man in her life – and, who knew? Peter might come to New York again. She herself might cut loose and go to Scotland – whether or not it was a wise career move according to Lorenzo. She was mobile; her studio apartment was empty except for a futon and a few ramshackle chairs and heaps of clothing. She was painting – stage sets, maybe, rather than canvases, but every night people saw them – and at least ten reviews of *Dreams* had mentioned her work: her Viennese rooms whose wallpaper turned into shadowy forests when the stage went dark; whose gaslights turned into gargoyles. Deep down she knew her sets for *Dreams* were probably the best work she had ever done.

She was happy.

One morning at the end of June, her phone rang at the crack of dawn. 'Jesus,' she groaned, and reached for it. Through sheer laziness she kept a phone at both the bed and kitchen ends of her apartment.

'Tasha?' The far-away voice wavered. 'I'm sorry. I just realised . . . what time is it over there?'

'I don't know, but I'm asleep.'

'Gosh, I . . . I'm sorry, Tash. I – must have got it the wrong way round.'

'Are you all right, Kristin?'

'No. Not really.'

'What's happened?'

'I've lost the baby, Tasha.'

'Oh, no. You had a –'

'A miscarriage. Yes.'

'But it was still early . . .'

'Three months, almost. They say after three months the chances are better . . .' Kristin's voice trailed off for a second. 'Things aren't right with Alex. He's stopped speaking to me.'

'But why?'

'Oh, it's a long story. I had – some fertility treatment, and I never told him. It was never a very big deal. Only drugs. He just thought he should know. I let it slip out –'

'Oh, no.' Tasha stared into the phone receiver. *You never told me, either*, she thought. Perhaps in her case there was the excuse that she had never been a hundred percent fascinated by the subjects of babies and pregnancy. But for Alex . . .

'Don't tell me you're on his side?'

'No. No, of course not.'

'Because sometimes it feels as if – everyone agrees with him.' Kristin's voice twisted into a sob.

'Kristin, who? Who's everyone?'

'No one. I'm alone. There's no one here. Alex has gone away . . .'

'Away where?'

'To Zurich . . . I feel so awful. I don't know if he's left me. He never said when he'd be coming back . . .'

'Kristin. Kristin? Are you there? Do you know what I think you should do . . .?'

Kristin flew into New York on the night of 3 July. Tasha ran towards her with open arms at the arrivals gate.

As they collided, Kristin gasped out, 'But you're different. You've cut your hair. You've changed.'

'Yeah. I hate my hair.' Tasha grabbed the handle of Kristin's suitcase and started to trundle it on its wheels along the ground. 'I blew a hundred and fifty bucks getting six inches lopped off, and now I look in the mirror and I'm like, "How quick can it grow back?" *You* look just the same as ever.'

'God. I wish I felt the same.'

Tasha manoeuvred them through the doors and up to the head of the taxi queue. 'Lorenzo wanted us all to get together for dinner. But I told him not tonight.'

'Thanks.' Kristin gave a wan smile. 'I don't quite think I'd be up to it.'

A cab pulled up and Tasha hauled Kristin's bag in. 'But you can come and see *Dreams* any night you want.' She leaned forward to give the driver her address. 'Better hold your breath,' she told Kristin, 'when we get to the front door. It kind of reeks. There're a lot of bums around.'

Kristin wrinkled her nose. 'What kind of a place is it you're living in?'

Tasha beamed at her friend. 'You've got to overlook the outside. It's cool when you get in. You'll see.'

Kristin unpacked her suitcase into a rickety-looking chest, which sat on a platform built on to the exposed brick wall, above the futon.

'Don't worry,' said Tasha. 'It won't fall. What can I get you? Coffee? Tea? Decaf, peppermint, camomile, rose-hip . . .'

'Do you have any Earl Grey?'

'That, too.' Tasha burrowed in the single cupboard that, alongside a miniature cooker and fridge, made up her kitchen.

'You're well supplied.'

'Tea and coffee are about all I've got. I never eat in.'

'So do you like being back in New York?' As discreetly as she could, Kristin wiped the dust her fingers had gathered from Tasha's bureau off on the inside of her jumper. Peeking through the slats of an extremely dirty Venetian blind above the futon, she could see a fire escape zigzagging its way up a wall.

'Yeah, it's great. Expensive, though. I was lucky to get this place. It's a sublet. Friend of a friend of a friend.'

'I see.' Kristin searched her mind for something polite to say about it, but couldn't come up with anything. She had never imagined Tasha actually enjoying living alone; even in her first few minutes here, she had found herself scanning the room for signs of another occupant – even a part-time one. Tasha always had some sort of man in her life. So who was it now?

Tasha crossed the room with a tray and two mugs and a bag of bagels. 'So were you able to get a message through to Alex that you were coming here?'

'I suppose. I spoke to his secretary. She said he's in Zurich for another week. Let it slip, rather. She seemed to assume I'd been informed.' Kristin sighed.

'Oh.'

'So if he comes home, it'll be to an empty flat. Let him see how *he* likes it.' Kristin blew on her hot tea.

'So what exactly happened with you two?'

With a slow letting out of breath, as if the telling had become a sort of nuisance, Kristin told her. 'Miscarrying,' she said, halfway through, 'by the way, hurts. It hurts like hell. And in my case it took two days.'

'Jeez.'

'So Alex went off to London and there I was at Tewne Abbot, bleeding. Then he rang to say he was going to Zurich and was I all right? So I said yes.'

'So do you think you two are going to separate?'

Kristin's eyes widened, as if the idea had never occurred to her. 'No.'

'But when you said on the phone – you thought he'd left you . . .'

'Yes. Maybe. But he'll come back. Things aren't as bad as that.'

'Just how bad do they have to get?'

'What on earth do you mean?' Kristin studied her friend's open face. 'In my book, marriage is permanent. I've put far too much into what we have to . . .'

'Are you still in love with Alex?'

'That's beside the point. I –'

'How can it be beside the point?'

283

'You don't understand. We've built a life together, we share things.'

'You mean that house?'

'Yes, Tewne Abbot. And other things,' Kristin added defensively. 'I'm not about to give it all up.'

'How does Alex feel?'

But Kristin chose not to answer that question. 'I think,' she said, her voice abruptly changing timbre, 'I'm really going to enjoy seeing New York again. After all these years. I'd love to see your parents. And what was that place we used to go to for coffee? You know, by the ice rink?'

Perplexed lines crossed Tasha's forehead but she got up to fix them both more tea. 'Honey,' she said, in a fake, flat Southern accent, 'this is your holiday. We'll go wherever you want.'

They went to Saks and Bloomingdale's. They went to Little Italy and bought pastries; they went to films in the middle of the afternoon. Ever since *Dreams* had opened, Tasha had existed in an enjoyable limbo, still receiving salary cheques, on call when set repairs were needed; but until Lorenzo found a new Broadway site and her designing work began again, her days were free.

She took Kristin to see *Dreams* on a Tuesday, which was usually a quiet night. Even having grown used to the play herself, and seen its emotional impact on dozens of audiences, Tasha was pleased to see Kristin's face grow solemn and still as the show proceeded . . .

'Gosh,' she said in a quavering voice at the end, just after the dying Sigmund Freud's big speech, in which he voiced his fears for the Jews and the whole of Europe. 'I never knew Lorenzo could write like that.'

Tasha snorted. 'He can't. Come on, let's go see him.'

They met up backstage, and after that a group, including some of the cast, went on to dinner at a Cuban restaurant. Lorenzo, on his habitual post-performance high, talked nonstop about old times and the Academy and what the people he and Kristin and Tasha had known there were all doing now.

'Steve,' he said, 'is like VP for his father's firm, he got married to this gorgeous Southern debutante last year. And Rachel's in med school, and – hey, you'll know about this, Kristin – Courtney's got a book out, that she wrote in England.'

Kristin grimaced. 'I saw her on the telly at home. Going on about how she was one of the new post-feminists, and how Oxford had radicalised her.'

'Her book got a review in *The Times*,' offered Lorenzo. 'Smaller than mine for the play, of course.' He smirked.

'This,' announced Tasha, draining her glass, 'is depressing me. I want to know about all the *failures* who were with us at Elliott.'

Kristin's eyes were bright, ranging around the table. 'Well, there's me. No career, no baby, marriage on its last legs.' She gave a nervous laugh. Feeling a sudden, desperate craving for a cigarette – there were none in her handbag – she eyed Lorenzo's.

He handed her one and said easily, 'Tell me about it.'

She only laughed again. 'Nothing much to tell.'

Slowly the table fell silent. Lorenzo, glancing perfunctorily at his watch, announced that he had an early appointment in the morning. The group drifted in twos and threes from the restaurant.

'It'd be all right,' said Kristin to Tasha, while they waited in the street for a cab, 'if he didn't have to *gloat* so.'

'Why do you say that? I like Lorenzo.'

'And he likes himself.'

'Listen, if you think you're a failure you can change that.' Tasha turned, suddenly angry, towards Kristin. 'If you put up with a marriage you're not happy with, well, that's your choice. You can have a career if you want one. Don't start acting as if your life's over.'

'Oh, is this your idea of helping me?' Kristin's voice rose unsteadily, and she turned away.

'Yes! If it's the only way I can.'

'And how are you qualified to preach? Is your life perfect?'

On the point of retaliating, Tasha stopped herself. She studied the set line of Kristin's jaw: the face upturned, above the wild gold hair, towards the streetlamps. 'Look, this is silly,' she said.

'Of course it is.' Kristin sighed slowly.

'We can agree to differ about Lorenzo, okay?'

Kristin gave a shallow laugh. 'I've always thought he was a prat. I don't think I ever made a secret of it. But of course he's your friend, and of course you should be grateful to him. Not *too* grateful, perhaps.'

'What do you mean?'

'Oh – never mind. Just . . . I think you should look out for yourself. Don't rely on him too much.'

'I don't,' Tasha said defensively. A silence followed, which she broke again. 'Look. There's something I really ought to tell you. I've been meaning to. Do you remember Peter Conaway?'

Kristin laughed, then turned her head towards Tasha, with a slow, careful smile. 'Yes, I should think so. Why?'

'Because . . .' Christ, thought Tasha, this was difficult. But it had to be done.

The cab dropped them off outside Tasha's building. 'Hold your breath,' said Tasha, as always, hopping out.

'Tasha,' said Kristin when, giving up on the rickety lift, they started to climb the stairs, 'are you sure about all this, with Peter?' She hoped her voice didn't give anything away. She knew that, in fairness, she ought to tell Tasha about those few days, in London, before she was engaged to Alex. The fact that Tasha had been holding back on her – hiding the fact of her own meeting with Peter, in New Haven, until just now – had washed over her without troubling her too much. Such deceptions seemed to her to be in the course of human nature. Besides, she, Kristin, had been in a fragile state when they met up in Paris. It was no wonder Tasha hadn't wanted to say anything that might upset her.

Still, Kristin felt a stab of something. Indignation. Concern. A few letters didn't seem like much of a foundation for the kind of plans Tasha seemed to be making. 'I still think,' she said, not waiting for Tasha to answer her previous question, 'Lorenzo's right. If you really care about doing set design in New York, you ought to stick around, and not go off travelling, looking for Peter.'

'Oh, I wouldn't be *looking* for him. I'd just be wandering around. I'd come to London, too, and see you.'

'Well, of course I'd like that. I just don't think –'

'I don't expect anything from him, honestly. The thing is, I just can't believe how well we seem to know each other by now. How well we're suited. I hope you don't mind my saying that –'

'No, of course not.'

'But sometimes I wonder if it's fate. Because somehow no man I meet ever seems to live up to him. I think about all the good times we've had together . . .'

'You and Peter?' *All the good times?* Kristin thought. When Tasha had seen Peter once in – what, five years?

She wondered once again if it might be kinder to come clean. But once again, her nerve failed her. 'Do you know where he is just now?' she said, praying that Tasha wouldn't – didn't. Because she, Kristin, did know. He was in Glasgow. She had heard so, from someone who had met him there: a woman, a guest at a drinks party.

'Oh, Scotland somewhere,' said Tasha airily. 'The address he's given me is care of somebody. But it's not that big a country.'

Kristin thought again of the bit of gossip she had heard, and of her instinctive dislike for the woman who had passed it on. Red-haired, the pretentious wife of a rich industrialist who kept an art gallery as a hobby: one of

Diana's acquaintances, by whom Kristin had found herself reluctantly buttonholed. She remembered the woman's words, and the uneasy feeling they had engendered in her.

'*Polypriapic, of course.*' The woman had waved her cigarette, evidently proud of her coinage. '*So many of these artists are. And I'm afraid –*' She had giggled. '*I couldn't get him to tell me his age for our catalogue. And when he did, he lied. He was really five years older. I'm afraid you really just can't trust them!*'

No, Kristin told herself resolutely now, you couldn't. You had, she supposed, to doubt everyone a little: the gallery owner, Peter, her own instincts. The truth probably lay somewhere in between the lies all of them told.

Which was something she wished Tasha would learn. She sighed.

'What is it?' said Tasha. She was getting up, filling a kettle, searching for teabags. 'Look, I know you think I'm crazy. But I'm really not hooked on the guy. Maybe we belong together, maybe we don't. I'm happy being single.'

'Are you?' said Kristin in a faint voice.

'Beats marriage.' Tasha spoke resoundingly.

Kristin, momentarily annoyed, gave a faint laugh. 'You might just be right.'

The phone rang and rang. It was five a.m. For some reason the answer machine didn't click on – Tasha must have forgotten it – and so Kristin reached over her somnolent body for the receiver. 'Hallo?'

'Kristin. Patricia told me you'd flown to New York.'

'Yes.'

'You could have waited. I'd have taken you there if I'd known you wanted to go.'

Kristin rubbed her eyes. The voice sounded like Alex's, but the words didn't. 'Alex? Is that you?'

'I'm sorry. I know it's early. I couldn't wait any longer.'

'I didn't think you'd mind if I went away.'

'Naturally I mind. If I hadn't spoken to Patricia I'd have come home, expecting to find you . . .'

This was sounding more like Alex. 'I know. I needed a change. I'm at Tasha's.'

'If you'd let me know, you could have used my air miles at least. Flying out there must have cost –'

Kristin let out a slow sigh, which she supposed Alex heard.

'Look, darling, I'm sorry. I seem to be getting off on the wrong foot. What I'm trying to say is, I want you to come home.'

'Are you sure?'

'I'm willing to admit I was wrong. Not about . . . everything, perhaps. But for flying off the handle the way I did.'

'Oh.'

'And I – think we should try again.' Alex paused, and there was silence. 'What about you, Kristin? Don't you?'

'Yes. I suppose we should.'

'Well, then.'

Kristin felt as if she were abandoning a conversation – or was it a confrontation? – in midstream; but she was not sure where it was going to go. She knew that, in any attempt to lecture Tasha about Peter Conaway, she was standing on thin ice.

'Look,' she said, hugging Tasha goodbye while her cab to the airport waited beside them, 'just be careful. Look out for *yourself*.'

Tasha shoved a hank of hair back behind one ear. Her cheeks were rosy. 'Sure I will. Who are you talking about? Renzo or Peter?'

'Both.' Kristin bent awkwardly through the cab door in her miniskirt.

'Okay, I'll look out. But you do, too. Give my regards to Alex.'

They waved goodbye until each disappeared from the

other's view. Kristin felt distinctly uneasy. As if she had left a job undone, or at least unfinished. Though perhaps she could make no difference. Perhaps it wasn't her business to try.

She couldn't be sure, either, that she might not blurt out the wrong words from the wrong motives: from jealousy. Because, after all, she had had those same hopes once. She had dreamed of being in Paris with Peter.

But then, she thought, *I grew up*. She let out a dissatisfied sigh. She knew she had to think of something else. Of Tewne Abbot, which would be awaiting her. The roses would be flowery, full-blown, the days lengthening; the sun would shine on to the golden wood of the floorboards late into the evenings. She would wander out across the grass, into the orchard . . .

It did not occur to her to wonder why, in her comforting vision, she was alone, without Alex.

THE SECRET EXHIBITIONIST
Inside the Life and Art
of Peter Conaway

22 Tasha tugged the Sunday *New York Times Magazine* free from its weighty accompanying newspaper, and drank in the sight of it. The soft-focused, dark photo; the headline.

'Hey, lady, you trying to read the paper in the store?'

Tasha tore open the lid of her coffee and took a sip as she turned to the contents page, ignoring the glare coming her way from the man behind the counter. She just couldn't believe it. Peter, in the *New York Times Magazine*, today: 21 March 1993.

He had told her to look out for it. After a long silence, a letter had come, printed in unfamiliar type: another new computer, she had registered. That was the sign.

Whatever you do, make sure to buy the Times *Mag,* he'd said. *I think its this week or the one after.*

Whatever else you could say about him, Peter had never been one to hide his light under a bushel. Tasha had watched the articles multiply over the last year: at first, just small pieces in British papers and magazines. Glorying in the attention, the tenuous beginnings of fame, he had sent her copies of every single one. And now this: the first piece in the American media. But the full treatment, from the magazine that counted. The *Times*.

She knew why it had all come about. Around last Christmas, a well-known London collector with an exotic name and his own private art gallery had decided to buy a huge bloc of Peter's work. Which – according to that last letter of his – had sent the galleries into a tailspin, trying to coax sculptures out of him on behalf of clients who had materialised out of nowhere. *They're all leeches*, his letter said, *the art world is like that, its worse than fashion or advertising. Well, the same thing actually, but hell, who am I to complain?*

She found that she was shaking so hard with excitement that she couldn't turn the magazine's pages to reach the actual article. 'Right,' she said, in sudden appeasement of the newsagent, and strode towards the counter. 'I'm buying. In fact I'll have three, but I only want the magazine. Throw the rest of the papers out for me, okay?'

The man shook his head and started to grumble, but Tasha, slapping down a five-dollar bill, had removed her three *Times Magazines* and escaped before his second volley of abuse could reach her.

Five minutes later, she let herself into her apartment. Opening up her coffee again, along with the bagel and cream cheese she had bought from the deli, she settled herself into her sofa to read. She reached the middle of the article fast.

> Is he a genuinely new force in the art world?
> Is his work ground-breaking, or merely a slick repackaging of concepts first launched in the sixties and seventies?

Tasha drew in her breath, indignant. It wasn't: of course it wasn't.

> From a friend's borrowed cottage in Fife – which he plans to trade in soon for a grander abode somewhere close to the London art scene – he eulogises the 'working man' as a Scot in his cups often will – except that Conaway drinks only sparingly. He calls himself a 'nationalist' but

> confesses to a restlessness that has spurred him
> to stray far from the middle-class Glasgow
> neighbourhood where he grew up, the son of a
> housewife and a high-school art teacher

'Huh?' said Tasha, aloud. This reporter must have got his facts wrong. Unless, for some reason, Peter had decided not to mention Dornoch and the biscuits and the sausage factory. Anyway, the *Times* had already misread him completely: all those corny images of hard-drinking Scots . . .

Suddenly Tasha wished she could phone him. She didn't have a number for him – only a temporary address in Glasgow. Well, that would change soon, if what the article said was true. If he moved to London.

At that thought, Tasha felt her face grow warm, and a sudden, hot happiness suffuse her. She put down the magazine, walked to the bathroom mirror and examined her round face: still youthful, the skin slightly grainier than it had once been, the corners of her mouth circumscribed by a couple of smile-lines. For twenty-nine, not bad. She thought of London, and knew that fate was finally going to bring her and Peter together. And the best thing about it was that he didn't know. She would surprise him.

On the other side of the door, the phone started ringing. Wrapped up as she was in pleasant fantasy, she let the machine take the call – then dashed to pick up the receiver when she heard Lorenzo's voice.

'Renzo, hi.'

'Hey, Tash, how're you doing? I was wondering, could you come over tonight?'

'Sure.' Tasha was mildly surprised by Lorenzo's efficiency: usually he dawdled for a long chat before getting down to business. 'What's up?'

'Not much. I've just been making some, uh, arrangements. Eight o'clock down here sound okay?'

Hanging up, Tasha wasted no more time on trying to

analyse Lorenzo's uncharacteristic brusqueness. He would be busy: at last, they were taking *Dreams* to London. She felt like an old hand at transformations now, having moved the show from 43rd Street to its current, larger venue, where it was still playing every night to packed houses. Through *Dreams*, and contacts of Lorenzo's, she had done sets for a couple of smaller shows off Broadway, but both had closed almost immediately; *Dreams* remained her main achievement. At any rate, it was still making her money. At first astonished when the play began to turn a profit, Tasha had come to take the regular royalty cheques for granted. They piled up in her bank account, largely unspent; she had thought, before, that she would use them to travel, but there was no need to, now that it looked like she and Lorenzo were heading for London . . .

The timing could hardly be better. Peter was back in Great Britain now – and of course there was Kristin. And Nat. After a string of different journalistic jobs, her brother had been taken on as a London correspondent by *Time* magazine, and showed no signs of homesickness whatsoever.

Tasha was sure she wouldn't, either. She was ready for a change. For one thing, she could do with an escape from her parents and their endless interrogations. 'Isn't there *anyone* special in your life?' her mother had taken to asking wistfully. 'You used to have so *many* boyfriends.'

'Rona, leave the girl alone,' Tasha's father would break in, in her defence; but it was a losing battle.

'Did I tell you, Natasha, I ran into Myra Wechsler at Bergdorf's and her son Ronald's just gotten divorced? I know it may not be exactly ideal, he's on the rebound, but at your age you can't be too choosy . . .'

Rona was always nagging Tasha about her weight, too. Which, though she failed to see it, was exactly the same as it had been for the last ten years. Fuming at the thought of her mother, Tasha decided to make herself an omelette to go with her bagel. While she tended the frying-pan with one hand, she read the rest of the article about Peter.

'I must be one of nature's loners,' says Conaway, still unmarried at 39.

Thirty-nine! thought Tasha. No way! He'd only turned thirty-seven a couple of months ago.

'I can't seem to find a woman prepared to live with me,' he says with a knowing smile. The obsessive nature of the artist . . .

Tasha skimmed the rest of the page. There was nothing here she didn't know. Then she let her gaze drift back to Peter's words. 'Peter Conaway,' she told the smiling, dark-eyed face in the photograph, 'your luck's about to change, and you don't even know it.'

She arrived at Lorenzo's early and hungry. Her omelette had been scorched by the time she remembered to haul it out of the pan, and she'd had no more eggs to try again.

'I've been thinking about the London sets,' she announced, handing him a bottle of wine. 'I was trying to paint this afternoon, but my mind just kept going around and around about the play. What I realised is, I don't want to build the same thing all over again in London. It'd be great to do totally *new* sets.' She fished in her canvas carryall for the sketches she'd done.

Lorenzo seemed oddly subdued, and absorbed in his stir-frying. 'Yeah,' he said, 'well . . .' And tipped the contents of his wok out on to a platter. 'If you look in the oven there're some spring rolls.'

'Okey.' It seemed unlike Lorenzo to be so lackadaisical about the presentation of food. He poured out the wine and took a swig without even attempting a toast.

'Lorenzo, what's up? You don't seem like your normal self.'

He gave a brief laugh. 'Normal? What's my normal self? That's a good question. Well. The thing is, uh, Tasha . . . Shit, I'm not much good at this. You're going to hate me.'

'What is it?'

'Well, I've been in touch with the management of the Arcadium – you know, the theatre on the South Bank where we're going – and everything's like, great, except . . .'

Tasha had a feeling for bad news, sometimes, before it came. 'Except?'

'Well, it's such a big space, they really want someone experienced for the sets. Um, there's this guy, John Roach . . . He's British, done a lot of productions over there. *Demon of Venice, Miracles* . . .'

'You're letting me go.' Tasha couldn't believe what she was hearing.

'Tash, don't take it like that. We're buddies. I knew you'd be really let down, but believe me, it took this to get the deal off the ground. I had the show to consider.'

'Oh.' She pushed back her chair.

'Hey, stick around for dinner. I mean, I'd really like to hear your ideas for designs and everything. John'll want you to contribute.'

'I doubt that.' Tasha heard an unfamiliar acidity in her voice.

'No, Tasha, listen. You own part of *Dreams*. Your opinion's not going to stop counting. I just need a big name in the credits in London, that's all.'

'Lorenzo, I think I'm going to go home now.'

'Tasha.' He looked perturbed. 'We go back a long way. *Dreams* deserves to go to London, you know that. You still have your percentage . . .'

'Fuck my percentage, Lorenzo.' Tasha bolted the last of the wine in her glass and made for the door, her vision blurred with tears. Then she turned to face Lorenzo for one last time, and spoke as sweetly, as calmly, as she could. 'Actually, I take that back. I want my percentage, I want

296

every last penny. You've screwed me over this, Lorenzo, but you're damn well not going to screw me out of anything else.'

She hadn't realised how much she had been counting on going to London. Now everything around her – her apartment, her future – looked bleak, and she knew why. Emotionally she had abandoned New York. She had been counting on a new start – on new chances she did not want to jinx, even by naming them to herself.

Kristin would be expecting her to call. Tasha supposed she would have to tell her. She let out a sigh as she picked up the phone: it was ten – so three a.m. in London. She couldn't even call now: too late. It would have to wait till morning.

'Oh, Tasha.' Kristin picked up the phone on the first ring. 'I'm so glad it's you.'

'How are you? You don't sound too great.'

'Oh, I don't know. I just hate being in London alone.'

'Alex away on business again?'

'Oh, he always is. I'd almost suspect him of having an affair, except he's so devoted to Chappell's it would seem to him like an infidelity.' Kristin gave an empty laugh. 'Oh, I don't know, Tasha. Maybe I just need to get away. Have a holiday. We both probably need to, but we can't afford it. We're supposed to be trying for a baby again. What a joke.'

'I'm sure it'll be okay, Kris.' Tasha spoke carefully, wary of Kristin's mood.

'At least you're coming soon. When's it going to be? Have you got a date yet?'

'Um . . .' Tasha took a deep breath.

'I suppose you'll need to tie things up in New York. Sublet your apartment.'

'No, actually I just have to give the keys back to the guy who owns it.' Tasha felt as if she were groping her way through fog, towards a clarity which had so far eluded her.

'But I definitely *want* to come. I mean, it should just be a matter of time . . .'

She didn't know what was possessing her: what right she had to say these things.

'Oh, Tash, I'm glad. It'll be wonderful to see you. Have you got your visa and everything sorted out?'

'Yeah,' said Tasha vaguely; and then she knew, with a sudden flash of inspiration, that in fact everything *was* sorted out. Lorenzo had made her and his other key people put in visa applications months ago. Hers had come back; it was fine; she could work in Britain for a year.

So what was stopping her?

'Gosh, I can't wait,' said Kristin. 'We'll have loads of things to do. And, you know' – she gave a sudden, bubbly laugh, quite different from her last one – 'Alex can bugger off to whatever bloody meetings he likes. When you get here, you and I are going to have *fun*.'

23   Tasha told herself it was because of Kristin. Kristin was feeling down; Kristin needed her.

Even as she made her arrangements to leave New York, depositing boxes of belongings at her parents', handing back the keys to her apartment and paying her last bills, she told herself that she was going over to London mainly to visit Kristin, and for a change of scene.

She hadn't heard from Peter, anyway, since the *Times Magazine* piece; and, not wishing to spoil the surprise of turning up on his doorstep, hadn't written him since then, either. Two months had passed; it was the middle of June now, as she scanned the luggage conveyors at Heathrow, feeling smartly superior to the other American tourists she could hear complaining of the cold all around her. Being, as she told herself, no mere tourist, she didn't mind it. Yet she scanned the streets with an outsider's curiosity as her cab wove its way in through suburban, then increasingly elegant and crowded streets of tall houses. Great West Road, Cromwell Road, Onslow Square. Finally, the early-Victorian town house, just as Kristin had described it: white front, dark bricks, black-painted railings.

Kristin burst through the front door just as Tasha was hauling her bags up the steps. 'Gosh, you're early. I feel rotten. Sometimes I *swear* to myself I must learn to drive, then I could have picked you up at the airport . . .'

'Hey, who cares? I'm here!' Tasha wrapped her up in a big bear hug, and they made their way, talking a mile a minute, up the carpeted staircase. 'So which floor are you?'

'First. Only one flight.' Kristin nudged open a high white door. Its paint was fresh, its brass knob and numbers shiny, the marbled wallpaper above and thick carpet below all equally plush and new.

'Nice,' said Tasha, nodding vaguely all around her. The inside of Kristin's flat continued the same effect: cushioned, luxurious. A little like a hotel. A hoover hummed faintly in the background.

Kristin shrugged. 'Mrs Keele's doing the sitting room, but we can go in the study. Have you eaten?'

'Mrs who?'

'She does for us Mondays and Wednesdays.'

'You have a *cleaning* lady?'

Kristin gave Tasha a very curious look.

'Gee, no rest for the wicked, I guess.' Tasha sank into a soft-looking sofa. 'I could handle a cup of coffee, if it's no trouble.'

Kristin left, and came back quite soon. 'If you'd like to use the phone, feel free. I suppose Lorenzo will be expecting to hear from you.'

'Who? Oh –' Tasha gave a quick smile that she knew probably looked shifty. 'There's plenty of time. I can make my calls later.'

When Kristin went away and came back again with two demitasses of dark coffee – a biscuit wouldn't have gone amiss, thought Tasha, or, say, a brownie, but Kristin had never quite got the hang of these things – Tasha put up her feet on the embroidered stool in front of her, and said, 'Well? What's up with you?' And for once Kristin didn't take much prompting.

'I've started,' she said, 'taking pictures again. And not just for myself anymore. I mean professionally. A friend of mine, Diana Barbour . . .'

And she was off. Tasha heard the words, 'magazine', 'go and shoot a house every other week or so', and 'since Alex is away so much, anyway . . .' She blinked and felt, despite the coffee, incredibly drowsy. Her head flopped to one side.

A minute or so later, Kristin noticed that Tasha seemed

atypically silent. 'Tash?' She looked over and smiled at her friend's slumped form, and went to fetch her a blanket.

The problem, Tasha realised, was that she couldn't decently try to locate Peter while she was still staying at Kristin's house. She could try to explain, but somehow she shrank from the prospect, and anyway, she had had the feeling, when she'd mentioned Peter the last time, that Kristin disliked hearing about him – disliked him, perhaps, or remembering him. So, she thought, finding Peter would have to wait until she had a place of her own.

It would have to be a cheap place: that way, the royalty money from *Dreams* could keep her going for quite a while. Though she had moments of wishing the whole play would go down the tubes, and take Lorenzo de Maas with it, she was usually sensible enough to see it as a handy source of income. It left her free, that was the important thing. To paint, to find a job here, maybe . . .

Her first night at Kristin's, she couldn't get to sleep, because she had dozed for so long on the sofa. She got out of bed and paced around the flat. It wasn't so enormous as it had seemed at first – just two bedrooms and a large sitting room and study – but it was nice. Very nice. Chintz curtains, fireplaces with marble mantles, paintings with little brass lights above them.

As she was examining the contents of the disappointingly empty fridge, she heard Kristin's voice behind her.

'Couldn't you sleep?' Kristin's face looked pale, almost childish in the dim light.

'Nope.' Tasha thwacked the door shut, embarrassed. 'Sorry. I shouldn't be pigging out on your food.'

'That's okay. Help yourself. I couldn't sleep either.' Kristin yawned and stretched. 'Too keyed up, I suppose. I was wondering – you never told me. When do you start work on the play?'

'Well, that's kind of a long story.'

'I've got time. Here we are, neither of us can sleep. Shall I make us tea?'

'Have you got cocoa?'

So as Kristin stood, stirring hot milk over a burner, Tasha told her. She supposed she had to, sometime.

Kristin turned round, her arms folded, aghast, when Tasha came to the part where Lorenzo gave her the sack. 'That little creep. I can't *believe* he'd do a thing like that. Anyway, this John whatsit – I've never heard of him. He can't be so fantastic as all that.'

Tasha shrugged. 'Lorenzo seems to think so.'

Kristin snorted. 'What a self-serving bastard he is.'

'It's not a hundred percent his fault –'

'Huh.' Kristin sniffed. 'I'll bet if he'd wanted you enough . . .' Her words trailed off. 'Sorry.'

'No, you're probably right.' Tasha sighed. 'He's a creep. You always said so.'

Kristin heard a sizzle, and spun to rescue the milk. A few seconds later, pouring out the cocoa, she said, 'But . . . if you're not with the play now, what are you going to do here?'

'Dunno. Paint a little? Travel around?' Tasha reached out for a mug.

'No – the other one's yours. Mine's got no sugar.'

'Cocoa without sugar? Kristin, that's foul.'

Kristin rolled her eyes and smiled, and Tasha let the subject drop. She could remember a time when Kristin wouldn't have drunk milk, let alone eaten sugar. 'So,' she said, 'I'm on the hunt for a job, I guess. Know anybody in London who needs a few sets designed?'

Kristin frowned thoughtfully for a moment. 'I just might . . .' Then she smiled. 'I'd no idea. Did you come just because of me, then? So we could have our visit?'

'Yeah, well, sort of.' Tasha smiled sheepishly. 'And Nat's here.'

'Of course he is. You said. I haven't run into him.'

'Well, London's a big place.'

'Not *that* big. I'll just run and fetch my address book. I'm sure there are a few theatre people in it, if I can only think . . .'

'So you found us.' Adrian Joseph stood up to shake hands. He was tall, beak-nosed and tousle-haired, and wore a black leather jacket. Nothing immediately identified him as gay, but Tasha suspected it, and registered a vague premonitory disappointment. Then she recalled herself. She was here to get a job: that was all.

'Kristin gave me directions,' she said, 'though at first I thought this place was a bingo hall . . .'

'Surely not because of the letters B-I-N-G-O fading away above the door? Use your imagination.'

Tasha grinned. She liked this man.

'So you're Kristin's friend from America.'

'And you're her friend from Littledene. She used to talk about you all the time.'

'Yeah, we've kind of lost touch though. Something to do with my not being a banker, I suspect. Listen, do you know what the Marlowe Theatre's all about?'

For a few minutes, Adrian Joseph talked on rapidly, easily. Tasha already knew she wanted to work here. It was just the kind of experience she needed. A small theatre, in what could only by a large stretch of the imagination be called the West End, with a small, devoted band of subscribers and a programme alternating new plays with seventeenth- and eighteenth-century revivals – hence the name. Not much money, but lots of sets to build every season – sets that had to be cheap and striking, as well as travel-proof. A chance at stage-managing, costumes, lighting . . . 'Sounds perfect,' she said.

'Whoa. Hold on. I know you've worked on Broadway, Tasha. You realise we probably can't afford you.'

Tasha listened blithely as he named a sum that was less than she had trickling in every month from *Dreams*. 'Yes, you can.'

Adrian gave a quirky smile. 'Any reason for this untoward generosity?'

Yes, thought Tasha instantly, *Peter Conaway*. But of course she didn't say that. She smiled. 'I just feel like being in London for a while.'

'Well, then.' Adrian shrugged and extended his hand. 'I guess you're on.'

Tasha clasped her new employer's hand and couldn't suppress a giggle. It had all been so easy, so far. Luck seemed to be on her side.

Alex Renfrew came back from his business trip three days after Tasha's arrival in London, and very rapidly made Tasha feel less comfortably settled in than she had been. One night when he and Kristin were out to dinner together, Tasha caught the tube up to her brother Nat's place, in Islington.

'Want a roommate?' she said, glancing round. Nat's was only a small basement flat, but it had the same quality of neatness and luxury she found so inviting in Kristin's, and which she seemed utterly incapable of creating around herself.

'No way.' Nat grinned, and his dark eyes sparkled. For a second he reminded Tasha of just about every attractive man she had ever known: Peter Conaway, Basil de Angelis, and ten or twenty-odd high school boyfriends and crushes whose names she had long forgotten. Why was that? Was her brother really the best catch of them all?

She banished the thought. 'Pretty please? For, like, two days?'

'Forty-eight hours. Max.' Nat gave her a mock-threatening look.

'So what are you hiding? Why don't you want me here? There's a woman in your life. That's it, right?'

'If only there were.' Nat shoved a coaster and a glass of wine across the table towards her.

'Come on.'

'No, you come on. There's nobody in the picture, and I don't want to talk about it.'

'You know what your problem is? You're too picky. So what happened to Gisela?'

'Warn me the next time I contemplate dating a woman with no last name.'

'Well, you keep going crazy over models, Nat! Half of them have no last name.'

'Oh, well. No more models, I guess, then.' Nat's voice was mellow, quasi-Californian. Unlike Tasha's other brothers, he had a reserved air about him; also unlike the others, he tended to think before he spoke. He smiled now. 'I know what you're going to tell me, Tash. I keep on falling for beauties, so it's my own fault they turn out to have all the emotional depth of Persian cats.'

'As much as that? I never noticed.'

'So find me my ideal woman.'

'That's just the problem! You should forget about ideals. Whatever happened to Melissa, anyway? I liked her.'

Nat's face took on a closed look. 'It ended.'

'More. I want to know more,' Tasha wheedled, putting on a spoilt-child face and flicking a drop of wine towards her brother.

'For Christ's sake, stop it. You'll stain the carpet.' Nat looked away.

He was really annoyed, thought Tasha. 'Sorry. What did I say?'

'If you'd grow up for a minute and stop fooling around I might tell you things.'

Tasha's eyes narrowed. 'Is it because I said Melissa? What is it about her?'

But Nat only shrugged and stalked off to the kitchen to find dinner, and not until a few hours later, when they had both eaten and drunk and forgotten about the scene before, did he tell her.

Tasha felt sheepish, then. She had presumed to know an awful lot about her brother, considering that she hadn't seen him in years. She had never guessed that he wanted to have a child. Perhaps because, as he'd said, he hadn't actually thought about it much, until Melissa accidentally got pregnant. And then he did want the baby: he wanted her to have it.

But she didn't. And, as he well knew, the decision was hers. The worst part of it was, she hadn't had the courage to tell him what she was going to do, until it was all over. *I hated her*, he told Tasha, *right then. I really hated her, I felt like part of me had died. She'd killed it off. I mean, I'm all for women's rights, but that was death. And she didn't even think of me.*

Tasha sat in the silent room and looked down at her hands. 'I'm sorry – I was so nosy,' she said at last.

'So if you start thinking about fixing me up with another girlfriend, bear in mind I'm an emotional cripple, okay?' Nat met her eyes for a second, and flashed her a faint half-smile.

'I don't believe that. But okay.' Tasha took a deep breath. 'I'm sorry I threw wine at you. I won't come to stay if you don't want me to.'

'No, do.' And he threw an arm around her. 'Just stop worrying about my love life, okay? Anyway, how's yours?'

'Not so bad.' Tasha beamed up. Now was the time to confide. 'Nat, I've met someone. Well, kind of met *again*.'

'Does he have a name?'

'Sure. Yeah. You'll meet him.' Tasha's gaze slid away from her brother's. 'But, hey, it's still early days.'

Kristin was secretly relieved when Tasha moved out. She had grown used to having control over her surroundings, and by the end of ten days Tasha's messiness was beginning to drive her crazy. As well as annoying Alex, who was being uncommunicative enough these days, anyway. He had been grouchy, in fact, ever since Kristin had decided to do the occasional photo shoot for Diana

Barbour. He complained because sometimes his shirts weren't back from the cleaner's on time, or the bath felt gritty because in Kristin's absence Mrs Keele hadn't bothered to clean it properly.

Well, bugger that, thought Kristin angrily, when he started in, again, the night Tasha left to go and stay with her brother.

'At least your friend's away. Thank goodness,' Alex pronounced. He was examining the edge of his wine glass for a chip, because he claimed Mrs Keele had already cracked two others.

'What do you mean, thank goodness?' Kristin broke a chunk off her bread roll and started tearing it into smaller and smaller pieces.

'We can have the place to ourselves again.'

'I don't see why you should care. You're hardly ever here.'

'Well, I'm back this week. I was thinking, we haven't had the Molyneuxs round in a while. Perhaps on Friday –'

'I'll be back late on Friday. I'm going out to a house near Northampton.'

'What on earth –' Alex looked annoyed, then drew in a careful breath. 'I really don't see why you bother. We're not *that* desperate for money. It brings in almost nothing anyway.'

'For myself,' said Kristin.

'That's rubbish. You have plenty to do. I thought you were too clever to buy into this women's-lib nonsense about deriving status from some silly little job.'

'It's not some silly little job! It's' – Kristin drew a deep breath – 'just about the only thing I enjoy these days.' Her face felt hot, and she stood up. Alex's steak was under the grill in the kitchen, and she had a vague notion of checking on it. Though, on balance, she was inclined to let it burn.

'For heaven's sake, don't get so worked up over nothing.'

'I'm not worked up. And I'm going to Northampton.'

Kristin spun away towards the kitchen, then changed direction and headed for the bathroom. She expected, when she slammed the door behind her, to be ostentatiously ignored by Alex. It was his usual way.

To her surprise, he came up behind her before she had even left the sitting room. 'Kristin.'

She half-turned, and eyed him warily.

'Is all this because nothing's happening on the baby front?'

'No,' she said coldly.

Alex seemed not to hear her. 'I've been thinking. If you're really worried – if you think that there actually is something, er, missing on your side, you could go back to that doctor of yours . . . You said, the last time, it was a quick thing to sort out.'

Kristin looked at him, bemused. 'Oh. Well, how kind of you. Only I think there's a little more to sort out than that. We're hardly likely to –' She stopped herself there. The end of the thought – *We're hardly likely to have a baby if we never have sex* – was not one which, she found, she wanted Alex to carry to its natural conclusion.

For a moment, he watched her, and she him. 'Well.' Alex shrugged and retreated. 'As you like. Is that my steak in the kitchen?'

Kristin nodded.

'Is it likely to be ready yet?'

'Why don't you go and check on it? You know how to use the grill.' Kristin walked on towards the bathroom, deciding that she probably wouldn't feel like coming out for quite some time.

She was damned, she decided that Friday, on the train up to Northampton, if she was going to let Alex's mood ruin this shoot. He could take the Molyneuxs out if he was so desperate to see them.

But in fact the shoot was a bit of a washout. The day was wet, the house more promising at a distance than close up.

The following Monday, she rang Diana to warn her not to expect too much.

'Oh, well, there are always a few that fizzle.' Diana sounded cheery. 'You're lucky, you've not had many disappointments so far. Listen, I was going to ring you anyway, because something's come up. It's awfully short notice.'

'What is it?' said Kristin eagerly. She was still on frosty enough terms with Alex that she rather relished the thought of announcing to him that she was off on yet another photo shoot.

'It's in Norfolk . . .'

'Fine.'

'Have you heard of the sculptor, Peter Conaway?'

Kristin felt her heart – at least she supposed it was her heart – sink like a stone in her chest. Then it rose again, and she felt happy. Almost giddy. 'Vaguely,' she said.

'He's just bought a new place in East Hingham. Why, heaven knows – he's got no connection with the place that I know of – but you know the Scots. They're often at their most patriotic the farther they get from the auld soil. Actually, the house is a modern one. Are you still interested?'

'Yes. Why not?' The giddiness was enduring, beguiling. *I can do this*, thought Kristin. *I am in control.*

'Would Wednesday be all right? I'll fax you the directions.'

When Diana had hung up, Kristin stood there for a moment, still holding the receiver. *Peter Conaway*. A dozen thoughts had flown through her mind when Diana spoke the name – none of which had been mentionable to her.

She thought of Peter's face, first, and how he would look when she turned up at his house without warning. Oh, he probably knew that she was living somewhere in London, just as she had known for – what, almost a year now, was it? – that he was back in Britain. But that still wouldn't spoil the surprise of it. She smiled.

She thought of Tasha, who ought to be warned. But somehow Kristin knew she wouldn't do it. What reason was there to? Either – as Kristin rather hoped, for Tasha's own sake – she had forgotten the mad notions she'd had last summer, about their sporadic correspondence meaning something; about meeting up, starting up all over again . . . Or she hadn't. In which case, Kristin would only do harm by reminding her.

Another, more unpleasant thought occurred to Kristin. That Tasha had come over expressly to seek Peter out – not for Kristin's sake, or Nat's either, whatever she claimed. The thought discomfited Kristin. But then, why should it? She didn't want Peter Conaway for herself. She wasn't jealous. Anyway, she knew for a certainty that should Tasha manage to track Peter down, he would only disappoint her.

24 Kristin felt strangely light as she climbed out of the cab. Overhead, she saw gulls wheeling. The land around her was flat, the path under her feet slightly sandy, an odour of marsh and sea borne up towards her by the cold wind. It was late July, but she wore trousers and a jumper and a long red raincoat; she imagined Peter in shirtsleeves. Rolled up, his arms bare. Yes, probably they would be.

Norfolk, she wondered. *Why?* She could think of no reason, nothing better than Diana's dismissive view that Scots were often happiest far from home. Peter had probably never owned a house before, she realised now. How odd and rootless that must feel. Perhaps he had wandered into this part of the country and simply thought, 'Here. Why not?'

She had arranged to arrive early, in the half-hope that Peter would not be here waiting, so that she would have a sort of advantage. Time to inspect. As she drew nearer to the house, she could see that it was no more than a low, plain block of gray carrstone with a red-tiled roof, similar to many others she had seen along the road. But then, as the driveway climbed slightly, she could see the large square lawn facing seawards, and the sculptures on it, large and primitive, like standing stones: a black obelisk, a row of thin pillars, a squat tanklike shape on wheels. The sculpture garden was edged by a gravel path, with low stone benches placed against a rockery of mosses and lichens. When she raised her head slightly to look beyond the distant trees, a line of flat blue came into sight. The sea.

For a second, perhaps even less, she remembered the

311

last time she had looked out at the sea with Peter. Maine. That first night, and the next morning . . .

She shook her head and wanted to shiver. *Madness*, she thought. She had cared then, somehow, about mystifying him: captivating him. Things were different now. She turned deliberately away from the view and back towards the house. The windows were made of darkened glass, but she still might be able to see into them. Shielding her eyes with one hand, she leaned close; she caught sight of a white shape she thought was a bed, and then heard steps on the gravel behind her.

Startled, she turned, ready to explain, but Peter's arms had already enveloped her.

'Peter?' Her voice came with a gasp, and a laugh. 'Peter, stop. I do hope it's you. I didn't even see you properly –'

He backed off, smiling. His hands still gripped her upper arms. 'Who needs to see? I would have known you anywhere.'

'Well, I do. You can't just –'

He was pulling her close again. She felt the tightness of his arms against her, the near alignment of their bodies. She didn't know what constricted her chest so that she could only laugh, and make a weak attempt at pulling away, until eventually, slowly, he released her.

'Why didn't you tell me you were coming?' he said.

'I thought *Décor* might.'

'Aye, they did. But Kristin Renfrew might have been anyone. I don't know any Kristin Renfrews.'

'My married name.'

'Ah. So you're still married?'

'Of course I am.'

Peter took her arm and led the way to the house. '*Décor*. That's a posh rag. I'm impressed. How long've you been taking pictures for them?'

She told him; he made a rubbery face, lifting his eyebrows as if in awe.

'Well, you've not done badly yourself.' Kristin nodded towards the door, then back at the garden.

Peter shrugged. She noticed that his face looked weathered in the outdoor light, his cheeks creasing into many lines, more than she remembered, around his smile. 'Ach, well, I thought if I was going to buy a house after all this time, I'd do it properly.'

'Why here?'

He shrugged. 'Why not? I like to look at the sea. The light's good, I've got good neighbours. Pub down the road's not bad, I'll take you down there for lunch –'

'Peter, that doesn't answer my question.'

He stopped and faced her. His smile was playful and his gaze flicked up and down her. 'Why does anybody settle down anyplace?'

She looked at him evenly. Two could play at evasions. 'Why not Scotland?'

He shrugged. 'I tried it. What's that saying, in America? "You can't go home again." 'Course' – he glanced quickly in her direction – 'you did.'

He didn't wait for her to comment, though. Kristin remembered how his patience with any line of conversation always used to run out after about five minutes; now he was opening the door to a tile-floored hallway whose centrepiece was a spiral staircase built of thin sheets of black metal. Through a low door to one side they reached the living room and kitchen, and then what Kristin supposed was a dining room, though it was empty except for a large orange and black mobile suspended from the ceiling.

She stopped in her tracks. 'That isn't really a . . .'

He winked at her. 'Got it at a discount.'

'Nobody sells Calders at a discount.'

'Neither they do. Ach, well, I tried to bargain them down.'

Kristin dug in her handbag for her notebook. She knew she should be writing down whatever Peter could tell her about the house. But as they moved through the next two rooms, then back into the first, large chamber, he proved more and more impossible to pin down. He would frown at a piece of furniture she had indicated, and rub his forehead. 'That table, eh? I don't know. Probably picked it up at some junk shop.'

'Peter, we can't put that in *Décor*. How about that picture up there?'

'Friend did that. No, wait a minute, I did.' Peter squinted at the signature. 'About ten years ago.'

Kristin stepped closer, looking more carefully at the long arc against a white background, which proved, on closer inspection, to be a line of coast: rocks, grasses, houses. 'It doesn't look like your style. I didn't think you did landscape.'

He shrugged. 'Experimental. Hey.' He looked accusingly at her notebook. 'Is this you asking me questions, or *Décor* magazine?'

'Both.'

'Well, I'd like to know which.' Peter planted himself in front of her, blocking her view of the painting and placing a hand on each of her shoulders. 'Because if it's *Décor*, I'll make up whatever rubbish I want to feed to them. If it's you, Kristin Ward, why don't you put away that notebook and let's go to lunch?'

'Renfrew,' said Kristin evenly. 'Kristin Renfrew.'

He smiled. 'You got married after all. I thought you might be losing your nerve. Last time I saw you.'

'Losing my nerve?' She gave a brittle laugh.

'Aye, that's why I took off. Didn't want to mess up your future. So how long's it been?'

'Six years.'

'Happy?'

She shrugged and nodded and started to turn away. He caught her by the shoulder.

'Do you mean that?'

She gave a bemused, practised smile and let her gaze

drift across his face and past it. 'Of course.' Then, slowly but decidedly, she turned away and took her camera out of its case to test the light. 'I might as well start.'

'I'll leave you to it.'

Kristin heard clattering in the kitchen. She wished she could focus on her work, but found that instead of seeing what lay through the camera lens, she was wondering what Peter was doing. While she was in the living room she heard the phone ring and the answer machine click on: Peter's brief message, then a female voice whose words she struggled to make out.

Silly. She knew she shouldn't be listening. None of her business. All over, all past, and what Peter was doing now, except for the purposes of her article, didn't matter.

She reached the bedroom last of all. Perhaps she had been avoiding it, because she had run through several films and this was the only room left. By now the light had improved; it was clear and white-neutral. She slid a roll of black-and-white into her camera as an experiment.

Peter came up behind her. 'Finished yet?'

She smiled and shook her head. 'Still this room to go.'

'How about a break for lunch?'

'It's still early.'

'I'm starved.'

So she agreed. For a moment or two, as they walked out along the path towards the road and the village, she wondered what they would find to say to each other, now that the excuses of the house and her photography had vanished. Then, as she should have guessed he would, Peter took over: talked about the house, the agents who sold it to him, the builders, the couple of years he'd spent up in Scotland, the few months in Dublin, the art gallery owner in London who kept trying to lure him south . . .

'Venetia?' said Kristin, at last getting a word in edge-ways as they faced each other across a plank table.

'Aye. How do you know her?'

'Oh –' Kristin shrugged. 'Through friends.' She thought

315

uncomfortably of Venetia Wilson's beaky face; her falsely intimate laugh; her words: *Polypriapic. Polypriapic.* 'You know her well, I think,' said Kristin.

Their eyes met. Peter's were opaque, pupils blending into irises. His mouth moved into a smile. 'In a way –'

'You slept with her.'

He cocked his head and looked sideways, past her. 'Aye, well, maybe I did. And I suppose you've had the odd fling since we last saw each other, haven't you, Kristin?'

'Actually, no.'

She found it hard to read the expression on his face. Surprised? Impressed? Mocking? His mouth curled and he rubbed his nose. 'You've had your chances, I imagine.'

'I wouldn't know. I've been . . .' Kristin took a deep breath. Heaven only knew why she was coming out with this. 'We've been trying to have a baby.'

'You have?' Peter raised his eyebrows, but looked otherwise unconcerned.

'It doesn't seem,' she said carefully, 'to be working out particularly well.'

'Sorry to hear that.' He looked at her evenly.

She felt strangely relieved that he didn't go into it further. He seemed to take the news as a sort of minor-scale disappointment: something to be acknowledged and passed by. And perhaps, after all, he was right. She felt a relieved warmth flood through her; and a happiness, simply at being here with him – as if she needed no more. She smiled, and let the smile linger. 'It's all right, really. I'm quite busy. I like my work.' She was sounding like a schoolgirl. She took a deep breath. 'I'm afraid I couldn't resist when Diana suggested I come to your house. I rather fancied surprising you.'

'Ach, I think we would have run into each other one day. Better this way, eh?'

'What do you mean?' Kristin frowned slightly.

'I imagine we know a few of the same people these days, Kristin Ward. Kristin Renfrew. Actually I'm surprised you haven't got two names. Kristin Ward-Renfrew,' Peter enunciated. 'Kristin Renfrew-Ward.'

'What's Venetia like in bed?'

He stared at her for a second, then laughed. 'Jesus! Here's your lunch. That gets me out of that one.' He glanced over at the barman who was carrying plates towards them.

'Go on.' She smiled. 'Tell me.'

'Is this for the benefit of that tape recorder of yours?'

'I didn't bring it.'

'So why all the curiosity about Venetia?'

Kristin shrugged.

'You getting bored?'

She had been studying her plate but looked up now. 'What?'

'Bored. With being married.'

She studied him coolly. 'No.'

He cocked his head, and started on his food. 'You sure?'

'Why should I be bored?'

'So you've never been unfaithful.'

She glanced around. 'No. Actually. Is this an interrogation?'

'Well, there you were – I thought you were wanting to interrogate me.' Peter grinned. And then he spoke under his breath, matter-of-factly. 'You know, all these years, I've never fucked anyone as good as you. Not really.'

Kristin drew back, trying to force her face into a controlled smile. 'Thank you. That's kind of you.'

'Do you see anything of Tasha these days?'

She felt as if he had hit her. 'Tasha,' she repeated.

'Aye, Tasha Seidelman. Or don't you two keep in touch?'

'She's in London, actually.' Why, Kristin wondered, even as the words came out, was she saying this? 'She's . . . got a job, with a friend of mine. At the Marlowe Theatre.'

It felt just as she imagined driving pins into her fingers might: with every word, a small kind of shooting pain. A punishment. Because of what had gone before. Because she had been tempted, had wanted him. She would make him this offering: Tasha. He might take it, or refuse it, but in any case he would stop tempting her.

She remembered too late why she shouldn't have said those words. *Forget it*, she wanted to say. *She's in love with you. You'll hurt her.*

'Tasha,' Peter said reflectively, and tilted his head back to drink.

'Oh, but – she's very busy.' Kristin knew the words were too lame.

'She's not married too, is she?'

Kristin glanced down at the table desperately, as if it would provide her with an adequate lie. 'No.'

But Peter dropped the subject then. 'So tell me, what's it like, going round shooting houses?'

So she told him about *Décor* and her work. They were on to leveller ground again, talking quickly, companionably. Kristin wasn't sure whether to be glad about that, or sorry.

They went back to the house. Five rolls of film later, he offered to drive her into Norwich for the train.

'Oh, no,' she said. 'That's too far. I'll get a taxi to Cromer.'

'It'll take you forever to get back to London that way.'

She shrugged. 'It doesn't matter. I like the views. Alex's working late.'

'Does he do that a lot?'

'Sometimes.'

'Would he care, do you think, if I ran you back to town?'

'Do you need to go?'

He looked at her steadily. 'No. Just want to.'

'You have a house in London, don't you?'

He laughed. 'You do your research well. What else have you found out about me?'

She fastened her case round her camera. 'Nothing, actually. *Décor*'s not exactly big on research.'

'Anything you want to know' – he grabbed her hand –

318

'just ring me.' And before she could free herself, he had penned a line of numbers across the inside of her palm.

'Oh, no,' she said, and backed away. 'You're not doing *that* again.'

'What again?'

She ignored his feigned innocence, and studied the numbers on her skin. 'This is for here, right? Is there a London one?'

'Not worth giving you. It's always the machine. I'm hardly ever there. So are you ready?' He was closing windows, switching off lights.

'You don't need to drive me back . . .'

'We've been through this before. I don't need to, but I want to. You've got your article, and your pictures, and your quotes, right? And I get to drive you back.' He touched her briefly under the chin. 'A few more hours. After all, who knows when we'll see each other again?'

Kristin wondered, if only briefly, at his reasoning, as they sped down the country road to Norwich. She thought this was the fastest she had ever been driven: certainly in this country. Perhaps anywhere. And yet she wasn't scared, and she wondered why.

Because, she realised, she felt charmed, as if nothing could touch her. Perhaps Peter felt this way all the time. It was intoxicating. She rested her head, for a moment, against the seat. Peter's hand touched her throat: stroked the curve of it, up and down. That meant he was driving one-handed.

'Don't,' she said.

But he went on. And it dawned on her slowly that the feeling which had begun, in these last few minutes, to overtake her, was no generalised exhilaration but quite a specific one. Arousal. She took hold of his hand and placed it back on the wheel.

'No,' she said. 'Really.'

'That for good? Or just for now.'

She didn't answer him.

319

*

Tracking Peter down proved harder than Tasha had expected it to be. He had no number listed in the London phone directory. No reason he should, though, she supposed. Either all that talk of moving, in the *Times* article, had been guff, or else he had changed his mind. She rang directory enquiries and tried his name in Glasgow. Nothing there, either. Experimentally, she tried Edinburgh, then Dornoch: 'Dornoch? Which one? Where's it near?' said the operator. Unsure of her geography, Tasha gave up.

He could, she thought, have moved to somewhere in the country. Was that what he had said he was doing, in the *Times*? When she dug the clipping out of her special envelope, it failed to enlighten her. For the moment, she gave up. If all else failed, she supposed, her mail from New York would reach her. There might be a letter from Peter, to help her find him. Or she would meet someone who knew where he was. Britain was a small country.

She was too busy just now to dwell on the problem longer. It was August, and the Marlowe was taking two plays up to the Edinburgh Festival. The answer machine on her desk was always busy with messages. Usually they came from props suppliers or actors – but occasionally, too, she heard from Kristin or Nat, or her father's cousins, the Sebergs. Like good Jewish relations they were still keen to fix her up with that nephew of theirs, now an orthopaedic surgeon. Tasha laughed off the suggestion. 'I am *not* going out with any doctors.'

Mattie Seberg was persistent. 'Are you telling me there's already a man in your life, Natasha?'

Tasha evaded the rest of her questions. She had divulged the truth to Nat at last, and rapidly regretted it.

'You're telling me,' he had responded, aghast, 'that you are trying to get together with someone you last saw almost eight years ago? Tasha, it won't work. Give it up. You both will have changed.' Then a sort of shadow had crossed his face. 'Now, this wouldn't be that guy from back at Elliott, that you and Kristin were both –'

Sometimes Tasha wished she hadn't confided so much in her brother before. 'Oh. No.'

The Sebergs and Nat might not understand the situation as it *really* was. Still, she was glad they all cared. It made her feel right at home in London, having this substitute family – ringing her up, inviting her over for meals. She had high hopes of a home-cooked meal – dinner, maybe – when she walked into her office on the second Monday of August, to find seven messages. She played them all off. Mattie Seberg, her mother, Mattie again, the Marlowe's cleaning lady, Kristin, Nat . . . and another.

She played it again, because her own astonished delight had kept her from hearing anything but the voice, the first time round.

'Tasha! I hope I've got the right place 'cause it's a long story how I found you. Anyway, I can't believe you're here in London. Give me a call.'

Then Peter left a number. Tasha searched frantically for a pen and couldn't find one, but it didn't matter. The digits were engraved on her memory. The only question was: call him now, or later?

Later, she thought at first. Tonight. But she found that she couldn't settle to anything – opening her mail, or answering her other calls. So she tried Peter's number. Lord, she hoped it wasn't someone else's house – some friend's, where he was staying. She didn't know what she would say to a stranger.

But, in the end, it was another machine. She blurted out a quick message, hoping, afterwards, that it had made some kind of sense. And that Peter would manage to reach her before she left for Edinburgh on Wednesday. Because after that she wouldn't be back for three weeks, and she just didn't think that she could possibly bear to wait so long to see him.

Kristin was surprised at her own persistence. 'You must,' she said softly, wheedlingly, into the phone, 'know someone who would have known him back then? Maybe one of his teachers?'

Décor, it was true, wasn't big on research. It usually cobbled together a sort of interview with a house's owner and left it at that. Still, just occasionally, an owner's personality pervaded a house to such an extent that it deserved some exploration. Diana had told her this. At least, Kristin thought, it made a good excuse.

'*Décor* magazine?' the secretary at the Glasgow School of Art had answered her, bemused; but she proved quite co-operative, even genial, when Kristin explained which ex-student she was writing about. She had passed on two names; one proved untraceable, the other elderly. He was laughing now, hoarsely, to himself.

'Well, I know who you should try,' he said. 'She won't want to talk to you, though.'

'Someone who taught him?'

'I suppose you could say so.' The old man put down the phone, then came back. He was apologetic. He had no number, only an address. 'It might be out of date –'

Kristin thanked him profusely.

'Alex?' she said that night. 'I'm going to be taking a quick trip up to Scotland.'

'I see.' Alex spoke from behind his *Evening Standard*. 'Another shoot, I suppose.' He spoke the word *shoot* disdainfully. 'You ought to call in on my parents, if you're near. They'd like to see you.'

'Oh, I won't be going that far north,' said Kristin hastily.

Alex shrugged.

Put down your paper, she thought. *Look at me. Care, at least, whether or not I'm going to have an affair.*

But he didn't.

25 Kate wondered why she felt watched, this morning, as she went down the path to meet the postman. It was a day no different from all the others this summer, cloudy, a strong wind blowing off the sea. As she opened the gate, waved at Jimmy, took the handful of envelopes, she felt extraordinarily conscious of her actions, as if she were performing them for a film. Yet she did not know why. The one woman she did see wandering up the street, a blonde in a red raincoat carrying a camera, was obviously a summer holiday-maker, probably the bored wife of some golfer, on the lookout for shops. The woman paid Kate no notice, nor did Kate acknowledge her. Instead, she wandered back inside, sifting through her mail.

In the hall, a pair of arms seized her round the waist. 'Oaf,' she said, and elbowed their owner away.

He nuzzled her cheek. ''Sthere any coffee?'

'Make it yourself, darling. I'm working.' She wandered upstairs. The light in her studio seemed stronger and brighter than it did outdoors. She glanced around the room at her works in progress, ticking them off on a mental list. For once, both the sculpting and painting were going well. Two of her clay sea serpents had been commissioned; three paintings were going off to a gallery in Edinburgh. She might pop down there herself, at the end of the week. She could do with the solitude. Not that she would ever dream of kicking Liam out. He was fun – but he had his limitations.

She looked out of the broad, high window and was almost tempted to start another painting. And then she saw the woman again: a speck of red in the street below, still wandering. For a moment Kate felt sorry for her. She felt sorry for all these women with too much money and not enough to do. How stale their lives must feel. Go away, speck of red, she thought. You're spoiling my view.

26 Kristin picked up the telephone. The number had long ago faded from her hand, but she had transferred it into a space in her address book under Diana's, and given it a false heading: '2d Fax'. Not, she supposed, that Alex cared, but she liked to be neat about such things. Not to leave any clues or trails. *Start as you mean to go on.*

She pushed the buttons. There was every chance he wouldn't answer. But she would catch him sometime, some night like this. When Alex was in bed – he always went to bed before she did, these days, discontinuing the formality of waiting up for her. Which, at the weekends, in the old days, had meant sex. Kristin was rather glad these weren't the old days anymore.

At the other end, the phone rang six times. She had almost given up and was putting down the receiver when something clicked.

'Conaway.'

Her heart gave a lurch of anticipation. 'Hello, Peter.'

'What kind of time is this to be calling a man?'

'You said to ring you. Anytime, I think you said.'

He gave a rough chuckle. 'But, Kristin, at two a.m. –'

'Are you busy? Is this a bad time?' There was a slight edge to Kristin's voice.

'No.' He laughed. 'I'm not even in bed yet. But I would have thought you'd be, with that husband of yours.'

'No.' She drew a deep breath. 'Peter, I'm bored.'

'Bored and rich. So there you are, Kristin Renfrew. Just where you always wanted to be.'

Kristin searched momentarily for a rejoinder, but Peter

spoke again, before she could. 'How'd the pictures come out?'

'Pictures?'

He laughed again. 'Of the house. I hope you had film in your camera? It'd be too bad if you had to come out here and start all over.'

'Would it?'

'What?'

She paused, measuring his silence. 'Be such a nuisance for you.'

'You know it wouldn't –' He paused, and gave a kind of sigh. 'The way I see it, Kristin, your life's your own. But what are you playing at?'

'Playing?'

'You can come out and see me anytime, you know that. But I don't want you thinking you can keep on dancing round the furniture and talking about houses as if you can fucking tease me to death.' He stopped, but just long enough to catch his breath. 'I won't let you.'

'What's that supposed to mean?' Kristin's face was growing warm, her heart pounding. This was working.

'You know well enough what I'd like to do with you.'

'Tell me.'

'Oh, no.' He laughed. 'I'm not playing those games again.'

'Why not? I . . . miss you. I've been thinking about you.'

'Well, that's just too bad.' Peter laughed again. 'I guess you'll have to keep on thinking.'

'No.' The air around Kristin felt heavy. She was going to make him do it. He would give in. 'Say it, Peter. Tell me you're not thinking about it. Tell me you're not turned on right now.'

'Are you?'

She let herself give way, just a little. Her voice came out low and rough. 'Yes. Of course I am.'

'Jesus. You know I want you. I wanted you last week.'

'To do what?'

He answered her, then, and the words were rude, rude as she wanted, and mocking. Dirty words for taking and using and discarding; and yet they charged her up. She felt something in her swelling and wanting him: wanting him, though he abased himself this far, saying what she wanted to hear, because she told him to. 'And?' she said.

'No, Mrs Renfrew. You say it.'

And she did. He was silent at the other end. Finally, he said, 'Well, then, you know what to do, Kristin Renfrew. So you're married. Stay married. I don't care.'

'No.' Kristin's voice grew suddenly light. 'Of course not. Why should you?'

'Well, then –'

'Because you're married yourself, aren't you, Peter?' Kristin waited, and heard nothing. She smiled. 'I've been to Crail. I've seen her. I know all about it.'

'Don't you fucking tell me you know everything! Because you don't.'

'All right.' Kristin grew still at the anger in his voice. 'I know her name and where she lives, that's all.'

'So you found out my little secret.' Peter didn't sound angry anymore.

'Why are you married if you don't live with her?'

'Well, that's a long story, Kristin.'

'You'll tell me, though. I'd tell you anything about Alex.'

He laughed again. 'But I'd guess there isn't so much to know.'

'You might be right.'

'So,' he said finally, 'when are you coming out here?'

Tasha charged up Hampstead High Street from the Tube station, on a surge of energy. She felt like singing, like dancing in the street like a character out of a Hollywood musical. Since she couldn't do that, she spent money. A bottle of wine, a hunk of cheese, a fruit tart, flowers from a greengrocer. Who said you couldn't give a man flowers?

Peter had tracked her down at last, in the office yesterday, her first day back after Edinburgh. She had been in the middle of a conversation with Adrian, too caught up to go self-conscious at the sound of Peter's voice. It had all been so easy: almost matter-of-fact. They were going to see each other again, for the first time in six years. Peter had given her directions to where he lived.

Now, as she turned in at a small street of mews houses, she glanced again at her scribbled notes. Surely she must have missed something? This was a fancy street, an expensive area. He couldn't be living *here*.

But there was the number, on the door of a tiny, thin house wedged between two others: 78b. It had one window and a sloping roof of glass above a sheer brick wall. She pressed the buzzer. The house, she decided, must belong to some friend of Peter's; mentally she prepared herself to be introduced to some stranger, to make small talk. It didn't matter. She and Peter would be alone eventually.

And then the door opened, and it was Peter. Himself; alone. He looked smaller than she remembered, and tanner, but his hair was still shaggy and the smile on his face creased his cheeks.

'Tasha!'

She fell into his open arms. Glancing up, she wondered if a kiss on the lips was appropriate. What the heck. It felt good. She pulled back. 'Hey. Long time no see.'

'Too long. How've you been keeping?'

'Oh, you know.' She followed him inside the house, and immediately started talking: about the Marlowe, the Festival, her tiny new flat in Islington. Somewhere at the back of her mind it occurred to her that Peter must know pretty much everything she had been doing all these years, because she had written him about it. But he acted as if he didn't.

He pulled her along through the narrow, dark corridor

and suddenly a space opened up all around them, bright and ceilingless, facing a wall of glass.

'Wow,' said Tasha. 'Whose house is this?'

'Mine.'

'Yours?'

'You know, leasehold, like everything in London. I own the other one, in the country, though.'

'You're kidding. I just cannot believe this. You have two houses?'

'Jesus, you're making me embarrassed.' Peter was rubbing his forehead. 'Wee boy from Glasgow makes good. Enough already.' He laid a hand on her back. 'Sit down, I'm starved, we'll eat. Christ, Tasha, you didn't. Did you bring all this?' He was emptying out the contents of the bags she had carried in with her. 'You shouldn't have. This looks amazing. Flowers! Are these tiger lilies or what? Maybe orchids. You know orchids grow without any soil or water or anything? Friend of mine collects them. He has this conservatory . . .'

And Peter was off: just like old times, Tasha thought. He would focus on any one topic for about thirty seconds, and then some wild notion would come along, some scrap of information . . . In the old days it used to be America, cars, other artists. Tasha wondered what had changed, exactly. Peter was talking about conservatories and houses and gardens. When he stopped for breath, she said, 'Funny, everybody here's so into property. They're like aghast that I'm still renting in New York. My parents wanted me to buy a place with the money I made from the play.'

'Play? Whoa, hold on a sec. What play?'

'You know! *The Interpretation of Dreams.* I was working on it with Lorenzo de Maas.'

'So are you still at that?'

'No. It's a long story.'

'So tell me.'

And he was focusing on her, leaning forward, elbows planted on the frayed knees of his jeans, nodding and prompting her with, 'Oh, aye,' and, 'You're joking,' and, 'Christ. The bastard!' And Tasha found that somehow it all came out: even the part about Lorenzo firing her. She didn't mind admitting the truth.

'Bastard!' Peter said again.

'You have such a way of saying that. Like, with your accent.'

'Scottish speciality. We've got to be useful at something.'

'So why did you come back here, after Japan? Why didn't you go back to the States?'

He shrugged. 'Worn it out, maybe. Everything was starting to seem too easy there. It's a comfortable life, but . . .' He shrugged again.

'What do you mean?'

'Tash, you're American, right? So it's hard to explain.'

'No, go on, try me.'

'It got like there was no challenge to it. Out in Seattle, people were so mellow they were halfway to the crematorium. You couldn't have a proper fight with anybody, they'd just give in. Like, I know about half the people I met out there totally hated my work. But they wouldn't say it. They wouldn't give themselves away. I could see them pretending. It was driving me spare.'

Tasha looked at him, uncomprehending. 'But they were *buying*. You had an audience, right? And you walked away from that?'

'Never mind.' He reached over and ruffled her hair. 'I'm going to make us lunch. Do you eat smoked salmon?'

'Do I eat smoked salmon?' She gave a sarcastic twist to the words. He ruffled her hair again, and grinned, and popped the cork on a bottle of something that tasted, to Tasha, suspiciously like real champagne, and while he scrambled eggs with smoked salmon in the corner of the kitchen – or rather the line of sleek black appliances at the back of the open ground floor of the house – he talked on, about Yale, which he said he just couldn't stick, since he

330

hated his boss; and Japan, where he was too much a foreigner to stay forever; and Scotland, where he had replanted himself, then started to feel restless again.

'Are you sure it's a good idea,' Tasha said, 'buying all these houses here, if you get bored everyplace you live?'

He shrugged. 'I figure you've got to try to settle sometime.' He eased the scrambled eggs out on to two plates and poured more champagne.

'So where's your other house?'

'Norfolk.'

'Norfolk?' Tasha repeated. It was a place which carried no particular associations for her. 'How come? I mean, what's your connection with there?'

He laughed. 'None. Don't know why I went there. I like the sea. Can't stick London all the time.'

'I like London. Even better than New York, some ways.'

'You don't miss your family?'

'I've practically got family here.' And she told him about the Sebergs and Nat, while they ate their way through eggs and bread and most of the fruit tart.

Afterwards, since the sky was looking clear, they went out for a walk on the Heath. Tasha watched the families running on and off the paths with their dogs; by herself here, she might have felt lonely, the odd one out. But not with Peter.

'I still can't believe I found you,' he said. 'I mean, there I was, Tasha, walking past the Marlowe Theatre, and there you were! I was just sure it was you. What do you suppose are the odds against that happening?'

'So *that* was why you called. I got your phone message. I'd actually been trying to get in touch with you, but I couldn't find a number for you anywhere.' Walking quickly, Tasha heard herself talking more and more loudly; she felt, though, as if she and Peter existed in a world of their own, brighter, more vivid than the one she saw around her: as if none of these families with their dogs would hear, or understand. 'First' – she counted off on her

331

fingers – 'I tried directory enquiries, but I didn't get anywhere. So I looked in that article – you know the one in the *New York Times Magazine*? They made a ton of mistakes, did you notice? They said something about your going to high school in Glasgow and your father being an art teacher.'

Peter was looking into the distance. 'Come again? They . . . Oh, aye.' He smiled. 'I remember now.'

'Cause you grew up in Dornoch, after all. You told us all about it at Elliott.'

'Aye, well.' He was looking at her directly now. 'You know these reporters, they just make things up.'

'So what do your parents make of it? All this success. Is it weird when you go back home?'

'Aye, well . . .' Peter rubbed his nose and looked absent for a moment; then Tasha saw him smile, switch on again. 'Ach, you know how people are. My brothers-in-law, they still work in the sausage factory, they wouldn't let me hear the end of it.'

'I'll bet. What about your sisters, then?'

'They're still in the old place, too. Both married, with kiddies. They're almost grown up now, some of them.'

Tasha had been sure he had lots of sisters: four, in fact. Oh, well, maybe he was only thinking of the married ones. 'What about –' she started to say, but Peter was pointing into the distance, at a cluster of people gathered on the grass.

'What do you think they're doing there? Rehearsing a play or something?'

So they wandered over to see what turned out to be only a couple of inept guitarists; as they were turning back towards the house, Peter said, 'I'm starving.'

'Again?'

'Did we bring any food?'

Tasha spluttered a laugh. 'No.'

'Tell you what. Let's run out of here.'

'Okay.' So Tasha grinned and took hold of his hand, and

kept up with no trouble. Her legs were long; she'd always liked running. She felt young, out of breath, her hair flying.

Within a minute or two she was gasping, and so was Peter. They stopped. She leaned against him for support – it seemed the natural thing to do – and as she did, felt his hand slide down her back underneath her denim jacket. She leaned closer and pressed her cheek against his shoulder, which was hard with muscle. Like in the old days. She allowed herself just to stand, and breathe in his smell. It had been so long.

He pulled away first, kissing her on the forehead. 'Home,' he said.

They stopped at a bakery on the way and picked up Cornish pasties, which were not Tasha's idea of a sexy meal; but she watched Peter devour two, plus most of hers, with all the old relish, and she couldn't help giggling. 'You haven't changed. I remember how you used to put away all that horrible food in the dining hall at Elliott. Stuff no one else would eat.'

And he laughed. 'Jesus, how long's it been? Ten years?'

'Eleven,' said Tasha automatically.

'Eleven. And here we are, Kristin's taking photos for posh magazines and you're designing sets on Broadway –'

'How did you know about Kristin's photos?'

'I don't actually know. Saw her name somewhere, I think. Where's she living now?'

'London. And some of the time in Wiltshire.'

'So has she got that country house she was always wanting?'

'She sure has.' Tasha didn't favour this particular topic of discussion. 'You know, I should be getting back. I've taken up your whole day.'

Peter smiled. 'Not as if I was doing much else. I'll run you home.'

She had hoped he would persuade her to stay around

333

longer, but, the words out, Tasha had no choice but to go along with his suggestion. 'Thanks.'

They climbed into Peter's car, which was low and pointy-nosed and, Tasha guessed, probably antique and worth something, though she didn't know much about cars. When the engine shuddered to a halt outside her flat, they both hesitated.

'You could come in,' she said, and turned to kiss him on the cheek. But somehow she missed, and their mouths were very near. They both laughed suddenly, at the awkwardness, and she knew that now was her time. Her chance. She planted her mouth against his.

It didn't trouble her that he didn't quite respond. She had lots of practice at taking the initiative. Men liked it.

She slid a careful tongue just inside the rim of his upper lip, and he laughed again. 'Old times, eh?'

'No,' she said, 'not old times. Now.' She tilted her head so that her hair would touch her shoulder. For a moment she wished she had the long sweep of it at her command again, as she had had at eighteen. She let her eyes linger on his. *I love you*, she thought. But there was no way she was saying that. Never. Too risky. 'Why don't you come upstairs?' she said.

'This is pretty sudden.'

'Depends on your way of looking at it.' She shrugged. 'We've known each other a long time.'

Peter looked ahead for a moment, as if thinking. Then he turned towards her, smiling. 'Well, all right, Tasha. Why the hell not?' And he crooked an arm round her neck and drew her into another kiss.

After a minute or two she slid out of his arms and led the way upstairs. As she turned on a lamp and began, matter-of-factly, to undress, he reached out and stopped her. 'No,' he said, 'let me. You have the most gorgeous body. Don't blind me all at once, eh?'

She shrugged and acceded, feeling suddenly shy. It wasn't as if men hadn't told her that before. But somehow it meant more, coming from Peter. 'Do you ever feel,' she started out, 'as if . . .' But then she lost her nerve.

'As if what?' He undid the last button on her second-hand cashmere cardigan. It fell back, revealing the bra she had bought specially the other day, an expensive one of goldeny satin and lace. She thought she saw him beam in appreciation before he kissed her through the cloth.

'As if I . . .' *As if it were meant to be*, she wanted to say. *Always. Ever since eleven years ago.* But she lost her nerve again. 'I don't remember.' She laughed. 'I've lost track of what I was saying. You distracted me.'

'Good.'

He took hold of her hands and leaned down towards the bed and she fell beneath him; but then he looked at her for a moment, considering, tracing the line of her lips and chin with one finger. Suddenly he swung back so that she was on top of him. 'Use me, Tasha. Do with me what you will.'

She laughed. 'All right.' One way was as agreeable to her as another. So he lay back and looked at her and stroked her hair while she did most of the work, letting her tongue trail a path across his chest, flicking over his nipples. 'Again,' he said and held her there. 'More.'

But she didn't mind. She had wanted for so long to have him back again, to hold and feel and smell, that she thought if her tongue traced every inch of his body, it wouldn't seem like too much.

She chose, though, to focus more particularly. She liked to hear Peter shout and curse this way. When she thought he wouldn't last much longer she climbed above him. He clung to her hips and watched her, still smiling, almost complacent as she rose and fell, except that his face had a pink sweaty sheen to it. She touched herself and arched her back and didn't mind his watching. In the end he said, 'Stop, Tasha. Tasha. It's over.'

'Oh.' She laughed and fell down beside him. 'Was it over ages ago?'

'Not really. Few seconds.' He slid an arm around her

335

shoulder and took a hank of her hair between his fingers. 'Why'd you cut it?'

'I thought I was getting too old for hair down to the middle of my back.'

'You aren't. You shouldn't have.'

'I'll grow it back.'

'Don't do that just for me.' He laughed. 'Anyway, maybe you're right. You can't get stuck in a rut just because you sort of like the way things used to be.'

Tasha felt a sudden chill cover her body. She wanted to pull up the blankets. 'I don't know . . .'

He laughed. 'I don't mean us, Tash. I mean life. Have you got any coffee?'

She leapt up, relieved. 'Brazilian? Kenyan?'

'This isn't fucking New York! I'm lucky enough it's not instant. Here, put on your robe, you'll get cold. I'll help you. Have you got anything to eat?'

'Again!'

'Engine's got to keep running.'

While she put the kettle on, wrapped up in her towelling dressing-gown, and he searched the refrigerator, Tasha thought how strange it was that eleven years could be swallowed so quickly into oblivion. That the only continuity which mattered was this.

She wondered if she had ever let herself become so cosily domestic with anyone else; probably not, she decided. But just now, with Peter, nothing could seem more natural. He drank his coffee and prowled her tiny flat, examining her stacked-up paintings and sketches: telling her which ones he thought she should exhibit.

'Exhibit? Where?' she said. 'I mean, I'd love to, but I've been so busy at the Marlowe. And I don't know anyone in the art business in London.'

'I can make a few calls for you. See who'd be interested.'

'Would you? Gee, thanks.' Tasha felt like taking a flying leap into his arms. 'That'd be amazing.'

He gave her a quirky smile. 'No big deal.'

'No.' She shrugged. 'I guess not. For you, these days.'

'Success, Tasha,' he said, 'is one step over the line from nobody wanting to know you. You could make it, and not just doing play sets. I mean the real thing. I'm not saying that just to be nice to you.'

She felt her face grow hot. 'Thanks.'

He gave her that strange smile again. 'Don't thank me.'

'All right. No thanks, then.'

'That's better.' He was gathering up his clothes. 'I ought to get home, Tash, but I'll ring you. Okay?'

Tasha nodded and beamed. Suddenly everything was going quite wonderfully.

'I didn't,' said Kristin deliberately, 'lie to him. He never asked what I was going to be doing while he was away.' Alex had flown off yesterday to Stuttgart; the journey out to Norfolk had taken half of today, by train, but she had insisted. It was just too risky to meet in London.

Above her, Peter laughed quickly. 'What? What's all this?' He propped himself up on his elbows above her, his fingers locked – dark, nicked, hairy – above the pale skin covering her rib cage. His body gave a quick jerk, inside hers.

'Peter, stop.'

'Why?' He jerked, again. 'We haven't got a lot of time.'

'I could go back tomorrow, instead.'

'Still.' He forced her chin up with one hand. 'You think I won't have fucked you five or six times by then?'

She laughed.

His hand found one of her nipples, and pinched it hard. 'You don't believe me? You'll pay for that, Kristin Ward.'

He pinched again, and that, or the rough edge to his voice when he spoke, began to make something seep and melt inside her. 'Again,' she said lazily.

'Oh, no. I don't work to order.' His body jolted, again, against hers, the rhythm accelerating.

She raised her hips slightly, against the weight of him.

337

'It's funny,' she breathed. 'I thought I could do without sex. I did for a long time, you know.'

'What about with Alex?'

'Doesn't count. I thought' – she was breathing quickly – 'if I didn't – care about it, that was the way it just had to be. That it didn't matter anyway.'

'Idiot.' He smiled. 'Of course it fucking does. Sometimes it seems like the only thing in the world. Does it seem like that now, Kristin?'

She reached up towards him, not answering, but he pinned her arms back.

'Say yes.'

She breathed out the word.

'Say it again, and look at me.'

'*Yes*.' She wanted to shout something else: to curse, or cry out with a wild animal mixture of joy and fear. She didn't, though. That would be giving in too easily.

The rain drummed on Tasha's window. She liked sitting in her one chair, beside it: the one outlook from the world of her narrow box of a flat, unless she counted the bathroom. The small terraced house, which had been carved into even smaller flats – bedsits, really – looked out on an alley filled by more of the same, in black and yellow brick. It wasn't an inspiring view, but after years of looking out on a dreary New York alley, Tasha was glad to have any view at all. And, until just recently, she would have been perfectly happy to sit in this chair, on a Sunday afternoon, and look out at it, dreaming, with only the vaguest of plans: call Nat, call Kristin, go out on her own to see a film.

But now, none of that really satisfied. She knew it was no big deal that Peter hadn't phoned her on Monday or Tuesday, the way he'd said he would. That, in fact, a whole week had passed without a word from him. He could have been called away on some urgent business, he could be busy . . .

She hoped he hadn't simply forgotten. No, he couldn't

have. Not after Sunday. As she got up to make herself another cup of coffee, the phone rang. Her heart gave a lurch, and she almost ran; then decided to wait. Keep calm, keep in control. Her machine was on.

'Natasha, honey. It's your mother. If you're there, would you mind picking up? I hate talking to these machines. . . .'

Tasha rolled her eyes and wandered into the bathroom. She knew that when she re-emerged, no matter how long she took, her mother would still be talking away. Sometimes she used up the whole tape so that no one else's messages got through.

This time, however, when Tasha wandered back into her main room, the machine was silent. Thankful, at least, for that, she looked at the clock and debated going out for a walk in the rain. But then, if she went out, the phone might ring.

Tasha, she told herself, *this is ridiculous*. In a burst of decisiveness, she dug out her address book and punched the buttons for Peter's number. Quickly. She would let it ring just eight times. Well, maybe ten. And if it was the machine, she would. . . .

'Peter Conaway.'

He had picked up in person. Taken aback, she said, 'Hi. This is, uh, this is Tasha. I hope this isn't a bad time —'

'Tasha! This is great. Where are you?'

'I'm just at home. . . .'

'Tasha, I was meaning to call you, honest. You know, about those galleries —'

'Galleries?'

'Listen, I have a friend, she has a little place in Faith Street. It's not the world's biggest, but. . . .'

'This is really nice of you. Thanks.' Tasha wondered why she couldn't work up more enthusiasm for the prospect of getting her paintings shown. Once upon a time, she would have been jumping up and down about it. Feeling oddly apprehensive, she listened to Peter talking about a woman

339

called Beryl who might be interested in seeing her work. 'That'd be great,' she said faintly.

'And, Tasha, about the other day. . . .'

Her heart sank. 'Really, it's all right, we don't have to talk about it.'

'Don't you want to?'

She thought she heard a laugh in his voice: a complacent smile.

'I mean,' he said, 'don't you ever fancy talking about it, when you're not there?'

'What do you mean?'

'I mean I get hot just thinking about you, Tasha Seidelman. Thinking about that body of yours. It drives me crazy.'

Tasha felt her face warm pleasingly. 'Gee,' she said. 'Yeah. Me, too.'

'If I could be with you now, right there, right inside your cunt –'

'What?' said Tasha. She gave an uneasy giggle.

'I said, inside your cunt.'

Tasha swallowed. 'Um, Peter, I. . . .'

He laughed. 'What's wrong?'

'I don't like that word.'

'Sorry.' He paused. 'Never mind, Tash. I guess it just came out.'

'It's just – I hate to be unliberated, but. . . .'

'I said never mind. Screw it. Or do you mind my saying that?'

'No –' Tasha wondered why Peter seemed to be in this funny mood, but before she could ask, he went on.

'So are you doing anything special just now?'

'No, not really.'

'Do you want to come over?'

Tasha was out of the door in under two minutes. She debated, for only a few seconds, changing into nicer underwear. Then she figured that getting hung up on lingerie was just a little bit kinky, like Peter's idea of phone sex, or whatever it was he'd been up to there. Well, she preferred the real thing. Out on Holloway Road she hailed a cab, thinking to herself that she would have to buy a car soon. It would make coming and going from Peter's place a lot quicker.

27 'And the next play we're working on's *The Duchess of Malfi*, I'm really excited about that, there should be room for cool sets, especially now that Adrian's got us a backer. How about you?' Tasha paused for the first time in a minute or so, forking into the warm, fluffy quiche Kristin had, somewhat surprisingly, provided, and was even more surprisingly eating herself.

'Oh, not much.' Kristin shrugged.

'How's the photography going?'

'Fine. Quite busy, really, I've been out in Norf— In Northamptonshire. And in Devon. Lovely houses, ghastly owners. Oh, and did I tell you, Alex and I bought a piano? For the country house. No room for it here. Perhaps one of us should learn to play properly. More wine?'

'No, thanks. I don't drink at lunch. It gets me woozy. Um, Kristin . . .' Tasha had been waiting and waiting for the right moment. It never seemed to come. All through September she and Kristin had planned and put off lunches together, because one or both of them turned out to be otherwise engaged. They had been on the phone a lot, but it seemed to Tasha that breaking this kind of news over the phone was wrong. 'I'm, um . . . Do you remember what I told you once, about Peter Conaway?'

Kristin's face was a model of pleasant opacity. 'That you two had been in touch? Yes, I remember that.'

'Well, I found him. I'd promised myself I wasn't really going to look. And then this weird thing happened. One day, on my answer machine at work . . . Kristin, you look strange.'

'What? Oh, sorry. Something tasted a bit off there. I hope the quiche is okay. You were going to say?'

So Tasha began, more slowly and searchingly, to talk. Kristin watched her with a face which she hoped was impassive.

'The thing is,' Tasha said at last, 'I hope you don't mind? I mean, really mind, because of, well, all that stuff that happened back at Elliott.'

Kristin gave a light laugh. 'Oh, no. That was ages ago.' She looked at Tasha, who was studying her in return with round, puppy-doggish brown eyes. There were one or two spots on her face, Kristin observed, which she would have done well to cover up. Going on thirty was rather pushing it for the makeupless look.

'Kristin, tell me the truth,' said Tasha. 'Please.'

Kristin was momentarily disconcerted. She folded and refolded her linen napkin. 'The truth? Well, the truth is, Tasha, I – worry about you.' Was that the truth? she wondered. Well, part of it. She wasn't lying. Suddenly everything had become so complicated. Again. She knew things about Peter which Tasha surely didn't, and she wondered now whether she ought to be cruel to be kind, and break all the bad news to Tasha at once. But then, that would mean landing herself in a very sticky place – for how would Tasha think she, Kristin, had come to know everything she did?

Kristin flattened her napkin again and spoke carefully. 'I only wonder if he's the sort of man who's capable of making any sort of ... long-term commitment.' She looked up at Tasha. 'I take it that's what you're looking for?'

'Well –' Tasha shrugged. 'Sure. I guess that'll come in time.'

'That's just it. Do you really think it will? Remember, he made a few promises before. Like one about meeting me in Paris. Not' – Kristin raised a hand to silence Tasha, who was looking apologetic as well as ready to protest – 'that I *mind* about that anymore. We were awfully young. But

343

you have to ask yourself if Peter's really changed. He's stayed unmarried all these years . . .'

'I don't care about *that*. I don't want to get married.'

Tasha sounded, Kristin thought, like a petulant teenager. *Grow up*, she wanted to say. But she restrained herself. Tasha talked on. Kristin heard the tones of voice, if not every single one of the words: justifying, excusing, explaining.

'Anyway,' Tasha finished up, 'I wouldn't ask him. It's a little soon.'

'Soon for what?'

'To move in with him.' Tasha spoke slightly impatiently, as if she had already said those words.

'Has he said he wants you to?'

'Well, it would make sense, wouldn't it? We live so near each other. Keeping two houses just gets silly. He's helping me get a show together, did I tell you?'

Kristin felt her heart, or some organ very near it, freeze into a stonelike lump. 'No.'

'He really, really wants to help me with my work. That's the amazing thing. He really wants me to succeed.'

A consolation prize? Kristin wondered. A kindness? A way of fobbing her off?

But she didn't know. Her earlier certainty – that Peter could only be using Tasha, playing games – was rapidly beginning to fail.

'Kristin, you don't look totally happy with all this. If you don't mind my saying so.'

'What?' Kristin gave a short laugh. 'Oh, no, I'm fine. A little shocked, of course. As you say, so much water under the bridge . . . But, honestly, I couldn't be happier. You know what? It might be fun to see Peter again. I mean all three of us, like in the old days.' Good Lord, why had she said that? She hoped Tasha would hate the idea.

'Hey, you know, maybe that'd be fun.'

'Why not?' Kristin heard her own voice answering,

344

faintly. And then she knew that she would do it: *must* do it. It would make Peter squirm. And he deserved no less.

'Peter, you shit!'

She heard him laugh uneasily at the other end of the phone. 'Guilty, Mrs Renfrew. So, all right, what have I done?'

'You know exactly what you've done. What you're doing. Do the initials T.S. give you any clue?'

'Holy shit, Kristin –'

'Bit improper of you to swear, I should think. When I'm the one who should be shocked.'

'Kristin, what has she been telling you? I meant to tell you, I swear it.'

'Peter, lay off. I know you find sex with anything that walks fairly hard to resist. You might have held off just this once, though.'

'Just wait a minute. Where do you get off, talking to me like that? You're the one who's married.'

'Peter, you're going to have to find a way out of this one. I don't much care how, but leading Tasha on like this – you're just not going to do it.'

There was a short silence at the other end of the phone line. 'I see what it's all about, Kris. You're jealous.'

Kristin forced a laugh. 'That would be far too simple. Of course I don't want to share you. Who would? But since in a technical sense I already am . . .'

'Hold on just a wee minute. What's sauce for the goose, Kristin –'

'But I've stopped sleeping with Alex.'

'I never asked you to do that.' Peter's voice was unexpectedly cool.

'Of course you didn't ask me. I wouldn't have done it because *you* wanted me to. Let's just say sex with Alex is eminently forgettable. We've both forgotten it, for the time being. It doesn't seem much of a loss.'

345

'Believe it or not, I couldn't care less what you get up to with your husband. So far as I'm concerned . . .'

Kristin gave an audible sigh. 'Obviously,' she said, 'we're never going to agree on this one. I do feel sorry for Tasha.'

'You don't care.' Peter's laugh slid into something close to a snarl. 'You know what I think? You're just weird enough, that if you thought about me and Tasha together it'd probably turn you on.'

'It's not something I care to think about.' Kristin shifted to her other foot and brushed back her hair with one hand. What she had said was not quite true. She had thought of it: had imagined it, with a stab of voyeuristic desire. Like Maine. Other people's ways of making love – in films, in photos – remained a subject of some interest to her. Interest, and mystification.

'I could be fucking three other women and you wouldn't care, Kristin. You'd probably want to know who they were, what they looked like, how they got off –'

'Stop it.'

'Are you coming out tomorrow?'

'Maybe.'

'Better say yes. I might be busy.'

'For Christ's sake –'

'If you want me to be your little whore, Kristin, and do your dirty work, you can't expect me to be a saint too.'

'All right. I'll be there.' Kristin let her voice soften. 'What do you want me to wear?'

He chuckled. 'Why not . . . something white? Like the good girl that you are.'

She hung up, thinking about tomorrow and the moment she climbed down off the train at Norwich station. She would not let Peter or Tasha spoil it for her. One way or another, they were going to drop each other. It was for Tasha's own good, anyway.

Hard to believe though it was, this Friday morning a week

into October was only the fourth time she had met Peter since August. She could, she supposed, have found ways to see him more often. They could have chanced meeting in Hampstead, for instance, but she liked the security of Norfolk. Another world. And she had to admit she rather enjoyed the elaborate arrangements of brazen lies that covered her journeys: photo assignments which turned out failures, shoots which had to be repeated. Of course, when Alex went away on business, it was easier. But almost boringly safe.

Today she only had a few hours. She and Alex were invited to the Molyneuxs' at nine tonight. Cutting it close, she thought. *So much the better.* She stood up and made her way to the door of the train as it slowed, coming into the station. She could feel the rush of air up the bare tops of her legs. She was wearing her highest heels – expensive rose suede, but inevitably tarty – and a dress that was no more than a shoulder-to-thigh-length wisp of cashmere, not really long enough to conceal the tops of her stockings when she sat down – or, should it ride up further, the panties that most decidedly weren't there. She had caught the ticket collector and two teenage boys ogling her on the train. Why, she wondered, had she not minded? Hadn't she once been shy?

Perhaps she still was, a little, because she pulled her fur coat carefully around herself as she climbed down on to the platform. The ticket collector shut the door behind her, calling out something about a safe journey.

Safe? she thought. *I'd rather it weren't.* Peter was standing at the end of the platform, frowning. As usual, he looked smaller and wirier at a distance than he did up close and without clothing. She walked along to him sedately, swinging her handbag.

'Jesus. You call that a skirt?'

'More or less,' she said, and stopped abruptly so that they collided. Peter did not bother kissing her – he knew well enough by now that, with her, it was a meaningless

347

formality – but his hands, it seemed, could not resist sliding around behind her, across the cashmere, where they met the bump of a suspender.

'You call this being a good girl?' he said, smiling.

'Pink and white.' She looked him up and down. 'Bad girls wear black. Don't they?'

'Does this mean I'm forgiven?'

'I'm not answering that.' She paused, watching him. They smiled at each other and he did not let go. 'You're turned on,' she said.

'Well, Jesus, who wouldn't be?'

'Let's go over there by that poster.' She twitched her head.

'What for?'

'A kiss.' She broke abruptly away and led him to the spot she had chosen.

'I thought you didn't like kissing,' he said, coming close to her again.

'Put your hand there. No, Peter. Up there. In.'

'Kristin.' He laughed. 'We don't need to do this kind of thing in railway stations. I have a house.'

She clung on to his retreating hand. 'No. Not yet.' She felt it relax, and tilted her head back to give him a peck on the lips. 'You know, I think kissing has its moments.'

A few hours later she told him that she was inviting him and Tasha to dinner at the end of the next week. He would hear the news from Tasha, of course, and must pretend it was a surprise.

'Sure as hell bloody is.' He sat up and ran a hand through his hair, which was damp. 'Kristin, why in God's name do you want to do this thing? How the hell am I supposed to act?'

'That's completely up to you.' Kristin studied her hands above the sheet for a moment. 'I think you told me you used to fantasise about our all getting together again. Like Maine.'

'But, Jesus, not in your house, with your husband right next to us.'

Kristin laughed. 'Alex won't have a clue what's going on.'

'Oh, I see. Just cannon fodder. So what about Tasha?'

Kristin frowned for a second. 'Have you thought of telling her about us?'

'Jesus, no. What good would it do, anyway?'

'Clear the air.'

'Any clearer and we'll be halfway up the fucking Andes.'

Kristin got up out of bed and walked to the window, stretching. She was glad nakedness had not yet become banal. She wondered when it would. Or perhaps it didn't, if you were careful and rationed it out properly. 'How long were you married to Kate?' she said. 'I mean married in the usual way. Living together.'

'What's that got to do with anything?'

'I just wondered.'

'Five years.'

'That's a long time.'

'Listen, this idea of yours about Friday night . . .'

'Did you break up because of the difference in your ages?'

'Kristin, if I want to talk about my marriage, I'll talk about it, okay? You went snooping around, I didn't know enough to stop you, but that doesn't mean I have to start answering questions.'

Kristin let out an impatient breath. 'All right. Seven-thirty on Friday. I do hope you can make it. *Tasha* sounded as if she was looking forward to it.'

'Kristin, you are sick, you know that?'

Kristin laughed. 'There's a simple way out,' she said. 'Tell Tasha you won't be seeing her anymore. After that I don't imagine she'll want to come.'

'Is that what this is all about?' Peter had got up out of bed and now he stood behind her, but didn't touch her.

Kristin heard the sound of liquid pouring and, when she

349

turned round, saw that Peter was drinking whisky out of a tumbler. She leaned back against the icy glass of the window. 'It would be better for all of us if you stopped seeing her.'

He grinned. 'Better for you, you mean. Kristin, I have to tell you this, I like her. She's a good person. And she can be pretty damned hard to resist after a few days of your mind games.'

Kristin turned her head away. 'Oh, so that's where you stand.'

He touched her cheek. 'Okay. I overstated it.'

She swallowed. 'I do mean what I said, about its being bad for all of us. The only difference with Tasha is, she's innocent. She's not cheating on anyone. You realise she might be expecting you to give her marriage? Some day, anyway.'

'I've told her I'm not getting married.'

They looked at each other steadily. 'How many women,' said Kristin, 'have heard that from precisely the men who do end up marrying them? And besides, it's not good enough. She'd probably settle for you without marriage. She wants to live with you. Are you really planning to go along with that?'

He shrugged and ran a hand through his hair again and poured more whisky. 'Look, she hasn't asked me about anything like that.'

'But she expects it.'

'I don't want to live with anyone.'

'Have you told her that?' Kristin paused. For a moment she eyed the whisky still in his glass. 'Don't you think you should go easy on that if you're driving me back to the station?'

For a second something flashed in Peter's eyes that she had not seen before: or at least she did not remember it. He tilted back the glass. 'You're pushing your luck, Kristin. Seems to me your husband can afford a cab.'

'So he can.' She spoke evenly, then turned away and

very slowly began to dress. Suspenders, stockings, bra, cashmere dress. Was it true, she wondered, that clothes were more of a turn-on for men than nakedness?

Peter smiled and turned suddenly towards her. 'Jesus, Kristin, you're a fucking tease, you know that? And you know what I'm going to do? I'm going to make you miss your train. It's the least I can do after the stunt you've just pulled on me.'

She inched back on the bed, then tried to slip sideways. But he caught her. His grip was hard around her wrist and, with his other hand, he slid the wispy woollen skirt up over her hips. 'Lie down,' he said.

'No. Peter, honestly, what am I going to do about the train?' Kristin heard her breath catch, giving her away. Her face felt hot.

'Stay the night and think up something to tell Alex in the morning.'

'I'm not very good at lies.'

Peter only laughed.

Tasha and Peter arrived nearly an hour late, by which time Alex was fuming and nearly finished with the first bottle of wine.

'*My* friends,' he said to Kristin, 'ring when they're going to be late.'

'For heaven's sakes, I'm sure they're on their way.'

'So who's this artist chap?'

'A friend of Tasha's. She asked if she could bring him along.' Kristin watched her husband pour himself another glass. 'Seriously, darling, you'd do as well to lay off that –'

Their argument was interrupted by the sound of the doorbell. Kristin ran out into the hallway to answer it and take coats. Tasha burst in first, pink-cheeked, Peter following after.

'No coat?' said Kristin, taking his hand and kissing the air by his cheek. 'You must be one of these hardy people who'd be quite happy in an igloo. They seem to abound these days, or perhaps I just have a frightfully low thermostat. Come and meet my husband.'

They drank and ate nuts, the four of them, for what seemed to Tasha like a very long time, with no sign of dinner on the way. Not even the smell of it. Kristin was bubbly, Alex taciturn, Peter unusually reserved, and Tasha wondered whatever had led her to think this was a good idea. The desire to establish her coupledom with Peter, perhaps: to demonstrate it, especially, to Kristin. A pretty childish desire, when you got right down to it. She wished the food would hurry up and come.

Just when she was beginning to give up, a small woman in vaguely servantlike garb nodded at Kristin from a doorway, and they all sat down at the table in a small alcove off the sitting room.

'So what exactly do you do?' Alex was saying to Peter.

'I'm an artist.'

'Are you?' said Kristin, and raised an eyebrow. 'How exciting. You must tell me, how does one go about it? Getting in shows and so on. Is it all dreadfully nepotistic?'

Tasha watched Peter smile at Kristin briefly, and eye her warily. 'A fair amount. It's not so different in London from what it is in Scotland.'

'Oh, is that where you come from? How silly of me, I should have been able to tell straightaway. Alex is from Scotland, you know.'

'Haven't lived there for some time,' he demurred.

'Well, they never do,' said Peter. 'Do they?'

Tasha watched him and couldn't tell what to make of his expression. Or the fact that Kristin was pretending never to have met him before. Reaching down for Peter's hand, she gave it a squeeze, for reassurance.

'Who do you mean by "they"?' said Alex.

'You know. Your professional Scot, who goes to boarding school or whatever, and comes down here and for the rest of his life goes on about how Scottish he is. Frankly, that's the sort of person that makes me sick.'

352

'I suppose you're one of these nationalists, then?' said Alex coldly.

'Darling,' said Kristin, casting her husband an admonishing look, 'whyever shouldn't he be? There's nothing in the least wrong with it. So, Peter, do tell me. Where exactly is it you come from?'

Tasha wasn't sure when it dawned on her that Kristin was virtually closing everyone out of the conversation, except herself and Peter. She had wondered already why Alex didn't seem to be in on the fact that they had all been at Elliott Academy together; now Tasha wondered why, every time she or Alex spoke, Kristin used what they had said to turn some question towards Peter: usually a question to which she already knew the answer. Tasha supposed she had never actually seen Kristin in action, as a giver of parties: perhaps this was just some kind of hypercharged hostess mode. Kristin seemed unusually excited, though, cheeks bright and pink, eyes sparkly. Once again, Tasha wished she had thought twice before saying yes to this invitation so quickly. Whatever this evening was all about, it wasn't turning out to be fun.

'So what's Glasgow like these days?' Kristin was asking, in this new, strangely gushy way of hers, over dessert.

'You mean to tell me,' Peter answered her, 'you've been married to a Scot all these years – sorry, Alex, I don't want to sound as if I'm talking behind your back . . . Anyway, Kristin, here you two are, up in Scotland two, three times a year, and you've never set foot in Glasgow!' He laughed. 'If you don't mind my saying so, that's just typical of the English.'

'I suppose' – Kristin gave an unnatural laugh – 'you wouldn't mind if I lumped all Scottish people together the same way you just did with us?'

'I don't know.' Peter looked at her evenly. 'You can do what you like with *me*.' He paused just long enough for the silence to become uncomfortable. Then he took a sip of his wine. 'Anyway, you're not totally English, are you? Your father was Hungarian or something.'

Alex looked puzzled. Kristin looked, for just a fraction of a second, as if someone had hit her in the face. Then she smiled quickly. 'I think you know more about me than you let on. Tasha, what on earth have you been telling him? Not, I'm sure, that there's much to tell. I wonder – are we all ready for coffee now? Yes? I'll speak to Hilda.'

As she disappeared, Peter went off in search of the bathroom. Tasha stood and looked aimlessly for a moment at one of the pictures on the wall, and then, disinclined to try to make conversation with a sour-looking Alex, wandered off towards the kitchen to join Kristin.

Except that Kristin wasn't there anymore: only Hilda, washing plates. Tasha heard the muted voices, which must be coming from the hallway. Quietly she made her way to the other kitchen door.

'All right,' said Peter, 'you've played me whatever way you liked for a couple of hours. So that's enough.'

Kristin laughed. 'It's no more than you deserve. Less, I should think.'

'So what do you deserve, Kristin?'

Through the door, Tasha heard a chuckle, then an inexplicable sort of murmuring. Then Peter's voice again.

'What did you tell them the other night?'

'Nothing. I made the last train, no thanks to you. Got to the Molyneuxs' in time for coffee. *He* was none too pleased.'

'You know, Kristin, I never gave a toss until now about that husband of yours, but I'm starting to feel bloody sorry for him.'

'So what do I deserve?' asked Kristin.

'What?'

'Are you going to punish me?'

'You're out of your bleeding mind.'

'Do it here, Peter.'

Tasha wanted to turn away, to run back towards the

living room, but she realised all too late that she was trapped. She heard the voices in the hall: she didn't want to hear them anymore, but she felt as powerless to go out there and confront them as she was to walk the other way and rejoin Alex.

She stood, drawing long breaths and pressing her fingers to her temples, for what seemed like an eternity.

'Are you all right, dear?' said Hilda.

'Fine.' Tasha blinked. She realised that the voices had stopped. 'Too much to drink, I guess. Better go back and join the celebrations.'

Later, as Alex was beginning to yawn and Peter – whom Kristin had more or less ignored for the last half-hour – was glancing at his watch, Tasha said to Kristin, 'Could you show me where my coat is?'

'Just through in the bedroom. I'll –' Kristin caught sight of Tasha's twitching head and meaningful look. 'Sure. I'll come with you.'

Once they were both in the bedroom, Tasha closed the door. She felt quite calm by now. 'I just want you to know,' she said, 'that as far as I'm concerned you are one weird, sick person.'

Kristin had been leaning over the coats. Now she stood, very straight, and ran a hand through her hair, considering. 'Well. It's actually all rather – complicated.'

'Oh, no it isn't. You knew I had him back, so you had to see if you could take him, too. That's all there is to it. You can't think any other way.'

Kristin blinked. 'I do see how it must look –'

'My mistake was to trust you. To think I could tell you the truth. I don't know why I ever tried to be friends with you again, after Elliott. I don't know why I bothered.'

'Tasha, believe it or not, everything that's happened tonight was for your own good. Peter's not what you think. He has – secrets.'

'Well, amazing.' Tasha's lip curled sarcastically. 'So do a few people I know.'

'But this is deep, Tasha. It's –'

'All I know is, *you* have no right to accuse him of anything.' Tasha was walking closer to Kristin. 'You bring Peter and me in here for your mind games . . . Well, what about your husband in there? Do you think about him?'

'This isn't about him.'

Tasha's eyes narrowed. 'Are you going to tell him, then? Are you guys going to get divorced?'

'Don't be ridiculous.'

'Then what's it all for? What do you want with Peter?'

'Sex.' Kristin shrugged; then shrugged again, nervously. Her eyes darted past Tasha. 'It's never been as good with anyone else. I know you won't believe me, because you think it's all perfectly easy, you've had God knows how many men –'

'I'll pretend I didn't hear that. Obviously I'm not going to get any kind of sense out of you.' Tasha threw her coat over one arm and made for the door.

'No. Tasha, wait.' Kristin came after her. 'Listen. Just for a minute. I'm trying to explain. The thing is – I've made a hash of my life. There's no undoing it. Alex and I are stuck. We have Tewne Abbot, but that's just about the only thing we have in common. And Peter . . .' She shook her head helplessly.

'Are you in love with him?' Tasha studied Kristin. If Kristin answered yes, she thought, then what she had done tonight, what she was doing, might almost seem understandable.

'No. He's –'

'You're out of your fucking mind, Kristin.' Tasha turned and walked back to the living room.

'You're quiet,' said Peter, steering the Jaguar out round a corner on to the Fulham Road.

'You would be, too, if you'd heard all the stuff I did tonight.'

'What?'

'If you'd heard' – Tasha took a deep breath – 'your best friend and the man you thought was your lover – your own, for once, not hers or anyone else's – if you'd heard them talking and doing, well, I don't know what else out in the hall tonight –'

'Tasha.' Peter sighed. He took one hand off the wheel and reached for hers. 'Christ. I'm sorry.'

'Just keep your eyes on the road, okay?'

'Tasha, it's not the way it looks.'

'I had the full sound effects, remember? I can guess pretty well what's going on. Listen, if it's Kristin you want –'

'That's what I'm trying to tell you. I don't. I don't even quite know how it happened. Or why. Just – there she was one day. She came out to the house in the country to take photos . . .'

'She never told me that. Come to think of it, you never did either.'

'It seemed like too much of a bother. Too complicated. To be honest, Tasha, that was how I found out you were working at the Marlowe. Kristin told me. I didn't see you there – not like I said.'

That silenced her for a moment. 'I see,' she said finally.

'So I called you. But you were away in Edinburgh. Then, before you got back, she came to me. She was all upset. About her marriage, or . . . Christ, you can see the type of stiff-upper-lip bastard she's married to. So, all right, I was weak. I thought, okay, just this once . . .'

'That doesn't exactly explain tonight.'

'You've got to believe me. I've only seen her two or three times, and I'm going to tell her it's all over as soon as I can.'

'So when's that?'

'Jesus Christ, don't start getting on to me.'

Tasha was silent again.

'Sorry,' said Peter. 'I shouldn't have said that.'

'Drop me off at my place, okay?'

But when they came to the street full of garages and mews houses, and he switched off the engine, neither one of them spoke or moved. Tasha looked over at him – sorrowfully, because this, after all, might be the last time she ever saw him. And she had loved him, she knew now, more surely than she had loved anyone, ever. She wished she could be wrong about tonight. Or just that she could spin back in time, to a week ago. A day ago, even . . .

Watching her, Peter reached out to stroke her cheek. Light caught the sharp bridge of his nose and the bump of his cheekbones; and suddenly Tasha had a vision of him – old, gaunt, about to die – and it was scary. For a moment she seemed to see the whole of the rest of her life pass away. She saw herself a middle-aged artist, alone. The one real love of her life come and gone.

And then she knew that she must be patient: she must trust. She must do whatever she could to keep loving it.

'Will you be all right, Tash?' Peter said, and his face approached hers.

'Peter, I'm scared. I just thought of the most horrible thing. I thought of dying . . .'

His lips silenced her, soft against hers, rough square fingers stroking her cheek.

'Just,' she gulped, through tears that she knew were coming, 'because I know it's over. It has to be.'

'Tasha, it doesn't have to be.'

And then somehow they were upstairs and in her flat, making love. Tasha clung on to Peter's body and wished the words were true. It didn't have to be over. They would find some way out of this mess; they would cling on to each other until it was all past, until they could be alone together. They had to.

Kristin thought she would go mad if she didn't speak to him soon. Yet there was no way to manage it. Alex, wired up by too many coffees, was meandering sleeplessly around the flat. Even if he did happen to go to sleep,

Kristin realised, to her own frustration, that she didn't have Peter's phone number in London, which she knew was unlisted. It had not seemed to matter before.

She pretended she was sleepy and went to bed, just to escape Alex's presence. There was nothing, nothing at all she could do, and she hated her impotence. Tasha and Peter had left together, in his car. They might have ended up at his place, or hers. She had no way of knowing.

She sat up in bed and stared into the darkness. She tried lying on her front. Then she stood at the window. Sleep would not come tonight – she knew herself too well even to hope for such an easy escape – and so, as the hours ticked by, she had time to think. More time than she needed.

Long before morning came, she knew that, rightly or wrongly, she could not bear to share Peter with anyone else. Of course, there was Kate. But Kristin could discount her.

She knew she had been telling Tasha the truth when she said she did not love Peter. It seemed to her that she knew him too well for that: neither her feelings nor his could be reduced to that banal, too common word.

If she was superior to love, then perhaps she ought to be superior to jealousy. Yet strangely, it seemed not to work that way. For she found the thought of his sharing his home with another woman, ever, quite intolerable.

Tasha wanted to be that woman. Kristin might have borne with her continuing, nagging presence, if it weren't for that. Without Tasha, the status quo could continue forever. She, Kristin, would stay married to Alex and see Peter when she chose to. *Divorce*. What an absurd idea. She didn't want to live alone or, God forbid, lose Tewne Abbot. Peter, anyway, preferred his freedom. Would Tasha finally come to realise that? And how long would it take?

For a moment, Kristin had a comforting vision of Tasha climbing on to a plane to New York. That moment – that disillusionment – would come, sooner or later. So, why not sooner? Why not very soon indeed?

28 Tasha thought that this must be war. Yet it felt more like an uneasy state of truce: of hiding behind barricades, refusing to ask questions, peeking out only occasionally to test whether the enemy was still there. And then she would wonder sometimes, disconcertingly, if the enemy was entirely who she had thought: if it really was Kristin.

One morning two weeks before Christmas, she and Peter lay upside down on the wide bed that sat in the middle of the upper loft of his house. They were watching the television downstairs in the main room, or pretending to watch, because it was too far away to see clearly. Peter flicked the remote control, and Tasha munched on a bagel.

'You'll get crumbs on the sheets,' he said.

'Mmf. Guess so, sorry. You want some?'

'I thought we'd go out for lunch soon.'

'Where? The Brasserie? Or how about if we go for dim sum?'

He laughed and flicked channels again. 'You think we're still in New York? Chinese food for breakfast . . .'

'This is when you eat dim sum. Look, forget it. We could make brunch here. I'll get dressed.' Standing up, Tasha noticed that her clothes had vanished. She was sure she had thrown them down on the floor there, the night before. 'Peter, where are my clothes?'

'At the top of the stairs.'

Tasha wandered there, naked, and found them in a neat pile at the very edge of the top step, alongside her boots. Any further, and they would have been out of the room. Out of the house. 'You don't need to bother folding up my stuff,' she said.

He shrugged. It reminded her of how she had suggested last week that she move a few useful items – a toothbrush, her favourite toothpaste and face cream – into his bathroom, instead of carrying them back and forth every time she came. In fact she hadn't suggested it, exactly, but just left them behind one time. The next time she came back she found them sitting on the kitchen table, in a sponge bag she had never seen before. She had decided not to make an issue of it. But now she wondered: why on earth did these little things – these small sharings – bother Peter so much?

In fact, she noticed now that down at the bottom of her pile of clothes lay a jumper she thought she had lost. She waved it at Peter. 'Hey, you found this. Thanks. Why don't I just leave it here, in case it gets cold?'

He turned slightly. 'Your belongings are like rabbits, Tash. They multiply.'

'Yeah, well, I'm always losing track of things.'

'Spoilt New York brat that you are.' Peter reached out a hand to summon her. 'Come on over here. Don't get dressed. Let me have a feel.'

'But, really, Peter –' He was nuzzling against her still-uncovered breasts.

'That's what used to drive me crazy about you,' he murmured. 'I thought I was in dreamland. I mean, who was I? A boy from Dornoch. Shagging this luscious girl from the Upper West Side. Perfect hair, perfect teeth. Rich parents. Not a care in the world.'

Tasha smiled and stroked his hair. 'I wish. I've been broke ever since I left college.'

He laughed. 'Your sort's never really skint.' A few seconds later, he drew back. Tasha's body followed his. 'Right,' he said. 'The Brasserie, then? I'm starved. Got an appointment at three.'

'An appointment?' This was the first Tasha had heard of it. She had been counting on the whole day together.

'Aye.' He touched her nose. 'And it's for your sake, it's with Beryl.'

'From the gallery? So shouldn't I maybe meet her?'

'Sure, sometime. She can be funny about getting on with other women, though. Better if I pave the way.'

Tasha didn't like to go on endlessly questioning, but it did occur to her that Peter had had a meeting with Beryl just last week. How many meetings did it take? Was he really meeting her again today?

'Where're you going, Tash?'

She had left him behind on the bed and wandered towards the loft railing. 'Just tell me the truth. I promise I won't get mad. Is it Kristin you're really seeing?'

'Jesus, how many times do I have to tell you I see her as little as I possibly can? Look, I'd stay out of her way totally except she keeps ringing me up. She rings me up with her husband in the other room, for Christ's sake! I don't want him coming after me with a loaded shotgun or whatever it is these tight-arsed English buggers like to use on the men who've been –' Peter cut off suddenly. 'Never mind.' He was standing at the railing beside her, now. 'You know, you make me feel like a bloody criminal with all these questions.'

'Okay.' She turned to face him. 'But just tell me the truth. How many times have you seen her since that dinner party?'

His eyes flicked away. 'Once. Well, twice, I guess.'

'Is that really all? Do you swear, Peter?'

He turned and smacked the railing with his hand. 'Jesus, do we have to keep going over and over this?' He turned around and started hauling clothes out of a chest of drawers. 'I'm getting dressed, right? And then we're going to go out, and try to have a halfway fucking decent meal, if you can stop pestering me with bloody questions.'

For a moment Tasha felt like storming out: *Forget it! I'm going home*, she would say. With anyone else, that was exactly what she would have done. But with Peter, she was afraid of going away angry. She could slip out of his life just so easily. Kristin was there, waiting to replace her.

She supposed that, before, she had never cared about the long term. She had always been aware of other men's deficiencies. She didn't like to think of these new sides she was discovering to Peter as deficiencies, exactly, though. His strange need for privacy; his sudden flares of temper. It was all Kristin's fault, really. If it weren't for her, they would never argue. He would see what was so clear to Tasha: that they were a couple. That they should live together; that it was, in a way, inevitable. She just wished there were some way of making him realise that *now*.

'You think he'd do it? Go along with it?' Nat sat on Tasha's floor, eating his way slowly through a quarter of a pecan pie.

'Nat, it's totally brilliant. Of course he will. I'll make him. Do you really think they'd do the feature on, like, the two of us as a couple?'

Nat shrugged. 'That was what Julia said they wanted.'

Tasha leaned over and gave her brother an impulsive hug. 'This is just too great. I didn't know you ever met British reporters.'

He shrugged lazily. 'Sometimes. It's one big club.' Then, spearing a stray pecan, he frowned. 'I just want to know, though. Is he really worth all this anguish?'

'Anguish? It's not anguish. We're happy together.'

'Tasha, you're saying that, and yet he spends half his time with your best friend –'

'Not half his time. Just as little as he can see her. He wants to let her down gently.' Tasha looked earnestly at her brother. 'If you'd ever met Kristin, you'd probably understand what I mean. She's a very mixed-up person. She's married to a creep. She wants babies but she can't seem to have any. She thinks Peter's the answer to her problems, but he isn't . . .'

'Frankly,' said Nat, 'I have no intention of meeting this

woman, ever. And I just don't want her problems to become yours, okay? I thought all this ended years ago, at Elliott. It should have, Tash. You're in over your head.'

'Says who? The emotional cripple? The guy who used to have hundreds of women after him and now won't even date?'

Tasha stopped suddenly. She watched Nat; she half-expected him to throw her out – tell her to get lost.

Instead, he only gave a wry, sad smile. 'You know, I wonder if the two of us'd be happier if we'd just lived about fifty years ago and let our parents matchmake for us.'

'Ugh.' Tasha laughed. 'Don't say that. The Sebergs are trying anyway. They keep talking about fixing me up with some orthopaedic surgeon.'

Nat laughed and Tasha gathered up their plates.

'You could do worse,' he called into the kitchen.

'Yeah, so could you.' Tasha turned on the tap and watched as the remains of their lunch, and, it seemed, their argument, vanished away with the running water.

'I don't know, Tash.' Peter frowned at her over his plate of fried dumplings. 'I really don't like to have the house filled up with photographers. It stops feeling like my own.'

'Right.' Tasha looked at him levelly. 'So Kristin was an exception?'

'*Décor* kind of caught me off guard.'

'Just one shot, Peter. They're not doing it for the pictures, it's really just an article about us and what we do on weekends.'

'And this is some friend of your brother's?'

He was proving harder to convince than Tasha had guessed he would be. She bit off the end of her spring roll. 'Yeah, she's really nice.' Well, she hoped the reporter would be. She had never actually met her.

'We don't spend weekends in Norfolk, Tash. You've never even been out there.'

'So? I want to. I'll drive my car.'

'Since when did you get a car?' Peter was instantly diverted. 'What kind?'

Tasha giggled; she could see him virtually panting for the keys. 'Don't get too excited. It's, like, an ancient Mini.'

'First car I ever owned was a Mini. What registration? Seriously, I'd better have a look at it before you start thinking about taking it out of the city.' Peter was polishing off his dumplings in gigantic bites. 'So how much did you pay?'

Tasha told him.

'Jesus. Too much. You should have asked me first.'

Tasha supposed, then, that he had accepted her proposal about East Hingham. At least he was no longer fighting it.

The photo session went well. Tasha spent twenty minutes putting on makeup, which was unusual for her, and Peter murmured into her ear, in between the reporter's questions, that she looked sexy as hell and he couldn't wait for these magazine people to leave so they could be alone together.

A few hours later, when Tasha's makeup was a good deal more smudged than it had started out, they went for a walk around the house, through the sculpture garden and towards the village. Tasha wanted to try out the pub there, but Peter said that wasn't a good idea, the food was bad and the landlord long-winded. It was a cold day, but Tasha could still smell the sea. 'I could get to like the country,' she announced, pulling in a great breath of air.

They went back into the house and mixed up a lunch out of tins and dried things, or rather Peter did, spaghetti and anchovies with overwhelming amounts of garlic, and it reminded Tasha of the old days. 'I thought you'd gotten more sophisticated,' she said. 'I remember this time when I was sitting on your floor at Elliott and drinking your wine and thinking, "This is the life", and, you know, it was great because it was, like, the first time at that place that I'd ever really felt like a grownup.' She was about to go on, but the phone rang.

Peter ducked away to answer it, and she didn't much mind his absence at first. There were objects all around to intrigue her: a Calder mobile – only it couldn't be, she would have to ask him about that when he came back – and chairs that looked like sculptures, and a stack of books in Japanese on the living-room floor, filled with beautiful plates of old calligraphy.

She got bored on her own eventually, though, because Peter was taking ages. She wandered down the hallway that led towards the bedroom, and then something in his voice stopped her in her tracks. It sounded low and rough, close to a whisper.

'Of course I do, Kristin. I want to f— you silly.'

Tasha's ears seemed to obliterate the word. She didn't want to hear it. She wasn't hearing it.

Finally the phone clicked down. Peter walked out of the room. He gave a start, seeing Tasha.

'That was Kristin?' she said.

He didn't meet her gaze. 'I feel like a drink. You want one?'

Tasha couldn't help feeling that something dread, momentous, was about to happen, and yet when Peter returned to the bedroom with a glass in his hand, he just stood by the window, saying nothing. Tasha lay down on the unmade bed.

'Sorry,' he said.

'This just goes on and on.'

He didn't answer.

'You know,' said Tasha, 'one of the reasons I don't just give up, is . . . I asked Kristin a while ago if she loved you. And she said no.'

Peter smiled.

How can he smile at that? she thought. 'Don't you care? She's just using you. She's never going to leave Alex. And you might think she's crazy or going to hurt herself or something, but sometimes I think she's as sane as anybody I know. Only more selfish. Why don't you just drop her?'

He shrugged and came over to stroke her back. 'I'm not awfully good at all this, Tasha.'

'Is it' – Tasha struggled with the thought, then admitted it – 'because you think of both of us together? You can't imagine being with me, and not her?'

He sighed. 'That might be part of it.' He ruffled her hair and bent down to kiss her head. 'Tash, you've been good to me. I don't want you to hate me.'

'I don't want to hate you either.' Tasha heard the tears behind her voice. 'I'm not going to blame you for what's really her fault.'

Again, Peter didn't answer.

On the first Sunday of the new year, Kristin was sitting in her kitchen at Tewne Abbot when she saw the article. As her eyes lit on it, her whole body went rigid. There could be no mistaking the place, or the people: the room with the wide window on to the sculpture garden. Peter and Tasha.

'Kristin, dear, how do you like it?'

It took Kristin a second to remember that her mother-in-law was still in the room. Margaret Renfrew smiled at her over the holly branches she was arranging in a vase. 'It was a bit of a scraggly plant, before, but now I think it looks rather festive.'

'Oh, yes. Lovely.' Methodically, Kristin folded the magazine in front of her, to hide the page that had been visible. Out in the sitting room, she knew, Alex and his brother Angus were competing over some New Year's news quiz; Geordie was out for a walk. It had been a slow torture, this Christmas: not so different from all the others before, but longer. She hadn't been able to speak to Peter, not even once. He had told her that he was going to be up in Scotland, with friends, where there wasn't a phone. Kristin had accepted this. She hadn't asked the questions that preyed on her mind. *Kate. Tasha.* He must be with one of them. She was the only one condemned to this marital misery . . .

Margaret made her way into the next room, carrying the vase, and cautiously Kristin unfolded the magazine.

Sunday Morning with:
PETER CONAWAY AND
TASHA SEIDELMAN
photo: Jane Harley

> Sundays find sculptor Peter Conaway and his stage-designer partner, New Yorker Tasha Seidelman, ensconced in Conaway's avant-garde country cottage in Norfolk. 'No,' Peter laughs, 'it's not at all your typical country cottage. Bauhaus-on-sea, more like.' Born in Glasgow in 1955, he first met Tasha, now 29, during a stint as artist-in-residence at the New England boarding school where Seidelman was a pupil. Encountering each other again, last year in London, they both thought . . .

Kristin felt like gagging. She forced down a mouthful of cold coffee. What galled her most of all was that the Norfolk house was *hers*. *Her* preserve: and Tasha had invaded it.

From the sitting room she heard a shout of exultation. Alex had probably trumped Angus at the quiz. She needed to go out. If only she had a number to dial, she would have been willing, just now, to walk miles to a phone box – if only to be able to imagine rousing Peter and Tasha from their cosy nest, wherever they were. They didn't deserve to be happy. They didn't deserve to waltz off together. Not while she was stuck here, where nothing could change . . .

She knew that all this hatred was wrong. That once she had cared about Tasha – that, somewhere deep down, she still did. But Tasha might have held back from gloating this way. Not while Peter didn't belong to her. When he wouldn't, ever: because he would always be Kristin's, too.

'You look pale, darling.'

Silently, Kristin pushed the magazine page across the restaurant table towards Diana.

'So who is this?' She gave it a quick look, frowning.

'That's Peter. And that's her.'

'You aren't serious.' Diana squinted, then fished her reading glasses out of her handbag. Quickly she scanned the article. '"Seidelman,"' she quoted, '"a neo-realist painter as well as the acclaimed set designer for the Broadway hit *The Interpretation of Dreams*, shares an exhibition next month with two other artists at the Faith Street Gallery. She is also working on an ambitious new *Duchess of Malfi* at the Marlowe Theatre . . ."'

Kristin winced. 'Yes, yes, I know, I've read it.'

'*I've* never heard of her. Is all this true?'

'I suppose so. Funny how some people's careers take off when they start sleeping with the right men.'

A waiter hovered, but when he saw that both women were ignoring their menus, he wandered off again. 'I do worry about you,' Diana said. 'Has Alex guessed?'

'Oh, he's too wrapped up in his latest takeover.' Kristin waved a careless hand.

'But are you going to break the news to him? I don't see how this sort of situation can go on forever.'

'I want her out of London.'

'Kristin, this other girl's not really your problem.'

'I don't care. She'll go back to America eventually. I want her to go *now*.'

Diana sighed and gave Kristin's hand a brief pat.

'Diana, I know you don't owe me anything really.' Kristin looked away, blinking; she didn't feel particularly tearful, but she knew she might just sound that way if she made a small effort. 'In fact I owe you all kinds of things, I know that. But – the woman who owns the Faith Street Gallery . . .'

'Beryl Stanwicke?'

'You know her, don't you?' Kristin looked up hopefully now. 'After all, you seem to know *everyone*.'

Diana laughed. 'Well, yes, I do know Beryl, though I can't say I've ever had a great deal of time for her.'

'So then . . .' Kristin held her breath. She knew Diana had clout: that a mention, or even better, a good review in *Décor*, would count for more to this Beryl person than the gratitude of a fledgling artist.

Diana's finger batted the magazine page. 'I don't see what you have to fear from *her*. Unless your Peter likes the blowsy sort.'

Kristin smiled, reassured.

'And I do wonder why we keep on being lumbered with all these Americans. I'll see if I can get hold of Beryl.' Diana picked up her menu, and Kristin knew that was the end of the topic, for better or for worse. 'Now, Kristin, are you eating fish these days? The sole *meunière* here would cheer you up immensely.'

'They're what?' Peter looked stunned. 'They're cancelling you?'

Tasha only nodded. There were tears in her eyes, but she was doing her best to contain them.

'They can't do that. It's totally ridiculous. There'll be something in your contract.'

Tasha looked fearful. 'I never exactly had a contract.'

'Never mind, Tash, we'll sort this out. I'll talk to Beryl.'

'I've tried. She's out of town.' Tasha paced over to Peter's fridge. She felt like laying siege to the chocolate cake that was sitting on the top shelf, but, thinking for a second of how she would look, consuming it, not to mention the effect on her complexion, decided against it. God, it was hard sometimes, keeping up appearances.

371

'Well, we'll go over to Faith Street and lean on their doorbell, if we have to.' Peter sounded indignant.

'I don't think it'll do any good.' Tasha sniffed. 'And now I've got all these paintings on my hands, that I got my parents to ship over. I can barely walk in my apartment . . .'

Peter put his arms around her. 'You can bring them here.'

'Really?' Tasha looked up through her tears. It was the first time he had ever offered to accommodate any of her belongings.

'Sure. And, believe me, when Beryl gets back, I'm going over to Faith Street personally to wring her neck.'

Tasha felt cheered, slightly, by his loyalty.

'Anyway,' he said, 'you've got the *Duchess* opening next month. They'll feel right idiots at Faith Street if that's a hit.'

'If it isn't' – Tasha smiled and wiped her eyes – 'the Marlowe'll want to sue me. Adrian says this is the most money they've ever spent on a play.'

Peter put his arms around her. 'Got to bet big to win.'

'And to lose.' Tasha sniffed again.

'Pessimist.' Peter smiled, and they stood holding each other. If it weren't for the times like this, Tasha thought, she would almost give up. But she wasn't going to. If she held out, she could have this forever.

The play opened at the beginning of February. Tasha looked forward to the day, and dreaded it too. It seemed so long, now, since she had sat behind the stage of *Dreams* and prayed it would not fail. Then, her work had meant everything to her. It was funny how, for all the time she had spent on the *Duchess*, painting flats and sorting out costumes and rehearsing lines with actors, none of it seemed to mean so much to her now. Once again, she sat in the wings: this time, it was with her stage-manager's book on a desk in front of her, so she couldn't let her attention flag for a moment. When the curtains closed after the first act, Adrian Joseph loped across the floor towards her.

'Tash, I think the sky in your left hand castle window's too bright. It looks different from the right one.'

'Well, that's where the sun's supposed to be.'

'No, it's more than that.'

'Well, maybe it's the lights. I'll talk to Mike.'

'Tash.' Adrian was still nervous; she had grown used to his first-night anxieties. 'I don't think it's the lights . . .'

Tasha did her best to talk down his misgivings. A few minutes later, the gong sounded for the end of the interval, and she heard the audience filtering back in. At the end of the play, there would be the opening party. She hoped Peter would make it. He had said he would try.

She followed the second half of the play now, turning the pages in her book, wishing she could duck her head around the front of the stage, just for a second, to check those windows. She had been trying to show the brilliant light of the Bay of Naples beyond the darkness of the palace where the play was set. Now Adrian's last-minute doubts nagged at her. She would have to ask Peter his honest opinion – if he was there.

Soon, to her relief, it was all over. The curtain calls, the applause, rising and dwindling, the actors rushing in from the stage on an adrenaline high, chattering, kissing. Tasha knew they would take a while to filter through to the lobby, where the party was being held, so she ducked into the bathroom to splash some water on her overheated face. She wished she had brought a change of clothing with her: too late. Peter was just going to have to see her as the drab backstage hand she was.

When she went out to the lobby, she didn't see him at first; Adrian asked her to entertain a couple of female journalists. Chatting away, she glanced into the crowd past their shoulders. Peter still wasn't there, but a flash of gold caught her eye, and she heard a familiar, flutelike laugh.

'Oh, Aje. Don't fret so. Of course it was wonderful.'

Tasha couldn't help staring. Kristin, who stood with a hand still on Adrian's shoulder, was wearing a long, long-sleeved, gold-spangled dress. She was more dressed up than anyone else in the room – ridiculously so, Tasha told herself – and yet Tasha couldn't keep her eyes off her. Nor, she supposed, could many of the men in the room. Alex seemed not to be in attendance.

She saw Adrian whisper in Kristin's ear again; saw Kristin give a bemused smile as Adrian led her across the lobby. They were coming this way. Quickly Tasha tried to duck away, but she realised she was trapped in a throng of people.

Adrian was waving. 'Ah, here you are, Tash.'

Kristin glanced from side to side, as if looking for an escape; then her eyes met Tasha's and she gave a careful smile. 'Yes, here she is. Thank you, Aje.'

All too soon, Adrian had slipped back into the crowd. Tasha turned her head, searching desperately for her two journalists, but they, too, had vanished.

'Well,' Kristin said, 'I don't see why I shouldn't congratulate you.'

The words caught Tasha off-guard. She groped for an answer.

'Everyone around me was saying how clever it was, to have sunlight out of one window and twilight from the other. Most inventive. I could have told them that your talents were much overrated, but I didn't see that I needed to.' Kristin paused to adjust the chunky gold bangle on one wrist. 'After all, Beryl Stanwicke must have figured that out for herself.'

'The theme of the show changed,' Tasha managed, through gritted teeth.

'Well, yes, darling, or perhaps she needed reminding who her real friends were.' The bangle twisted and turned.

'It needn't have happened, but you would push your luck.' Kristin met Tasha's puzzled gaze. 'That Sunday magazine piece last month. So cosy. I liked the touches about East Hingham, when you'd never been there before.'

'You don't know –' Tasha started out, prepared to lie.

Kristin raised a hand as if to silence her. 'Oh, but I do. Peter told me you'd never been there before then. That it was all harmless publicity. Which I was prepared to accept' – Kristin broke off, to wave at someone in the crowd, with a dazzling smile – 'except that it involved you. Presumptuous, I would say. Pretending you share that house. You're never going to, Tasha. He's never going to let you move in with him.'

'That is none of your business.' Tasha finally found the words that had lain jumbled in her brain, beneath the outrage. 'And you have no business coming here and ruining my opening night.'

'Adrian's my friend, too,' Kristin interjected. 'And I should bear in mind, if I were you, that he and I will be here a lot longer than you. And so will Peter. We belong here. You don't. Why don't you just go back home, Tasha?'

'Maybe I feel like staying.' Tasha stretched her arms out in front of her, cracking her knuckles. It was a gesture which used to make her feel strong, macho, but it seemed to have no effect on Kristin.

'I don't see why you should, when you're unwelcome. Beryl didn't kick you out of her show because of any silly theme change. She did it because I wanted her to. I have friends here, Tasha. You should remember that. Whereas you really have no one.'

'I have Peter.'

'So where is he tonight?' Kristin glanced around. She caught sight of another acquaintance; gave another smile, another wave. Then she laid her hand on Tasha's arm. 'When you read the reviews of this play, remember: I have friends. We're all friends, here in London, those of us who

375

belong. And we don't really owe you any favours, do we now, Tasha?' Kristin removed her hand, studying her fingers for a moment. 'I know you spent a bomb on this play. Adrian told me. More than the Marlowe can afford to lose. Am I right?' She smiled briefly. ''Bye.' Squeezing Tasha's arm quickly, she was off.

All at once Tasha felt like going home: escaping. But Adrian grabbed her as she was making her way towards the dressing rooms. 'Darling! We've hardly got started.'

'I'm not feeling too well.' But, glancing around again, Tasha saw that Kristin was at the door, putting on her fur coat to leave. For a second she wondered if Kristin had come all this way specifically to torture her.

'Come on back, Tash,' said Adrian. 'I think what you need is a drink.'

Since Peter was still nowhere in sight, and she had nothing in particular to look forward to, except going home to her empty flat and wondering whether to ring him – wondering where he was tonight, if he couldn't even make it to something as important to her as this – Tasha followed Adrian back in.

Kristin flagged down an empty cab a few yards from the theatre, relieved that at least she would be home soon now. Tonight had hardly been an unqualified success.

She supposed she ought to be glad Peter had not turned up. Tasha would be disappointed. She must have been sure he would come to her opening. That was why Kristin had decided to go: not so much to speak to either one of them as to hover, luminescent, discomfiting, at the edge of their vision. They could not celebrate without her: they could not forget her. They had no right.

Still, she had taken the wind out of Tasha's sails. And about time, too. Tasha wouldn't be putting any further failures down to bad luck, now. Kristin knew well that she had been pushing it – hinting that she could influence theatre critics the way she had influenced Beryl Stan-wicke. But the important thing was that Tasha should believe she could.

Alex was still out at work when Kristin got home, so she rang Peter's Norfolk number. She was preparing herself to plant some casually perverse message on his machine when he picked up in person.

'Conaway. Whoever this is, you woke me up.'

'Peter. Sorry. But, wait a minute, you don't go to bed this early. What are you up to?' Kristin paused. 'Or are you in hiding?'

'Working, believe it or not. Some of us do have to work for a living.'

'The less you do, the more they'll want you, darling. Did you forget all about Tasha's opening?'

'Christ, that. How'd you know I wasn't there? Did you go?'

'For a bit.'

Peter laughed. 'Then I'm glad I didn't make it. Don't think I could face that particular – scene. Like another one of your dinner parties.'

'Are you all right?' Kristin frowned into the receiver. 'You sound drunk.'

'Mildly. Slightly. So how was it tonight? Did you two speak? You on speaking terms these days?'

'If we aren't, you know exactly why. When are you going to stop stringing her along, Peter?'

'I'm not getting into this, Kristin. I'm tired.'

Annoyed at herself for having broken her cardinal rule – not to nag – Kristin contemplated the silence. 'Well. Sweet dreams,' she said, and heard Peter grunt assent and hang up.

Nothing about tonight was going quite the way she had planned it.

'Read the next one,' Tasha demanded. 'I can't do it.' She was spreading cream cheese on a bagel and layering it carefully with smoked salmon. She was superstitious. If the reviews were bad, she wanted something good to eat while she heard them, to soften the blow.

'"An enigmatic interpretation,"' Peter began.

'No, no. You read that one already, remember? Try the one underneath.'

Peter sighed. Then he started to rattle off the headline and the words. '"Christopher Stephens's Bosola . . ."' he read on.

'That's all the stuff about the actors. What does it say about the sets?'

'Hold on, hold on, let me get there. ". . . an expensive new production, whose poorly balanced sets by Broadway import Natasha Seidelman rather overwhelm the small stage . . ." Tash, are you sure you want to hear this?'

'Yes.' She gritted her teeth and closed her eyes. This was the second bad review. And the others hadn't mentioned the sets at all. At all. Was it deliberate?

Peter went on. '"Though the notion of bestowing a supernumerary sun upon the Amalfi coast is an original one . . ."'

'Oh, no! Not that about the windows again.'

'What happened with the windows, Tash? Could be they just don't understand your idea.'

'Nope.' Tasha munched her bagel glumly. 'I made a mistake. I got the perspective wrong. I thought I'd looked at the thing a hundred times, but I missed it somehow. Some great realist I am.'

Peter came over and put his arms round her. 'Just you forget it. These reviewers don't know anything. Folk who see the play won't even notice the windows.' He paused. 'So what happened, Tash? You're usually so careful.'

'I don't know.' Tasha stared at the reflecting surface of her coffee. She couldn't say it to Peter, but she knew exactly how the sets had gone wrong. Because she was in charge, and Adrian was famously nearsighted – because the lighting people, who were answerable to her, probably hadn't dared mention anything that looked wrong . . . And the actors never saw the sets from far away; and nor had she. At least not often enough. Her mind hadn't been on them – not a hundred per cent. And she hated to think why.

'Want me to read any more?' said Peter.

'Not just now.' She wondered if what Kristin had said was true. That she could make sure Tasha got bad reviews, whether she deserved them or not. 'I'm depressed,' Tasha said.

Peter stroked her back. 'Anything I can do to make you feel better?' His fingers wove in through the roots of her hair and rubbed the base of her neck.

She buried her face against his shirt. 'If you mean the usual, I'm not sure I'm up to it.' She gave a helpless laugh. 'For once.'

'Ach, why not? It might help.' Peter smiled, and brushed a tear away.

Soon, inevitably, they were joining, shedding clothes, stroking each other. Tasha felt the pace of her heartbeat quickening. She wished she could dissolve all her worries this way. Her body always answered his; she felt her skin thrill to his touch; she murmured and cried out. And then everything went quiet, and she knew nothing had really changed.

Peter said, 'Any better?'

'A little.' Tasha turned on her side to look at him. 'Listen, I've been wondering. I have an idea. Would you like to come back to the States with me?'

Peter's expression didn't change; he didn't speak, either.

'I'm beginning to feel like I don't belong here.'

'Why do you think that?' He reached down to twist a lock of her hair around his finger.

'I think you know.'

He was silent.

'She wants me gone. She is making me very uncomfortable.'

'You'd go back because of that?' Peter looked mildly disapproving.

'Not just that. I feel like I'm in limbo here. My six-months' lease on my flat is almost up. I could renew, but, well, it's expensive, and my visa only lasts me till June . . .' Tasha drew a deep breath. 'Peter. Have you ever thought about whether we should move in together?'

He frowned; rubbed his forehead. 'Tasha, that's a big step.'

'I know. But, look, we're together a lot anyway. And we wouldn't have to be in the same place all the time. I wouldn't get in your way, I promise.'

Peter raked his hands through his hair. 'That's not the problem. Not exactly.'

'Then what is? Is it Kristin?'

'For Christ's sake, no. She's out of the picture. Forget her.'

'You're afraid I'm trying to drag you into marriage. Look, I don't want marriage. I don't care about that.'

'What'll you do when your visa runs out, then?' Peter gave a thin smile.

'Oh, go back to the States for a while or something. Get another. I'll sort it out. Look, my problem just now is really with my flat and the landlord.'

'I'd . . . need to clear some space.'

Was that a yes? Tasha's heart jumped. 'You don't have to clear space. I hardly have any stuff with me. And I'll try not to mess up your place, either. I'll be really neat. I promise.'

He squeezed her round the shoulders. 'Sure, and Scotland'll win the Cup.'

'Huh?'

'The World Cup. We're already out of it. Never mind.'

Tasha smiled. This was like the old days: Peter talking about unfamiliar things – unfamiliar, because she had been young then, and American, and he had seemed so engagingly foreign.

He didn't anymore. She almost missed that. She wondered now what new things she might still find out about him, once they moved in together. And when that would be: he hadn't mentioned a date. She decided, just now, not to ask, not to press him. He had said she could move in. That was enough.

At first, she did not worry when Peter was unreachable for almost two weeks. She was busy at the theatre; the *Duchess*, unfortunately, was running out of steam fast. Adrian had hoped to get a couple of months' run from her, but now he was talking about closing. When Tasha started to blame herself, he told her not to worry: sets never made or broke a show.

'But I spent more money than anyone,' Tasha reminded him in an agonised voice.

'True. So you did,' he said equably, and went off to make some phone calls, leaving Tasha to mull over everything that was going wrong. The lease on her flat was due to end in the middle of March. She had had two letters from the letting agency asking if she wished to extend, but she kept putting off answering them. She just had to track Peter down, soon. She had even contemplated driving out to Norfolk, just in case he was out there working, with the phone off the hook. But for some reason, she couldn't bring herself to do it. She didn't know what she might find there.

Kristin.

She had not hated Kristin before: not absolutely. But, after that night at her opening party, she did. She had half-believed, before, that Kristin might have been trying to protect her, whatever bizarre form that protection took. Now she knew Kristin was just out for herself.

The wrecker. The deliberate, selfish wrecker: snarling up other people's lives without the least concern. What about Peter himself? What about Tasha? And poor old Alex?

Tasha had never been exactly crazy about Alex, but she was beginning to feel sorry for him now.

She was sketching desultorily in her office one afternoon when Adrian ambled in and sat down beside her.

'Hi,' she said. 'Want to see these?'

'Are you busy just now, Tasha?'

'Not really.'

She looked up and half-turned her chair towards Adrian. He had an odd, shifty look on his face.

'Tasha, I hate to have to tell you this,' he said.

'What?' She frowned.

'You know . . . we've been in financial straits. The *Duchess* hasn't helped.'

'Aje, I know. I wish . . .'

'I'm sorry, Tasha, but you know your job here was never permanent. I'm afraid it's going to have to end.'

'Oh.' Tasha felt as if he had punched her in the stomach. 'I see.' She took a deep breath. 'Look, if it'd help you could pay me less.'

Adrian studied the ground. 'That's not – exactly the point. This is – I'm sorry, it's awfully unpleasant.'

More unpleasant for me, thought Tasha, but she held her tongue. And then it dawned on her. 'This is something to do with Kristin, isn't it? She's put you up to this.'

'No,' Adrian said. He was still looking firmly at the floor.

'Look, Kristin and I may not be the best of friends anymore, but that's nothing to do with me and my work here. I don't know what she's told you . . .'

Adrian looked up, then sideways. 'You might at least have told me, Tasha. About that business in New York. To be honest, I did wonder why you'd left *Dreams* so suddenly.'

'Wait a sec. What business?'

'Look, it's all old news. I know the sums involved weren't very large on a Broadway scale . . .'

'Adrian, I don't know what Kristin's told you, but I *didn't do anything wrong*.'

382

But he was looking at her in open disbelief. 'Tasha, you've done good work here, but enough is enough. It's not worth fighting. Your visa's up in less than six months anyway.'

Tasha knew when she was defeated. She didn't know what Kristin had told Adrian. Nor did it really matter. Any half-baked story would do: some petty misdemeanour . . .

She had thought she and Adrian had become friends in these last few months. But obviously they weren't as good friends as Adrian and Kristin. They hadn't spent their childhood together; they didn't exchange whispers and kisses at openings. Kristin's words came back to Tasha again. *We belong here. You don't.*

They were getting harder and harder to fight.

The pub was half-empty. Tasha guessed, from the high round tables and stools, that it used to pretend to be something more sophisticated, a wine bar maybe, but now it looked neither here nor there, and she wondered why Alex had named it as the place they should meet. Probably, she decided, because he didn't want to spend more than the bare minimum of money or time on her, and this sort of place limited both.

She sighed, annoyed. It wasn't as if she was exactly looking forward to this encounter either, but it was necessary. Just as she was glancing around the walls in search of a clock, she noticed a tall, bespectacled figure ducking in through the doors. Alex headed to the bar, claiming two glasses of white wine, and then came to Tasha.

'Sorry I'm late,' he said, pushing a glass in her direction. What, thought Tasha whimsically, if I hadn't wanted wine? However, she did, very much at this moment. She took several quick gulps.

'Thanks,' she said.

'So what was it you wanted to see me about?'

'Alex, do you know that . . .' This was harder than Tasha

had thought it would be. 'That Kristin – she's seeing somebody.'

Alex's expression did not alter. He pushed his spectacles higher on to his nose. 'I see.'

'I thought you ought to know,' said Tasha lamely.

'Well. I expected something of the sort.'

'Oh.' Tasha drained her glass. 'Don't you, um, mind?'

Alex studied the small spill of wine that remained to him. 'No, not really. Rather, I mean – yes, for God's sake, of course I mind. Tasha, why are you asking me all this? I fail to see that it's any of your –'

'Alex, do you remember the man I brought to your house a couple of months ago? Peter Conaway?'

Alex nodded slightly.

'He's the one.'

Alex nodded again. 'I see. You feel she's – stolen him from you.'

He sounded, Tasha thought, like an actor in a melo-drama who clearly thought that the piece he was performing was beneath his dignity. 'Alex, don't you know anything? We all go back a long way. I mean, Kristin and Peter and me. We met each other at Elliott Academy. Twelve years ago.' Tasha tilted her glass, regretting that it was empty.

'Here. Let me get you a refill.'

Alex came back with two refills. By the time he did, Tasha had composed herself a little. She could see this was not going to work out as planned. She had hoped to keep cool: to arrange the sort of crisp confrontation Kristin managed so effortlessly. But she had been hopeless. She might as well give up. Relax a little.

'Thanks, again.' She forced a smile, and pulled her glass towards her. Steady now, she thought, and took a deep breath. 'Well, I'm sorry, Alex. If you don't mind what's going on, I'm wasting your time.'

'Oh, no. That's all right. We're not busy.'

'Not busy –'

'At Chappell's. Where I work, you know.'

'Oh. Right. I remember.'

'How did you and Kristin get to be such great friends, anyway?'

The question surprised Tasha. She almost smiled, and drank some more of her wine. 'We were roommates at Elliott. I mean, don't you know? Doesn't Kristin ever talk about back then?'

'Not much.'

'She came in our second-to-last year. I didn't think I was going to have a roommate . . .' Tasha was feeling maudlin, as well as slightly drunk. Both states tended to make her talk. Alex was a good listener: he seemed genuinely interested, as if he hadn't heard any of this before.

So she came, before long, to the part about Peter. And Quincy Adams and the sculpture classes and the winter and the spring; and then finally Maine. Why the hell not? It might at least provoke some kind of reaction from Alex.

'I see,' he said.

'So she never told you.'

'No. None of this. Not in the least.' Alex looked merely mildly surprised.

Tasha went on. College, Paris, René. She finished off her fourth glass of wine.

Alex was frowning slightly, she noticed now. 'You say . . . she was living in this man's flat?' he said.

'Yeah, it was gorgeous. Right in the Marais, full of antiques. It had these, like, big high ceilings –'

'But, hold on. It was his? How did she . . . How could she afford it?'

Tasha laughed. 'Kristin wasn't affording anything, Alex. René was paying the bills.'

She wondered what she had said wrong. All the colour seemed to have drained from Alex's face.

'Paying her,' he said.

'Not in so many words. I mean, I don't know what their

exact arrangements were. You didn't – know anything about this?'

He shook his head very slightly.

'What *has* she told you?' asked Tasha softly.

'Not much, I'm beginning to realise.'

'As far as René went, it might not have been the way it looked. She didn't tell me a whole lot of details. I'm only assuming . . .'

'So then she found out he was married,' said Alex in a lifeless voice, as if he were repeating something learned by rote.

'Oh, she always knew he was married. He had a wife and two sons. They lived around the corner –'

Alex was staring down at his drink, and not saying a word.

Belatedly it dawned on Tasha that this had all come as a shock to him: less the part about Peter, which he had guessed at, than, perhaps, René. It occurred to her that Alex might not, after all, be a very worldly person: that he was, perhaps, a man who held to traditional moral values. Who had thought Kristin was more or less the same.

'I'm sorry,' said Tasha.

Alex looked up with a thin smile. 'I suppose I deserve to know the truth.'

'Deserve? I don't know . . .' Tasha was at a loss for words. 'I really am sorry.'

'Tasha, do you suppose she's in love with this chap? This Conaway?'

'She told me she wasn't.'

'Do you have any idea why she married me?'

Alex was looking straight across at Tasha. For a moment she felt the urge to lie: to say Kristin loved him. But she could see that, in the end, there was no point. 'I wouldn't know. I think – she always thought you had a lot in common.'

'Never mind.' Alex shook his head. 'I ought to go.'

'Listen, I talk too much. I've been shooting off my mouth. You shouldn't pay me much attention.'

'Maybe.' Alex gave a small, queasy smile. Then he emptied his glass. 'Queer how you can think you know someone, when you don't.'

'I wouldn't say that. I'm sure if you've been married . . .'

'She must have required a replacement for René. She was never the sort of girl, I suppose, who'd care to live on what she could earn.'

'Alex, I'm sure it's all really complicated.'

'Or not.'

'What?'

'Funny how sometimes it only takes a moment to see someone clearly. That was my mistake, perhaps. I never thought about – what she was. I thought she was simply – a nice person.' Alex shrugged, and gave an apologetic smile. 'Nice to me. She was nice to my parents . . .'

'Alex, maybe it's time we both went home.'

'Yes. Yes, Tasha. Thank you. I imagine it is.'

29 The arrangements fell quickly into place. It seemed to take only days.

'Why,' Kristin said that first night, 'are you in such a hurry, Alex?'

'Because when one finds out one's wasted six years – '

'Alex, for heaven's sake. What's got into you? All right, I've seen someone else. Occasionally. That doesn't mean . . .'

'To you, perhaps, it doesn't. To me it does.'

And so Kristin found, to her increasing bewilderment, that Alex no longer wanted to live with her. And he wouldn't say why. He had found out about Peter – she could only assume some bit of gossip had drifted his way – and he wouldn't even listen to her reasoning; her pleading. 'Our marriage matters more to me than anything else ever could,' she'd said.

But Alex had made up his mind.

From a colleague of his at Chappell's, he heard of a flat in Pimlico, which he arranged to rent for Kristin. So far as their mutual property went, he would keep the flat in South Kensington, which he had owned before their marriage, and they would divide any profit from the sale of Tewne Abbot evenly between them.

'But we don't need to sell,' Kristin objected. 'We don't have to – '

Alex ignored her. 'Of course we may lose money. In which case I would be prepared to give you – '

'Wait a minute. *We don't have to sell.*'

But Alex was implacable.

Why? she asked him, again and again. And he wouldn't tell her. *Alex, talk*, she said. *What is it? What have I done?*

'I thought I knew you.'

'What?' Kristin's voice flew high. 'Of course you – '

'I didn't know you. You didn't tell me a thing about your past.' His upper lip curled.

'You didn't want to know! You never asked me . . .' They were standing in the kitchen of the Kensington flat. Lately they seemed to carry on every conversation standing up. Kristin took a deep breath. 'Alex, we must try to understand each other. All right, I admit I haven't told you everything that ever happened to me – how could I? In every detail? It would take forever.'

'Don't quibble, Kristin. Your time in France is hardly a detail. Here I was thinking you were just another art student when you were actually a married man's paid mistress – '

'Who's been talking to you? Who's been telling you this?'

Alex was silent then, and Kristin knew.

'I've arranged,' he said eventually, without emotion, 'for an estate agent and an antiques appraiser to meet us at Tewne Abbot tomorrow.'

They couldn't seem to sit down at Tewne Abbot, either. Kristin stood, her back stiff against the drawing-room wall, while the estate agent walked around with his measuring tape.

'You're right,' she said to Alex. 'We'll lose money. I really don't see the point.'

'Better sometimes to get clear of a bad investment than to keep hanging on in the hope it'll put itself right. We've given it time.'

'What exactly are you talking about? The house? *Us*?'

'Stop it, Kristin.' Alex drew a deep breath. 'Of course I mean the house.'

'I can't believe you're so soulless that you can see it as that. An investment.'

'Well, that was what it was meant to be.'

'It was meant to be a *home*.' She had thought he understood. A house like this wasn't a commodity to sell. It lasted longer than the flimsy paper that bought it: longer, sometimes, than the structures of the families that owned it, longer than it took for children to grow up, longer than husbands and wives stayed in love. Because a house like this survived all those things. It was stronger than human beings: sometimes they had to give way to it, because it was greater than they.

Not that she could expect Alex to understand, if he didn't already. The love for a place like this was in the blood; Kristin knew she possessed it. Love had made her study this house in its every detail; strip paint and struggle over marbling patches of wall; plant new trees in the orchard. Love had made her search for gifts to fill its rooms – offerings. Love made her want to feel only happiness here: to raise a family within these walls. And that was where she had failed it.

'Would it be different,' she said now, 'if we'd been able to have children?' She turned towards him with wide, measuring eyes. The estate agent had wandered upstairs, away from them.

Alex gave a grunt of frustration. 'It might. But we didn't. It's probably just as well.'

'We didn't try hard enough . . .'

'Kristin, I'm sick of this sort of conversation.'

Before the antiques man came, Alex mentioned that they might each want to choose a few objects of sentimental value, to keep. Whatever she wanted for herself, she had only to indicate. He wouldn't quibble.

Kristin chose twelve glass vases from the kitchen, the piano stool and the mantelpiece clock and the coffee table from the living room. She pointed at mirror after mirror as they climbed the main staircase.

'Kristin, this is ridiculous,' said Alex. 'You're only moving into a small flat. What are you going to do with fourteen mirrors?'

'You said to choose. I'm choosing.'

Up in the master bedroom, the antiques man took measurements. 'I don't see how you're going to get this out through that doorway,' he said, nodding at the big bed.

'It came in in pieces,' said Kristin.

'Well, it'd have to be taken apart again.'

'I'm not sure it can.'

'Don't be silly,' said Alex.

But the antiques man was examining the joins with a doubtful look on his face. 'Someone used glue here. It doesn't look like it'll come apart very easily.'

'It isn't meant to,' said Kristin.

Alex looked impatient. 'Of course it will. We spent a fortune on that bed.'

But in the end Kristin was right. The appraiser tugged various pieces of the bed in different directions. 'I hope,' he said finally, 'whoever buys this house likes this piece, because I think they're going to be stuck with it.'

Kristin smiled. She walked up to the bed, and stroked a tall, carved post. Her bed. She had watched the building of it: designed the frame for the new canopy. It belonged in this room, nowhere else. And now it would stay. That was one small consolation.

When only she and Alex were left in the house, she walked out into the garden. Her garden: her very own. And she was going to lose it. Tears rose to her eyes. It felt like losing her father, losing Littledene all over again. She heard Alex's footsteps behind her. 'You wouldn't make us do this,' she said, 'if you understood a single thing of what I'm feeling.'

'For God's sake, Kristin, it's only a house. You're going on as if you'd lost a child or something –'

'Don't talk about children!' The words were sudden and sharp, almost a cry, and Kristin ran over to the brick wall and leaned against it, the grooved stone biting into her forehead. *How could he*? she thought. How could he possibly be so cruel as to remind her of what she could

391

never have? After so many years of trying, of growing used to failing, she knew now that what Mr Jenkyns had told her, years ago, must be true: it was possible that she would never conceive a child without medical help. And even that was less likely to work as she grew older. Next month she would be thirty . . .

She thought the sobs would dissolve her. She was losing Tewne Abbot. Losing everything. And it was wrong of Alex to go on as if she'd let this house take the place of a child. Because she knew that if there were anything she wanted more – anything she would trade Tewne Abbot for without a moment's hesitation – it was that.

She felt, rather than heard, him come closer. 'I'm sorry,' he said, belatedly. 'That was unfair.'

'Forget it,' she said. 'It doesn't matter.'

'Well.' Peter smiled. 'To independence, eh?'

They touched glasses; two days had passed since Kristin had moved into her new flat. It was a bright, clear Friday in the middle of March, and the sun shone in through curtainless windows, glinting off the fourteen mirrors leaning against the skirting boards.

'It feels so odd living here,' she said. 'Quiet.'

'You'll get used to it.'

'Do you like living alone?'

Peter looked suddenly wary.

'Never mind, I know you must. Still, I'm not sure about me. Either I'll love it or hate it. Peter, stop looking at me that way. I'm not asking you to move in with me.'

He laughed. 'Sorry. I've just been feeling under a bit of pressure in that direction.'

Kristin tilted her head and studied her wine glass. 'From her?' They almost never discussed Tasha. Kristin was not sure that she wanted to now.

'Don't know if she wants to be together all the time, or just sees me as a handy rent-free place to live.' Peter smiled and spun the stem of his glass.

'I think you know the answer to that.' Kristin paused. It was strange to feel her heart beating so: hard and fiercely, as if it would jump out through her sweater. She registered the feeling with a certain alarm. If it meant she cared – that what Peter said next mattered, that she would be hurt if he said he was going to let Tasha move in with him – then she had better not hear his next words. 'Anyway, never mind,' she said quickly.

'Kristin –' He gave her a curious look. 'I can't figure you out. Either you're bothered about me and Tasha –'

'Listen, that's your business. Would you like lunch now?'

'In America I think they call this denial. What I'm trying to tell you is –'

'Maybe I don't want to hear what you're trying to tell me.' Kristin spoke quickly as she stood up.

'You mean you'd go on the same way we are?'

She could hear the incredulity in his voice, behind her. 'Maybe. Look, what I told you in the beginning was, I don't want to see Tasha hurt. That still stands.'

'You have some funny ways of showing your affection for your friends, then. That night at Tasha's opening –'

'Look, shut up, will you, Peter?'

'I think you love me.' He had come up behind her very quietly. His fingers sneaked around her waist and met in front of her.

'What on earth can it possibly accomplish to force something like that out of me?'

'Don't know.' He laughed and swept her hair up with one hand, then kissed her neck. 'It'd feel good to hear it, though.'

'Peter, you're a greedy sod.' She half-turned towards him. 'No. Christ.' She pushed his face away from hers. 'Don't kiss me. You know I hate it.'

'Do you?' He kissed her chin.

She flinched back. 'Promise me one thing. You won't let her move in with you.'

He nodded. 'Okay. Promise me something? That you won't go back to four-eyes.'

'He's not so bad. I've treated him rottenly.'

'So we rotters should stick together, eh?' He stood back and looked at her.

She sighed. 'All right. I'll tell you the truth. I want Tasha to go home. Away to America. And not really for her own good, because her own good can go hang! She drove my husband away. If she didn't stop at something as low as telling tales behind my back –'

'Whoa, hold on, wait a minute. What are we talking about here?'

'I think she found Alex somewhere and told him a bunch of tales, all right? Enough said. Can we stop this conversation?'

'So you want Tasha to go?'

Kristin sighed. 'All right, I admit it. I want you to myself, Peter.'

'I know.' He smiled, and then, for a second, looked thoughtful. 'Well. I'll see what I can do.'

Kristin had had enough of all this. She gave a shiver and pulled Peter's hands away from her waist. Then she walked slowly to one of the spaces between the windows facing the street, and started to peel off her clothing.

He stared, then smiled again suddenly. 'Jesus, Kristin. What do you expect me to do now?'

'Undress, yourself. Then come over. On your hands and knees.' Kristin's eyes sparkled. 'Otherwise people will see you.'

He did part of what he told her. Then he reached up and unbalanced her, pulling her down to the floor on top of him.

'You're not my wee girl anymore,' he said.

Kristin looked quizzical. 'What?'

'Never mind.'

'No. What do you mean, wee girl? How old are you really, Peter, anyway?'

He sighed. 'Forty.'

'Do you swear? Is that the truth this time?'

He nodded.

'So you lied every time before.' She slapped his face.

When he had gone, she thought things over and decided that she did not want to share a house with him. Why ruin a good thing?

Why, in fact, do anything at all to change a situation that might be more agreeable to her, after all, than she had ever suspected? She had lived alone in London before, and not particularly enjoyed it – but then she had been staying in a grubby bedsit with no money, no friends and a dead-end job. Things were different now. Suddenly new vistas of happiness seemed to open out before her, and they were nothing like what she had previously imagined happiness to be. *What if I were to travel?* she thought. She scanned the ads in the papers for airfares to Japan, China, India. *Why not?* She would take her camera; maybe Peter would even come with her. Or meet her there.

She imagined buying her own little house, when the money from Tewne Abbot came through. A terraced house, maybe, with two little windows and flowers trailing from pots on the sills: a house just big enough for one, or two, and everything inside as she wished it. She would live there, and Peter in Hampstead, and they would visit each other and share dinner and bed. Why share any of the dreariness of life – the drudgery? Very possibly there was something in domesticity that killed off sex. And that was the last thing she wanted.

She told Peter as much, exultant, on the day Diana offered her a three-week assignment shooting country houses in Ireland.

'It'll be lovely,' she said, twisting the cork from a bottle of white wine. 'All by myself. I've never been there.'

'My grandparents came from there. Donegal.'

'Do you want to come with me?' asked Kristin suddenly.

She didn't know why she hadn't thought of it before: it would be even better than going alone. And yet not in the least domestic.

'Sure. That'd be great.' His eyes slid away from hers. 'But . . .'

Kristin looked at him closely. 'It's *her*, isn't it? That's what's stopping you.'

He sipped his wine and looked up at her now. 'No,' he said. 'Just that it's too much like being married.'

'Why *are* you still married?'

He shrugged. 'Kate's religious. The Church –'

Kristin shook her head slowly. 'The Catholic Church, isn't it? But *you*'re not religious. You could get divorced. She'd just have to lump it. And just not get married again if she couldn't square it with her conscience.'

'Mm.' Peter looked uneasy and swallowed more wine.

'So that's not the reason, is it?' Kristin stood up and refilled his glass with some concentration. 'I think it's because you still love her. She was your teacher at art school and then she supported you all those years when you were trying to get started, so perhaps you think you owe her something. I don't know.'

Peter stood up and walked to the window.

'I don't know what goes on in your mind, and I hardly ever ask you, Peter. I don't like people prying into my thoughts –'

'Right.' He smiled and turned to face her. 'So stop prying into mine.'

'I only wanted to know' – she took a deep breath – 'if you had some particular reason for not coming to Ireland? I didn't mean to get into – Kate.'

He frowned, and his brows shadowed his eyes. 'How do you know so much anyway, Kristin? I didn't tell you.'

'Oh, that old professor of yours from the art school – the one I found when I was working on that article for *Décor*? He was surprisingly talkative.'

Peter grimaced. 'He must be going senile. He's never talked to anyone before.'

Kristin shrugged. Then she walked closer to Peter and trailed a hand across the line of his shoulder and down his arm. 'What I don't understand is why she puts up with what she does.'

'Kate?' He smiled. 'Why do you?'

'Oh, no. But I don't. I know all about you, which makes a difference.'

He gave a short, uneasy laugh. 'Right. So you do.'

'So why does she pretend you're still married? Why do you let her pretend?'

He touched her chin, pushing it up until her mouth was closed. 'Enough interrogation.'

Later, when he had gone, Kristin's thoughts returned to Ireland, and she felt distinctly dissatisfied. She had thought she would be happy with the current state of play. That she didn't care about living with Peter – or, God forbid, marrying him, since her first attempt at marriage had gone so badly wrong. Still, she did not feel that her control was complete enough. She did not have even partial possession.

She postponed the trip to Ireland, from one week to the next. She didn't want to go off and leave Peter, not while Tasha was still here. Diana came up with other assignments; in one week Kristin travelled to Cornwall, Sussex and Edinburgh. Her diary filled up with appointments and grew congested with scribblings – so full, in fact, that for a long time she failed completely to realise what was missing from its pages.

'All right, all right. Just give me another month.'

'If you really don't want me to move in, just say so. I have to admit though, if you don't want me to, I'd have to ask myself where we're going after all this time. And that would really hurt. I'm being honest with you, Peter . . .'

He gave a fleeting, placating smile, then pressed his forehead to the glass back wall of his city house.

'What is it, Peter? Talk to me. Tell me.'

'You know, Tasha, for someone who's so fucking good in bed, you certainly can ruin it when you open your mouth.'

'Oh. I see.' Tasha felt tears bubbling to the surface, and retreated among the sleek black enamel and chrome of the kitchen. It was all hard here. Too neat. Nothing cosy or comforting or steaming. Nothing to console her.

Peter sighed and turned. 'This is hard for me.'

'Ever since Kristin left Alex you've been this way.'

'Believe me, this is nothing to do with Kristin.'

'Then it's me.' Tasha couldn't help herself. She threw her head and arms down on a countertop and started to sob.

She'd done everything wrong: messed everything up. Even talking to Alex – her clever idea. That had been a complete mistake. She had been so sure that the slightest threat to her marriage would send Kristin running back, obedient, to her country house and her clothing allowance. What Tasha hadn't reckoned on was that Alex wouldn't let her.

So there Kristin was, solo, in her expensive little flat. A loose cannon. There for Peter at all hours of the day and night. *I screwed up*, Tasha thought. *Screwed up totally*.

She noticed that Peter's hands were on her back, stroking.

'Come on, Tash, I'm famished. Let's go out to the bakery and get something.'

'Don't you ever stop thinking about food?' She rubbed her eyes and turned. 'This thing with me and Kristin's not going to go away. You're going to have to make some kind of a decision.'

His eyes met hers: dark, sparkling, unreadable. 'But, you see, Tash, that's just what I can't face. We're all so tangled up in this thing together.'

Tasha had the strange feeling that he was telling her the truth for the first time. 'I know.' She rested a hand on his shoulder. 'But you've got to make up your mind.' She took a deep breath. 'Unless you want rid of both of us. If that's the only way it can be.'

'I'd have to be an idiot to want rid of you, Tasha.' Peter brushed the hair back from her face.

She had the feeling, as he spoke, that the real Peter she had seemed to glimpse for a second was retreating. 'So,' she said quietly. 'When?'

He sighed and kissed the side of her face. 'Next month, at the latest. I promise.'

She did not like to tell him that he had already said that a month ago: that she had had to renew her lease in the end. Because it just might be true, what he said now. If she gave it another month – two – she might still win.

'Tash, I think if I hear the names "Kristin" or "Peter" one more time I'm going to have to send you home.' Nat poured out the dregs of his afternoon coffee. 'Cheers.'

'I'm sorry. I've landed on you at a bad time. Were you in the middle of an article?'

'Sort of.'

'It was just, I haven't been able to get him on the phone for three days. He doesn't normally go out to the country in the middle of the week. But he must have. He must be with her. The thing is, he told me last week we were going to move in together. How can we, Nat? If this is still –'

Nat gave a small groan. 'You're sure he told you that?'

'He *said* it.'

'You're sure you're not just hearing what you want to hear?'

'What do you mean?'

'Listen, count me out of this. I've been telling you for a couple of months now you ought to let go. Call it good riddance. Obviously Kristin's poison, and he's not a whole lot –'

399

Tasha ignored the last few words. 'If you ever met her, you wouldn't think she was poison. You'd want to go to bed with her. All men do.' She gave an unhappy sniff.

'Well, there's no way in the world I would. Anyway, did it ever occur to you that maybe those two deserve each other? That he's just two-faced enough and she's enough of a schemer . . .'

'Nat, stop it. He's not. He's in a bind, but she's put him there. He deserves somebody better. Sane, at least.'

'You mean you.' Nat smiled. 'That is, if you stay sane for much longer.'

'Stop it, Nat.'

'Tell him, then. An ultimatum.'

'I've tried that. At least I think I have.'

'Try again.'

Tasha looked at him with a puppy-doggish trust. 'You really think so?'

Coolly, sagely – almost resignedly, she thought – her brother nodded.

At ten that night, she paced the floor with the phone in her hand. Engaged. Still goddamned engaged. Were they having one of their dirty talks, then? Was he going to say, when Tasha finally got through, that he'd been talking all the while to some art dealer? To his parents? There was always some story.

Tasha put down the receiver and took a deep breath. She was getting out of control.

Ten minutes later, she tried again. This time, the phone rang at the other end.

'Conaway.'

'Hi. It's me.' Tasha waited for a response and heard none. 'I just – well, I hadn't heard from you in a few days, so . . .'

'Well, then. You okay? Is everything okay?'

'Peter, I need to know . . .' Nat had said an ultimatum,

she reminded herself. *Calm. In control.* 'If we're going to move in together, when's it going to happen?'

She heard him laugh. 'This is coming a bit out of the blue, at ten o'clock on a Friday night.'

'I tried earlier. Peter, this is starting to eat me up. I really need to know.'

'Right. Well.' Tasha heard a sound like floorboards: the floor of the Norfolk house below his feet. 'Fine.'

'So when, Peter?'

'This is really not a great time to be, uh . . .' His voice trailed off.

'What's the difference? Between now and any other time? Every time I ask you, you keep putting me off. When?'

'Tasha, you sound just a little hysterical.'

'That's because I need to know. Next month, next month, you keep saying. Well, that's fine for you, but my life is in limbo, and . . . Peter?

It was very odd. He hadn't hung up – at least she didn't think so – but at the other end of the phone, she heard only silence.

'How about lunch with our friend across the road? And then we'll cruise out to Sandbourne.'

'You seem happy.' Kristin smiled and looped an arm through Peter's as they strolled out to his car. *She* felt happy: almost absurdly lighthearted.

They pulled up at the pub, whose landlord, as usual, gave her the once-over, but she didn't mind. Peter procured a tabloid and ordered a pint and a glass of wine.

'Oh. No,' she called towards the bar. 'Cancel the wine this time. I'll have a mineral water.' Then they settled in at a wooden booth in a corner and waited for their plough-man's lunches. Peter flipped through the paper.

'These ministers. Keep on biting the dust at this rate, and soon we won't have any government. I'm almost starting to feel sorry for them.'

'Why? They try to lead a double life. Why shouldn't they pay the price?'

Peter pulled a long face, and just then their lunches came.

The landlord leered at Kristin. 'Nice day for it, eh?'

She blinked up innocently. 'We were going to drive out to Sandbourne.'

'Good day for that, too.' He deposited their plates.

'Sometimes,' Kristin murmured, 'I want to decapitate that man.' Peter smiled, and they ate their lunches, peacefully, silently. There would be plenty of time, as Kristin reminded herself, for talk. Once they were really alone.

The roads were empty, and it didn't take long to get out to Sandbourne, one of the fringe of coastal towns near East Hingham – if it could properly be called a town. The sky had started to cloud over, and the sea gave off a faint rank smell, yet Kristin felt happy as Peter's Jaguar bowled out along the road to the shore. She felt her heart soar as he built up speed, and said giddily, 'You know, I think I'm beginning to understand about driving. Why people like it so much, after all.'

'Why don't you learn?'

She made a face.

'It'd get you out to your assignments a hell of a lot quicker than BR. Why don't you try now?' Peter grinned and took a hand off the wheel.

She laid hers down on the warm patch where it had been: felt the wheel vibrate to the hum of the engine. 'It scares me.' She shrugged.

'Sometimes you have to face what you're scared of.'

'I suppose you're right.'

They came to the end of the road, which turned into a gravelly parking lot at the edge of the sea. Peter shifted to a lower gear, and then, unexpectedly, instead of parking, steered the car towards the right.

'Peter.' She laughed. 'What the hell are you doing? Going up on the cliffs? There's no road.'

'No policemen either.' The car bumped along the footpath, climbing steadily higher, struggling at times, fenders brushed by tall grasses.

'Darling, are you mad? Don't you see the signs? "Cliffs eroding". This is a *footpath*, Peter.'

He only smiled. 'Do you ever like to go as far as you think you can – and then take it just a little bit further?'

'No.' Kristin laughed, perturbed. And then she understood. Or began to. *Yes, maybe after all I do.*

He pulled up on the rough grass at the edge of the cliff. Gusts beat at the car's windows.

'I don't like it much up here,' she said.

'We'll only stay a minute.' He grinned over at her.

'Peter.' She took a deep breath. 'I've got something to tell you.'

'You've got your divorce.'

'For heaven's sakes, that's going to take two years. No.'

'Then what?' He looked at her evenly. 'Bad news or good?'

'Oh, good,' she said, beaming suddenly. 'The best.'

30 Tasha was beginning to think she had made a big mistake. *Damn it,* she thought. *He's avoiding me.*

Maybe Nat had been wrong, and confrontation wasn't the best policy. Because ever since that odd phone conversation from which Peter had disappeared in midstream, she had been completely unable to reach him. Not in Norfolk, not in Hampstead. She tried and got his answer machines, again and again.

She decided to give him the weekend to cool off. And then Monday and Tuesday. She had gotten overanxious before. She didn't want to nag him.

When Wednesday came, she started to feel annoyed again. And restless. Without a job, she sometimes found the days long – only her and her painting, which wasn't going at all well – and so she decided, in the end, to drive over to Hampstead just to find out whether he was there at all.

It looked as if he wasn't. No lights were on, and when she peered through the slit of a window by the door, she could see mail piled up on the mat.

She rang the bell at the house next door. The old lady there was unhelpful. 'He's in and out so much, dear. These artists . . . He has a place in the country, doesn't he?'

What the hell? Tasha thought, and filled up her petrol tank and drove, in an increasingly black mood, to East Hingham. How were you supposed to move in with a guy who wouldn't even tell you his whereabouts? Who'd just take off like this, without an explanation? Privacy was one thing, but . . .

The long low house looked unpromisingly dark. Tasha climbed out of her car and walked around, peering in the windows. No, there were definitely no lights on. There were four bottles of milk queued up on the front doorstep, though, which made her feel more hopeful. Surely if he was away for long he would have cancelled the milk?

She drove to the pub across the road, which she had never been inside before. At first the landlord only shook his head at her questions. 'Well, I did see them on Sunday,' he said finally. 'Him and his girlfriend. They were going down the shore at Sandbourne.'

'His girlfriend?'

'You know, the blonde one. Blonder than you. Sorry, love, but you know what I mean. You a friend of his, or a relative?'

'Friend.' Tasha started to back towards the door, wondering if that were quite true.

'The house all right? Nothing gone wrong, is there?' the landlord called after her.

'No, everything's fine,' Tasha shouted back, and fled.

Back in her car, she studied the road atlas and found Sandbourne. Only ten miles away. It didn't seem a very likely destination for a couple about to run off together. To disappear for good.

She had to swallow to ease the feeling of panic that was rising in her throat. *Don't be silly*, she told herself. *They wouldn't run off. Why should they? What would they do, elope? They couldn't. Kristin's still married.*

She felt better then. She started the engine and drove down empty roads and felt almost calm by the time she reached Sandbourne. She'd probably find nothing. Just to give herself a rest, she parked and walked up the slope of the cliff; and that was where she found Kristin.

'I'm going to have to leave the country,' Kristin said.

'They'll find you out.' Tasha stood a few feet back from the edge now. At first she had thought she was going to faint. Then, with a deep gulp of air, she had recovered, enough to keep standing. But she wasn't going to look down again.

Not that what could be seen was particularly gruesome: the exposed underside of a car, strewn with sand. It was gruesome only when you thought about it. And when Tasha did, she felt nauseous and scared. The best thing she could do was get far away from Kristin. It occurred to her that Kristin might be dangerous: that she ought to say something appeasing. 'Listen,' she said, 'I'm not going to put anyone on to you. Try and get away if you want. You do what you have to do.'

'Not you, too.' Kristin's voice was cold, sarcastic.

'What?'

'Telling me to do what I have to do. Don't you care?'

'Kristin, why the hell should I care? I hate you, you hate me.'

'I don't hate you.' Kristin looked down and clenched her arms more tightly around herself. 'I wish you'd understand that.'

'Oh, and I suppose everything you've done is for my own good? Look.' Tasha took a quick, deep breath. 'This is stupid. I'm going.'

'Don't –'

'First you want me to keep away, now you want me to stay. Which is it?'

'Don't. Not yet . . .' Kristin looked up, and for the first time her eyes were anxious.

Tasha relented a little. 'How'd you get here?'

'I took a cab.'

Tasha looked down, briefly, at the beach again. Then she covered her face with her hands. *This is not your problem. Get out now.* 'I don't know what you're going to do,' she said, speaking slowly. This was totally against her better judgment. 'And I don't want you telling me things. I don't want to know. But I'll give you a ride back to London. If you want it.'

For most of the way in from the coast, they didn't speak. Tasha was beginning to wish she could dump Kristin – in Sandbourne, in Cromer, in Norwich, anywhere – but she couldn't seem to bring herself to stop. Driving, she felt safe. Once or twice, Kristin began to talk, and Tasha silenced her.

'Tasha, do you think –' Kristin started again, as they wound their way through the suburbs of Norwich.

'Kristin, I don't want to hear anything you've got to say. I go out there, I haven't seen Peter in a week, the milk's piling up on his doorstep and there's his car turned over and buried in the sand –'

'It was an accident.'

'Listen, I don't care what kind of accident. I don't want to know. I'm taking you back to London, and then as far as I'm concerned –'

'Tasha, you're in the wrong lane.'

So she was. Tasha took a deep breath and steered back over to the left. Her hands and arms were shaking. Perhaps she needed to stop.

They came to rest in a side street lined with semi-detached houses. Nowhere in particular. Nowhere they were known. 'I think,' said Tasha at last, 'you'd better tell me what happened, after all.'

Kristin closed her eyes and rested her head against the seat. 'So. That's it.'

'That's it? But, Kristin, what you said doesn't mean . . .'

Kristin thought that Tasha's voice sounded very far away. Everything had felt far away, since Sunday. Kristin had wandered through the days – Monday, yesterday, today – without noticing much, even the passage of time. Even now she was not sure how she had found her way back into Sandbourne that Sunday night. She must have walked. She remembered walking in through the front door of an empty-looking hotel; telling the receptionist she needed a room.

The other woman gave her a kindly once-over. 'Trouble with your car? Oh, dear. Your coat's all muddy.'

And then somehow she was upstairs, and sleeping, not waking until the middle of the next morning; and then she was back in London. She was holding the phone in her hand.

'Yes,' she said. 'Dead.'

But she couldn't remember to whom she was talking, or why she had called. Frightened, she hung up abruptly.

She was cracking up. She would give herself away soon. She had to leave here. She pressed her fingers into her forehead, hard, because she felt a wave of nausea coming on. The phone rang again.

God, no. They had found her.

It rang, eight, nine, ten times, then stopped. Then it started up again.

She picked it up quickly, prepared to slam it down.

'Kristin? I tried a moment ago. Is that you?'

The voice was a woman's. Kristin held the receiver out in mid-air, then drew it closer. 'Diana.'

'So it is you. For goodness' sake,' said Diana, and immediately started chattering away. Kristin didn't really hear what she was saying.

'Diana,' she started in, when a break came, 'did I just ring you? Speak to you?'

'No!' Diana laughed. 'Why do you think I was trying to ring you? Silly girl. Now, listen . . .'

Diana started talking again. She seemed to be saying something about Kristin's last shoot. 'Well, if you think you missed something, go back,' she said. 'You can ring them up and explain.'

'Yes,' Kristin said. The words seemed to stick in her head. *If you think you missed something, go back. Go back.* Perhaps Diana was right. She might have left fingerprints. Some clue. She must make sure she hadn't. Or if she had, remove them.

So she had gone back. Caught the connecting trains,

took a cab. She made sure the cab left her in the middle of Sandbourne. When it was out of sight she started the long walk to the beach.

And then, incredibly, there it was. The Jaguar. Still buried in the sand. Peter's last proper words to her came back again, echoing, cold, in the wind. *You do what you have to do.*

'That's not an answer,' Kristin said.

'It's all I can tell you.'

She felt the anger rising then: surging within her.

'Kristin! What the hell are you –'

She didn't answer him. She locked her fingers around the bumper of the Jaguar and pushed. *He loves this car. More than he loves me. Us. He cares for it. I want to destroy it.* She remembered the signs about cliffs eroding. He had been a fool to drive up here.

When at first nothing gave way, it surprised her. The car was heavy. Peter was fighting her. 'For Christ's sake, Kristin, are you crazy? Let go. God damn it –'

But she threw him off, and her arm, lashing out, caught him on the jaw. He staggered. He was near the edge. Kristin gave the car one last push.

It went.

All of it. Its heavy metallic bulk, the ground beneath – grass, sand, clods flying. She saw Peter stagger, and then capsize. *Like a ship*, she thought. Only not so graceful.

She was on the edge of the crumbling ground, herself: on all fours. She scrabbled backwards. And then suddenly she felt lightheaded and very weak, and closed her eyes.

She opened them again, not sure how much time had passed or what had happened. Everything around her was silent.

'*Peter?*' she called. Then more quietly, afraid of giving herself away. 'Peter.'

No answer came.

'Kristin, why?' Tasha said at last.

409

Kristin shrugged. 'I was angry.'

'But why? What happened?'

'It just – all came out. He didn't care.' Kristin stared at the blank façades of the houses beside her, above their neat grass lawns. *I should move on,* she thought. *I can't stay here.* 'Look. I shouldn't be talking to you. I need to go home.'

'What did you tell him? Why did you guys argue?'

Do what you have to do.

She had been so happy. It was ironic. She had wondered, at first, how to break the news, but somehow he had made it easy. 'Let's get out,' she had said. She felt a sudden need for fresh air. So they climbed out, and stood leaning against the side of the Jaguar. They didn't hold hands or touch, but she felt that they were in harmony, as one. She told him she had news. *What?* he said. *Bad news or good?*

Good. The best. 'Peter. I'm going to have a baby.'

'What?' he said again.

'Peter, I'm pregnant.' She turned her head towards him, smiling. 'Believe me, it's a complete surprise. I told you about all the trouble I'd had. I didn't think it could happen. I never bothered taking precautions.'

'Jesus Christ, Kristin. What?' Peter's hand slammed down hard against the roof of the car.

'I told you, I didn't think I could ever have a baby anyway. But it's all right, I did a test at home, I've been to the doctor . . .' She noticed then that his expression was not what it should be. Before, she had put his strange reaction down to shock. But now, he looked no more pleased than he had a moment ago. In fact, he looked angry.

'I can't believe I've been so stupid,' he said.

'What?' Something was going cold inside her chest. 'What do you mean?'

'I really thought you were different. I didn't think you'd try to trap me.'

410

'Trap you? What?'

'I've been through this before. I don't want babies. I don't *like* them.'

'Peter, that's silly.' Kristin forced a laugh. 'Not everyone likes babies, but most people like their own children. And I'm not trying to trap you. I know we can't get married. I only wanted to tell you because I thought you should know. I thought you'd be . . . interested.'

He looked down at her coolly. 'You're just like all the others, aren't you?'

'What?'

'Other women. They're all into babies. Kate said she wasn't, but it happened to her. I tell you, you can do what you want, but I'm not going down that road again.'

'Not going there again? What do you mean?'

He sighed. 'I have a son, Kristin. He's nineteen. His name's Liam.'

Kristin fell back, slowly, against the side of the car. 'You never told me.'

'You were starting to know everything else about me. You'd have found out. Why should I tell you?' He drummed his fingers on the car door, and then took a deep breath. 'Kate fell pregnant. Just like you. Don't know to this day whether she meant to, but there it was. Said it was her last chance of a baby. She was thirty-five. I was twenty-one. She said she had the money to look after me. Look after all of us. And so she did.' He gave a hollow laugh. 'Oh, did she. But that baby . . . Cried day and night. I was trying to finish my degree, trying to work. It was driving me crazy. Kate was so wrapped up in it. I kept thinking to myself, what am I doing here? A fucking father. I'm twenty-one. I haven't even lived my own life yet. I've never had a chance.' Peter stopped talking and looked, expressionless, out to sea. 'But it was crazy. I still cared about Kate, I still wanted her. When I figured that out I thought, all right, I'll give her the choice. It's me or that baby. She chose Liam.'

'What on earth else could she do? You can't give up a child.'

'That's what she said. Said I was drinking too much, anyway. Maybe it was better if I wasn't around.'

'This is all in the past, Peter. It isn't us.'

But he didn't seem to hear. Kristin tried to ignore the defeated feeling inside herself: tried to ignore the hurt, the knowledge that this would not be his first child. All right, so he and Kate had a son. But Peter was older now. Not twenty. He would feel differently. Kristin talked and hoped and reasoned: she talked for such a long time that she wondered if she was repeating herself, and fear tinged her voice. *Peter, you have to stay with me. I can't do this alone.* 'I'm not asking you to be around all the time,' she said. 'Just to be there some of the time, for the baby. So it knows its father.'

'Kristin.' He spoke roughly. 'I want you to know, you got yourself into this mess, and you can get yourself out of it however you like. I don't want anything to do with it.'

'What are you saying? That you'd ignore your own child?' Her voice grew cold, like his, and her eyes narrowed. 'I'll have you know, I'm not giving this up. I wouldn't for all the world. Whether or not you –'

'You do what you have to do.'

'That's not an answer.'

'It's all I can tell you.'

And then came the fury, and the blur, and the darkness. But she would never undo it, Kristin thought now. Not for anything.

Tasha nodded. 'He said he didn't want a baby . . .'

'Because –' Kristin knew she ought to say it. But she was sure Tasha didn't know, yet. Not about Kate. And somehow fear defeated her. This was the wrong time for explanations. 'He said he didn't like babies,' she said finally.

'That was *it*?' Tasha was incredulous.

412

'Yes. More or less. I tried to reason with him . . .'

'How could he just say he doesn't like babies? How does he know? I mean, how could he . . .'

'I know, Tasha. Maybe I should have tried harder to convince him, but I just got upset. Because he was so set against it. And because I'd been so happy, I never thought I was going to be able to . . .'

'I know, Kristin. I know.' It struck Tasha quite forcibly for a moment that she was falling back into her old ways. Pitying Kristin. That she must stop: remember what Kristin had done. 'Well,' she said more harshly, 'you're in for it now. I can't say I blame you for the way you felt, but . . .' She turned her key in the ignition. The engine coughed and refused to start. After a few tries, she had to give up and let it rest. 'Look, Kristin. Unbelievable as this may seem, I'm pretty angry at you. If I had half a brain I'd be turning you in to the police right now.'

'Tasha. No.' Kristin reached out and touched her arm.

'I wish I could believe you weren't guilty of murder.' Tasha leaned her forehead against the steering wheel, and then took a deep breath and threw back her hair. 'Look. Are you totally sure he . . . went down with the car?'

'Tasha, I think I – saw him.'

'But did you? Did you see it happen?'

'I don't know where else he could have gone.'

'But you didn't actually see it. You blacked out.'

'I saw the car falling . . .'

'Kristin, he might not be there. Did you ever actually look? Did you go down there?'

'I was going to, today, but . . .' Kristin shook her head.

Tasha tried the engine again, suddenly businesslike. 'That's it, then. We've got to go back to Sandbourne.' The engine coughed and then caught. 'We'll go back right now.' She pulled out into the road.

'Tasha, we can't. It's dark. And if we did – I realised when I was up there today – if I went any nearer I'd leave footprints. Probably other things the police could find, too.

413

At least anything I left before might have washed away . . .'

Tasha sighed. 'So what do we do?'

She didn't notice, this time, that she was thinking as if she were on Kristin's side, again.

'Wait, I guess.'

'Somebody's bound to notice there's a car lying on the beach.'

'You're right. For all I know, they might have already.'

'But, wait a minute. If there were a . . .' Tasha hesitated to say the word 'body'. 'My God, I can't believe I'm saying this. Look, if he were really . . . down there, wouldn't somebody – something – have been noticed?'

'I don't know! I don't know.' Kristin bent her head and dug her fingers against her forehead. 'Sandbourne's not a very big place. Maybe nobody's walked out that far. The weather's been bad . . . Tasha? Can you stop for a bit? I don't feel well.'

Tasha pulled over, and Kristin sat and took deep breaths for a moment.

'What does it feel like?' said Tasha eventually.

Kristin looked over at her: the slightly lumpy, worried face, orange in the light of the streetlamps. 'What?' she said.

'Being pregnant.'

The question made Kristin want to laugh. 'Nothing much, really. A mild case of the 'flu.' A smile crept across her face. 'Do you think it really might be true? That Peter might be . . . all right? Alive somewhere?'

'Unfortunately, yes.' Tasha started up the engine again. 'I'm beginning to think if anyone could be in two places at once, he could.'

Kristin made no comment.

They sat, still in Tasha's Mini, by the kerb outside Kristin's flat.

'We'll just have to wait,' Tasha said. 'He might turn up.'

'I want him to, and yet I don't.'

'Better for you if he does.' Tasha paused. 'Kristin, there's one thing I just don't get. How could you have done it? I mean, pushed a whole car over the edge like that.'

Kristin sighed and looked around, and finally smiled. 'Gosh. I don't know. I just tried, and it happened. Funny. For a moment it was the most wonderful feeling. As if I had so much strength, and I'd never known it. He loved that bloody car so much. Going on about the year and what a great model it was –'

''64 or something?'

''63.'

'I just told him to shut up when he got going. I couldn't care less about cars. Do you remember that one he had at Elliott? The Corvette?'

'Tasha, don't.'

'I know.' Tasha sighed. 'Life moves on.' And then, 'You know, I wish it could have been me. Who did what you did. I was starting to want to.'

'Tasha, there's something I ought to tell you. Something I found out – about Peter . . .'

Tasha gave her a weary look. 'I'm not sure I'm up to any more revelations just now. Can you just, like, keep it for later?'

Kristin considered. 'Yeah, I suppose so.'

'I'll call you sometime.'

'You don't have to. I'll be all right.'

Tasha shrugged and reached over to open the passenger door.

'Thanks for the lift.'

Tasha shrugged again and watched, unsmiling, as Kristin ran up the steps of her building.

31 For a week, Tasha didn't leave her flat except to go out for milk and supplies of tins when her food ran out. She unplugged her phone and answer machine and didn't wash her hair.

On the eighth day, she woke up to a pounding at her door. 'Go away,' she shouted.

'Tasha? For Christ's sake, let me in. It's Nat.'

She dug her way out from under the bedclothes and felt her way to the door.

'Tash, what the hell's happened? Are you all right?' Nat blinked into the darkness of the room. 'This place smells. Have you got the 'flu or something? You should have called.'

'Peter's disappeared.'

Nat said nothing. Then he took a careful look around him, opened the heavy curtains and the window, rolled up his sleeves and started stacking dishes in the sink.

'Nat, you don't have to do that. Listen, I . . . I'm sorry.'

He gave her a curious look. 'Don't be sorry. What happened?' Steaming hot water and bubbles were filling the sink.

'It kind of sunk in, once I came back from . . . I mean, I thought I was taking it okay at first. I kind of broke down.'

'Looks like it.'

'Don't be sarcastic.'

'Sorry.' Nat glanced up. He looked contrite. 'Listen, if you'd been out during the last week, you'd realise it's been all over the papers. His car washed up on some beach in Norfolk. The police have been searching for him, but they haven't found . . . Tash?' Nat stopped what he was doing and came over to her with open arms, dripping soap. 'I'm sorry. I really am. Don't cry, Tasha. Please.'

Tasha buried her face in his clean-smelling shirt. 'I can't help it. I don't know what's worse. Thinking he's dead, or – or wishing he was. Wishing I'd done it. Because I do sometimes.'

He held her close. 'You feel what you've got to feel.'

'Don't be so bloody Californian.'

He chuckled. 'I'm not. And you're not English either, so don't start talking like one of them.' A while later, he let her go and looked her hard in the face. 'You should go and take a shower.'

'Nat, I don't feel like it. I don't care. I don't think I ever want to leave this house again.'

'Just do it,' he said, insistent but patient. 'And we'll see how you feel after that.'

So she did.

By the time they got to the restaurant, which purported to be Russian and kosher, Tasha felt surprisingly hungry. She ordered the chicken soup with dumplings. 'Not like Grandma's,' she said.

'Nope. Not even close. But about as close as you'll get in London.' Nat tore off a chunk of bread. 'Listen, you don't have to tell me what's going on. But you can, if it'll make you feel better.'

Tasha sighed. 'I don't even know where to start. Peter's gone. He might be –' She lowered her voice. 'He might be dead. And Kristin's . . . Kristin's pregnant.'

Nat's eyes widened. Then he shook his head. 'How's she handling it?'

'Nat.' Tasha felt hurt. 'What about me?'

'I know.' He laid a hand on hers. 'Sorry. So is it . . . his?'

Tasha nodded silently. 'I don't want to be jealous. I know I wouldn't want to be . . . stuck, in her position, but . . .' She shook her head and found that tears were

417

flooding her eyes. 'It hurts. Just because – she's got something I know I'll never have now.'

'She's got a ton of problems and you should be glad you don't. For a start, the tabloids are probably hounding her.'

'Tabloids?'

'Sure. Conaway was like minor-league famous. And when he disappears . . . Look, it's pretty definite he's not dead. They dug up the car and dredged the beach. There was no body.'

Tasha felt a strange lightening inside her chest: an easing of tension. 'Are you sure? But . . . it could have washed out to sea.' *He's alive*, she thought. And felt a new hope: a fleeting happiness. Until she remembered. It could never be the same again. Not now.

Kristin is having his child.

She felt heavy again, inside. 'I don't know why I should care,' she said. 'He two-timed me all along. Right up until the . . . right up till last week, he was telling me I could move in with him. He just kept putting it off. But I thought he meant it. I wanted to believe him so much, I . . .' She shrugged. 'I just kept on waiting. I thought it was meant to be. That's why I can't stand to think about Kristin. And the baby.'

Nat nodded. 'I know.'

'Nat, what am I going to do?'

He smiled quickly. 'Eat,' he said, and pushed a dish of *pirogis* towards her. 'Eat now. Think later.'

Tasha smiled back faintly. She supposed he was right.

The next day, she ventured into a newsagents' and saw that he had been right, too, about the papers. Peter's disappearance didn't quite get headline status, but two of the tabloids carried inside stories, featuring photos of Peter's house in East Hingham and an old one of Kristin in a miniskirt. '*Renfrew: Love child?*' said one of the captions, and Tasha shook her head. How did they find out these things?

When she had finished reading, she sat and stared at her phone. Nat had made her promise to plug it back in. She thought for a moment about the emptiness in her life, and then about the fact that, in a way, she was lucky. Nobody from the tabloids was bothering her. Either they hadn't noticed that Sunday magazine piece about her and Peter, or the rumours about Kristin seemed more scintillating. For whatever reason, she was being left alone. She could put her life back together again. She wasn't pregnant. . . .

Finally she picked up the phone and tried Kristin's number.

The answering voice sounded stiff and guarded.

'Kristin?'

'I'm sorry, she's not here.'

'Kristin, I know it's you. It's Tasha.'

'Oh. Hi.'

'Have the papers been bugging you?'

'Some of them.' Kristin still sounded wary.

'I was just wondering . . . how you were doing.' Tasha paused. 'Are you feeling okay?'

'Not great. A bit sick these days.'

'Do you want to come over?'

'Maybe you'd better come over here.'

Half an hour later, wondering what on earth she was doing, Tasha pulled her Mini up in front of the mansion block in Pimlico. She had brought a strawberry tart with her, in a box. Though it was hard, she reflected, to guess what a person with morning sickness might feel like eating.

'I've gone off coffee.' Kristin poured out some water from a bottle.

'That's all right.' Tasha wondered again what she was doing here. 'Have the police, um . . . wanted to talk to you?'

'They did. They came here. Before the reporters or anything, so God knows how they found me. The only way I can think of is that landlord. You know – the one at

419

the pub by Peter's house? I always thought he was a nosy creep.'

Tasha smiled faintly.

'It's strange, I felt almost relieved. I kept waiting for them to say they were going to arrest me, take me away. I thought about trying to cover things up, but I didn't know where to start lying. In the end it all just came out. And then they just said, "Goodbye, Mrs Renfrew, thank you." That was all!' Kristin laughed, slightly edgily, and ran a hand through her hair. 'They seemed more pissed off that Peter had driven his car up on to the cliff path than anything else. They said he was looking for an accident.' She shrugged. 'Chivalrous of them, I suppose. I asked them if I ought to phone my solicitors, if there'd be any charges. They laughed.' She shook her head in disbelief. 'I can't believe that's it. That it's all over.'

'So are they going to find Peter now?'

'They said that wasn't really their job. So long as they could be sure there'd been no wrongdoing, he's within his rights to disappear. Isn't that strange?'

'It sounds,' said Tasha grimly, 'like a great way for Peter to land even more publicity. When he gets back here, at least.'

'I know.' Kristin gave a thin smile. 'But something tells me he won't be hurrying home.'

Tasha blinked, confounded. 'He won't be afraid of us.'

'Oh, no?'

Tasha watched Kristin smiling. Sometimes it seemed to her that she understood less than ever.

'I think,' said Kristin eventually, 'that he was beginning to feel hounded. Pursued.'

'By us?' Tasha gave a bewildered smile. 'What could we do to bother him?'

'Perhaps more than we might have thought.'

'So does anyone have any idea where he's gone?'

Kristin shrugged.

'I mean, I want to know. Don't you? There're a lot of

things about him I just don't understand. If he comes back again –'

'Tasha, forget it.'

She blinked and looked up at Kristin, startled. Kristin had sounded unusually forceful.

'Look,' she said. 'They . . . went into both his houses. They had a warrant, and there was nothing there. Or only a few bits of furniture. No clothes, nothing personal. He's cleared out completely.'

'But where?'

'We might as well give up asking that. We're not getting him back. You're not and I'm not. And even if I could, I wouldn't want him. I know what he's like now. I thought I did, before . . .'

'Sure,' said Tasha stiffly. 'But don't you wonder . . .'

'Frankly, no.' Kristin sipped her water and walked over towards the window.

It seemed to Tasha then that there were a lot of things she wanted to ask Kristin: about how it felt to be her. Alone, pregnant, about to divorce. And whether she was afraid. But she knew that it was equally impossible to ask any of these questions. Instead, she said lamely, 'Are you all right?'

'Of course,' Kristin answered. And Tasha didn't believe her.

Tasha thought, as she drove home that evening, that nothing at all was solved. That the police were a pathetic bunch if they couldn't even find out where Peter was: if they didn't even care. Unless Kristin was holding back . . .

She thought of the house in Hampstead, and the house in Norfolk. Were they going to sit there vacant for good? Peter wasn't the sort of person to run off and leave unfinished business behind. Whenever he had moved on before, he had made a clean break: from Lawrencetown, from New Haven . . . Tasha wondered for a moment which

421

other places he had left behind: perhaps places she didn't even know about.

And then it came to her that there was a way she could find out if he had left any clues. Not in Hampstead, where the house was too closely packed among its neighbours. But out in East Hingham. Peter had never given her a key to the house – to either of his houses, she realised now, to her chagrin. But she knew the code for the burglar alarm, and there was nothing else to stop her trying.

Once the notion had come to her, she grew restless. She knew that she should wait until the morning. But somehow she couldn't. There was still some light in the sky. Why not drive out? she asked herself.

Why not do it now?

The country road after the turn-off for the village was completely dark. Tasha thought she knew its twists and turns, but several times they surprised her; the Mini's engine struggled over bumps, and just when she caught sight of the first houses of East Hingham, a van came whizzing towards her down the centre of the road, and she had to pull over. When she tried to start up again, the engine died.

She glanced down at the indicator lights, all of which seemed to be blazing away; after three false starts with the ignition, she gave up. She wasn't so far from Peter's house now. She could walk the rest of the way.

So she locked up and got out. The darkness and quiet of the empty road spooked her slightly, but she kept her eyes fixed on the lights ahead. Just before the pub sign, there would be the turning for Peter's house. When she got near it, she started to run.

Gravel flew into her shoes and she had serious second thoughts as she came to the clump of trees that guarded the drive. An empty house, total darkness: she did not like to dwell on those prospects. Nor had she figured out yet exactly how she would get in.

So when she saw light shining out of the windows, she felt relieved. Someone was home. Peter was home. She might be angry at him, but just now she would be so glad to see him. She ran up the rest of the drive and thumped hard on the door.

It took some time before anyone came, and then the footsteps were light and hesitant.

'Yes? Who is it?'

A female voice. For a moment it paralysed Tasha. 'I'm – looking for Peter Conaway.'

'I'm his wife. Can I help you?'

The door opened slowly.

His wife? thought Tasha. *But she can't be. She looks like Katey. Katey's dead.*

'Are you all right?' said the other woman. 'Do you want to come in?'

32 'I suppose I should introduce myself,' said the woman at the door. 'My name's Kate. Are you Tasha?'

'How did you know that?' Tasha was still staring at the figure opposite her in the dim light of the doorway: tall and rangy with a mass of dark hair and thick eyebrows. She remembered how Peter had mentioned the eyebrows. Thinking of that – of the day, long ago at Elliott, when she came upon the diaries, the letters to 'Katey' on his computer, it struck her that she could almost be dreaming this. Katey was dead. Not a real, living person. Peter had said so.

Yet there she was, strikingly like the girl – woman – his descriptions had conjured, only older: late forties, perhaps, or even fifties. She had the kind of finely lined, high-cheekboned face Tasha had seen in pictures of ageing actresses; her hair was threaded through with grey. She wore a long skirt above bare feet, which slapped on the tiled floor as she turned towards the inside of the house. 'Do you want to come in?' she said neutrally.

'I think there's got to be a mistake,' said Tasha, who was beginning to feel afraid, for some reason, of entering. 'I'm looking,' she said again, 'for Peter Conaway.'

'Yes. Well, perhaps he never told you about me? We don't go by the same name.'

'How did you, um . . . . How did you get here?' said Tasha. She wanted to ask, *What are you doing here?*

'Shouldn't I be asking you that?'

Tasha looked around. They were at the dining-room doorway now. Something seemed different. The table, which Peter always kept bare, was strewn with papers – and then Tasha saw it. The Calder mobile had gone.

Relief flooded through her, as it had not before, whatever Kristin told her, whatever private conclusions she had drawn. If the mobile was gone, Peter had taken it with him: collected it, then calmly made his exit. So he was somewhere – far away, perhaps. But somewhere. And quite all right.

'Where is he?' said Tasha bluntly. And Kate shook her head.

'He wouldn't tell *me* that. Shall I make us tea?'

She was English, Tasha thought to herself as she waited in the living room. Her voice sounded nothing like Peter's. So his story that they had met in Dornoch was a lie. Besides which – how much older was she than he? Ten years, at least? They couldn't have been teenagers together. Ever.

Kate came back into the room a few minutes later, carrying a tray laid with a teapot and mugs decorated in what looked like graffiti. Peter's had always been white: Japanese.

'I'm sorry,' said Tasha, and she knew her voice sounded hostile, 'but I just don't know what's going on. Where you fit in.'

'Oh, I should think *I* fit in,' said Kate calmly, starting to pour. 'The question is, where you do. Or perhaps we should begin at the beginning.'

'So you're still married?' said Tasha. The tea leaves had clumped at the bottom of her cup. She thought, irrelevantly, that someone who knew about these things might venture to tell her future by them. Probably a miserable and lonely one.

'Oh, yes, in the eyes of the law. And the Church. We were never divorced.' Kate spoke with an airy certainty, and Tasha stared at her. *How dare she? How can she? Acting as if she possesses him.* She struggled to keep her face, her voice, calm.

'Isn't that kind of weird if you don't live together?'

'It suits us.'

'When did you get married?'

'1974.'

'But, wait a minute.' Tasha frowned, struggling with numbers. 'That doesn't add up. Peter was born in –'

'1952.'

'No, he wasn't. I mean, he said –'

Kate laughed. 'Whatever he told you, he was born in 1952 because when he came to the College of Art he was eighteen. It was in his records. I saw them.'

Tasha was liking this woman less and less. She wished she could puncture Kate's smugness, but she didn't know how.

'Perhaps,' said Kate charitably, 'when he met you and Kristin he wanted to seem younger. It would hardly have appealed to girls your age, would it, to know that he was married? The father of a little boy.'

'The father of a –'

'Liam's nineteen. He's lived with me, mostly. Except when he's away at school. He's at art school right now, in London. He did that drawing over the fireplace.' Kate inclined her head towards the picture Tasha had noticed before: the black arc of coastline, isolated on a white ground. 'That's Crail,' she said.

'Where?'

'Where I live,' Kate said. Then she shrugged. 'The East Neuk of Fife. I more or less washed up there, after Glasgow, and a spell in London. It seemed a good place to bring Liam up. And I didn't have much money once I stopped teaching. My parents had left me something, and that kept me and Liam going. Peter too, when he was in the States, and struggling.'

'But why?' Tasha seized hold of the only ammunition she had. 'Why should you pay for him to go away to the States and leave you behind?'

Kate looked hard at her. 'I rather think that's between us.'

Tasha studied her cup again. She felt as if she was assembling a puzzle whose parts consistently refused to fit. Whatever she did, a piece here or there remained missing. '*Why* did he go to the States?' she said doggedly.

'I always knew,' said Kate, 'that he had talent, but that it isn't enough, these days, to be appreciated here. One has to travel. You see, he was better than anyone else I ever taught. Better than me.' She gave a small laugh.

Tasha realised Kate was dodging her question. She opened her mouth, preparing to ask it yet again.

'More tea, Tasha?' said Kate.

'No – thanks. I'm all right.'

'I'd been meaning to ask you. You didn't phone me, about a week ago, did you? To say Peter was dead.'

'What?'

'The voice didn't sound American, but I wasn't sure.'

Kristin, thought Tasha suddenly. But she said nothing. Kristin could have made such a call and then forgotten it. Though that would mean that she knew who and where Kate was . . .

'It had me worried,' said Kate briskly, now, 'until I finally realised the sensible thing to do, since I couldn't get through to Peter, was to ring the police here. They came to check on the house and said everything seemed all right. And then I had a letter from Peter's solicitors.'

'His solicitors?'

'Because they had the keys to his houses. Apparently he's made them both over to me.'

Tasha grappled with different thoughts, different questions. Finally, she said only, 'Why?'

Kate looked at her evenly. 'He owed me a little, I think. I'm not exactly *very* rich. And then I suppose – he might have wanted to be free.'

'Free?'

'From material things. Surely you must have realised that about him? He never liked to be tied down.'

'He always liked –' Tasha swallowed. 'He likes cars, and things.'

'Oh, yes, because they move. But houses . . .' Kate smiled and shook her head. 'I must say I always thought it odd that he ended up owning any property at all. It was so unlike him. Of course, he could have been thinking they'd make him money. He was never averse to that.'

'So where is he now?'

'I don't know.' Kate laughed briefly. 'I got the impression even his solicitors don't.' She paused. 'I still do wonder about that phone call, though. Why should anyone have thought he was dead?'

Tasha looked at the ground.

'Tell me, what is this Kristin like?'

'We . . . used to be friends at school,' said Tasha weakly.

'Yes. I know.'

'Well. You know how it's hard to describe anyone you know too well. It's like that with Kristin.'

Kate shrugged, excusing herself, and took the tea things away to the kitchen.

When she came back, Tasha asked her, 'Did Peter ever write you . . . letters, on his computer?'

'Oh, yes, all the time.'

'Oh.'

'Why, does he write to you too?' Kate gave a light laugh. 'Quite the scribbler, isn't he? He writes to me, he used to write to Liam. Until they fell out over the computer thing.'

'Computer thing?'

'Peter did this piece called *Intimations*. A sort of great computer with a broken screen, and a hand sticking out –'

'*That* one. I've seen the posters.'

'He got the idea from a sketch Liam did and sent to him. He was only ten at the time and at first he was proud as anything that his dad had used his idea. Then he started to think he deserved some credit. His name on the posters.

Some of the royalties, even! Liam can be quite the prima donna too, sometimes. For years the two of them hardly spoke. But it's better now.'

Tasha scratched at a drop of paint which had caught in the furrows of her corduroy trousers. It was taking her some time to adjust to all this. A wife. A son. She had never expected marriage from Peter – she had been quite sure it didn't matter to her, whether she ever got married or had children – but now that she knew Peter was married, already, and had a child, so that perhaps he wouldn't want any more ... 'I don't see the point,' she said now, aggressively, 'of you two staying married if you didn't live together.'

'You don't understand.' Kate's chiselled face was calm. 'We're both Catholic – oh, yes, Peter is, too, he was raised that way. And in the eyes of God we'll always be married. Some piece of paper, some flimsy so-called divorce, isn't going to make a bit of difference to that.' She had delivered all this without changing expression. Now she smiled slightly and ran a hand over the greying tendrils of her hair. 'And we don't want to be divorced, either. We may not see each other often, but Peter always comes home. Every Christmas and every summer.'

'And – other times?' A vague memory was returning to Tasha, from the interview in the *New York Times Magazine*. It had said something about his living in a friend's borrowed cottage in Fife . . .

'Oh, other times, too. I never quite know when he's going to turn up. But he does. And then, you see, we're happy. We weren't particularly, living together when Liam was small. But now . . .' A dreaming smile crossed Kate's face.

'So why doesn't he tell anybody he's married to you? Why does he keep it a secret?'

The smile disappeared and a thin, sour line appeared at each corner of Kate's mouth. Then she shrugged, her fingers twining themselves in her hair. 'Our marriage is our business. Why should it be anybody else's?'

'How can you call somebody your husband who won't even admit to knowing you?'

'Peter's his own man. He's beyond being owned by anybody. You must realise at least that much, Tasha.'

'I'm not like that. I never wanted to own him.'

'Well, I'm glad, because then you won't mind, now he's gone. You didn't really know him anyway.'

'You can't say that.' Tasha's voice spluttered, blocked by incipient tears. 'We talked about everything. Art and work and life –'

'Don't you realise? Talk is nothing to Peter. It doesn't count. He could talk to you for ten years running, you still wouldn't know him. You have to learn what he doesn't say. You have to learn about the lies. The other women. Oh, yes, there were plenty of those. Not just me. Not just you and Kristin.'

'Sure.' The tears stung Tasha's eyes now. 'Of course. I mean, we always both understood, we were going to see other people . . .'

'The odd thing was the way he stuck with you and Kristin. I suppose at first it was just the novelty.' Kate shrugged. 'What man could resist that, after all? Running two girls at once. Girls not even out of school. Creating little rivalries . . .'

Tasha didn't think she could listen to any more. 'Excuse me,' she said, and ran out to the bathroom.

Once she was there, she took a deep breath, and the tears receded. She knew what she wanted: just a minute or two alone in the house. To see that it was empty, and mourn the fact that everything was over.

The inside of her mouth tasted bitter. *Three women. Not just two. There were three of us.* She splashed cold water on her face and opened the door quietly; the hall was dark. Kate must still be through in the living room.

On Tasha's left lay the bedroom door. She moved

quietly over and opened it. The room was dark, empty, and she didn't dare put on a light. She didn't know, after all, what she was looking for.

She wondered if he had taken away every last piece of clothing – not that he owned many clothes. Every computer disc: every personal possession. She went over to the bare desktop where his latest computer had once been, and opened the drawer beneath. Something rattled behind it, and seemed to fall.

She knelt on the ground, and picked it up. A little book. A passport. *Republic of Ireland*.

She opened the cover and saw the photograph: black and white, his face craggy and puffy in a cruel light. She saw the name: Peter Michael Conaway. The date of birth: 20 October 1952, East Kilbride, Scotland.

A place he had never mentioned. Not Dornoch, not Glasgow. And it seemed to her then that Dornoch might or might not exist, that what she had read in the *Times* article – that he was the son of an art teacher in Glasgow – might or might not be true. That nothing was certain, except what she saw before her. The photo. The few bare facts.

She looked again at the dates – the date of issue – and saw that the passport had expired. He must have got hold of it because he had Irish grandparents, and then, using his British one, not missed it when he ran away. Well, he wouldn't be back for it now. Tasha put it in her pocket.

Walking back into the living room, she felt almost calm. 'I've got to go home now,' she said.

'Well.' Kate smoothed her skirt and stood.

'There was just one thing I wondered. Did he ever talk to you much about Dornoch?'

'Dornoch?' Kate frowned. 'I don't think so.'

'Some kind of town on the Firth of Clyde? With a factory?'

'Oh, yes. I remember him talking about someplace . . . I don't remember the name, but it was somewhere outside Glasgow, and he used to go and visit his cousins. You see, because he was an only child and his parents were elderly – they're both dead now – they must have thought it would be good for him to be with other children. Why?'

'Oh . . . no reason.' Tasha felt something crumbling inside her. Another certainty. Kate was right: she knew nothing. 'He grew up in Glasgow, then?'

'Yes.'

'Funny, how he ended up down here. In the country and everything.'

'Oh, I don't think so at all. You see, what he told me, Tasha, after he bought this house, was that we both looked out on the same sea. However far apart we were.'

'Oh.' Tasha backed down the corridor, towards the door, which Kate reached and opened.

'You know, I'm glad I met you after all this time. I'd be quite curious to meet Kristin.'

'Why?' said Tasha blankly.

'Well, I can't imagine *you* were the one Peter was so afraid of.'

Tasha couldn't seem to find the words for an answer. 'Afraid,' she repeated.

'Oh, yes. You see, he told me what was going on down here. I knew he'd try to spin it out as long as he could. He's like that. But I think something was making him nervous. Crowding him in.'

Me, thought Tasha. *Wanting to move in*. Or Kristin, wanting . . . Wanting what?

Kate was holding the door open. 'I think your friend Kristin might have got at one or two of his secrets. Oh, well. I'm glad I met you, anyway. Funny, but I feel a sort of link with you both. None of the others have managed to hold him.'

Tasha mumbled something – it must have been 'goodbye' – and ducked her head and ran out along the gravel pathway. She heard the door slam closed, and felt an immense relief. She remembered only a minute or so later, when she reached the road, that she should have asked

Kate if she could make a phone call. She was going to have to do something about her car. If she couldn't get it started and had to go back to the house, she'd feel like an idiot.

As if that matters. You are an idiot, Tasha. He had you fooled all along.

Tears came up and overflowed, blurring her sight. Sometimes she felt grass under her feet, sometimes asphalt. She couldn't see her car yet; now she heard the hum of a motor behind her, growing quickly louder.

She felt a thump at the base of her spine; and then nothing. She was spinning into blackness.

'Hello. I'm trying to get hold of Tasha –'

Kristin heard a silence at the other end of the phone. A male voice had answered it, sounding strangely familiar, and not just because it was American. 'I do have the right number, don't I?' she said.

'Sure, uh . . . yeah. This is her brother. Nat.'

'Nat! I used to talk to you ages ago. This is Kristin.'

'Oh.'

Kristin wondered at the voice's hostility, then gave an inward shrug. There could be a thousand explanations. 'So is Tasha there?'

'No. Actually she's in hospital.'

'What?'

'She's had an accident. A car crashed into her out on a road in Norfolk. I'm just here to pick up a few of her things before I go out and see her.'

'But is she all right? Is she very badly hurt?'

'I'm surprised you sound so concerned.'

Kristin fell silent. So, he knew. Knew something. Knew enough for him to begin to dislike her. She said at last, 'You shouldn't be. It's all rather complicated. But I have every reason in the world to worry about Tasha. I hope she's okay.'

'She came out not too badly,' said Nat laconically. 'It sounds like just a concussion. Some guy driving home

433

from the pub bumped into her. For some reason she was walking in the middle of the road.'

'I see.'

'It seems like her car broke down. Listen' – Nat's voice was reluctant, slow – 'if you want to go out to Norfolk and see her, feel free.'

'I would, but it's a bit awkward. I don't drive.'

Nat sounded even more reluctant this time. 'I'm driving out in about half an hour. Do you want to come with me?'

Tasha gave a hazy smile up at the face above hers. Sun was washing, bright, across the room, so she could see little of the face except that it was male and friendly-looking, surrounded by chestnut curls.

'You look not too bad for someone who got knocked down by a car less than twelve hours ago.'

'Twelve hours? Is it that long?' Tasha rubbed her eyes. 'What happened, exactly? Do you know?'

'You were walking on the wrong side of the road. A man ran into you. Phoned for an ambulance.'

'A man?' For some reason this surprised Tasha: then she realised. Insofar as she remembered the accident – recalled her thoughts in her odd moments of consciousness last night – she had been convinced that it must have been a woman. Kate. Pulling out of the drive in a car, then running her down. How ridiculous.

'You're American, aren't you?' The man – he must be a doctor – glanced again at Tasha's notes. 'Seidelman. My father used to have some cousins called that, in New York. Funny. So where are you from?'

'New York.'

The doctor looked up sharply from his notes. His eyes were a very bright blue. 'New York? Are you serious?'

'Yeah. So what . . .'

'You're Natasha Seidelman.'

Tasha's head was aching. She reached up carefully to touch the source of the pain, which turned out to be a crusty-feeling lump above her left eye. Her hand quickly retreated.

'I'm sorry.' The doctor put the notes down again. 'I should have explained. We must be cousins. Well, distant ones anyway. I'm Jonathan Seberg.'

'Jonathan . . .' Tasha squinted, bringing back the sharp pain in her head, and let out an involuntary groan. 'You mean you're . . .' Her memory seemed to have gone rather hazy. *Seberg. Orthopaedics . . .*

'I'm not normally on this ward. I'm in orthopaedics.'

'I think I've heard of you.'

'I think I've heard of you, too.' The doctor – Jonathan – grinned.

Nice teeth, Tasha thought. And nice hair. Definitely nice hair. *Tasha Seidelman, you are incorrigible.*

'I've got to go now. But listen, I'll come back and see you before you go. With any luck, they'll let you out this afternoon. Looks like you have some visitors.' Jonathan Seberg glanced towards the door.

Tasha looked over and blinked. Nat and Kristin. Kristin and Nat. There was something very strange about seeing them together, but just now she couldn't quite identify what it was. They were standing a foot or so apart, like people who weren't quite strangers but would rather remain so. Now Jonathan headed towards them and spoke briefly to Nat. The two men nodded, grinned, shook hands. Jonathan must be explaining, Tasha thought. Explaining that we're cousins . . .

When Jonathan had gone, Nat came over to Tasha's bed. He handed her a box covered in Hebrew lettering.

'Halva! You're sweet. I don't think I can chew it, though.' Tasha tilted her face for a kiss. 'My whole head hurts.'

'I'm not surprised. You look like the rehearsal for a low-budget horror film.'

'Thanks a lot, bro.'

Nat glanced back towards Kristin. For a second he

looked strangely aloof, almost hostile. His hands were buried in his pockets.

'Why don't you come in?' Tasha called, and Kristin moved forward, with a wary look at Nat. For a second they seemed to measure each other up, neither of them smiling, but their locked gazes had a curious intensity Tasha couldn't seem to place. And then she remembered. Of course: they had never met before. Talked on the phone, but never met. And yet they must know all kinds of things about each other.

Nat smiled and broke the silence. 'So what I want to know is, how did you get run down by a car in the middle of Norfolk?'

'Long story,' said Tasha.

'Your Mini's at a garage for repairs. If you ask me, it's not worth –'

'Yeah, well, I didn't ask.'

Nat backed away from the bed. 'See?' He spoke to Kristin for the first time. 'Won't listen to sense. She's all yours.'

He went out into the hall, leaving them together. Every now and then his head would appear in the doorway; he glanced at Tasha, and then at Kristin, with the same guarded hostility as before. Tasha wanted to laugh. *She's not going to bite you*, she thought. And then it struck her that her brother might be afraid of women: afraid, at least, of the ones who attracted him. In case history might repeat itself.

Then she dismissed the thought and concentrated on what Kristin was saying.

'So yesterday I went for a scan. Do you want to see the picture?' Kristin's voice was brisk, her cheeks flushed, echoing the bright red of her long flared dress. Beneath it she still looked bony, insubstantial, and not the least bit pregnant.

Since Tasha hadn't refused her offer, she dug in her handbag and finally produced a slip of shiny paper. Tasha saw a grey, blurred background with a white beanlike shape in the middle of it.

'All the nurses said it came out really well,' said Kristin eagerly. 'Eleven weeks.'

'So does this mean you're going to . . .' Tasha swallowed. She couldn't seem to come out with the words. 'Going to, like, have it? Keep the baby?'

'Of course! What else could I do?' Kristin looked perplexed. 'You didn't think – just because Peter's gone . . .'

'I don't know.'

'I could hardly do anything else. Don't you see?' Kristin's eyes looked a more intense shade of blue than usual. 'If you're about to tell me it's going to be hard, don't bother. I know that, Tasha.'

'I wasn't. To tell you the truth, I hadn't actually thought that far.'

'Well, I have.' Kristin closed her handbag neatly. 'It'll be born at the beginning of October. I can go on working up till near the time. I shall need to find a house, and hopefully learn to drive. I shall be very busy.'

'A house –'

'A cottage, I hope. I've been thinking perhaps of Oxfordshire. I don't want to stay in London. With a baby . . .'

'So this is really going to happen?'

Kristin looked down at Tasha and took her hand. 'I do know how you must feel. I'm sorry.'

'Sorry?' Tasha's head was aching again.

'You have to believe me. I never *planned* to have Peter's baby. If anyone had told me ten years ago that I was going to end up a single mum, I'd have said they were right off their head!' Kristin gave a faint laugh. 'My mother's quite horrified.'

'You mean you're talking to her?'

'I finally rang her. I think she's more shocked at the

notion of becoming a grandmother than by the fact that I'm not married anymore.'

Tasha smiled. 'How about Alex?'

'Alex is . . . all right,' said Kristin carefully. 'He's seeing another woman actually. Someone called Naomi. A solicitor.' Kristin tossed her hair back. 'Well. That's quite enough about me. How about you? How did all this happen?'

So Tasha told her. She wondered why Kristin didn't seem very surprised to hear of Kate's existence; then gradually forgot to wonder, as she kept on talking.

'I picked up something,' she said finally. 'It's in my bag, if you can find it.'

Kristin searched for a moment in the bedside cabinet, and eventually took out the Irish passport. She opened it; studied the photograph impassively. 'Why did you keep this?'

'I don't know.' Tasha shrugged. 'Maybe because it made him real again. I was starting to think I didn't know anything about him at all. He'd told us so many stories.'

'So,' said Kristin, 'he's an only child. I always thought those brothers and sisters he talked about didn't have much substance to them.'

Tasha giggled. 'I think sometimes he lost track of how many there were supposed to be.' Then her face grew sombre. 'Did you know about Kate?'

'Kate, yes. I tracked her down . . . when I was doing a photo shoot, at Peter's house. I don't suppose I told you.'

'Never mind.'

'But I didn't know then about Liam.'

A silence fell. They both looked at each other, then away. 'It wasn't,' Tasha said at last, 'as if he had *that* much to hide. His age – well, big deal. A wife and son.'

'So what was Kate actually like? I've seen her, but somehow – we never spoke.'

Tasha tried to tell Kristin, sensing her own ineptitude with words. 'She didn't seem like a bad person,' she said at last. 'Just kind of pathetic. The funny thing is, I knew about her all along.' She told Kristin about the day, long ago at Elliott, when she had come across Peter's letter to Kate on the computer. 'He made up this story. He said she was a girl back in Dornoch, who died.'

Kristin laughed faintly. 'But Dornoch doesn't exist.'

'I know. I went looking for it when I was over here the last time – before I saw you in Paris. There turned out to be towns with names like it, but never in the right place to be the one he was talking about.'

Kristin frowned. 'But why did you go looking for it then? That year? You wouldn't have seen Peter in . . .'

Tasha sighed. 'I had just seen him. In New Haven, that summer. Do you remember? I told you.'

'Of course you did. It seems such an age ago.' Kristin studied her fingers. 'I suppose I was never strictly honest with you, myself. Because actually – I ran into him, too, in London, just before I was married. I was wandering through the Tate, and there he was, at work.'

'Does it begin to seem as if it wasn't entirely an accident?'

'But it must have been. I don't know how else . . .'

'Fate?'

'I was so sure I'd see him again when I got back from my trip to Europe. But he'd just disappeared. To Japan. The guy who'd rented his house –'

Kristin interrupted, almost as if she hadn't heard. 'Yes, he disappeared. That was it exactly. He left me a note, saying he didn't want to ruin my plans . . .'

'We started writing letters . . .'

They caught each other's eye, then, and stopped.

'It's over,' said Kristin.

'It was always going to be, wasn't it?'

Neither of them answered the question. Tasha shifted in bed. Her head was starting to throb. 'Are you going to be – all right, on your own?' she said at last.

'Of course,' said Kristin brightly. And then, 'Well, I hope

so. What can I say? I don't know much about babies. Silly of me, when for so many years I'd been trying so hard to have one.'

'Are you scared?' said Tasha. 'You know. Labour and all that. And after.'

Kristin got up and walked towards the window, not answering.

'It's all right. I think everybody is, a little.'

Kristin turned sharply, forcing a smile. 'Of course I'm scared. Scared out of my wits when I think about it. All I can do is not think, really.' She grasped the rail at the side of Tasha's bed and began to knead it, the tips of her fingers turning white. 'Oh, I've got certain things all worked out. I know I can fend off anyone who's nosy enough to start asking about the baby's father. I don't think people will, not these days. But then I wonder sometimes what I'll tell *it*. I mean, the baby. Him or her . . .'

'You've got time to think about that.'

Kristin gave a brief laugh. 'He's nothing to be ashamed of really, is he? For a father. He's clever and good-looking and talented. I suppose. Not that I ever could figure that out. Even after all these years, I've still got no idea whether he was any good or not. I'm so hopeless at modern art. Isn't that queer?'

Tasha sighed. She felt the tension in her sore forehead start to ease. She was glad of a question she could answer, at least. Or begin to. 'Kate said he was more talented than anyone she'd ever taught. I think he's talented, too. But he did less than he could. He could have been a really good artist, a really good draughtsman, a real sculptor instead of someone who just stuck old scraps together. But he knew what'd sell. What would get him known. An idea like *Intimations* . . .' Which, she added mentally, was not even his.

'I guessed it was something like that.' Kristin rubbed the bar of the bed.

Tasha took a deep breath. For some odd reason, she felt

440

better. There had been something she understood about Peter, then, that Kristin hadn't. 'Listen,' she said. 'Nat'll be up here again soon. I just wanted to say,' – she looked up earnestly, almost nervously – 'if you need any help with the baby – you know, when the time comes . . .'

Kristin's eyes met hers. 'It seems rather a lot to ask, under the circumstances.'

'If I'm in the States, I can fly over. It's no problem.'

Kristin looked down. 'Tasha, you're too nice. Too kind. Stop it!'

Tasha stared at her, wounded. And then, without looking at her, Kristin reached out with one hand. She twined it around Tasha's. 'Forgive me.'

'That's what I'm trying to tell you.' Tasha's voice sounded blurred and watery. 'I have.'

Kristin didn't answer but her hand clasped more tightly around Tasha's. It shook a little from the strength of her grip, and the nails dug in.

When Nat reappeared, Kristin wondered what he and Tasha found to talk about. It felt intrusive staying with them, so she stood out in the hospital corridor, trying to grow used to the idea that she would be spending time in such a place six months or so down the line. It still seemed unreal, whatever the doctor told her: whatever the scan showed. Did she deserve to be so lucky – so blessed?

Sometimes she thought that whatever else she did with her life now wouldn't matter so much. She would have her baby. Not at the perfect time, in the perfect house, with the perfect husband: but a baby all the same, and the rest might come, or not. People would be bound to see her as flawed, slightly fallible. She saw herself that way. And, strangely, it made everything easier.

Through the glass window of the ward she could see Nat Seidelman coming towards her. There was something aggressive about the unsmiling line of his mouth, and hostility – or she thought so – in his dark eyes. He opened

441

the door and jerked his head back towards Tasha. 'Do you want to see her again before we go find lunch? I talked to the doctors. They're going to let her go this afternoon but they want to check a couple of things first.'

'Good. No,' Kristin answered Nat's question belatedly. 'We had plenty of time to talk, before. I'll let her have some peace now.' She gave Tasha a nod and a wave through the window. Then she and Nat walked away down the corridor.

'You know the way into Norwich from here?'

'Sort of.'

'I thought we could see the cathedral.'

Kristin shrugged and walked on. She wondered why someone who rather obviously disliked her was proposing lunch. Out of a sense of obligation, perhaps? They reached the exit to the car park. 'You know,' she said, 'you don't have to entertain me for lunch. Go on your own if you like.'

Nat turned, his hand on the door, and smiled slightly. 'But I don't like.'

Kristin walked out past him. For the first time, she sensed his physical presence: the vague warmth emanating from his body. Nat was not particularly tall, and more wiry than Tasha or his other brothers. Yet, she suspected now, he was strong. He gave off that feeling.

A minute or so later, he was unlocking the door on her side of the car. 'Actually, if you know the way, why don't you drive?' he said. 'This car's insured for anybody.'

'I don't drive,' said Kristin quickly.

He stared at her as if she were crazy.

'Yes, I know, there must be something wrong with me, everyone drives. Especially in America. Actually, I'm thinking of learning.'

'When?'

'When what?'

'When're you going to learn?'

'Well, sometime, when –'

'How about now?' He tossed the keys up towards her, over the roof of the car.

'Nat, I don't know – ' Surprising herself, Kristin caught them.

'Look, I've been in three car crashes already. Nothing's going to faze me.'

Kristin studied the keys. 'Three? I didn't know that.'

'There's probably a lot you don't know about me. So. I'll tell you what to do.' He was watching her. In the daylight, his eyes held a hint of green. 'Believe me, if you fuck up, I'll let you know.' He smiled.

She wondered for a second why she had felt the old thrill, the quickening, at the words: *I'll tell you what to do.* Nat was a perfectly normal man. He was talking about driving. And yet . . .

Something fluttered in her stomach as she sat down in the driver's seat. She found the ignition. The keys wouldn't go in at first. Finally she jabbed them in, turning them, and heard the engine cough and die. She felt a fool.

'I can see,' Nat said, 'we're going to have to start at the beginning.'

'You know, I don't have a learner's permit yet –'

'Pull out the choke when you turn the key. That thing. There.'

Kristin did as she was told. She was, she had time to reflect as the car reversed very slowly out of its space, rather good, by now, at doing what she was told.

Yet perhaps she would like to take the lead, sometime. To do the telling. She glanced over at Nat's profile as the car moved unsteadily, but in a reasonably straight line, towards the exit gate. She saw the faintly contemptuous curl of his upper lip: the veiled eyes. Suddenly, vividly, she imagined him looking up with those eyes from beneath her.

'Don't look at me, look at the road,' he said.

'You've been in three car crashes. Why not go for four?' she said, smiling, as she took the car out into the traffic.

443

Jonathan Seberg set two mugs down on the bedside cabinet. 'The real stuff,' he announced. 'Doctors' brew, from the staff canteen.'

Tasha squinted up. 'Thanks.'

'Sorry. Were you asleep?'

'No. I'm not sure. Just tired, I think. My head's kind of swimming.'

'That'll be the knock you took.'

Tasha, who was not sure that was the reason anymore, didn't say so.

Jonathan handed her a bar of chocolate and proceeded to unwrap one of his own. 'Lunch,' he said.

'You're kidding. It's four o'clock.'

'I had people to see until five minutes ago. And' – he glanced at his watch – 'more people to see about five minutes from now. But I wanted to catch you before you left.'

Tasha nibbled at her chocolate. It tasted better than lunch had. Then she noticed that Jonathan's was already gone. 'Here.' She held out the bar. 'You have this. Chocolate isn't much to keep you going all day.'

'You sound like my mother.' Jonathan's eyes lit on the wrapper. They were, Tasha noticed, very blue. Almost turquoise. 'You sure?'

Tasha grinned. 'I can't wait to tell Aunt Mattie I met you. I'll have to see her before I go back to New York.'

'You're going back to New York? When?'

'As soon as I can.'

Jonathan leaned forward on his elbows and looked at her. 'So. You hate it that much here, do you?'

She laughed. 'No. I like it. It's just . . .' She shook her head. 'Some weird things have happened to me here. And my visa's running out. I'm starting to miss home.'

'I've heard the drivers are quite relaxed in New York. They pull over when they see somebody who wants to walk up the middle of the road.'

Tasha laughed. 'Enough. I was stupid. My car broke down, and I wasn't thinking.'

Jonathan smiled and glanced at his watch.

'Don't hang around for me. I'm okay on my own.'

'I'm not.' He swigged his tea. 'I'm just thinking how it's too bad you're leaving so soon. I've never met any poets before.'

'Poets?'

'Aren't you a poet? Aunt Mattie said –'

'I'm a painter.' Tasha laughed again and gathered back her hair. 'I paint, and I design sets for plays.' Her hair, at least the ends of it, felt clean. She hated to think what her face must look like, though.

'So what I've always wondered is, how do you get the scale right? I mean, painting something as big as that. Do you have to keep running backwards and forwards?' Jonathan's forehead, under the curly hair, was wrinkling, in what looked like genuine puzzlement.

'Yeah, that's the least of it. You can plot your designs out ahead of time and transfer them. You know. To scale.'

He shook his head. 'I can't imagine it. That's what comes of staring for too long at anatomy textbooks. Part of your brain shrivels and dies.'

'But anatomy's useful. Knowing how bodies are constructed. I mean, look at Lucian Freud.'

Jonathan looked puzzled again.

'You know, the painter?'

He looked sheepish now. 'I thought he was an author or something.'

It took Tasha a second to overcome her shock. Then she grinned suddenly. 'Who cares?'

'What?'

'Everybody has the stuff they know. You have yours, I have mine. Why's one thing any more important than another? By the way, what about your patients?'

Jonathan grimaced at his watch. 'Right. Well. You know, I wonder sometimes. There's a whole world out there – plays, art, books, the kind of things you do – and I'm missing it. All so a few people's bones can get glued together again, in a worse position than they started out in the first place.' Then he ran a hand through his hair and smiled again. 'Listen. Are you going back to London? I mean, are you going to be around there?'

'Yeah, for a couple of weeks. I haven't exactly –'

'Can I meet you sometime?'

Tasha ducked her head. 'Gee. I'm not sure. I . . .' She felt ashamed. Here was a nice man – they had nothing in common of course – but *nice*. Cute. It seemed to her that she owed him the truth. But it was all so complicated. 'I'd . . . like to see you, but maybe it's just too much. I've just – broken up with someone, and . . .' Her voice trailed off.

'That's okay. I understand.' Jonathan stood.

She looked up at him. 'Thanks for the tea.'

'Sure.' He picked up the mugs, and just then Nat and Kristin came in. Nat was smiling, and Kristin's cheeks were flushed.

Tasha tried not to feel her heart sinking slightly. Tried not to think why. If the tension between those two had gone, so much the better. In the doorway, Jonathan spoke to Nat again, briefly, and gave her a wave. Then he was gone.

Stupid, Tasha, she told herself. *Stupid.* She shouldn't have turned him down: not so flatly.

But then, she was going home soon. To New York. And for now, back to London. Nat had already slung her bag over his shoulder, and Tasha took hold of his hand and Kristin's and slid gingerly down off the bed.

33 Tasha was thinking of having a farewell bash before she went back to New York. Every now and then she turned the idea over in her mind, wondering how she could fit more than three or four people in her flat – wondering if she knew more than three or four people in London who would want to come. But when she thought about it, she did. There were the actors and all the other people she'd met who helped out at the Marlowe. There was Adrian Joseph, with whom she was on speaking terms again. A few days after her accident in Norfolk, she had swallowed her pride and called him; and he had been the first to apologise. 'Look. I can't tell you how sorry I am. Kristin has told me she came up with a pack of lies. Tasha, what can I say? Do you want your job back?'

But she had told him she thought not. It was time to move on.

May, she thought. In a week it would be May, and if she held out another week or two there was every chance it would be sunny enough to hold a party outside. In a park, or even in the disused little patio at the back of her building. Which brought her back to the guest list. She sat by the window with her address book and started to write it down. Kristin, of course, and Nat, and Adrian and the Sebergs.

Jonathan Seberg. She hadn't been thinking about him: hadn't been meaning to, but somehow, there he was. Popping into her mind again, curly-haired, blue-eyed, grinning. She had been mean with him, she knew, that day at the hospital. Though perhaps it was forgivable, under the circumstances.

Should she invite him?

Sometimes decisions came rashly, quickly. She reached down under the table for her phone book, then realised that of course he was in Norfolk. She would have to phone enquiries. What had the name of that hospital been?

A few minutes later, she heard the line ringing. She could hardly believe she was doing this.

'Dr Seberg.'

'Oh. Hi. Got you in person. I wasn't expecting to.' Tasha giggled, feeling foolish.

'Is that Tasha?' Jonathan sounded groggy.

He had recognised her voice right away, though. Tasha felt absurdly pleased. 'Yeah.'

'Sorry if I sound out of it. You woke me up. I'm on call.'

'Oh. Sorry.' Tasha drew a deep breath. 'Listen, I was thinking . . .' *The party,* she thought. *The party.* Yet suddenly it seemed cowardly: inadequate. 'Do you ever come into London? Because if you do, it'd be nice to see you. I could cook you dinner. Or lunch or something. We could go to a gallery. Or a play . . .'

'Which one, then? Am I supposed to pick?'

She heard his faint laughter, and felt foolish again. *You should have been definite, Tasha. Decisive.*

'Well, yes,' he said. 'To whichever.'

'Are you free this weekend?' Tasha stood up with the phone cradled against her ear, on her shoulder. She felt light and free. Like flying. When Jonathan said he had to work this weekend and couldn't come in till the next one, she didn't mind. 'Fine,' she said. 'I'm also thinking of having a kind of going-away party. But I'm not sure when. Depends on the weather.' *Idiot,* she told herself. You should never invite someone to two things in a row. What if the first one doesn't work out?

'Great,' he said. 'I'm just sorry about the reason.'

'The reason?'

'That it's a going-away party.'

'Oh.' She laughed. And then she heard a bleeping noise

in the background. When Jonathan had to hang up, then, because he was being called, she held on to the receiver for a moment, smiling to herself. Next weekend, he was coming in. That wasn't so far away.

Her door buzzer sounded then, and she ran down the stairs, surprised at the sight of a red mail van parked outside. She couldn't think of anyone who would be sending her a package. She took the box, which was long and narrow and neatly wrapped, covered in stamps and black Oriental lettering.

Japan. She didn't know why, but she guessed at once that was where this came from. Upstairs in her flat, she tore open the paper, then cut away the tape and layers of bubble wrap. Whatever was in here, someone had packed it up professionally.

The box, when it came out, was actually quite light. It had a sliding black lacquered lid, with an elaborate inlay of tall flowers. She opened it. There was a tiny scroll of paper inside. Hand-written.

FOR TASHA. GOOD LUCK IN ALL YOU DO. LOVE, PETER.

She flipped the piece of paper to and fro in the light. Whatever she did, it refused to tell her any more. The box, she realised on studying it longer, was for paintbrushes. She tried to ignore the strange stirring she felt in the region of her heart as she slid the lid to and fro. It reminded her a little of the teapot Alex and Kristin had once given her. Too expensive, too breakable: out of place, somehow, in her clumsy life, yet too fine to give away.

Yet perhaps it was sturdier than that. She gave it an experimental knock; then she wrapped it up in its tissue again, and called Kristin.

'That's funny,' Kristin said. 'I had a parcel, too. Do you want to see it?'

So – Tasha was not sure quite why, for she had no more desire to dwell on Kristin's gift than contemplate her own – she found herself revving up the engine of her repaired Mini and fighting her way south through lunchtime traffic. It was a day of intermittent sunshine: hints of summer in the drifting clouds. As she pulled in at the kerb, Kristin called down from her upstairs window.

'I'm glad you came anyway. I was wanting to show you – I've found a house.'

Tasha called back, 'A what?'

'A house! Never mind, come up, I've got coffee on, I'll show you the particulars.'

Tasha climbed the stairs and Kristin met her halfway, planting a kiss on her cheek. She smelt sweet and watery, and she took Tasha's hand and tugged her towards the door. It seemed an oddly childlike gesture in a woman four months pregnant, whose long flowery dress drifted out below her waist, over the slightest of bumps; whose dining-room table was loaded with camera equipment and who was talking at a rapid rate about book assignments, estate agents and houses.

'Book?' said Tasha in midstream. 'Wait a minute, what book?'

'The one I'm doing for that friend of Diana's.' Kristin beamed and poured coffee. 'Poland and Lithuania. All the fantastic old houses and palaces . . . I'm going to take pictures and find out who's living there now. Next spring, I hope. Or summer.'

'What about the baby?'

'She'll come with me! Or he. Of course.' Kristin gave an indefatigable smile. 'I'll just have to take things slowly. Diana's already on to me about a nanny but I don't know how I'd afford one. Anyway, I don't want it. Nat's going to be over in the Czech Republic and he said if it'd make it any easier –'

'Yeah. I know.' Tasha watched Kristin, who was studying her coffee. She knew that Nat was expecting to be transferred to Prague, but not much else.

'I'll show you what Peter sent.' Kristin hopped up abruptly from the table. A minute later she came back from her bedroom. 'It's just this. There was no note.' She

450

held out a picture in a frame; Tasha peered through the reflections in the glass. She saw a mother and child – long-limbed, oval-faced, stylised, almost hidden by the details of their antique costumes and the pagodas and mountains in the background. The paper they were painted on was brown and looked very old.

'I'm thinking,' Kristin said, 'of selling it. If I took it to Christie's . . .'

'Would you?' Tasha gasped, startled. 'Could you . . .'

'Of course I could. This is guilt money. I need a new camera.' Kristin studied the painting for a second. 'It is very beautiful.'

'If you sell yours,' said Tasha suddenly, 'I'll sell mine. Or give it away.'

Kristin looked at her, puzzled. 'Why? It doesn't matter.'

Tasha stood up and stretched. 'Because you're right. It's over. You know, I think it's almost sinister, the way he's trying to make some claim on us from over there. Trying to remind us of him.'

'We don't have to remember.'

'Leave that to Kate.' The sound of the name still hurt, slightly: the effort of saying it. Yet perhaps each time she said it, it would hurt less. Kate. Kate. Kate.

For a moment the rogue notion of sending Kate the paintbrush box flitted into Tasha's mind, and away again. And yet, maybe she would. 'Poor old Kate,' she said.

'Don't feel sorry for her. She's chosen the way she lives her life.' Kristin walked over towards the window.

'Kristin –' Tasha knew she had to say it. Now, or eventually. 'Be nice to Nat.'

Kristin turned, and there was a strange look on her face. Pinkness in her cheeks, and an expression of puzzlement. 'I couldn't do anything else.'

'He's had a hard time. I mean, from women.'

'Yes, I know. He's told me.'

'And – you see, he's my brother, and I don't want him to be –'

'Trust me.' Kristin looked at Tasha hard, then turned her head away, swiping at her eyes. 'I do want it to be different this time. I want to change.'

It seemed to Tasha that there was no way of answering that.

'He knows about the baby. Anyway, Tasha, I think your brother can take care of himself. Anyone who's survived three car crashes – '

'Three what?'

Kristin was fidgeting with the window lock. 'Maybe he never told you. I suppose he didn't want you to worry.'

'But it's my right to worry! What the hell does he expect? I'm his sister!'

Kristin shrugged; and then so did Tasha. She felt the weight in her chest lifting. Kristin was right. You couldn't control other people's lives. Or, perhaps, even your own. She walked up to the window and stood beside Kristin. 'Actually, I've got something to tell you.'

'Shall I give you a clue?' Idly Kristin's finger traced a shape in the dust on the glass: the letter 'J'. Then an 'S'. And, together, they laughed.